FLAME SEEKER

Flame Seeker

KAY DANELLA

HEAT | NEW YORK

THE BERKLEY PUBLISHING GROUP
Published by the Penguin Group
Penguin Group (USA) Inc.
375 Hudson Street, New York, New York 10014, USA
Penguin Group (Canada), 90 Eglinton Avenue East, Suite 700, Toronto, Ontario M4P 2Y3, Canada
(a division of Pearson Penguin Canada Inc.)
Penguin Books Ltd., 80 Strand, London WC2R 0RL, England
Penguin Group Ireland, 25 St. Stephen's Green, Dublin 2, Ireland (a division of Penguin Books Ltd.)
Penguin Group (Australia), 250 Camberwell Road, Camberwell, Victoria 3124, Australia
(a division of Pearson Australia Group Pty. Ltd.)
Penguin Books India Pvt. Ltd., 11 Community Centre, Panchsheel Park, New Delhi—110 017, India
Penguin Group (NZ), 67 Apollo Drive, Rosedale, North Shore 0632, New Zealand
(a division of Pearson New Zealand Ltd.)
Penguin Books (South Africa) (Pty.) Ltd., 24 Sturdee Avenue, Rosebank, Johannesburg 2196,
South Africa

Penguin Books Ltd., Registered Offices: 80 Strand, London WC2R 0RL, England

This book is an original publication of The Berkley Publishing Group.

Cover art by Phil Heffernan.
Cover design by George Long.
Text design by Kristin del Rosario.

PRINTING HISTORY
Heat trade paperback edition / December 2009

Library of Congress Cataloging-in-Publication Data

Danella, Kay.
Flame seeker / Kay Danella.
p. cm.
ISBN 978-0-425-23082-4
I. Title.
PS3604.A513F53 2009
813'.6—dc22 2009019540

PRINTED IN THE UNITED STATES OF AMERICA

10 9 8 7 6 5 4 3 2 1

Thanks to my agent, Roberta M. Brown,
for her continued enthusiasm and support;
to my editor, Leis Pederson,
for taking a chance on Flame Seeker;
and to the members of the writers_warren Yahoo group
for all the smiles.

FLAME SEEKER

Prologue

"No, child, you cannot travel Hurrann unattended."

Alithia frowned in frustration. She thought she had an excellent command of Hurranni, but the emphasis placed on the last word by the old trader the clan retained to teach the language implied some nuance that evaded her grasp. "I would not be alone. I will have my usual retinue."

She had summoned him to discuss the necessities for the journey, so certain the mothers would see the rightness of her plan once she could present them with specifics; instead, she had been met with opposition—and from a man not of her clan. The debate had gone on for so long the tea in their bowls had turned cold and her backside had become numb. Training and determination kept her seated and her fingers from toying with her red hair.

Shaking his white head, Curghann crossed his arms, the etched *mythir* bands he was never without catching the weak spring light. The white metal bracers were a testament of his wealth; few could afford even one small piece, and he wore the two so casually. She had often wondered what whim made him accept the clan's retainer when he had no need for money. "Child, it is forbidden . . . and for good reason."

"What do you mean?"

It was so simple. Alithia needed to travel to the mountain realm's fabled north and retrieve the tablet of mysteries some bedamned foremother had sent to Sentinel Reach—wherever that be—for safekeeping. The flood that swept the Perfumers District had quenched the holy fire in the clan altar, and ordinary flame would not do to render the sanctified oils, incenses, and attars demanded by the Goddess's temples. They had sufficient inventory to last the next winter—less than a cycle of seasons—but without the second mystery to rekindle the holy fire, the clan would be ruined, cast down to trade among the lesser clans and make obeisance to the priestesses of the temple.

No one knew what the second mystery was or how it worked. The Fire had been lit for generations, fueled by the Goddess's presence, burning without need for tinder or firewood—since before the great-grandmothers' great-grandmothers' time. But what was certain was that it had to be retrieved; that much was clear from her scouring of the clan's records.

Alithia had turned her attention to mustering arguments to convince the mothers of the rightness of her conclusion. Astred, Alithia's grandmother, might lead clan Redgrove, but even she needed the consent of the mothers—the women of the clan blessed by the Goddess with children.

The last person she had expected to balk her was Curghann; the kindly trader had always been a gracious teacher and quick to offer trenchant advice. This resistance was most unlike him.

"Girl children are special in my home. The Lady gives us so few of them; thus they must be protected. By temple law, girl children who have seen four and twenty of the Lady's turns—

such as yourself—must be given to husbands' attendance." He politely ignored her gape. "It is different here, in the lands beyond the peaks, I know. But the mountains are dangerous. There, a woman needs her husbands' protection."

Curghann's use of the plural possessive form penetrated her astoundment.

"*Husbands'?*" Alithia repeated, wondering if her wits were failing her. Duty to the clan required her to provide a daughter to take her place, which meant a husband for the duration—but to take *more than one*? "At the *same* time?"

Surely the Goddess would never require a woman to submit to such!

"Shield pairs," the old trader added, apparently in clarification, his hand stroking scuffed *mythir* nostalgically.

She noted his curious action. "You are married?" While their lessons had touched on Hurranni clans in general, Curghann had never spoken of his own.

He startled as though he had forgotten she was there, then extended his arms in formal presentation, his back straightening to the fullness of his formidable height, a vestige of some warrior past peeking from behind his aged mien. "I am widowed." His crisp tone of correction said she shouldn't have had to ask, his mouth a thin line above his wispy beard.

His use of *widowed* suggested something more than a contract ended by the death of one of the parties. She couldn't think of a comparable word in Lydian.

"I do not understand," Alithia admitted freely. The Goddess taught there was no shame in confessing ignorance—even to a man not of her clan—only in the willful refusal to correct that state of affairs.

The severity on Curghann's face melted into a smile, a sea of wrinkles drowning all hint of sternness. "The fault is mine, child. You speak Hurranni so well, I forget it is not your milk tongue.

Of course, you would not know." He seemed to lose himself in his thoughts once more, much like the great-grandmothers and others of that age.

She exercised patience, knowing he couldn't be rushed. There were accounts to see to, but her cousins could handle them. This was more important. The survival of the clan depended on her success.

"Forgive an old man his wandering. This is not something I have had to speak of. But I see I have been remiss in my tutorship." Once more he extended his arms as though for her inspection, the broad *mythir* bands wrapped around his forearms almost glowing in the morning light. "A Hurrann who is widowed wears two *idkhet*."

The term *idkhet* sounded like a compound, a conjunction of the Hurranni words for *life* and *ring*. "You mean those bracers?"

"Perhaps a more accurate translation would be *marriage bands*."

"And wearing two means you are widowed?"

"On a man. On a woman, it means she is married."

"But why—" She didn't know how to phrase her question. Shouldn't the meanings be similar? It seemed illogical.

Curghann took pity on her confusion. "*Idkhet* are made in pairs. During the pledging, a woman receives an *idkhet* from each of her husbands, both the half of a pair. She wears one on each arm, and her husbands wear theirs on one arm. Once sealed, the *idkhet* cannot be opened except by the death of the wearer. A man wearing one is a husband, bound to attend to his wife. A man with two is widowed, and in her memory he wears the *idkhet* he gave his wife."

Except by death. The term of Hurranni marriages was for life?

"But a woman . . ."

"Is too precious to remain a widow, if she is of childbearing age. If she is a matron who has lost both husbands, she is settled beyond the peaks, as it is too dangerous for her to remain unattended. Brigands are the least of the perils."

Horror made Alithia's stomach roil. Wrested from home and clan? It took strength of will to recall the purpose of their discussion. "But I will have my retinue. I go only to retrieve what is the clan's."

The old trader straightened his robes, the delay a gesture of disagreement. "That is of no import. The priestesses of the Lady forbid it. You would not be allowed your retinue. Your female guards would be unattended. Your male servants are not your husbands nor are they widowed—they would not be allowed to accompany a child."

Alithia stared at Curghann, finally understanding his meaning. To Hurranns, a woman was not an adult unless she was married. He persisted in addressing her as *child* not because of his great age but because she had no husband.

Not knowing what to say, she stood up and walked to the window, gripping the sill as she fought to master her turmoil. The cool breeze was a welcome slap to the cheeks. She needed it to clear her mind, to consider what would best serve the good of the clan. The mud-covered garden below struggling to throw off the leftover muck from the flood filled her sight, an inescapable reminder of the moons' tide that had raised the river and drawn waters higher than any recorded in the archives—and extinguished the holy fire.

She stared at the heart of the clan house, the flame trees that were their greatest claim to fame, from which they took their clan name. The bare branches sported fresh growth, the sprigs flushing a dark red. Soon they would flower and release their fragrance throughout her home. But without the Fire, her clan could not render their oil to sell to the temples—the first time in all the long history of clan Redgrove that the blooms would not be gathered for that purpose.

Alithia deliberately avoided looking west toward the sanctuary where even now the mothers continued to attempt to rekindle the holy fire. If her reading of the records Eldora had found were correct, their efforts were futile.

The Fire in the clan altar was visible proof of the Goddess's favor. Her blessing of fire took many forms: the flames gave warmth and life in the winter; they transformed in the cooking of food and the smelting of metals; but in transformation, fire destroyed, reducing wood to ash that was then used to make lye or simply worked back into the soil to feed the plants. Burning incense encompassed all that.

By virtue of the holy fire, clan Redgrove was one of the few that could provide sanctified oils and incenses. It gave them a near monopoly over the temple trade in Lydia and her neighboring states. It allowed them some independence from the Goddess's priestesses—the freedom to decide what and how much or how little to make, with whom to trade, what price to set on their incenses and perfumes—and at the same time raised the Lydian temple to preeminence among the Goddess's temples.

Without the Fire, all that would be lost. They would be tied to the whims of the priestesses of the Lydian temple, a pawn in political games, with the good of the clan merely an afterthought. The Goddess in Her faces of Maiden, Mother, and Crone may rule the Cycle of Life, but Her servants were as prone to squabbles as women elsewhere.

She couldn't leave the fate of clan Redgrove to their fickle care.

"You have a brother." The suggestion was offered in a tone of reconciliation.

Alithia turned her back on the garden and its gloom. "The mothers would never send a son on women's business." It embarrassed her to say so to the old trader, but it was only the truth. The only alternative was one of her female cousins . . . and likely Curghann would offer the same objections.

If the journey was so dangerous, she couldn't in good conscience ask someone else to take her place. This plan was hers; the danger should be hers as well. Taking uncles or male cousins for her retinue wasn't an option, as none of them were trained as guards.

"I could hire men—warriors—to protect me."

Even before she finished speaking, Curghann was shaking his head. "No Lydian man would know the route, and no Hurrann would contract to lead honorless men. For they would have to be bereft of honor to be unmarried yet attend a child not their kin." The smile he gave her conveyed sympathy but no hope for leniency. "I have seen the warriors here. Such hirelings would be considered brigands, especially as they would not be shield pairs. You would be . . . rescued from their clutches. And given to husbands' attendance." He spread his hands in a gesture of apology, one that acknowledged the unfairness of the world. "Girl children are the domain of the temple, their protection paramount. As a child, your objections would carry no weight."

Frustration welled up at his answer, a bitter draught that roiled her stomach. Never had she felt so powerless. But railing against Hurranni strictures was fruitless. Curghann could no more change them than she could swim through ice.

"But I have to go." As the first daughter of her age, if the tablet of mysteries held the answer to rekindling the holy fire, it was her duty to travel to Sentinel Reach to retrieve it. The second mystery was the only hope of her clan.

His eyes narrowed in sudden thought. "Then we must find you suitable husbands."

Trial

One

Staring up at the two moons sailing through the cloud-swept sky, Alithia ignored the priceless scroll of Hurranni herb lore lying unfurled on her lap and the swaying of the palanquin, the jostling of the gargant's stride as familiar as the rocking of a ship at sea after nearly a season of travel. Red Adal and pale Egon, the fox and the erne in their eternal chase. Their presence was a potent reminder of that debate with Curghann last spring.

"In the same way as the Horned Lords attend to the Lady of Heaven, so do husbands attend to their wife." The old trader had gestured toward the wakening grove and the sky above it—at the crescent moons and the sun.

Two husbands. How strange Hurranni ways were. Husbands were for cementing alliances and begetting children to enrich the clan, daughters to carry on the ways of mothers, not this constant *attendance* that Curghann insisted upon. What need for two, when one would suffice for breeding? Two men meant pleasure—that natural celebration of life. And yet if she did not bow to their ways, she would not be allowed to travel to Sentinel Reach, and the clan would lose its temple trade come the new cycle—the highest in the Perfumers' Guild reduced to ordinary scents. The priestesses of the Goddess would never accept unsanctified oils.

Without the temple trade, clan Redgrove would have to pay levies on their sales, no longer exempt by the Goddess's favor. The clan's alliances would suffer, any negotiation starting from a disadvantage. Some of their trading partners might sue to have existing contracts declared void. The value of the marriage contracts of Redgrove men may even suffer, tainted by the loss of the holy fire.

Compared to the downfall of her clan, taking two husbands was of little consequence, however extraordinary it might seem in Lydia. She had until they entered the mountains to reconcile herself to such an alien outlook—just a few more days, according to the old trader. She had expected it to be sooner. The snow-capped peaks stretched across the north horizon as far as the eye could see, the lower slopes a blue green band cloaked with trees and wreathed in clouds, growing larger with each sunset. They had already surmounted the foothills. Even now, the caravan of gargants was climbing the steep shoulders.

Yet Barda, the town guarding the border into Hurrann, was farther still, he had said.

"You're enjoying yourself."

Alithia looked at Gilsor in surprise. She had thought her brother fast asleep, inured to travel. They had gone by gargant from the very beginning—first because of lingering snows and mud, then because of rougher roads that culminated in this mountain trail. There wasn't much else to do on the beast, save ride. There were no accounts to tally, no errands to run, and he could stand only so much leathercraft and needlework. They sometimes gathered herbs while the servants pitched camp for the night, but bundling those didn't take long.

"No mothers to convince or cajole into agreement," he expanded. "No endless arguments, no second-guessing."

Allowing the curtain to drop back into place, Alithia turned away from the window with its startling vistas so unlike the flat plains and crashing surf of home. Thinking back, she realized she was happy, not merely content, despite the deprivations inherent in travel. This was the first time she had been gone from clan for so long; the trips to neighboring states took less than a season. It allowed her to focus on a single goal without constant interference. She smiled at his insight. "I believe you're correct."

"Do you truly intend to travel Hurrann?" Gilsor stared at her from across the expansive palanquin, patiently awaiting an answer, the bright sun picking out strands of gold in his foxy brown hair. As her brother, his presence at her side was deemed acceptable. He was relieved only by Curghann, who was also acceptable by dint of his widowed state.

At the start of their journey, Alithia and Gilsor had spoken often, all speculation and commentary, on the rich appointments Curghann had insisted on using for her palanquin, on flowers and plants seen, on people and beasts chance-met, as they traversed the land of their birth and ventured beyond its familiar sights, the sound of Lydian words a respite from the constant Hurranni they practiced with Curghann and his servants. Of late, silence prevailed, their conversations reduced to short words and quicker gestures—much in the same way bushels of bright velvet petals become a few drops of spirit oil redolent with seasons of blooming.

"You know what we stand to lose if I don't." They had discussed this before. Did he hope she would change her mind? Perhaps his questions now were due to the imminence of their parting. As a dutiful son and brother, he had expressed only support once the mothers had given their consent to her journey. But he wouldn't accompany her beyond Barda.

She pulled her shawl closer around her shoulders. Though the days had grown steadily warmer as they traveled north, the summer sun seemed to lose strength the higher they climbed. The return to spring chill impressed upon her the passage of time.

Only two seasons remained. She had to return to Lydia with the tablet of mysteries before winter's end—else the clan would be ruined come springtide and the budtime festival.

"Still, it's dangerous for you to be gone for so long."

Understanding that he didn't mean physical danger, she spread her hands in acknowledgment of his concern. "But it would be worse for the clan if I don't go. I believe this offers the best chance of rekindling the holy fire."

"But marriage . . . I can't imagine the mothers not wanting a voice in whom you marry, in your choice of *husbands*." Gilsor pronounced the last as if it were a distasteful word. He wasn't mistaken. The mothers' endorsement of her plan hadn't been unanimous—especially on the matter of marriage to Hurranns—not that she had expected to win the support of Bera's coterie. "And would you truly refrain from taking pleasure loves?"

"They would be my choice, not just strangers pressed on me." The decision to honor a Hurranni marriage and forswear pleasure loves was part of that choice.

Her brother wore such an air of puzzlement that Alithia could not resist a tease. "That's not all. They'll pay for the honor of marrying me."

His sea green eyes bid fair to leap from their sockets. "*They'll* pay? What recompense for their clan?" A logical question and one of abiding interest to him, since the mothers had been estimating the value of the first of his marriage contracts when they left. Upon his return to Lydia, he could expect to stand the sire soon enough.

"Nothing." She tilted her hands in bafflement, showing empty palms. "That's what Curghann said: they take the wife into their protection and will pay the clan for the honor. Of course it was in Hurranni, but I asked what we'd have to pay, and his answer was 'Nothing.' "

She still couldn't make sense of it—and she didn't like not understanding. It could lead to unforeseen complications, more difficulties in this unprecedented journey.

"Huh." He scratched his jaw thoughtfully. "I suppose it's a good thing they're the ones paying. Then they'll take better care of you." He peeked at her sidelong. "I've heard stories."

Alithia smiled indulgently. "You always hear stories."

Gilsor made a face at her. "Baillin said ferocious monsters dwell in the north, serpents that kill gargants and nest in trees as high as mountains, dragons with wings larger than a galley." He spread his arms wide as though about to take flight. Though only two springs separated their births, her younger brother was merely a son and as yet not overly laden with duty; he still had time to gossip with servants, swallowing the fanciful tales like a basse in water, and Curghann's servant delighted in his credulity.

"Those are just stories."

"Dragonblood must come from somewhere."

She didn't have any answer to that. For certain, all the old apothecary records claimed the dark blue powder known as dragonblood came from dragons living in the north—in Hurrann.

He turned away, staring out the window on his side, the fingers drumming his thigh conveying his doubt without words. The creaking of the ropes securing the palanquin to the gargant's harness filled the long silence, interspersed with the beast's heavy trudge and occasional grunt of complaint. "I can go. You don't have to marry. I'll go in your stead."

Affection swelled in Alithia's heart at the resolute offer. "It has to be me."

"Why?"

She composed her thoughts, trying to remember the precise intonation of the voice from the Goddess's own hearth—the message from Sentinel Reach. The Fire had leaped up when it spoke, so high the heat licked her face where she stood several paces away. "I asked at the temple. They said, 'A Blood Claim must be made by a Daughter of the House.'" She mimicked the speaking as best she could, trying to inform her words with the pregnant weight of the original. "If not me, it would have been Blas. Do you think she would agree to a permanent marriage to Hurranns, much less do her best to succeed?" Their cousin was only a spring younger than she, and many in the clan expected her to maneuver for advantage.

That was perhaps one reason why Bera's coterie hadn't been so vehement in their opposition to Alithia's quest: her absence would weaken Arilde's standing, or so they hoped. Their mother's eldest cousins could be aggravating in the extreme, hoarding their spite to the detriment of all. She stifled revenant guilt and the suspicion that she fled her responsibilities to Arilde and the clan for the comfort of action—any action.

What was done was done, decided, and acceded. To turn back now would be the height of folly, providing the very spark for what she wanted to prevent.

Gilsor bit his lip, his brow creasing in thought and perhaps a touch of disappointment. His offer was probably motivated as much by the prospect of adventure as brotherly feeling. She hadn't missed the gleam of excitement in his eyes when he had spoken of monsters and dragons. Yet she would have to leave him behind—leave them all behind—when she entered Hurrann; her husbands would handle the arrangements for the journey to Sentinel Reach.

A shout of exultation came from without. Alithia stood up, balancing easily on the swaying palanquin, and pushed aside the curtain across the door to investigate the furor. A cool mist kissed her cheeks, the air heavy with the musk of gargants, the tang of tree sap, and an undertone of decaying leaves.

On the gargant ahead, Curghann waved at her, his azure robes a bright spot of color against the beast's short, cream coat. He pointed beyond the ridge, a proud grin rearranging the wrinkles of his bronzed face.

Across the steep valley, stone ramparts loomed, cradled between two far taller peaks, a fortress of black granite with walls higher than those of the Goddess's main temple in Lydia. A warrior place, stark and unwelcoming. The mountain trail wound round and up, leading to its massive bossed gates, the entrance to Hurrann itself. If there had been a bridge, they could have ended the first stretch of her journey within the day—but the valley ran long and deep, curving with its head out of sight and its foot far below.

Now she understood why it would take a few more days to reach the border town. But understanding was not what set her heart to thundering. Soon she would meet the men who wished to marry her . . . and she would have to choose. Quickly. Despite the spring chill, summer had to be nearing its end in Lydia. Travel to Sentinel Reach would take till the middle of autumn—weather and wildlife permitting—longer if luck was against them.

But how to make a choice?

Curghann had proposed what he had called a "traditional" trial of arms: shield pairs battling for supremacy with the winners as her husbands. It sounded barbaric to her, but he didn't seem to see anything exceptionable about his suggestion. His calm demeanor had shaken her.

For all that she had known the old trader for several springs—since before her Maiden rites—she didn't really know much about Hurranns. The differences between their marriage customs alone made that clear. What other assumptions had she made that would prove founded on shifting sands?

Suddenly the enormity of what she had agreed to crashed home on Alithia. She had wrestled with these thoughts before, to no decisive conclusion, and now she had only days left. How could she choose when she had never met her prospective husbands—and did not have the luxury of time to become acquainted? Knowing next to nothing of her options, she couldn't base her decision on the merits of clan alliance the way the mothers would prefer—if that were even possible. To try would take too long; such maneuverings took seasons.

And in her secret heart she wondered. Did they make love the same way? Would she have to take her husbands by turns, or did they share? What other surprises awaited her?

More worries raised their heads. What would happen after she retrieved the tablet of mysteries? She would still be married. Would the mothers object to her not being available for alliances? As the first daughter of her age, her own more valuable marriage contracts were supposed to consolidate the clan's position as the preeminent perfumers of the south.

A cloud slid before the sun, casting the mountainside into ominous shadow. Alithia shivered at the inauspicious timing.

She would take two Hurranni husbands because marriage would enable her to fulfill her duty as she understood it.

But what if this attempt to rekindle the holy fire failed?

Phelan watched Taith hone his axe, the soft keen of the whet- stone soothing to the ears. Even stripped down to woolen trews and the shirt he wore beneath his dragon-scale tunic, his sword brother was a warrior without equal—Phelan's continued survival was testament to his skill. It was just like him to be putting an edge to his favorite weapon, though they hadn't been in a fight since reaching Barda.

Taith's battle prowess would be an advantage in the coming trial, but that wasn't what interested Phelan right then. A caravan had been sighted across the valley the other day—perhaps the very caravan carrying their hoped-for wife—and now his thoughts bubbled over with possibilities. "What d'you think it'll be like?"

The steady keen continued unabated. "Do not go forming preconceptions. They would likely be wrong."

"Huh? How would you know?" He leaned forward, all agog. Did his kinsman and sword brother have some experience Phelan knew nothing of? Had some matron inveigled Taith to lie with her and put those lessons to practice? He'd have said it was impossible; not only did they go everywhere together, but all the women they'd ever seen had been properly attended. Even his mother had always been in the company of one or both of his fathers.

Taith made a face at him, clearly divining his rioting thoughts. "Simple logic, mush head. I prefer the axe; Slann prefers the sword. If you judged him by my preferences, you would be wrong. The same with pledging."

"But it will be pleasure."

His sword brother set down his axe to swipe a hand over his face, something he did when exasperated. "Fighting is also pleasure," he grumbled to his palm. "Phelan, enough with the questions! We will know when we know."

"But don't you wonder?" Phelan threw himself down on their plank bed, ignoring the shudder it gave as its thin mattress failed to cushion his impact. He'd never understood how Taith could display so little curiosity about so essential and fascinating a mystery. Even in their boyhood, his kinsman had been frustratingly stolid during the lectures on pleasing a woman, while he had suffered an endless parade of heat dreams, spilling his seed on his sheets from lack of control.

He took a deep breath, remembering some of those dreams. It was his misfortune that he'd never had the opportunity to practice those techniques they'd been taught as they were meant to be done, but they provided rich fodder in sleep. He adjusted his trews, the fit suddenly tight, his flesh's blade responding to his thoughts. The touch of his own hand was sweet fire on his length, spark to its tinder.

"Enough already." As always, his sword brother was the voice of reason. Taith gave him a gimlet eye. "We do not have time for that."

Phelan grinned, the familiar banter a comfort in this moment of uncertainty. "You sure?"

A warm, reluctant smile answered him, tacit acknowledgment of temptation. "More than sure. The caravan should arrive sometime today. You do not want us caught unready."

"Oh, very well." A new thought distracted him. "What about her, what d'you think she's like?" A maiden of age to pledge. But not a timid one, to brave the jungle passage to Sentinel Reach with the rainy season coming. Would she be of a mind to try those positions their long-ago tutors hinted at?

"Lords above, Phelan! You heard the same message I did. You faced the Fire with me, heard the invitation. You know as much."

Truth. Nearly two fortnights past, they'd returned to the Black Python clan house to a summons from the temple and an incredible message from Taith's old father offering them a chance to win a wife. It was flattering to know they were held in such high esteem—the opportunity alone was a compliment, but communication between temple hearths cost a whole silver crescent.

The reminder of the unusualness of the offer brought to mind another departure from tradition. "She's a southerner. What if we don't suit?" He held back the real question on the forefront of his mind. What if she was too small for Taith? Phelan knew himself as unexceptional in build, but his sword brother was big—in every way.

"Phelan." The growl emerged low, with strained patience. "We worked for turns, taking jobs and risks many shield pairs would have second thoughts about—all so we can afford to pledge. You were the one pushing to get to Barda the soonest possible. *Now* you entertain second thoughts?" Taith picked up a knife in its sheath and flung it at Phelan's head. "Meet her first, then decide if you want us to fight for her bond."

He snatched the knife from the air before it hit, the hard leather stinging his palm. "That supposes we'll win."

"And if we fail, we wasted no energy tying ourselves in knots," his sword brother countered repressively, then stilled, his head canted in a posture of pointed attention.

Reaching for his sword on the floor by his plank bed, Phelan jerked upright, planting his feet squarely on cold stone. "What? What is it?"

Taith stood with his eyes narrowed, listening to something Phelan couldn't hear. His sharper senses were part of the reason he was Sword and Phelan was Shield. "Gate is opening."

Sure enough, the squeal of metal followed, long and piercing. Too loud to be just any gate, it had to be the great door—the portal to beyond the peaks—and it was opened only for caravans.

Their eyes met in silent agreement. Arming themselves in haste, they joined the flood of warriors jostling for space at the parapet, claiming a spot just as the gate opened to its fullest extent. A line of gargants entered, healthy adults, to judge by their deadly swooping tusks, their thick, pale fur announcing their southern lineage.

Heads bowed—Taith's and Phelan's among them—at the sight of the old man standing on the beast second in line. Taith's old father.

She was here.

Phelan's heart raced, determination in every beat.

The long wait was almost over.

If they were lucky, Taith and he would leave Barda with a wife.

Two

After a season of nothing but small towns and smaller villages, the mountain fastness that was Barda with its architecture scaled to heroic proportions should have overwhelmed. It nestled between the shoulders of two peaks, the pass guarded by towering walls. Past that first immense gate was a meadow with pasturage for the caravan's gargants, then what looked to be a minor city carved from the bones of the mountains and another high wall beyond. Its people bustled with brisk purpose.

Groomed to oversee the business of her clan, Alithia quickly identified storehouses much like those on the docks of Lydia, too large and too many simply to supply the needs of Barda. To her mind, that could only mean transshipment. Goods for and from trade with the south were gathered here for transport hither and yon. Caravans went laden, coming and going.

It helped explain the other buildings: temporary lodging for traders and their teams; the various trades necessary to support Barda's inhabitants, especially the garrison; and the inevitable taverns. There were more of the latter than she expected, yet most were clearly prosperous, forcing her to increase her estimate of the border town's trade volumes.

The day after their arrival, the weather warmed, the soft breeze whispering of summer and the passage of time.

Alithia dressed carefully, arranging her hair with the help of Gilsor, then inspected the results in the polished metal mirror in their room. The very image of a well-born Lydian woman. No matter that Hurranns wouldn't consider her an adult until married, she knew what she was.

Today, she would meet the men Curghann had invited—two of whom would become her husbands. She had to appear her best. She supposed she should be grateful she would have two if she had to have a permanent marriage; surely just one for all time would pall after a while.

A knock sounded on the door. Curghann awaited her.

She nodded approval and turned away.

It was time.

On any other day, the great hall of Barda's garrison would have merited a closer inspection from Alithia. The ceiling soared high above, supported by massive arches, of a height to accommodate a rearing gargant. Its small windows should have rendered it dark, but the walls sparkled with color—the tiles that were the mountain realm's other source of fame—reflecting light in countless shades.

But not today.

Today it was the hall's occupants that held her attention; not that the hall was crowded, but the men in it seemed to take up more space than they actually did. They bristled with weapons—swords and daggers, knives and axes—buckled and belted on their persons. In the gallery were more men, similarly bladed yet standing closer together.

She shivered inwardly at the thought of their using those weapons on each other, drawing blood simply because their laws demanded she have a husband—two husbands. Worse, she had to choose among shield pairs—men already partnered. She couldn't choose separately, judging each man by his own merits.

A closer scrutiny suggested that not all were there to vie for her bond. By the walls, she spied men with the double bands of widowhood, many with short beards or mustaches. Sprinkled among them were others with the single band of husbands. It seemed her options were the ten unbanded men—five shield pairs—nearest her and Curghann.

Focusing on them helped Alithia push back the sense of overwhelming masculinity.

The candidates were all tall men, corded with muscle, straight-backed, and alert. Black hair hanging past broad shoulders. Clean-shaven faces mostly sun-tinted bronze and copper and gold, their expressions set, eyes sharp. These were not youths like Gilsor behind her, still adjusting to their final growth and awkward in their bodies. They wore an aura of command around them, as comfortable as a soft blanket—warriors, quite unlike the pleasure loves she had left behind in Lydia.

All that darkness made her conscious of her own fair skin and red hair, so different from theirs. Imagining them touching her sent a lick of Goddess heat unfurling in her belly. Perhaps duty need not be so bleak?

Alithia prayed for guidance. If this was the Goddess's will . . .

Curghann gestured to the leftmost pair and intoned in the stilted formality of introduction: "Slann and Arghal, clan Dancing Wyvern of Sky Cavern Mountain." They nodded in turn, the former lowering long, thick lashes in a rather bashful manner.

Alithia nodded back, keeping her expression courteous. From the old trader's lectures during their journey, she knew their clan made silk, and it showed in their attire. Over his armor, Slann wore a teal green robe of silk brocade with gold embroidery that made his dark skin look darker and contrasted with the belts of knives crossed over his chest and the enormous sword he rested his hands on. Arghal's, on the other hand, was a rich, bright red—a color made possible only by exotic and expensive northern dyes—that gave his sharp features a coppery glow; he sported knives on his upper arms and on his thighs.

His hand continuing to the right, Curghann announced: "Mahon and Rhi, clan Stone Bridge by Sentinel Reach."

Another exchange of nods as she veiled a surge of interest. Their clan had its seat near her destination; that familiarity could be an advantage on her journey. Mahon was a bear of a man—among already large men—and one of the three tallest, standing head and shoulders above most of the others. Under a leather robe tasseled with curving claws at least as long as her fingers, bronzed muscle bunched. His arms were easily the size of her thighs, while one big hand gripped a spear taller than he was with a long, curving blade at the top. Rhi came only to his partner's wide shoulders, a lean, golden shadow in comparison, though no less dangerous, if the knives dotting his leather robe were any indication. He smiled at her just then, the quirk of his lips revealing an old thin scar high on one cheek.

"Bronn and Lughann, clan Iron Wood of Dragon's Foot."

Bronn looked so like Mahon that Alithia wondered if they were cousins, though Curghann's lectures had not mentioned any special connection between their clans. The similarity went beyond their powerful build; she could see it in the shape of their faces, the strong jut of their brows, and the hard line of their jaws. Bronn's nose, though, was somewhat crooked, as though it had been broken. And as his shadow, Lughann was taller and much darker, his grin a bright slash in his face, like Egon at crescent in the night sky. Lughann smoothed a hand over the colorful beadwork on his leather robe as if it held some significance beyond a display of wealth.

Was she missing something of import? Many of the Hurranns she had seen since arriving at Barda wore beads, either sewn on their clothes or braided into their hair. Her potential husbands were no exception. She reined in the frustration she felt at her ignorance, forcing away the frown that wanted to knit her brows.

"Deighann and Kail, clan Crystal Bell of Crescent Bay."

Theirs was another clan that had roused Alithia's curiosity. They fished, but not just for food, harvesting from the sea rare plants and substances demanded by apothecaries in the south. The mothers would not object to obtaining some of that trade for the clan. Deighann and Kail wore no robes; instead, they had tunics of large, iridescent blue scales that clung to their chests in a most complimentary way. The two could have been twice-born, so alike were they in appearance and height, save that Deighann had his hair pulled away from his face into a tail like hers and had a sword on his back, while Kail wore his loose around his shoulders and carried an axe.

Finally, Curghann gestured to the rightmost pair. "And Taith and Phelan, clan Black Python of the Lady's Hills."

Black Python also supplied the southern apothecary trade with items such as the dragonblood of Gilsor's speculation. But that was not what was responsible for Alithia's sudden interest. Taith was the third of the tallest among the shield pairs, and what looked like a double-headed axe peeked over his broad shoulders, so large the blades arched like metal wings to either side of his head. Phelan was another with a lean, compact build—compared with the others. They, too, wore tunics instead of robes, but these were of some shimmery material—not cloth—that had a strange pattern of blues, greens, and black.

These then were the . . . brethren, the shield pairs who would compete for her. Following Hurranni custom, Curghann had introduced them in order of Sword and Shield, their chosen roles in a woman's—their wife's—defense.

Alithia suppressed a shiver at their obvious readiness for violence. While the Goddess taught that violence and dissolution had their place lest the world grow overfull—sickness, death, and decay being the Crone's domain—the Maiden favored creation and the celebration of life. Yet if Alithia was to claim her clan's tablet of mysteries in Sentinel Reach, she would have to accept two of these men as her husbands.

And take them to her bed.

Goddess heat suffused her, a flash of understanding of what she had to do. While she had to take husbands to satisfy Hurranni law, there was a way for her to also obey the Maiden.

Her audience's avid scrutiny stiffened Alithia's determination. Smiling, she gathered her thoughts, choosing her words with care. She wanted to be certain there would be no misunderstanding. "It is taken for granted that your presence here is guarantee of your martial prowess." Curghann had implied as much. Only men the old trader deemed capable of protecting her from the perils of her journey had been invited to the trial. His continued calm assured her the situation had not changed. "Therefore, I have a different test for you who wish to be my"—*Goddess help me*—"my husbands."

Frowns met her announcement. Even Curghann turned to face her, his wrinkles growing pronounced.

"The ones I will choose as my husbands are the shield pair that can pleasure me best."

*The soft, confident words hit Taith like a blow to the belly, driv*ing the air from his lungs and leaving his heart stuttering. He was not the only one in shock. Phelan was struck dumb—a miracle in itself. The other pairs were equally stunned, white-eyed and gape-jawed, rocking on their heels.

They had expected a trial of arms, had come prepared to strive their utmost to win. But none of them could have foretold the sort of blades their hoped-for wife would require.

A quick glance at the old father standing attendant beside her caught a flash of disbelief—even he had not expected such a development, though her kinsman hid a smile.

But the answering heat in his belly stunned Taith more. Never had his body so rebelled against his control at so little provocation.

He sent a silent prayer of gratitude winging up to the Horned Lords for the weight of dragon scales that hid his inconvenient response. Phelan would be merciless in his teasing if he knew. Luckily, his shield brother appeared too stunned to notice—another reason to be thankful.

His first sight of their hoped-for wife had shocked. She had pale skin—not merely a soft, golden brown, but the color of milk—and large nipples like pretty flowers. He had heard the peoples in the south, beyond the peaks, were unlike any Hurrann, but he had thought that meant they followed other customs. He never suspected that, much like their gargants, their differences extended to skin and hair.

But unlike those beasts, she had hair the rich red of the Lady's trees in bloom—when they were most holy. Gathered into a thick tail at the top of her head, it spilled in a frothy cascade down her back; and just like the tree's bell-like flowers, it looked as though a single strand should set whatever it touched ablaze.

Her calm self-assurance standing on the low platform and flanked only by the old father and an unbanded young man could have rivaled the Lady of Heaven. But it would have taken more than that for Taith to overlook the rest of her.

She was slender, even compared to Phelan's leaner form, and small—the top of her bright head would come only to the middle of his chest were she not on the platform. How she could be so small when her legs, bared by a skirt that ended at the tops of her thighs, went on forever, he could not understand.

And her legs were not all that was revealed. The shawl about her shoulders did nothing to hide the pert breasts bared and upraised by her laced bodice. No woman would dress so scantily in Hurrann. But though the old father beside her drew her aside for a quiet question, he behaved as though he saw nothing strange in her attire.

That could only be to the good. Taith did not want a temple-raised Hurranni maiden for their wife.

She glanced around as she listened to the old father.

Her eyes struck Taith like sudden lightning, a shiver of recognition sweeping through him. They were the sometimes blue, sometimes green of the waters of Crescent Bay, the waters he had played in, in his boyhood, sparkling with life. He had never conceived of eyes the color of the sea.

"Do you think—" Phelan grabbed Taith's arm, his wits recovered, despite wide-eyed glances at their hoped-for wife.

Taith could imagine the wild speculation flying through his shield brother's head. "Wait," he whispered beneath the outpouring of murmurs from around them. Surely she did not mean that as it had sounded, though her Hurranni flowed easily, like a mountain spring flush with snowmelt.

After some discussion, the old father stepped forward, raising his hand for their attention. "The trial shall not include union. Any who attempts union will forfeit his place."

He agrees with her proposal?

Taith heard the rest of the rules through a roar of shock.

Three

"This is ridiculous. What's wrong with a simple trial by combat?" Mahon grumbled loudly over the noon meal, his plate piled high with curried rice and fried mountain tree serpent. Clearly his disgruntlement hadn't affected his appetite, Phelan noted, though very little probably could. To travel the breadth of Hurrann meant learning to eat and sleep whenever they could. No one survived as many turns as the older Sword had by having a tetchy stomach.

Across from Phelan, Taith held his customary silence, watching their brethren at the other tables and crunching on bony snake meat with evident relish. The northern caravaners preferred this dining hall because its cook had a deft hand with spices, a good man to have in the peaks where most of the meat available was snake, snake, snake, and snake—gargant meat was too tough, requiring a fortnight of tenderizing, and sheep and goat were stringy.

"Of course, you'd ask that since your size gives you an edge in strength. But the manner of trial is the girl's choice and her prerogative, though seldom exercised. Are you going to challenge it?" Rhi shook his head at his sword brother. "Both my fathers would advise against such. It's one thing to offer a wife guidance; it's something else entirely to make your disagreement public. The temple would say there is no harm in her plan." Having grown up less than a day's ride from Sentinel Reach, he would know.

Lots had been drawn to decide the order of precedence, and Mahon and Rhi would be the first shield pair to stand trial. They had a day to prepare, but the unprecedented proposal had rumor and speculation running rife and rampant.

Had she truly meant bed play? A rumble rose from that corner of the dining hall, Mahon and Rhi's men sticking their blades in. It seemed everyone had an opinion.

"Any plans?" Devyn prompted in a low voice, careful to keep his face from the other tables. The third in command of their crew, he had taken to sharing the knowledge he'd accumulated in his five and fifty turns, treating them like the family he'd lost—wife, shield brother, and sons—to a pack of direwolves.

Phelan looked at Taith, wondering how he would answer. As luck would have it, they were the last in line for trial, but that also made their wait longer.

"We watch and learn." His sword brother continued to eat, steadily consuming the food on his plate as he surveyed the other tables. His face betrayed little of his thoughts as wild speculation was bantered back and forth. One might think he had no stake in the outcome of the trial, so calm he looked.

Nothing more would be forthcoming. Once Taith had chosen his position, neither rampaging gargant nor stampeding uruxi would move him.

Nine of the Lady's turns of brotherhood didn't lessen Phelan's disgruntlement at the answer, though he did try to view their brethren—their competition—the way his sword brother might. Or as a wife might—a southerner at that.

If the trial to come were a test of arms, he knew who he'd consider their strongest rivals: Bronn and Lughann. Though Mahon had height over Bronn, Rhi's quickness didn't make up for the concord between those two. They were a formidable shield pair.

But for bed play, how could he tell who held the advantage?

Deighann and Kail were peacocks with a taste for finery, as were Slann and Arghal, but the latter pair traded in silks, so it was only to be expected. Mahon and Bronn were big men—tall and muscled—bigger than Taith even, while Rhi and Lughann were about his size. Did that make them about equal? Or did that mean they'd have to be more careful? Rough play was not a problem with men, but he imagined it would be different with a wife.

The boisterous discussions at the other tables ventured into salacious territory.

Phelan huffed in disgust, shooting a grimace at his sword brother as he returned to his meal. Nothing he could see gave any hint of their chances of winning.

How Taith could be so patient was an old point of frustration for him, but Taith had been correct to advise him to wait. Phelan's fears of not suiting seemed foolish in hindsight. Now that he'd seen Alithia, he couldn't imagine wanting anyone else as wife. The proud slopes of her creamy breasts, the lush flow of red hair, the long, slender line of her legs, the sight of so much that was denied to unbanded men . . . To be allowed to touch her—he swallowed down a groan at the thought—was a gift from the Lady Herself. How could any other woman compare?

"The child has claws," Devyn murmured into his mug, the narrow, gray braids at his temples swinging forward and veiling a faint smile and the crinkles at the corners of his eyes.

"What d'you mean by that?" The older man was wont to make obscure statements and delighted in having explanations drawn out of him—with mock threats of violence if necessary.

"Pleasure's important to women. Don't ever forget that. She's willing to outrage custom to get what she wants." He tipped the mug toward Phelan in toast. "'Sides, what use would you be as protectors if you get yourselves hacked up winning her? Claws and brains, good to have in a wife. You'll be lucky to have her." A healthy gulp of grog signaled the end to his advice—for now.

Eoghann wondered aloud if all southern girls were so bold, arching his brows meaningfully at his sword brother, Gair, who answered with a low laugh. With the exception of Devyn, their men were all much younger shield pairs still amassing funds for a wife. The *idkhet* alone were worth several turns' hard work. But at twenty turns, the two were the youngest of their crew and still took a lighthearted view of pledging.

Phelan frowned, ignoring the speculation at their table. Taith and he wouldn't lose much if they didn't win the trial. They were younger than most shield pairs ready to pledge and had come to Barda with goods to sell. They could find cargo meant for destinations other than Sentinel Reach.

But the next chance to win a wife would be at the start of the next turn, and their competition would be every worthy shield pair in Hurrann. The odds of success then would be much lower. It was certain to be a trial of arms—as a rule, the temple required proof of the shield pairs' fitness to protect a wife—and accidents could be fatal; two of Taith's brothers had met their deaths there. Too, the fact that Alithia was a southerner meant the pledge gift wouldn't have to be the tithe due the temple; as Taith had pointed out when they discussed the invitation, they could offer something more moderate without giving insult. That was a blessing that might never come their way again.

Morning came too soon, especially for those with lodgings near the stables. Why his sword brother had chosen a room there when they'd had their choice of quieter rooms, Phelan was in no mood to contemplate kindly. Howls and bellows came from the runs, loud and frequent, the beasts scenting something in the air.

He sensed it, too. Anticipation. Excitement. Trepidation. Daring the unknown. The first trial was that afternoon. Mahon and Rhi were expected to *pleasure* Alithia. What would happen then? His thoughts churned, streaking in all directions like lightning in a summer storm. His heart started pounding and, as if in response, fresh cries rose in chorus, the trumpet of a bull gargant drowning out the rest.

Taith somehow managed to sleep through the clamor, yet opened a disgustingly sharp eye when Phelan gave up his futile attempt at more sleep and reached for his whetstone. "Up early."

He gave the wit a baleful sand-rimmed glare. "And whose fault is that?" He struggled free of the blanket twisted about his hips—the fruit of his restless night—and pulled out the knife he'd tucked under his pillow.

"You cannot blame your tossing and turning on me." His sword brother swept his hair over the pillow, then folded his arms behind his head, apparently content to remain abed.

Another howl resounded, the start of a dissonant chorus that shook the very air.

"Ha! But that"—Phelan used the whetstone to point toward the stables—"that, I can." Luckily, he didn't recognize any of the voices raised—their mounts could be fractious when roused—so their presence wasn't required.

The raillery passed the time, as did some arms practice, but even that helped little. His thoughts twisted and coiled upon themselves like tangled old rope, returning time and again to the trial to come. It seemed to take forever for the Lady to rise to noon and begin her departure for the west. How much slower must it feel for Mahon and Rhi, about to perform for all of them to see?

That pair and their crew didn't make an appearance in the practice yard where everyone else was venting their tension on innocent targets or equally blameless brethren. No one sparred with bare blade though, reluctant to risk injury and forfeit their trial.

"That won't help, you know. You should just accept the inevitable and retire from the field."

Yanking the last arrow free of the straw dragon, Phelan glanced over his shoulder to see Lughann grinning confidently, his teeth a bright slash against his darker skin. He shook his head as he slid the arrow back into his quiver, an answering grin on his lips. "Unless you've been getting some practice of the other sort, I don't think it's that cut and dried."

"We're not talking herbs here. Pleasuring a southern girl will take more than old lessons prated by those creaky tutors, who'd probably forgotten more than they remembered."

He frowned at the other Shield, wondering if his talk was just the usual chaff, Lughann trying to unnerve him, or if he truly knew something Phelan didn't. "Can't win if we don't try."

Bronn walked up at that point and slung an arm across his shield brother's shoulders. "Come. Sorcha is acting up."

"Don't say I didn't warn you," Lughann called back, waving as he allowed himself to be led away.

With a snort, Phelan gave the Shield the finger, twisting his hand for emphasis.

A hearty laugh was all the answer he got in return. Someone was awfully cheerful—too cheerful for Phelan's peace of mind. He glared at the back of the departing Shield, eyeing the point between Lughann's shoulders, his quiver of arrows temptingly close to hand.

"Leave be. He is just trying to unsettle you. Do not give him that satisfaction."

He glanced at Taith and shrugged, guilt at his thoughts twisting his mouth. He really shouldn't have dignified Lughann's chaff with a response, but be damned if he'd roll over and play dead. They weren't giving up that easily.

"Come." Taith slung his arm across Phelan's shoulders, tucking him against his bigger body—obviously in deliberate mimicry. He usually didn't play up his size this way. "Kail wants our opinion on some spicewood they bought."

Phelan poked him in the ribs and put some distance between them, enough that his left arm wasn't blocked, but he allowed himself to be diverted, affection welling up inside. Just when you thought Taith was all serious, he did something like this.

When the appointed time came, Taith and he trooped with their brethren to the inn where the southbound caravaners had taken up abode, a short distance from the garrison. They filed past Mahon and Rhi's crew into the chamber where the trials would be held. As the old man had announced, the other four shield pairs had the right to witness the trial, to ensure that no one attempted union. Naturally, not one of them declined the opportunity to keep an eye on their competition.

Questions swirled in Phelan's head, giving him no respite. Did southerners think nothing of performing such intimacies in the presence of others? Another more daunting thought occurred to him. Would she expect it of her husbands? That fresh worry was banished by the sight that greeted them.

A bed occupied the center of the room. No simple pallet, it was large enough to host a feast, piled high with furs and Alithia curled on top, all serene confidence, like the Lady Herself awaiting Her worshippers. Her bright hair spilled over her pale shoulders, shielding her breasts from their avid gaze.

Transfixed by her vivid sensuality, Phelan stared, unmindful of her kinsman and the old man standing behind the bed. Propriety demanded their attendance as protection for Alithia and as witnesses to the trial, but they could very well have been absent for all the notice they were given.

Then she straightened her legs, and he caught a glimpse of bright curls between her thighs and realized she wore nothing at all. He sucked in air sharply, his body hardening without his volition, his heart suddenly racing, like a boy's at the first hint of the forbidden. She was so different, with her rounded curves so unlike a man's. None of those long-ago lessons, those tantalizing lectures on the techniques of pleasing a woman, prepared him for this.

A yearning woke deep inside. To touch and feel all that creamy skin. To have the right to sheathe his swollen blade in her body. To sleep with her in his arms, pillowed against her softness. What man wouldn't fight for the privilege?

He struggled for breath, shocked by the raw, clawing intensity of his need. The ache ran to his very bones.

Phelan wanted to wrap her in the furs, away from the covetous stares of their brethren. She was theirs—Taith's and his! But now Mahon and Rhi strode forward, looking odd without Mahon's favorite spear, and Phelan choked on the urge to demand they step away.

The old man inspected the shield pair for beads of power, to ensure no spell would influence Alithia's choice. He had Rhi undo his braid to prove the Shield wore no beads. With great solemnity, he nodded acceptance, no expression crossing his stern face.

Ignoring their audience, Mahon and Rhi undressed quickly, intent on beginning their trial. Direwolf claws and throwing knives clattered as they folded their leather robes and set them on the floor. Shirts and trews joined the pile until they stood before Alithia proudly naked, displaying their battle-scarred bodies the way a trader displayed prime goods.

Having finally seen their hoped-for wife, Phelan found his concerns multiplying like slither-roots in the rainy season. Standing before the bed, Alithia was even smaller than he'd thought—she barely came to Rhi's chin, and Phelan was a thumb or so taller than the Shield. She looked so fragile beside Mahon—and he suspected she would look just as fragile beside Taith.

By the swelling of Mahon's blade, it seemed likely he would cleave her into two, were he to attempt union. Surely her body was too fragile to sheathe him? Phelan frowned at his sword brother, who was nearly an equal of Mahon in size, his worries redoubled.

Taith had that stolid look on his face, as though watching a brigand attack instead of one of the most secretive and speculated of activities. One might think he had seen it before.

"Come." Alithia extended her hand to Mahon, a smile starting in her blue eyes then spreading to her pink lips as she settled back on the furs, her entire body an invitation.

Despite the unprecedented trial she'd proposed, her confidence surprised them all, especially the Sword, who hung back even when she repeated her summons. Shouldn't she be more uncertain? Did she truly see nothing unusual in having two naked men before her?

Mahon finally stepped to the bed, the flexing of his shoulders betraying his tension. Phelan held his breath, wondering what the Sword would do.

But it wasn't Mahon who moved.

Alithia's hand dropped, cupping Mahon's turgid flesh in her palm. With a hum of judicious reflection, she worked her hand around him, encouraging his thickening with not a hint of hesitation in her bold caresses.

A sound swept the chamber—almost a gasp—as the brethren stared at Mahon. He did nothing, unusual for so decisive a warrior and trader. He just stood there, arms and eyes startled wide, as her other hand joined the first in its squeezing and stroking, and his already swollen length grew.

Phelan swallowed, his own blade aching inside his trews, throbbing in time to the motion of Alithia's hands. He could almost feel her hands on him, milking him for his strength. He tore his gaze from that fascinating sight, for fear he'd embarrass himself with release.

Rhi seemed equally stunned, his hands clenched by his waist, as though reaching for knives that weren't there. He simply watched, slack-jawed, as Alithia played with his sword brother.

The shield pair almost seemed besotted, too drunk with excitement to move.

A soft murmur of approval dragged Phelan's attention back to Mahon's and Alithia's hands. Her pale fingers looked so delicate around his ruddy length, yet the confidence of her strokes pronounced her no maiden fresh from the temple who—if Phelan's long-forgotten instructors were to be believed—needed to be coaxed into bed play. She'd taken the reins and was driving Mahon unerringly.

Was this the true trial? A test of their control?

Her thumbs circled the tip of Mahon's blade, spreading the dew she found there into a clear sheen.

Phelan could only imagine the delight streaking through the Sword; if it were he, he would have been on his knees, that part of him was that sensitive. It now throbbed in concert, a yearning that strengthened the longer he watched.

She sped her caresses, her eyes intent on her prize.

With a choked exclamation, Mahon released, his pleasure spurting in a sudden gush of white.

Someone groaned.

Phelan winced, embarrassed for the Sword. The inadequate control that release implied! He wasn't the only one empathizing with the big warrior. Brethren exchanged pained glances across the chamber. Mahon should have given himself ease before the trial.

Alithia smiled, delighted by Mahon's honest response, tempted to lick her fingers to taste the cream of his body. But he jerked away, dragging his heavy shaft from her hand, his face a picture of horror. His reaction startled her. Before she could attempt to soothe his distress, a touch distracted her—Rhi embracing her from behind and kissing her shoulder.

A Lydian man wouldn't have made the first move.

Surprise held her still before his attentions. But she excused his presumption as Goddess heat bloomed within her, the simple delight of sensual contact sweeping her body. It had been so long since she had enjoyed more than the pleasure of her own fingers. Too long.

She twisted around to take Rhi's mouth, running her hands over corded muscle. That was another difference she noticed. Lydian men didn't run to excess, but none of her pleasure loves had been warriors. Rhi felt other—hotter, harder, somehow huskier. The stiff ridges of the scars on his golden skin only served to heighten the contrast.

Like Mahon, his chest was bare—a natural smoothness, not the temporary effect of shaving, with no stubble to prickle beneath her caress. Unlike Lydian men, the hairs around their groins started as a thin line below the navel, not a fan across the chest to draw the eye. A modesty at variance with Rhi's forward manner. His heart pounded under her hand, its frenzied beat honest, his excitement fanning hers.

Purring approval, Alithia tasted him, dipping her tongue into his mouth and discovering spice. He had made the effort to chew fennel seeds to sweeten his breath.

Rhi met her kisses with fervor, his eagerness verging on aggression. He reciprocated her caresses, rough hands rasping over her skin in erotic friction. Here was a man who didn't doubt his purpose.

She rubbed herself against him, savoring the feel of his chest against her tingling breasts, the smoothness so different from Lydian men—yet there was no mistaking him as anything but male. The hardness of the muscle bunching under her hands left her in no doubt as to that.

Still kissing her, he urged her down, his weight pressing her into the furs, his shaft a hot brand against her thigh.

Alithia shivered at the searing contact, need roiling the emptiness in the center of her being. Yet she clutched at his shoulders as desire clashed with ambivalence at the atypical position, the tinge of subservience scraping at her delight.

As though he understood her hesitation, Rhi sat up, taking his weight off her. Instead, he used his hair like a gentle brush, drawing the ends across her breasts and her belly. Knowing lips lingered on her skin. His hands roamed her sides, the restless caresses almost possessive in their errantry. He paused at the curve of her waist, lingered to squeeze, then wandered lower. Calloused fingers scraped sweetly against her groin, sparking shivers of delight that fed the Goddess heat inside her. There he dallied, drawing circles within circles on the tender skin, teasing her heightened senses with the promise of more intimate contact—a partner in the great dance.

She writhed against the furs, borne on a wave of tingling, quivering, seething anticipation. Need grew, a carnal hunger too long denied. "Give me more." She forced the words through her tight throat, needing a moment to recall her Hurranni.

Those bold fingers moved then, reaching the juncture of her thighs and the flesh that ached for a man's touch, for the blunt homage of a man's shaft. Rhi seemed to hesitate, drawing out her suspense with every heartbeat of stillness. Finally—*Maiden be praised!*—he parted her wet curls and ventured deeper, finding the bud of her pleasure.

Bliss shivered through her, settling with a flutter of delicate wings in the center of her being. Purring in approval, she spread her legs and arched up for more of his play. The barest tip of his finger in her cleft elicited a lightning flash of hot delight.

Yet this was just Rhi.

Surely Mahon would join them?

The Sword stood back, an unreadable expression on his broad face. Alithia couldn't help but stare, despite the delight of Rhi's caresses. Why did he keep his distance? He hadn't been so reserved earlier. The unsettling memory of his inexplicable horror pricked her enjoyment.

Only when Mahon noticed her attention did he approach, his body held stiffly, climbing onto the bed on her other side. His touch on her shoulder was awkward—as though he didn't know what to do. He nearly succeeded in suppressing a flinch when she reached for his hand, but she felt his muscles twitch, and that bothered her, tearing at the veil of pleasure Rhi wove.

Once again, the Shield distracted her, sliding down to nibble on her folds, his tongue delving into her channel.

Sweet pleasure pooled in Alithia's core, desire swirling in a eddy of gathering rapture. She arched up, lifting her hips and pressing closer, wanting a deeper touch. Need throbbed, suffusing her blood with thrilling, prickling hunger.

Rhi pierced her with his fingers, stretching her delicate flesh while he continued to feast. The contrast of vigor and finesse, cunningly blended, cast a net of pure delight across her senses and reduced her concern over Mahon's withdrawal to trivial shadow.

Hard hands brushed her nipples, featherlight, too gentle, hesitant in their caresses. They fell far short of what she wanted—firm and fervent, the sure knowledge she lay with a man.

But it had been too long since she last swayed to the Goddess's dance. Even this simple frisk built to a climax. Ecstasy bloomed in a warm rush of sensation, sweet as a stick of honey crystals, surging through her veins and onward.

Alithia welcomed the final step, the rapture made fuller by seasons without. Her release swept her body in breath-stealing waves of bliss, each exultant surge a reassurance of life.

As she lay panting on the furs, her body flushed with heat, Mahon then Rhi slid off the bed, ending their trial. Before the silent regard of other shield pairs, they dressed themselves and withdrew, Mahon rushing ahead as if flames licked his heels. Once they were out of sight, the rest followed, strangely silent, their unusual behavior piercing her euphoria.

Alithia dressed in turn, the lingering tremors of sweetness

resonating within her tempered by a niggle of bewilderment. She couldn't escape the feeling something had gone wrong.

Back in her and Gilsor's room, she turned to the old trader. "What happened? Why were they like that?"

"What do you mean, child?"

"Mahon acted . . . upset after his release. The other shield pairs seemed troubled."

Curghann gave her a forbearant smile. "They are young, and the young have certain illusions about their capabilities. I suspect what you saw was Mahon's disappointment in his performance. He failed to meet the lofty standards he had set for himself."

"Failed?" Alithia shook her head, impatient at his indirection. "That makes no sense."

The old trader combed his fingers through his beard, a gleam of amusement in his dark eyes. "He sees his release as failure at restraint."

"What?" Doubting her ears, she turned to stare at Gilsor, who spread his hands in perplexity. "I would understand if Rhi were resentful, but for Mahon not to want release . . . ?"

She shook her head in incredulity. *Hurranns!*

Taith walked past the warehouses that on other days and other trips would have been their destination. This time they would not trade with brokers. By the old father's invitation, the shield pairs had first option on the goods the southern caravan had brought, and he intended to take full advantage.

Phelan was silent, in all likelihood still brooding over Mahon's devastating show. Why he stewed over such events Taith could not understand. He preferred to acknowledge the problem or mistake and take action or move on to other activities. His shield brother, however, delighted in conjecture, proposing and entertaining even the most outlandish circumstances—and worrying about them. Granted, the habit had been useful and profitable on more than one occasion. But he could not see the appeal of worrying about events that might never come to pass. The futility of trying to anticipate every possible contingency was the path to madness. All the time Phelan had spent wondering about winning a wife had been for naught. Neither of them could have dreamed of the trial Alithia proposed.

By the same coin, his lively mind was the reason Taith had agreed to form a shield pair with Phelan. Left to himself, he might have taken the slower, surer road set down by clan expectations and tradition—and would have hated it. His shield brother's hunger to pledge was what had driven them this far, this fast. It was because of him that Taith had the stake to try for a wife—at least two turns sooner than his blade kin. Pride swelled at the reminder of that accomplishment.

All due to Phelan.

The storehouse they entered was a confusion of casks, bundles, and stacks, an assault of a thousand scents unlike any broker's warehouse they'd ever visited. A shouted greeting heralded the approach of the old father's steward, a wiry, grizzled man the age of his fathers.

"You're in luck. You're the first," Baillin announced as they exchanged warrior grips, his bare forearm like hard leather under Taith's fingers. "Not letting moss grow on you, that's good. Of course, the two of you never did that."

"The others are distracted," Taith explained as the steward extended his hand to Phelan in turn.

"I heard what happened." A wince crossed the voluble man's face. "Was it as bad as they tell it?"

"Probably worse." Phelan shook his head and hopefully his brooding with it.

With a grimace of apology for raising the uncomfortable topic, Baillin waved invitation, the gesture encompassing the entire storehouse. They set off, going down the nearest aisle by silent agreement. "Not all the regular stuff, this time. We didn't go by the usual route because—well, you know." Alithia's presence attended by only the old father and a young kinsman meant they had had to take greater care.

Taith nodded understanding. He ignored the sacks of wheat and other grains, the tin and copper ingots for northern forges piled high like dark gryphon eggs, searching out the smaller and more expensive—thus easier to transport but potentially more profitable—southern goods. Mead, tree syrup, linen, resins, furs, he found all that and more. But profit was more than having rarities that would sell well; it depended on knowing where to sell them and who would buy at the price they set.

Then there was the question of how much coin to spend when there was still the pledge gift and *idkhet* to consider—supposing they won—and how much the entire flight could carry while maintaining their speed and agility. Too heavy a cargo could kill man and mount alike. Or slow the journey to Sentinel Reach.

It was a fine balance to strike.

"What's she like?" Phelan asked as Taith continued his survey of the goods on offer.

"Strong-minded but kind. Himself was opposed to this expedition," Baillin said, referring to the old father. "She brought him around. She's like a daughter to Himself."

Fingering a sample of linen, Taith listened with half an ear. He refused to trance over fair skin . . . likely smoother than the cloth he held . . . red hair that brought to mind Lady's trees in full bloom . . . slender limbs—

He wrested his mind back to the task on hand.

If they waited until they knew for certain Sentinel Reach was their destination, he could make better choices, perhaps even risk special items for specific customers. But if they did wait, their brethren would leave them with fewer choices.

He glanced at Phelan, raising a brow.

"Sentinel Reach." His shield brother barely waited for the gesture, knowing he would ask. "Even if we don't go there, there'll be buyers elsewhere who'll want the same."

Taith smiled, glad Phelan was now focused on business. As he saw it, there was no point in tying oneself in knots over possible failure. "Have you dragonblood?"

The old father's invitation had reached them at the Lady's Hills, fresh from another trip. They had had to sell their stash of the precious powder in order to resupply quickly enough to get to Barda in time for the trial.

Surprise crossed Baillin's face, then as expected he shook his head. "You know dragonblood fetches a much higher price in the south. You won't find any to buy, not here, not for a reasonable price."

Though he had not expected otherwise, Taith grimaced. They preferred to have some dragonblood on their travels, in case of grave wounds, but if he insisted on buying, they probably would not have funds left for other goods, might not even have enough for an acceptable pledge gift.

He exchanged a look of resignation with Phelan. They would have to wait until after Barda to replenish.

"Gems?" Star rubies were highly prized because of their connection to the Lady, while red white onyx was sought for the Horned Lords' favor.

A broad grin answered Taith's question, and Baillin led them to the small office and its strongbox.

The rest of the afternoon passed in trade as Taith and Phelan settled on what to buy and negotiated for good prices with delivery scheduled for after the trials. All three came away satisfied with the results.

After the spurt of normalcy, the sober mood in the dining hall that evening was jarring. Conversations were hushed as the other shield pairs and their crews grappled with the outcome of the first trial. Even Devyn and the others spoke in low tones, as though respecting grief.

Taith ate as quickly as he could, not lingering over the food. The last thing he wanted was for his shield brother to resume brooding. Phelan in a flurry of excitement was a whirlwind of ideas; him in a stew made life uncomfortable with all his relentless questions.

Four

Alithia plumped up the furs behind her, still undecided on how to handle the next shield pair. Yesterday's trial had left her with mixed emotions. While Rhi was talented with both mouth and hands, Mahon was awkward, though stouthearted, persevering despite his baseless embarrassment. Irritation stirred at such wrongheaded thinking. Did that mean she had to limit her play to save her potential husbands from what any Lydian would consider pleasure?

She rather wished Curghann hadn't objected to union—talent with mouth and hands didn't always mean talent in the final step of the Goddess's dance, though she couldn't deny Rhi's shaft was well-formed. She had offered to use a pessary, but the old trader argued that such methods didn't always suffice to prevent breeding—and they already strained tradition by holding the trial without temple sanction. To ask Hurranni husbands to risk a child not of their shield pair may be tempting the demons of chance to mischief. She had heard the wisdom in his words. Thus, she would have to abide by her agreement.

In Lydia, such things didn't matter, since any child was of the mother's clan, and the husband returned to his own clan after the birthing. Not so in Hurrann. Another strangeness she would have to adapt to, if not accept.

Would today's trial be similarly mixed?

Deighann and Kail entered side by side, already bare-chested. With their hair loose, she couldn't tell them apart—a matched set ready to bring her pleasure if the tenting of their trews was any indication. They played up the similarity in their appearance, mirroring the pose of the other. She had heard of other women taking twice-born as lovers but had never had the opportunity herself. Now she understood the appeal. Her fingers itched to touch them, to explore the virile territory they presented, to learn if they responded in the same way and enjoyed the same caresses.

She sat through Curghann's inspection of them, impatience singeing the edges of her restraint. Goddess heat kindled inside her, awaiting the spark of pleasure. She shifted, the furs beneath her rubbing skin tender with anticipation. If only she could roll in them to ease the ache. She hadn't danced the Goddess's dance since spring in Lydia, and yesterday's trial had served as a reminder of how much she had sacrificed.

Once the old trader indicated his satisfaction, Alithia called them both to her, her breasts already swelling for their touch. This trial promised to be better than yesterday's. From the way Deighann and Kail acted, they intended to share.

They moved together, catching her between them, both demanding her lips and raining kisses on her. Without any hesitation, they climbed onto the bed, urging her down on the furs. Unlike Mahon and Rhi, neither took the lead.

Surprise held her pliant before their enthusiasm. Deighann and Kail didn't waste time with the courtesies, plunging straight into the dance. Their hands roamed her body, fondling and teasing, touching her as though they had every right. As though she were already their wife and they her husbands. The Lydian woman in her was piqued by such presumption—but their combined focus overwhelmed her starving senses.

Alithia couldn't tell who touched her or whose body she stroked. But both of them bent down and kissed her aching breasts . . . then found her nipples.

And sucked.

Delight leaped from their tugging lips to the center of her being, desire flaring to vivid life. Moaning, she pulled them closer, fingers tangling in silken hair. She throbbed with need, her skin too tight, the emptiness inside her demanding fulfillment. It had been too long since she had taken a man into herself.

She writhed, finding hard muscle under her hands, over her belly, against her legs, bracketing her with male strength. Their musk filled her every breath and gasp.

This was what yesterday's trial lacked, this harmony of mouths and hands. The promise of two lovers at once. That synchronism magnified the effect of their artless caresses, so unlike Rhi's expertise.

Truly, Deighann and Kail were twice-born, moving with one spirit and a genius for discovery. They found her wet flesh, hard fingers weaving together to tease the sensitive bud within her folds, not a word spoken between them.

Goddess heat spiraled within her. Alithia gasped, her thighs parting unbidden, welcoming their caresses. Her hips rose, urging them deeper.

Low groans answered her. They delved into her wet channel, calloused fingers dancing against her delicate flesh. Firm lips tugged on the tips of her breasts, teeth grazed their slopes, even their hair caressed her.

But it wasn't enough.

Hunger for more than this meager passion woke. She wanted

them stretching her, needed to be filled, craved the heat of a man's shaft, the hard thrusts that scorched the blood. She reached down. Woolen trews denied her the prize she sought—the heavy proof of their desire.

Someone caught her hand. "No."

The fingers at the juncture of her thighs withdrew.

Alithia stilled in shock, disappointment cooling her passion. "No?"

"If you do, we'll break the rules," one murmured, tousled hair veiling narrowed eyes hard and burning.

"No union," the other reminded her, kissing her neck while caressing her breasts with a slick hand. His pelvis against her thigh made his readiness clear, his shaft a thick presence. Only his trews separated them.

Need clawed the center of her being, demanding appeasement, a feral hunger baited by their cunning fingers. She was tempted to declare them her choice in order to have them inside her, filling her the way a woman should be filled.

Only the training of a first daughter stifled the impulse. One raised to direct the affairs of her clan could not afford thoughtless haste. Deighann and Kail were not pleasure loves, to have and send off on the morrow.

*Taith's face felt stiff, his cheeks heavy with the mask of dis-*passionate duty. The weight was familiar, as though it had been merely a sennight since he last wore it instead of several turns of the Lady, during his boyhood at Crescent Bay. He might have been back at the temple, witnessing the Harrowing—the rite before planting that ensured the fertility of the fields.

In his mind's eye, he saw the three priestesses with their husbands on the pallets before the altar, limbs entwined. Heard the gasps and groans of their sacrifice . . . performed before the entire temple. As ever, the memory sent a chill through him, unmitigated by his time with clan Black Python. The prospect of a priest's duties had been the bane of his boyhood.

And yet . . .

He wanted Alithia—for more than the deliverance she represented. He wanted her hands on him. Wanted her voice crying out his name. Wanted to be the reason for her pleasure.

Just then Alithia arched above Kail, her pale body flushed the deep pink that betokened arousal. She was so open with her delight, hiding nothing.

If he breathed deeply, he imagined he could smell her musk. His heart thundered in his ears as he watched Deighann kiss his way to the juncture of her thighs, unable to look away while the Sword laid his mouth where Taith wanted his.

She gasped, tossing her head in delight. Her eagerness for bed play meant her husbands would not have to temper their approach, as one boyhood instructor had said was often needed for more timid wives. On the contrary, she had such confidence in the art of pleasure that he suspected she could have taught that old priest a new skill or three.

Taith was certainly willing to learn, if she wanted to teach him—anything to smell that heady fragrance for himself. It took all his training to maintain his dispassion and to not adjust the fit of his trews.

Phelan's color was high, his pulse fluttering in his throat. Taith did not want to consider what thoughts were running wild in his shield brother's head. He had enough to contend with as it was and did not need more suggestions.

Kail whispered something that made Alithia laugh, a husky chuckle that sent a thrill through Taith as well as a spear of envy. He wanted her to laugh for him, to reach for him, to cry *his* name when she found her release. Watching her lie with another shield pair was difficult when he wanted nothing more than to tear her from their arms and claim her for—

For him and Phelan.

He stifled the selfish voice that tried to contradict him.

Phelan shifted just then, restless with carnal hunger. Taith slung an arm around him, digging his fingers into a tight shoulder to distract his shield brother—and ease his own guilt.

Of course he wanted to claim her for the two of them. They were a shield pair.

Jaw aching, Taith forced himself to watch as together Deighann and Kail brought Alithia to gasping, moaning release—in his mind's eye, seeing himself and Phelan in the shield pair's stead. That was how they were meant to be.

He had known those two had a reputation for bed play, but that was among brethren; he had not thought beyond it to . . . this, their expertise extending to the pleasure of women. His stomach flopped and writhed like a landed fish as Deighann and Kail made the most of their mouths and hands, wringing a final sigh of delight from Alithia.

Taith could not help shaking his head in grudging admiration when the two staggered off the bed, chests heaving, their loins still heavy with unspent desire, their sweaty faces dark with the effort to control themselves, and glowing with proud triumph.

Deighann and Kail had done it, damn them to the Red Lord's hells. If he and Phelan wanted to win Alithia, they would have to perform better—with their brethren standing witness.

The effects of Deighann and Kail's success spread throughout Barda. Men walked about with grins on their faces, exchanging hearty backslaps with uncustomary geniality—almost as though celebrating the birth of a daughter. The way they were carrying on, one might think they'd had a hand in pleasuring Alithia.

Passing another rowdy group already floating in their cups toasting the shield pair, Phelan scowled as he followed Taith around a fountain on their way to the dining hall with Devyn and the rest of their crew behind them. There would be scuffles at the very least tonight, and sore heads in the morning. He didn't mind the occasional dustup himself, but their behavior seemed to make mock of the trials.

Deighann and Kail's table was boisterous that night, a celebration under way. Blood mead flowed freely, as if from a mountain spring instead of the expensive southern liquor it was. The relief of the shield pair was palpable.

Even the tables of the other shield pairs were infected with their high spirits. One of their brethren had succeeded! It made the prospect of their own trial easier to face—and yet more difficult. There was the knowledge that an early release was not inevitable, true; but for the shield pairs still to face trial, the need to surpass that performance preyed on their minds.

Or at least it did on Phelan's.

"So, what'd you learn?" Setting down his eating knife, Devyn propped his elbows on the table, clearly intent on an answer. Like a stern father with recalcitrant sons.

Phelan made a face. "Nothing we can use." He buried his mouth in his tankard, wishing the cold springwater was blood mead, but they couldn't risk having their wits addled with the trial still ahead. A glance at his sword brother told him no help would be forthcoming from that quarter. When Taith got it into his head to watch and learn, he could be frustratingly stubborn about withholding comment lest they be misled.

"Why not?" Gair, one of the younger Swords in their crew, leaned forward to ask from down the table.

"It's simple. I look nothing like Taith. He's taller. He's bigger. He's meaner." Stabbing a chunk of meat, Phelan ducked a swipe at his head that proved his sword brother was listening, despite appearances to the contrary. "See?"

Devyn gave a grunt of dismay. Even he couldn't argue with

the proof of his own eyes, and anyone could see Deighann and Kail were as alike as matched pearls.

"But you'll win, right? I have ten crescents riding on it." Despite his question, Eoghann's grin held no doubt whatsoever.

Phelan stared, the meat skewered on his eating knife forgotten. He shouldn't have been surprised people were betting on the outcome; they laid odds even on traditional trials of arms. If he hadn't been so focused on finally having a wife, he'd have expected the wagers. But ten silver crescents was just two crescents short of the gold flame that was the Shield's pay for the trip. "That much?"

Most of the crew admitted to backing them as well, if not as heavily. Few shield pairs passed on a chance for a windfall.

"Even you, Devyn?"

"I'm too old for that. I have other uses for my coin."

"There's that dragon hide of yours," someone pointed out.

The older man merely shook his head. "That's spoken for."

"What are the odds?" Phelan tallied their funds, wondering how much they could safely risk. He had no intention of losing, but the final decision was Alithia's.

"About even when they were laid."

A surge of determination lifted his spirits. "They still taking bets?"

"You know that's not the way it works."

He pounded the table then remembered his food, biting down in surly disgust at the lost opportunity.

Taith laughed, breaking his silence. "He would not be Phelan if he did not try." His sword brother reached over to pat him on the shoulder. "Not to worry. I put two flames and six crescents down on us."

By the Horned Lords, how had he missed that? He must have been lost in a fog not to have noticed Taith place the bet. Then it hit him. *Two flames and six crescents?* That was nearly their entire profit on the previous trip!

* * *

Back in their room, Phelan shifted restlessly. He lay with his head on Taith's shoulder, an arm and leg slung across Taith; he slept that way almost from the start of their brotherhood. Taith had learned not to mind the heat along his side and the weight anchoring him to the bed.

But at that moment his shield brother was not asleep. "I can't believe you placed a bet, and I didn't notice."

Taith shrugged, amused by Phelan's persistence. "You were distracted. Thinking too much, again. You have to stop that." Not that he expected him to. Even Eoghann would not consider the odds of Phelan changing his ways worth a bet.

While he might not understand the attraction such speculation held for his shield brother, that fertile mind was what made Phelan stand out from the other boys in Crescent Bay, when Phelan was a fosterling. On the escapades he had dragged Taith into, Phelan would speak of traveling the length and breadth of Hurrann. Taith had known Phelan would go far—and far was what Taith wanted.

As far from Crescent Bay and its temple as he could get, though he had never thought to venture beyond the peaks.

When they announced their brotherhood, everyone expected Phelan to be Sword and Taith Shield, even Phelan. That would not have suited Taith at all; at least Black Python's clan house was in the Lady's Hills at the feet of the peaks, not by the sea. Phelan had been surprised and relieved when Taith offered to be Shield, little realizing it had been no sacrifice at all.

"If you want me to stop thinking, you know what you can do." Phelan grinned up at Taith, a hand already tracing patterns on Taith's belly, ruffling the line of hair below his navel. "Volunteering?"

Their room was warded and no one expected. Neither of them had taken release since they arrived in Barda. There was no reason for restraint tonight. Their hoped-for wife had arrived.

Desire roused a heavy ache in Taith's loins. Though the past days had stirred unwelcome boyhood nightmares, watching their brethren pleasure Alithia had also sharpened his hunger to throbbing hardness.

He had taken release with Phelan before. As a shield pair, it was inevitable they would engage in bed play, honing the skills that would pleasure their wife. Few brethren did not, not when it took at least a grand turn—two and ten turns of the Lady—to save enough to be worthy of pledging. But tonight his shield brother was distracted, his touch meandering with little of his usual haste.

Certain Phelan would share his thoughts soon enough, Taith reciprocated the slow caress, enjoying the novelty of a gradual ascent to the heights of pleasure. He avoided the small nipples, keeping to the less sensitive chest muscles given definition by constant sword practice. The heat beneath his palm was a comfort, the strong, steady heartbeat reassurance. His shield brother who did not hesitate to reach for what he wanted.

There was something intensely satisfying about touching and being touched. In sharing a moment of intimacy. In knowing he was not alone.

"Do you think bed play with a wife will be different?"

For once, Phelan's question did not puzzle Taith; instead, it infected him with some of his shield brother's curiosity. Remembering Alithia's enthusiasm for bed play, he could not help but imagine touching and being touched by Alithia.

"Of course it is."

Phelan stilled. "How d'you know?"

"We are taught to use a gentle touch on the breasts—breasts are soft, unlike muscle." Taith scraped short nails over the firm slabs of Phelan's chest to make his point. Alithia's breasts were not the first he had seen, though they were certainly the fairest—like cream topped with petal candy.

"Hmmm . . ."

"As with Alithia, girls do not have this strange ripple in their bellies." He brought his hand down, skimming said ripple.

Phelan laughed. "You mean like this?" He poked Taith's belly in mock accusation.

"And they do not have such bony hips." Taith rubbed a calloused finger over Phelan's hipbone where the skin was thin and his shield brother especially sensitive.

A hiss and a shiver rewarded his teasing. "You're always so logical." His shield brother arched up to give him a hard kiss tangy with the ghost of spices as he rolled on top of him, his hands doing some teasing of their own.

"Most importantly, they have a sheath, not a blade." Taith reached down, catching Phelan's in a knowing grip and stroking him in time to his words. "Said to be wet and warm and tight." The ultimate mystery and the closest any man could approach the Lady of Heaven.

Memory confirmed the priests' teachings; the sacrifices he had witnessed attested to their truth. He thrust aside the thought of countless eyes upon him, watching and judging—only he and Phelan were here. When they stood trial, there would only be ten witnesses—ten too many for his comfort, but better than an entire temple. Still, his rocks prickled at the reminder, dread touching him with tiny claws.

Phelan groaned, grinding his flesh into Taith's fist. "Wet and warm and tight?" A shudder passed through him, likely his imagination catching fire.

Taith found himself grinning at Phelan's fervent response. In some ways, his shield brother was very predictable. "Slow, now. You are always in a rush." His protest was halfhearted, gratified as he was at his success.

"If I hadn't been, you'd be Lughann's Sword now."

The unexpected reply gave Taith pause. "That was turns and turns ago. You still think of that?" He made a face as he sank his hand in Phelan's hair and cradled his head.

Phelan levered himself up, his gaze unyielding. "Of course I do. I won, didn't I?" His next kiss was more aggressive, a clash of firm lips and sharp teeth—perhaps too aggressive for bed play with a wife, but not unusual between them. His hands went straight for Taith's nipples, rasping and tweaking, sparking a burst of delight that heated the blood.

Need awakened, uncoiled, stretching itself through Taith. He exhaled with a growl of approval, his pulse throbbing insistently in his loins. As well as he knew Phelan's pleasure points, so did his shield brother know his.

Their play turned vigorous, the inevitable challenge between two men such as they, especially when Phelan's patience snapped its bonds. They wrestled with soft chuckles, grunts, and sudden gasps, the planks of the bed creaking beneath them.

Taith's larger body gave him an edge, but it also gave Phelan more skin to touch—an advantage his shield brother exploited to the fullest.

Excitement rose, built on the quick thrill of little nips, the steady rasp of calloused fingers, the familiar breath-stealing friction of hot, sweaty skin on bare blade. Fire kindled in Taith's rocks, licked the length of his blade. Need spiraled up, like a hungry wyvern taking flight.

They arched against each other, intent now on satisfaction. Rubbing. Stroking. Struggling against breathless desire as they scaled the heights of passion.

Release came on a sudden stroke of freedom, a fountain of sheer delight purging all tension from the body. They groaned as one, united in pleasure as in all else in their brotherhood.

A feeling of well-being suffused Taith, a lightness of spirit that was its own soporific.

Phelan stretched, stifling a yawn behind a fist as he settled back into his usual position, his head on Taith's shoulder. "Do you mind that we came to Barda? We could always wait until the next turn, go to the temple as is proper."

The sleepy question roused Taith faster than a shove from his wyvern. Turn away from the trial? Surrender all hope of winning Alithia and concede defeat?

"Banish the thought." Until the old father's invitation, Taith had never considered the possibility of a southern wife. But if he truly wished to avoid priesthood, pledging themselves to Alithia was surely the best way to ensure it.

Five

For the third time, Taith and Phelan filed into the trial chamber with their brethren to see Alithia on the bed, the embodiment of everything feminine. Each time Taith saw her in all her pale glory was a punch in the gut. It amazed him that someone so small could contain so much of the Lady's blessings.

And she had the will to pursue her goals—claws, as Devyn had said. Taith had to agree, remembering the stipulation in the old father's invitation that her husbands convey her to Sentinel Reach and accompany her to the south, beyond the peaks. Despite the trial's lack of martial flavor, it was no whim on her part.

Slann and Arghal entered the chamber wearing their silk robes, though not their knife belts. Bare chests were visible between their lapels. No tunic. No trews, either. When the old father inspected them, it immediately became clear they were naked under the robes.

Phelan's grip on his arm demanded Taith's attention.

He glanced at his frowning shield brother. "What?"

"They're gambling on contrast. Deighann and Kail didn't risk removing their trews, so they did."

Taith could not dispute Phelan's conclusion. Yet when the shield pair began their trial, they did not remove their robes. What were Slann and Arghal about?

Their strategy quickly became obvious.

Leaving the robes to gape open, they teased Alithia with glimpses of their bodies while trying the usual preliminaries. Taith could almost see her interest stirring, much like a swamp leopard with prey. Then Slann caught her wrists behind her, and Arghal slipped off his robe, using it over her belly.

Even as Alithia gasped, objections rose, Phelan's among them. Gritting his teeth, Taith held his peace, knowing how the old father must answer.

"It is not power. There is no spell. You may proceed."

Phelan turned outraged eyes to Taith in silent demand that he add his voice to the protests.

Taith could only shake his head in admiration. "They have the right of it. Use of spells and attempting union are the only ways to violate the rules, not silk. It was astute of them to realize that."

"But—"

A purr of approval emphasized the soundness of Slann and Arghal's tactic—and no other shield pair could match them in their weapon of choice. The sounds of Alithia's pleasure hardened Taith's determination. He and Phelan had to find another way to compete—to excel—if they wanted to win.

Slann's grip on her wrists trapped Alithia's hands behind her, a hold no Lydian man would have dared. She would have protested—should have protested—except Arghal was doing something with his silk robe that had her squirming with delight. The expensive fabric sliding over her made her body tingle, so cool yet evoking so much Goddess heat. That smooth slither and the contrast with his rough palms sent an exquisite thrill through her unlike anything the other shield pairs had wrought.

Pleasure shimmered, spreading from Arghal's hands to her tight nipples and the very tips of her toes. He plied the silk all over her body, burnishing her skin until she fairly glittered with delight.

She writhed from the indulgence of her senses—too much, too quick, too vulnerable. Too selfish. Something woke inside her, protesting her simple acceptance. No first daughter would submit to such impertinence without exacting a price.

Contradictory impulses. But that didn't mean she couldn't assuage both.

Alithia reached back, her fingers finding Slann's flesh through his robe. Thick and warm and pulsing. So very thick and male. It was a good thing his hold prevented her from twisting around, or she might have flung caution and fairness overboard and attempted union. But even just the sensation of a man's shaft in her hand was a delight in its own. She squeezed him—carefully—to avoid a repeat of the upset of the first trial.

Still he gasped.

Kneeling over her, Arghal paused to stare at his sword brother, his hands stopping their lovely motions. "Slann?"

She couldn't have that. Stretching her leg, she stroked the inside of his thigh with her toes, then slid the top of her foot against his crisp nether curls and the orbs they veiled. Her toes curled at the light contact. Even those parts of him were hot and firm.

Arghal shuddered, his focus transferring to her, his fierce gaze, the flare of his nostrils and the taut skin across his cheeks giving him a feral expression. "What did you do?"

"He is fine. I just thought he might want some pleasure of his own." Riding a wave of triumph, Alithia tipped her head back to consider the expression on Slann's face and smiled. There was not a hint of that first bashful smile now. He looked like he was thoroughly enjoying her caresses. She danced her fingers along his length, dragging her nails over the delicate head of his shaft, using the silk of his robe on him in the same way his shield brother was using his on her. "Like that?"

With a growl, Slann took her mouth, his hands pressing hers harder against him, his hips rocking to her touch. "That is so—" His voice broke on a gasp when she squeezed again.

She laughed against his lips, delighted by the success of her ploy. Just because they had the advantage of strength didn't mean she had no wiles of her own. The first daughter within her approved of the change in balance.

Taith's hand slashed out in warning as he stopped in his tracks. When Phelan glanced at his sword brother for an explanation, Taith tilted his head toward the wyvern run they were passing and drifted closer to the fence.

Wondering what had caught Taith's attention, Phelan joined him. All he could hear were the wyverns' low hoots. Seeing no one around, he strained to listen. Voices carried on the still air, a phrase, a grunt, no conversation he could make out.

Taith lifted a brow in question.

Having no preference one way or another, Phelan flapped a hand, leaving the choice to him.

His sword brother walked along the fence, his steps as silent as a hunting swamp leopard's. Of necessity, Phelan stalked his heels. A good Shield guarded his Sword's back, and he prided himself in being a good Shield. Nearly ten turns together was no guarantee of continued brotherhood, only pledging to a wife. It wasn't unheard of for a shield pair to part ways, and he had no intention of losing Taith to some ambitious would-be Shield.

The voices became louder, clearer, and it was obvious what the shield pair—the two speakers had to be a shield pair, though no one Phelan recognized—were about.

"Did you hear her?" A lecherous groan followed. "I swear,

hearing her moans was enough to make me hard. Can you imagine touching her? Those breasts!"

A coarse laugh answered. "I won't last if I do. I'd love to show her my horn."

Phelan exchanged a look of disgust with Taith. There was nothing to gain in lessoning such boors. He jerked his head at his sword brother, urging him away. This time, when he walked, Taith was behind him.

"What was that about?" It wasn't like Taith to be so curious when there was no danger nor chance for profit.

His sword brother scowled. "They were talking about Alithia. They said her name. That was why I sought them out."

Phelan stopped in the middle of the lane between two runs, righteous anger striking him dumb. *They what?!* He was sorely tempted to hunt the two down to teach them some manners, but that wouldn't solve Taith and his problem. It would relieve their frustration but not the source—and they didn't have time to indulge a whim.

He tugged on his braid, trying to uproot temptation. The negligible hurt didn't distract him nearly enough. He exhaled sharply, forcing out the tension knotting his shoulders. "No profit there. Let it go."

In silence, they continued to the stable for their discussion. Rather than haul their belongings to their room and assign one of their crew to guard them, they'd left most of it in Bulla's stall. Taith's mount was choosy about whom he allowed inside and was better protection than a spell—nastier, too.

Taith helped him unpack, the fractious wyvern watching them from the opening to the communal wyvern run while Dinglis sprawled outside on the grass and soaked up the afternoon heat.

Dry scales crunching underfoot, Phelan paced, staring in perplexity at the small assortment of baggage—mainly weapons and treasure. He'd spread it out, everything they'd brought with them to Barda, hoping he'd overlooked something useful. His heart dropped at the limited options. They'd packed for speed and a trial of arms, leaving the trinkets that they considered nonessential at Black Python's clan house in the Lady's Hills. The goods they'd brought for trade had been sold shortly after their arrival in Barda. What could they possibly use for the trial? They didn't have matching appearances. They didn't have silks. After Slann and Arghal's performance, they'd need the Horned Lords' own luck to win their hoped-for wife. That pair even managed to retain their control!

He paused long enough to wonder what Bronn and Lughann planned for the morrow. They had the same problem but didn't seemed worried at all, despite the showing of the last two pairs. Was there something after all to Lughann's hints? What did they know that made them so confident? Was it something Taith and he could adapt for their trial?

"Focus on what we know."

The impatient sound of Taith's voice recalled Phelan to himself. What had they been discussing again? What they knew, that's it.

"She likes her breasts touched and sucked." He swallowed as the thought of putting old lessons to practice brought his blade to full and aching hardness, looking away as he wiped off the sweat gathering above his lip. "That technique of the mouth between her thighs."

"And hand techniques for there." Sitting on their strongbox, Taith oiled his saddle, a never-ending duty if one was to avoid sores in both rider and wyvern, but this time Phelan didn't find the familiar activity reassuring, suspecting as he did that his sword brother just wanted to occupy his hands—busywork since they had no idea how to surpass Slann and Arghal's ingenuity.

But the repetitive motion was hypnotic.

Hand techniques.

"Yes, that, too." His rocks throbbed, their sac tighter. He fought to ignore them. Now wasn't the time for that—as Taith would be sure to point out. And anyway, he wasn't about to risk some shield pair catching him seeking release out in the open like those oafs.

"Teeth."

"What?"

"Rhi nibbled her shoulders."

Phelan turned wide eyes at his sword brother. "How d'you know he did?"

Taith tapped the base of his neck. "I saw the marks. Believe me, Rhi nibbled."

And no one could deny the Shield's success, despite Mahon's poor showing. "Teeth, then. I wonder if she likes it everywhere or just on her shoulders." The thought of using his teeth on her petals sent another jab of need through his rocks. He licked dry lips as he contemplated performing that intimacy.

"More important is what she does not like."

"Not like?" Stopping in the middle of the stall, Phelan searched his memory of the trials for Taith's meaning. Nothing came to mind to contradict his impression of confident, knowledgeable enthusiasm on Alithia's part.

"Rhi was on top of her on the bed."

He blinked at the reminder—and its implication—indignation stirring belatedly. "That was almost sacrilege. The woman isn't supposed to be under the man; that would be like the Lady of Heaven submitting to one of the Horned Lords!"

Taith gave him a wry smile before bending back over his saddle. "He forgot himself. But I am certain that was not what Alithia was thinking at the time. There was no outrage for any disrespect. She simply did not like it."

"We'll have to remember that." Phelan settled on his haunches to stare at their useless weapons. Was all the trouble they were taking to prepare for this trial truly justified? A trial of arms didn't require all this planning. They just had to go out and fight to win and prove to the temple their worthiness of pledging. He had few doubts as to their success if presented with a traditional trial.

When it came down to it, they were almost certain to have sufficient funds for the temple's tithe, come the next turn of the Lady. They could take their chances then. There was no need to subject themselves to potential embarrassment.

Don't be a mush head, Phelan. That's cowardice speaking. Truth be told, he simply didn't relish the thought of coming up short in the eyes of Alithia. He'd always wanted to form a shield pair and pledge his bond to a wife. This was no time to lose heart at the first chance of attaining his dream.

He supposed it was balance he sought, a marriage like what his fathers have and the priests of his childhood. He missed that simple happiness. One was lonely, two a game of push and pull—although amusing at times, it was as though something was missing. Three was just right—stable like a brazier's tripod. That was what a wife brought to the shield pair bound to her.

Then, too, he couldn't forget the mysterious, indescribable air of satisfaction he remembered on his fathers' and other husbands' faces after a bout of bed play—hinting at pleasure beyond what he could achieve with his own hands. To a young boy, it had been a forbidden secret he'd yearned to know.

A secret for husbands.

Permitted only to husbands.

Through union.

That boyhood fascination had driven him since then. He wanted that intimacy, that affection, that love he'd witnessed between his fathers and mother for himself. He couldn't back down now.

There was also Taith to think of. He couldn't disappoint his sword brother this late in the trial by proposing they surrender their chance to pledge their bonds without even trying.

As early as now, Taith seemed to be waking to himself, to want Alithia for more reasons than just custom and fulfilling clan expectations or Phelan's need—reasons of his own. If they didn't win the trial, would his sword brother return to his sleep, not asking anything for himself? It wasn't fair that they as a shield pair always worked toward Phelan's goals, Phelan's ambitions, never Taith's.

Surely his sword brother deserved better?

Like a prod from the Red Lord's sword, that fear slashed through the confusion of his churning thoughts. Phelan pounded his fist on the straw-covered floor. "We're going about this the wrong way."

Not bothering to straighten, Taith merely cast him a questioning glance as he continued oiling his saddle. "How so?"

Trembling with excitement, Phelan met his sword brother's gaze. "By treating it as if it's still a trial of arms—it's not. The rules are no beads and no union. The trial ends when the shield pair concedes an end to their attempt. Nothing requires us to wait to start." A sense of exaltation stretched his lips in a wide grin.

"Come." He led Taith out of the stables and up the mountainside, borne on a fever of certainty.

"What are we to do here?" His sword brother surveyed the grassy slope that was too steep for gargants. Bereft of frequent grazing, it was dotted with the yellows and reds of blooming serpentroot as high as their knees.

"Baillin said she likes flowers, so we bring her some." Drawing a knife, Phelan stalked a likely clump of color. They couldn't get just any blown flower; it had to be pretty to be worthy of Alithia. "See, because the trial is one of pleasure, there's no reason not to approach her. And why not bring her a gift? Women like gifts."

"You know this . . . how?"

"My blade father gives my mother little things. It makes her smile." He smiled at the memory of his mother's delight.

When Taith continued to frown, Phelan gripped his shoulder. "Remember, we need every advantage. The trial might be held in that chamber, but that's the final stage."

* * *

Alithia leaned back against the sun-warmed stone wall, the cool night breeze caressing her bare breasts, her whirling thoughts returning to the day's trial like a leaf caught in a vortex. Had she been wrong to accept Curghann's advice? The need for completion burned inside her. Her body craved fulfillment. She had never been one to deny the Goddess her due, and the pleasure loves of spring had been so long ago. In Lydia, union was the obvious step, the culmination of the celebration of life—yet she had given her word to refrain from union.

The stars twinkled, mocking her confusion. Here in the mountains, the heavens looked so near, as though she could reach out and pluck one of the multitude of stars from the sky the way one might choose a diamond from a jeweler's tray. In Lydia, the torches lit the night until only the brightest stars remained in the sky—them and the two moons—much diminished in splendor. So diminished, Adal and Egon were merely a fox and an erne, not warrior lords worthy to serve the Goddess.

The curtain twitched behind her, disgorging her brother, his breath smelling of the spicy stew they had for supper. "You've been standing there all evening. What's wrong?"

"Just wondering if I made the correct decision."

Gilsor stepped up to the balcony rail to rest his forearms on it and study the dark streets of Barda. "Why?"

"I denied the Goddess Her due again."

He glanced back at her in surprise, brow upraised. "All I saw was pleasure freely given. How's that a denial of Her?"

"No union, though I wanted it." She still wanted it, now more than ever. The morrow's trial would be more difficult because of her growing need. Sweet though it was, the pleasure she received during the trials was meager fare compared with the ecstasy of union.

Her restless hands stroked the rough stone, remembering firm male flesh. She hadn't felt an ache like this before, had never had to refrain from union for so long. There were always willing men if she wanted, drawn by the prestige of a first daughter's interest. Yet it was her duty now to abstain. She had given her word, the word of a first daughter of clan Redgrove.

Twisting around to face her fully, Gilsor grinned. "'Pleasure postponed is pleasure increased.' Didn't someone tell me that at some point? It bears repeating."

Alithia laughed, reluctantly amused. "What did I know?"

His smile faded. "Do you have a preference among them?"

She tilted her head back, resting it on the wall. She had difficulty finding the Fisher, the first constellation she had learned to recognize as a child because it was one of the brightest in summer; she found it sparkling lower in the sky than in Lydia, its stars simply greater lights in the crowded heavens. To see its shape, she had to ignore the twinkling of the multitude, the fish in the Night Sea filling its net. Hurranns had to see other constellations. By seeking the Fisher, was she blinding herself to those shapes?

"Better not to. The mothers would tell you preference should have nothing to do with marriage."

Gilsor grunted, a furrow between his brows. Disappointment?

Lughann's bright grin flashed before her eyes, followed by Rhi's easy smile. Of the brethren vying to marry her, they seemed the ones most like the pleasure loves Alithia had left behind in Lydia. But such trifles shouldn't matter to a first daughter, one who would lead the clan when her time came. "I know too little to have a preference."

"But this marriage would be . . . permanent, no end written into the contract. What if you don't like them outside the Goddess's dance?"

"I pray She will guide the trial, that the most suitable shield pair wins." Alithia raised her eyes to the stars once more. Gilsor went back inside shortly after, perhaps sensing her need for solitude.

As she stood there, two men turned onto the street, bearing themselves with the confidence of warriors, their stride smooth and unhurried. There was something seductive about all that confidence and control and the smooth flow of muscle. Why had she never taken a warrior to her bed? Surely there had been some in Lydia with that virile grace that now made her pulse skip?

They drew nearer, and Alithia recognized them as one of the shield pairs: Taith and Phelan. Clan Black Python.

Their walk was purposeful, stopping beneath her balcony. They looked up at her, Phelan with a wide smile that gleamed in the starlight. Then Taith with some reluctance helped the Shield climb to his shoulders, raising him high enough to grab the balcony.

Phelan scrambled the rest of the way up to perch on the rail. "Good eve, lady."

She hid a smile behind her hand. "Good eve to you both. Phelan, I believe, and Taith."

"We come bearing gifts." Excitement glittered in his eyes as he reached behind him. When he brought his fist back, it was full of bright yellow flowers, slightly bruised. Each wide cup had five dark red spots clustered around the center that seemed to glow in Adal's light.

The thoughtfulness of their gift warmed her heart. Clearly it had been chosen with her in mind. Simple flowers wouldn't impress most first daughters.

"They are beautiful. Thank you." On impulse, Alithia kissed Phelan on the cheek and blew a kiss to Taith. Accepting the bouquet, she traced a delicate petal with a wondering finger. So soft and fragrant, sweet spice with an undertone of green. She had never seen their like. "What are they called?"

"Serpentroot."

Alithia glanced at Phelan in surprise. She couldn't recall any mention of serpentroot in the scrolls of Hurranni herb lore she studied. "How did it come to have such a name?"

He blinked at the question, nonplussed, then glanced down at Taith.

"The sap of its roots is potent against snakebite," the Sword explained, seeming content to wait below. He made no move to join them.

"A useful herb." She would have to remember to ask Curghann about serpentroot.

"To whom do you speak, child?" As if summoned by her thought, the old trader stepped through the curtain. At the sight of her companion, he grunted, a frown knitting his thick, white brows. "Climbing balconies now?"

Undaunted by Curghann's dry welcome, Phelan grinned, exuding good-natured charm. "We didn't want to bother anyone." He gave them a respectful bow, then slid off the rail—to be caught by Taith in an amazing display of trust and strength.

The shield pair left Alithia clutching their gift, an unbidden smile on her face and a strange warmth in her heart.

Six

Curghann completed his inspection, leaving Bronn and Lughann to approach Alithia, clothed in plain shirts and trews, though unarmed. The other shield pairs stood in a crescent behind them, watchful, silent, and motionless. In the previous days, she hadn't paid much heed to their presence. But today she was conscious of Phelan's eyes on her as a prickling on her skin.

Bronn and Lughann traded glances, that silent communication she had noticed between shield pairs, then Bronn pointed his chin at his shield brother. The big man so similar to Mahon took a step back, clearly yielding the initiative for their trial.

Lughann met her gaze with a grin, his eyes sweeping her body with such an appreciative glance that she had to smile back when they returned to her face. He toyed with the tail of his shirt in pretend uncertainty.

Relaxing against the bed's furs, Alithia extended a hand in invitation, his flirtation an approach that was familiar from her pleasure loves. "No need to be shy."

"Promise you'll be gentle?"

She laughed, delight in his game bubbling up irrepressibly despite her inner tension. All the others had been so serious, treating the trial as if it were a matter of life and death. "You will have to take your chances and see."

Lughann took her hand and raised it to his mouth for a kiss, his gaze modest yet hopeful, polite with but a hint of boldness. Taking a finger between his lips, he nibbled gently then sucked it deeper, teasing her with a mimicry of forbidden union.

The first stirrings of Goddess heat swirled in Alithia's veins, titillated by the promise of more and better to come. At the same time, doubt woke to nibble at her equanimity. Should she encourage Bronn and Lughann when she now hoped Taith and Phelan would win?

Bending his head almost diffidently, Lughann transferred his attentions to her wrist, his mouth brushing the thin skin in the softest of kisses.

Her heart leaped as though goaded, her arm throbbing where he laid his lips. His measured overture called up memories of her pleasure loves, partners accustomed to treading the steps of the great dance. A breath of home in this alien place.

The reminder made her smile. Here was no chance of inflicting humiliation.

By his actions, Lughann knew the rules and accepted them. He offered himself to her, waited until she tugged at his shirt before pulling it off, letting her explore his body at her leisure—much like a Lydian man would.

However much she might wish to end the trial, it wouldn't be fair not to give them a chance. Duty and training demanded she give each shield pair due consideration. Impulse had no place here, not when the fate of clan Redgrove hung in the balance. She had to trust that the Goddess would guide her decision.

Alithia hooked her hand behind Lughann's neck and drew him closer, burying her fingers into his hair. Coarse silk to the touch.

She could imagine how it would feel across her breasts. Drawing a black lock to her face, she rubbed it against her cheek, smelling cedar and clean male.

Desire flared as the scent woke more memories—of passion and carefree laughter, of a time before duty became her foremost consideration.

Despite the unabashed hunger in his eyes, he made no presumptions, didn't touch her more intimately until she placed his dark hand on her breast. Still, his touch was fleeting, sliding over her, almost more shadow than man against her pale skin. The contrast was exotic—that beautiful darkness in one nearly Lydian in his manners. But it wasn't enough.

"Lughann," Alithia protested, wanting what he withheld.

"Command me," he whispered against her lips, sweat gleaming on his taut cheeks, his nostrils flared.

Excitement filled her, throbbed in the center of her being. "Touch me. Everywhere," she ordered, and his caresses grew surer.

His eyes blazed with black fire. "Watch me."

Half sprawled on the bed, he bent over her, pressing her breasts together with calloused hands and nuzzling his face against their slopes. The sight of that darkness against her skin sent an incredible thrill singing through her. His tongue lashed out for a quick flick across her nipple, but then he stilled. The next lick was slow, lavishing a wet stroke around her nipple and urging it to aching tightness. "Horned Lords, you're so sweet."

Delight sparkled, burnished with each tender, lingering stroke. Alithia lay back, the softness of the furs beneath her heightening the sensations. His hair spilled over his shoulders, a silken caress across her body all the more potent for its abruptness, but it was as nothing compared to his mouth. She lifted her breasts for more of his attention.

Lughann drew on them, his suction stoking the Goddess heat in the center of her being, a blazing brand thrown into the bonfire that was her hungry flesh. He sought her gaze as he suckled, his own ardent, urging her to watch as his dusky lips pulled on her nipple, as his lean, night-dark cheeks nestled against her breasts, as his jaw worked in time with the unseen flicks of his tongue.

The indescribable intimacy of that look—as though he was offering her the very essence of himself—shook Alithia to the core. Her body thrummed to the beat of his strokes, the connection between them unfettered.

She pressed her thighs together, trying to ease the emptiness blooming inside. The insidious caress of the thick furs beneath her was no help. Finding no respite from the ache, she caught Lughann's head and pressed his mouth closer. With her other hand, she rubbed his hair over her yearning body in a vain attempt to slake her growing hunger. "Harder."

He nibbled on her, the edges of his teeth sparking a shiver she felt all the way to her toes. His hands wandered over her, growing in fervor, touching and kneading and squeezing.

But it wasn't enough.

When she pushed at his trews, he quickly stood up and discarded them, obediently baring himself to her avid gaze. His shaft was almost as dark as the rest of him, rising straight and proud and long. Just the sight of him renewed the tingling of her nipples.

Knowing how that much flesh would feel inside her, Alithia bit her lip, struggling against temptation. It had to be enough that she could touch him. Until the trials were completed, that was all she could do.

But when she reached for him, Lughann gasped, his muscles tensing under her fingers. He didn't quite flinch, and he relaxed immediately, but she couldn't believe that his apprehension was gone—his reaction was too sudden not to be truth. The reckless tumult of her passion cooled, the sense of a special trust between them fading as she recalled herself to the purpose of the trial.

Forcing her hand from his shaft, she stroked his hip instead, exploring the tender flesh of his inner thigh. So very dark. She had never imagined skin that could make hers look like snow. There was something unbelievably titillating about seeing her hands on his ebony darkness—he put that wood to shame.

Lughann shuddered under her touch, his shaft twitching and curving higher. So sensitive. There were so many things she could think of doing with one so responsive in bed play.

She slid off the bed to kneel beside him and nibble on his hip, taking the thin skin between her teeth in teasing menace.

He gulped audibly, the eye of his shaft weeping musky dew. There was no mistaking his surprise or delight—more dew seeped down his length when she licked the bite.

Alithia could not help smiling. Here, as in other ways, this Hurrann proved himself no different from her Lydian pleasure loves. A pity that the salt on her tongue was his sweat—not his dew, which she couldn't allow herself to taste.

Her knees complained at the hardness of the floor. Not one for discomfort, she returned to the furs.

Despite his earlier start, Lughann climbed onto the bed after her without any apparent hesitation and lay down when she pushed on his shoulder.

As Alithia made to resume their game, Bronn's eyes glowing with eagerness caught her attention over Lughann's shoulder. He had stripped off his clothes while his shield brother occupied her attention. Would he wait his turn if she decided to take them one at a time? He appeared willing to stand beside the bed until Lughann was done, but that didn't seem fair. She was choosing two, not merely one husband. Would they share?

Her hand went out to Bronn even before the thought was complete, the invitation as natural as breathing.

The Sword approached her with similar diffidence, waiting for her to indicate her desires before touching her. He was a large man—nearly as large all over as Mahon. The similarity was enough of a reminder to keep her hands away from his shaft.

He added his hands to Lughann's, equally obedient to her instructions, doing no more than she commanded. His touch was slow, not necessarily awkward but certainly cautious—caressing her as if she were a precious jewel or some fragile flower that would bruise if he breathed too hard on her.

Alithia nearly laughed. A first daughter wasn't anything so delicate. The demands of clan and Goddess wouldn't permit it.

Such diffidence in so large a man intrigued—she suspected that was as he and Lughann planned. But from the tentative way Bronn continued to stroke her, one might think he had never been with a woman before!

She pulled him down into her kiss, showing him how she wanted to be touched and where. While their Lydian manners were nice, she much preferred it when her pleasure loves lost control and forgot themselves in the urgency of passion.

Their restraint was a challenge to her womanhood. She was tempted to test their control, to see if they truly could hold out against her wiles as Slann and Arghal had. But Mahon's reaction and Lughann's own apprehension reined in that impulse, a pang of guilt following in memory's trail.

If they refused to take release at her hands, was it fair to stoke their desire? If they would not take that last step, perhaps it would be kinder to simply leave them to pleasure her and not draw them into the fullness of the great dance—though it gave her less basis to judge their suitability.

Phelan stared, unable to look away as Alithia responded to Bronn's and Lughann's caresses. Theirs was an approach he hadn't anticipated. Who noticed skin? Lughann's was dark—but nothing out of the ordinary. Many of the clans from around Dragon's Foot and the western peaks were similarly dark—nothing like the milk-white skin of their hoped-for wife, now tinted a beautiful pink.

Was her skin as soft as it looked? As sweet as Lughann whispered? Or was that just more of the shield pair's tactics? His cheek tingled where she kissed him last night, taunting him with the memory of the softness of her lips.

As uncertain as it looked, their hesitant approach—as though she were a swamp leopard they wanted to tame—seemed to appeal to Alithia. She showed none of the surprise of the previous trials, her body losing a hint of tension he hadn't realized had been there until it was gone.

Could Taith and he adapt Bronn and Lughann's approach without appearing false? Taith might have the patience, but Phelan doubted either of them could wait that long to touch her when it was finally their trial.

She laughed when Lughann made some teasing comment about her fairness and his "fear" that he would leave smudges on her body, her low chuckle full of confidence. Clearly she didn't mind; in fact, she seemed to delight in their differences. It seemed the Shield's earlier confidence hadn't been misplaced.

Phelan glanced at Taith, then his own hand, instinctively comparing their brownness to the Shield's darkness. Nothing his sword brother nor he could do would change their skins tonight.

He wrapped his fingers around his belt, his knuckles aching from his grip. Alithia's cries of pleasure made his heart and blade leap even as his stomach roiled, overset by misgivings.

How could they surpass the performances of the other shield pairs? He hated the helplessness assailing him, constrained by the rules to await their own trial. Action had always been his answer, not standing around while doubts pecked him.

For once, Taith's dispassionate mien did little to dispel his fears. In the light of Lughann's unique approach, he couldn't help but wonder at his sword brother's thoughts. Appreciation of the shield pair's strategy, ideas for their own trial or . . . Lady forbid, regret that he was Phelan's Sword instead of Lughann's? That old worry rasped at his equanimity with the stiffness of dried leather.

Bronn moved with some of the uncertainty of Mahon, cautious despite Alithia's obvious approval, leaving her to lead him where she wanted. How much of that was stratagem and how much was Bronn's innate reserve? He even left that technique of the mouth to Lughann!

Despite Phelan's doubts about the Sword, Alithia clearly had none about Bronn's performance. She writhed in ever more voluptuous motions, her gasps and moans whispering through the tension-filled chamber, her vivid hair the flame that should have burned the charwood that was the shield pair.

Phelan averted his eyes, his racing heart plugged in his throat, too perturbed to watch. Unfortunately for him, not looking was of little help. The sounds building up to release nearly unmanned him, spurring the seed in his rocks to rise and threaten to spill free.

He stared at the other shield pairs, hoping the reminder of their presence would strengthen his control. Across from Taith and him, Deighann and Kail leaned against each other, seemingly unmoved, but their eyes were fixed on the bed. Mahon's throat worked, his jaw tense, his face darker than usual. Rhi didn't reveal much, but the scar on his cheek seemed more prominent than usual. He couldn't see Slann standing on the other side of Arghal, but the Shield was restless on his feet, the tenting of his silk tunic betraying his arousal.

A tug on his braid startled Phelan out of the fervid stew of his thoughts in time to hear Alithia's drawn-out cry of delight. His arms prickled on a shiver of pent-up desire.

Unable to stop himself, Phelan turned to the bed where Alithia lay in boneless languor, her breasts rising and falling in fascinating regularity, a smile of satisfaction on her lips.

Kneeling on all fours, Bronn dropped his head to the furs, his hair hiding his expression, but from the deliberate way he left the bed, he was at the verge of release. Now that the trial was over, Lughann was gasping for breath, equally careful in his motions.

But there was no denying the shield pair's success.

* * *

*"That leaves the dragonblood, amber, copal, and various bal*sams for delivery on the morrow." Curghann made a notation on a scrap of vellum, his char stick wielded with great precision. The figures he drew made no sense to Alithia; the old trader didn't use the letters she knew. While he had taught her to speak Hurranni, his lessons hadn't included writing.

She glanced at Gilsor, pausing over the last bit of roasted meat on her platter. "Did you get that?"

From memory, her brother recited the goods they had ordered for the clan, naming the amounts and prices, which merchants would provide them, and the schedules for delivery, without hesitation or error. Alithia smiled, knowing they would be safe in his hands. The materials would cushion the losses from the temple trade, should her return be delayed—only delayed—she refused to consider the possibility of failure. It was unfortunate that sanctified oil was not among those listed; she had hoped to find some in Barda to shore up the clan's inventory, but it seemed the temple's requirements weren't so large that the local perfume merchants kept stock on hand.

Curghann nodded in approval. "You managed to buy far more than I expected."

She finished chewing and set down her knife. "It seems to be a novelty to negotiate with a Lydian woman. They might have been humoring me."

The old trader chuckled. "Do not complain. An advantage is still an advantage, especially with the trials nearly at an end. And speaking of trials, what did you think of this last pair?"

He had asked the same question the past three nights, and each time Alithia wasn't sure how to answer him. She tried to be impartial, keeping in mind that he had personally selected the five shield pairs.

"They were good," Gilsor commented, buying her time to gather her thoughts.

"Polite, you mean."

"That, too." He fidgeted in his seat, impatient now that supper was over.

"I think Gilsor would like to explore." She smiled at her brother, knowing the constant attendance required of him chafed his adventuresome spirit. Throughout this journey, he had been tied to her side, save for the occasional foray on his own. Forced to watch and listen while she and Curghann discussed trade, and to witness the trials. Once he was back in Lydia, the mothers would soon settle him into the first of his marriages. This may be the last time he would be free of duty.

Taking the hint, the old trader nodded. "I shall remain until you return, lad. Take Baillin with you, if you wish."

Seven

Leaning on the parapet, Taith stared out into the night. The Gray Lord lurked in the star-washed blackness, a thin slash of white, laying an ambush for the Lady's enemies. The Red Lord waxed full, almost shield, His dark face turning the snow on the peaks the color of fresh blood. Taith tried not to take the sight as an omen for their trial.

Rhi had done very well, perhaps well enough for Alithia in her kindness to overlook Mahon's loss of control—she seemed the sort to give allowances for a man's shortcomings, not as an excuse, but acceptance of reality. Deighann and Kail had worked together like a well-practiced team—though they had refused to display themselves for her inspection, which might count against them. Slann and Arghal had used their silks to good effect. Bronn and Lughann had played up the contrast of Lughann's darkness against Alithia's pale skin, canny trader's tactics that seemed to have worked to their advantage.

And he and Phelan?

They had yet to decide how to approach the morrow's trial. But one thing was certain: they could not imitate the hesitant approach that had served Bronn and Lughann so well. Those two were cautious; that approach came naturally to them. By the same token, he and Phelan were more apt to seize opportunity—Phelan, especially.

A cry came from beyond the wall, some night hunter stalking the forest. Another one not content with easy prey.

Taith could empathize. He was not one to string dreams about the wife they would have—that he had always left in the hands of the Lady. Now, though the original urgency to pledge to a wife had been Phelan's, he found he wanted Alithia—her in particular—as wife. Her confidence. Her daring. Her claws. Her un-Hurranni manner. Which gave the prospect of failure another reason to eat at him.

Another reason, because despite his own advice, he was already worried—not for his sake but for his shield brother's; Phelan had tranced over a wife for so long. How he would react if they missed this chance, Taith did not know. Despite his earlier halfhearted offer to wait, his shield brother wanted to pledge his bond to Alithia.

"Now you're the one brooding." Phelan's teasing reproach held a note of concern. His shield brother stood facing the walkway, on guard against attack. They had left Devyn and the rest of their crew to prowl Barda but had ended up on the wall facing south, toward the homeland of their hoped-for wife, as if the air would bring them understanding of Alithia's mind.

"Just considering our options."

"And how's that different from what I do?"

The familiar banter failed to disguise his shield brother's worry, but Taith answered him in the same vein: "You speculate. I evaluate."

"And has your evaluation produced a conclusion?"

"Yes, that we need more information."

"We're not going to get that from the old man," Phelan pointed out, patting the hilts of his knives as Taith made to move on, a habit his shield brother had developed after losing a favorite knife at a tavern in the back end of nowhere. "However, I think I know just the one to talk to and where to find him."

They found Alithia's kinsman, Gilsor, by the gates to outer Barda—the section of the garrison where Hurrann-bound travelers stabled their beasts. Phelan flashed Taith a grin claiming victory.

"Looking for something?"

The southerner spun around to face them, his face a picture of startlement in the torchlight. "No, I was just wandering around." His attempt at offhand dismissal was belied by a quick glance toward the stables from where several low cries erupted.

Phelan lifted his chin at Taith, urging him to speak. They had long ago agreed to leave trading to Taith, as Phelan's quick tongue was often too quick to accept terms.

"Is there anything in particular you want to see?"

This time Gilsor stared openly at the gates, his curiosity plain for all to see. For one who had traveled far from his homeland, the southerner seemed exceptionally young, not because of height or build—he was only a thumb or two shorter than Rhi, and Taith had met men just as lanky who were fathers—but because of a certain air of softness. As though he were unseasoned.

Taith finally set his finger on the source of his puzzlement: a Hurrann of a similar age would have more scars. Foolishness to make comparisons. Of course, a southerner was not like a Hurrann. That point settled in his mind, he opened negotiations. "We can show you around."

"Why offer?" Gilsor asked, his strange green eyes narrowed, though his hands remained easy by his sides. In another man, his stance would not have signified much, but the southerner bore no weapons, and his clothes had no bulges that might conceal such. He roamed Barda alone with only Curghann's influence as shield—

granted, a formidable one, given Barda's current complement—but Taith suspected the southerner did so in ignorance of the risk.

"Curiosity for curiosity. You wish to see what lies beyond the gates; we seek answers. A fair trade, no?"

"Questions about?"

"Alithia."

"Can I choose which questions to answer? I would not want to speak of anything that would discomfort her."

That was only as Taith and Phelan had expected.

Frowning, Gilsor pondered their proposal, then finally nodded. "A fair trade."

They led him to another gate, one closer to the stables they used. In their company, the guards merely glanced askance at the southerner and kept their counsel.

The clean scent of dry scales greeted them at the stable door, along with the flicker of forked tongues and several dartlike heads rearing above the stall walls. Smooth scales gleamed black and copper in the ruddy moonlight streaming through the open back of the stable.

Gilsor gaped. "Wyverns!" He took a hurried step back as another large head made an appearance over the nearest stall and released a low hoot they felt in the chest. Serrate teeth flashed as the narrow snout turned in their direction.

"Calm, Bulla." Taith interposed himself between the southerner and the beast, bracing himself as the fractious wyvern flicked his tongue around his legs and chest in greeting. Finally satisfied with his inspection, Bulla rocked him back on his heels with a nudge of his horny head.

"Don't worry. They're safe. Wyverns prefer fish, and they only need to eat once a sennight or so." Phelan's patter eased Gilsor's fears, enough that the southerner extended his hand to be tasted.

"I was told there were wyverns in Hurrann, but not that you use them as . . ."

"Mounts." Taith rubbed the soft skin at Bulla's throat, plucking off the flaking scales that irritated the wyvern.

"You do not use gargants?" Gilsor continued to eye the curious beasts watching them, his expression a mixture of caution and fascination.

Phelan chuckled, shaking his head in amusement, as he summoned power to light an amberlamp, which he hung on a wall hook. Imbued with the Lady's gift, the glowing chunks of amber were safer than oil lamps and torches though more expensive. "Gargants would get mired in the swamps or eaten by dragons. The drier routes would take too long. We'd lose trade to competition."

"This one is impatient." Taith tilted his head at his shield brother.

"Truth," Phelan confessed with a wry smile. "The regular caravans that supply Barda use gargants. It's steady business, hauling grain and ingots and the like, but not as profitable."

Gilsor nodded slowly in thoughtful understanding. "Of course. Wyverns would carry less but are faster. If you trade in small, valuable cargo . . . that makes perfect sense."

They spent the next long while introducing the southerner to their mounts and asking their questions in return. Phelan's Dinglis delighted in meeting another person to tickle her, the playful wyvern banishing the last of Gilsor's fears. Taith suspected she was what tipped the balance in their favor. After that, the southerner seemed more willing to discuss Alithia and less guarded in his answers.

"Lydian women like to . . ." Trailing off, Gilsor licked his lips in thought, clearly choosing his words for accuracy. "Play."

"Play?" Phelan raised his brows at the southerner in inquiry from where he sat on their pile of bags.

The younger man frowned at the cobbles underfoot, his hands on his hips. "Remember that first trial, when the big one—"

"Mahon." His shield brother made a face.

"Yes, him. When he released at her touch, and he was so embarrassed?"

Taith exchanged discomfited glances with Phelan, the memory stoking their own fears. "Yes."

"What about it?" his shield brother urged.

"I noticed she did not do it later—perhaps because Mahon was so embarrassed—but Lydian women like to touch. My sister is fond of touching flowers or soft cloth like silk and velvet."

Truth. The memory of her delight when she stroked the petals of the serpentroot flowers—and Mahon's blade—haunted Taith's dreams.

"Letting her touch, letting her bring you release, that would be play. Lydian women like making a man lose control, but only if they are pleasured as well. Letting her strain your control to the point of release should add to her pleasure." Gilsor looked up, a toothy grin stretching his mouth, his eyes old as though he had knowledge beyond his age. "Since union is not allowed, it does not matter if you release early, yes?"

"But—" Thoughts flew behind Phelan's eyes.

"But what?"

Taith waved away the objection. They were there to get information, not debate methods. "What else can you tell us?"

Resuming his scratching of Dinglis's flank, the southerner frowned in thought, the lamplight casting golden sparks in his green eyes, his pale features remindful of the statue of the Gray Lord in the temples. "Alithia said she would choose as her husbands the shield pair that pleasures her best. All the others succeeded in pleasuring her. To win, your goal should not simply be to bring her release once, but to bring her release as many times as you can, for as long as you can."

She approved of daring, Taith realized, remembering her smile when Phelan presented the flowers. He realized something else: he wanted her smile for himself.

For as long as you can? Phelan mouthed the words, staring at

Taith, clearly daunted by the advice. But given time to consider, his shield brother was certain to think up some ideas.

For Taith's part, he already knew what he wanted to do with Alithia. He could see it in his mind's eye—and that was quite unlike him. Even more disconcerting, his body hardened in response to those visions, aching for her touch. The memory of how she had caressed the other men was an unexpected torment, wanting it for himself as he did.

"I have a question for you." Gilsor left the wyvern's side to lean on a stall rail, frowning at Phelan then Taith in turn. "What is the purpose of the inspection Curghann performs at the start of the trials?"

"He checks for beads of power."

"Yes, I understood that much. But why? What power do they have that he has to guard against them?"

Startled by the question, Taith traded blinks with Phelan. Southerners knew nothing of the Lady's gift?

"The beads protect the wearer. During the trial, it would be difficult—mayhap impossible—to prevent someone from attempting union if he wore beads. They also bear spells of various sorts, for easing pain, perhaps even the bringing of pleasure. Only the temples know all the spells possible."

What his shield brother did not mention were the stories told of beads that guaranteed a fair hearing for their wielder, not a theft of will—which would be contrary to the Lady's gift—but elimination of prejudice for the moment. If such did exist, Taith doubted there would be any in the hands of the shield pairs facing trial. The priestesses of the temple would be loath to allow such a potent bead out of their hands. But the possibility was there, thus the acceptance by all of that rule.

Bulla and Dinglis were curled up on the straw by the time the trade was completed with both sides satisfied. They left the wyverns to their sleep, picking their way through the copper-washed night, down deserted lanes to the nearest gate.

Once beyond the guard's earshot, his shield brother waved them to a halt. "Why'd you tell us this? You didn't have to share so much."

The southerner smiled, his face seeming as dark as a Hurrann's in the light of the Red Lord. "Because you asked. You are the only shield pair who did. It shows planning, concern, thoughtfulness. I want that for my sister. Besides, she liked your flowers."

His sword brother was silent when they left Gilsor by the gates to outer Barda, giving Phelan too much time to brood. His heart pounded at the dilemma he faced, its thundering shaking his chest. Let Alithia bring him to release early on—in front of their peers? The humiliation! And yet if he wanted to win her for their wife, he would have to. He couldn't ask Taith to take that role, not with Mahon Taith's kin through his blade father. He could imagine the rumors that would run wild, were he to ask—that the lack of control ran in their blood.

In silence they went to the baths, and in silence they returned to their room damp but free of wyvern scent.

"You are thinking too much again," Taith chided as he released his hair from its braid, set his beads aside, and started combing its braid-set waves free of snarls.

Phelan made a face as he dug through his bag for his own bone comb. There were some disadvantages to a sword brother who knew him so well.

"*I* will do it."

Shameful relief swept him at Taith's calm statement. "Do it?" Did he truly mean what Phelan thought he meant?

"Let her play with me."

"But—" He should be the one to do it. He was the one who pushed them to earn fast, so they'd be worthy of pledging sooner—all because he wanted what his fathers had with his mother. He should be the one to pay the price of his eagerness.

"She turned to Mahon," his sword brother said simply, as though that outweighed all other arguments.

He gritted his teeth against the enervating relief that threatened to swamp him. He couldn't let his cowardice win. "You don't have to. She— I can—"

"Phelan." Taith's impatient glance made the words dry up in his mouth. "I want her to play with me." Very rarely in all the Lady's turns as a shield pair did his sword brother issue such statements. Taith usually went along with whatever profitable job Phelan scrounged up, however risky.

When his sword brother made a decision, he rarely changed it. On such occasions, Phelan knew it was best not to argue, so he didn't.

He just wished he didn't feel this bone-melting relief at avoiding public humiliation.

Eight

As Taith and Phelan crossed the open ground for the inn, their crew crowded around them, feet shifting restlessly—acting so nervous one might think they were the ones facing trial. If they got any closer, they'd be limited to short sword thrusts should they be attacked.

Sensing the hand of Devyn behind the measure, Taith hid his amusement at their precaution. They had some cause for concern with the betting running high. Stripped of beads and the Lady's protection they bequeathed, he and Phelan were at their most vulnerable. It would be simple for some honorless cur to remove them from the trial. Few were fast enough to stop a well-shot arrow. If they had been among any other but brethren and kin, neither of them would have agreed to the risk.

"You've eased yourselves?" Devyn frowned at their empty hands, his own opening and fisting as though seeking a hilt to fill them. "What d'you plan?"

"We will be fine, old friend," Taith assured him as they entered the courtyard, which was already crowded with the crews of the other shield pairs and the old father's southbound caravaners. Critical eyes scrutinized them, searching for weakness, but now that the trial was upon them, Taith's heart beat steadily, filling him with a sense of strength and confidence.

Finally, it was their turn.

He could act.

Outside the trial chamber, Devyn clapped them on the shoulders. "May the Horned Lords guide you." The rest of the crew echoed his blessings as they arrayed themselves in the courtyard. Since only the five shield pairs standing trial were allowed inside to witness, they had to wait there.

"Do your best, now. I've got ten crescents riding on you," Eoghann whispered, then ducked quickly to avoid Devyn's swat.

Phelan stared at Taith, the whites showing around his eyes. Now that their time had come, his shield brother was at a loss for words. Probably remembering the two flames and six crescents Taith had put down on them.

"Mush head, you are tying yourself in knots again—as usual," he chided, tugging on Phelan's hair to give him something else to think about. The black mass was unusually straight, lax since neither of them had bothered with braids that morning.

"Ah, must you do that?" Making a face, his shield brother rubbed his scalp. But at least he no longer looked as though he were staring into a dragon's gaping maw without a weapon to his name.

"It works."

Pledging their bonds to Alithia would mean following her beyond the peaks into the south—more distance from the Lady's temples. Had Phelan taken that into account in his speculations about a southern wife? The embarrassment to come was a small price to pay compared to that.

Gilsor nodded at them when they entered, the ghost of a smile on his mouth. At least the southerner seemed confident.

* * *

Alithia's heart gave a flutter of gladness as Taith and Phelan approached. They looked well, moved well, the loose black hair hanging to the middle of their backs and the absence of weapons the only obvious differences from the previous days. Unlike the others, they came completely clothed, wearing even their strangely patterned tunics. A deliberate attempt to distinguish themselves from their competition, she suspected—in much the same way Deighann and Kail had used their similarity, Slann and Arghal their silks, and Bronn and Lughann the latter's much darker complexion.

Taith disrobed leisurely for Curghann's inspection, all the while gazing at her. His eyes dared her to watch him as he stripped off that unusual tunic, revealing a sleeveless shirt beneath, then bare chest with muscles so broad they might have been planks of wood. He held her attention so completely she missed what Phelan did.

Just as slowly, Taith removed his trews, tantalizing her with the gradual unveiling of his length. He was so thick, firmly rooted between sturdy thighs and curving upward like the blades of his axe, dusky with arousal.

She wanted to touch him.

Alithia clenched her hands, pressing them to her lap so as not to reach out. A season of abstinence and the temptations of the earlier trials tore at her restraint. Her nails dug into her palms as she fought for decorum. A first daughter should have better discipline than this, no matter the provocation.

Only the memory of Mahon's embarrassment kept her on the bed. She wrenched her eyes away, forcing herself to consider Taith's shield brother—the other third of this trial.

Phelan was slighter in build, lean and compact, almost slender in comparison, though he hadn't seemed so the other night. The top of his head reached Taith's chin. His hips were narrower, and so was his shaft—though longer than Taith's. His skin was a similar golden brown, bronzed at the arms and face from the sun. Neither man was as dark as Lughann.

Curghann's inspection passed in a blur of Goddess heat.

Without waiting for her invitation, Taith approached the bed and took her fist, his thumb coaxing her fingers to open. Then, holding her gaze, he placed her palm on his chest and slowly—oh so slowly—dragged it down to his smooth, flat belly.

And lower, along the crisp line of hair there . . .

Until she cupped his hot, swollen flesh.

Alithia reared back to stare at Taith, her heart racing, disbelief warring with excitement. She hadn't expected such an overture from a Hurrann—much less from a man who had been content to wait below her balcony.

He smiled down at her, the corners of his mouth lifted in secret invitation, daring her to accept. The confidence of his stance beguiled. He closed their hands around him to stroke his length, showing her how he liked to be touched.

The heft of him had her melting inside. Firm yet delicate. Velvet softness over strong flesh. She couldn't span his girth. She licked her lips, swallowing against the dryness of her throat, her channel melting in readiness. He promised to fill her yearning body to overflowing.

Taith's eyes blazed, his chest expanding around a deep breath, dark nipples furling into tight studs. "Touch me."

In a daze, she brought up her other hand slowly, waiting for his protest.

But none came.

He only stared down at her, his chest rising, flushing beneath his golden skin. When she touched him, his other hand came up to guide her, wrapping her fingers around him. As she squeezed him, using both hands to milk his swollen length, his lashes fluttered down, his lips parting around a sigh. "Oh, yes." His hips rocked to her caresses, the motion slow and hypnotic, such a sensual response in so imposing a warrior.

Alithia watched in a fog of disbelief as Taith gave himself over to her hands. By the Maiden, he actually seemed to revel in the caresses that brought him to greater hardness. Of all the Hur-ranns, he alone didn't treat her exploration with wary caution. After Mahon, she hadn't imagined any of the shield pairs would risk her touching their shafts. Yet Taith deliberately invited her to fondle him with nothing in between to separate them.

He warmed her palms, the very part of him that made him male so resilient and pulsing with life. The dew of his desire seeped down his length, anointing her hands and perfuming the air with his eagerness, a heady enticement to one of her clan. The sight of him sliding between her slick fingers stole her breath, such dark candy inviting a taste.

A quick glance found Taith apparently caught up in his plea-sure, his eyes half shuttered as he moved to her strokes.

How far could she go before he pulled back?

You won't know unless you try. The thought of discovering his limits seduced her. How else to test his suitability?

Throwing caution to the winds, she bent down.

Taith's lungs seized, surprise holding him motionless. Surely Alithia did not mean to—

Groans erupted around him.

Unheard of! A wife did not lavish such attentions upon a hus-band. Shield pairs might give pleasure with mouth on blade, but no woman did that. The temple taught that it was the husbands' duty to pleasure their wife. As the embodiment of the Lady, through whom men approached Her, the woman had the right to expect release. Her ecstasy was paramount.

And yet Alithia seemed not to care.

Her breath was the veriest caress, the touch of a petal from the flower of the Lady's tree. Perhaps only a fantasy, did he but shut his eyes. Then she took the tip between her lips and lightning streaked through his body—fiery sweetness, like a slug of moon blossom nectar only more, burning delight unlike anything he had ever felt before. The delicacy of her kiss shook him to the bone. He could only wish it would never end.

She stroked his length and the sac beneath, fondling him with playful caresses. She knew just how to touch a man; yet it was different from Phelan's bed play or when he brought himself release, her fingers smoother and somehow more gentle.

But her mouth was a wonderment he never dreamed possible. Nothing in all the lessons, in any the stories and lore, not even his turns of brotherhood with Phelan, could have prepared him for the hot, slick clasp of her mouth on him.

Pleasure flayed him, striking deep. *By the Lady, how can anyone survive such rapture?* He could not think, could only feel as her tongue explored him, licking him like one might lick honey crystals—slow and lingering, swirling over his tip and teasing out every throbbing bit of flesh.

Savoring him as though he were a treat!

Taith gasped, struggling for control as need coiled in his loins, winding tight around his rocks. His hands tangled in her hair, the soft curls defeating his attempt to restrain her. They betrayed him, drawing her closer instead of holding her away, pressing her lips harder against his blade.

Release threatened.

Too soon! He wanted more—to stretch out the pleasure, to absorb into memory what he might never have again if he and Phelan did not win.

He glared at his shield brother kneeling behind Alithia, gaping like some lackwit—doing nothing. If Phelan did not distract her, the game would be over, and letting her play was their main strategy.

Phelan jerked upright, reminded of his part. He reached out, his hand hesitating over her shoulder for an endless moment while Alithia nibbled on Taith's rioting flesh.

* * *

An unexpected wave of envy held Phelan motionless, struck by the anticipation glowing on Alithia's face as she bent over his sword brother's blade . . . and *cherished* the turgid flesh. To be the reason for that look!

He nearly groaned, the thought of her touching him in a like manner slashing him with scorching need. The caress of her lips was surely the height of southern audacity.

Taith's glower shocked him back to himself—and their trial. Here he was dreaming of a future they had yet to secure. He truly was the mush head his sword brother named him.

Phelan's heart thundered like a stampede of uruxi, its strident beat shaking his throat. Here—this—was the realization of so many boyhood dreams.

His hand trembled above her shoulder; she was so pale he feared the slightest touch would bruise her. Reason argued against it: the other shield pairs hadn't done so, yet it took no mean effort to complete the motion.

The first brush against Alithia's skin was a surprise. So smooth, like cream. Finer than the finest silks. Temptation to rough fingertips. Irresistible.

The scent of her was heady sweet and unexpected. He'd dreamed of her for the past five nights, but that detail hadn't occurred to him. It reminded him of the gardens of the temple in the Lady's Hills, blooming at the end of the rainy season, a profusion of flowers filling the air with myriad perfumes.

Phelan found himself bending over her, his hands on her back, his lips on her narrow shoulders, so fragile compared to a man's. He nibbled gently, seduced by the texture of her skin. Again, that sweetness, not the salty musk of his sword brother.

Kneeling closer, he traced the strong yet graceful line of her spine, the small waist, the firm roundness of her rump. So delicate and soft and petal-smooth. Softer than the velvet fuzz on ripe horn pods, than the hairs on silkweed seeds. Over the past days, he'd envisioned this, touching as the others had touched her, had tried to imagine how she would feel.

None of those dreams compared.

And when his hand curved on her waist, he inhaled sharply. She filled his palm like the hilt of his sword, the feel of her comfortable and somehow just . . . right. As though he had been made to hold her—and only her—among all the daughters granted life by the Lady.

Then his hands slid front and found her breasts . . .

Lady of Heaven!

Nothing in Phelan's life had prepared him for the feel of those soft mounds in his tingling hands! He groaned at the thrill of their weight, the way they yielded to his touch, the tight nubs that rasped against his sword calluses. Nothing had ever felt so perfect.

Horned Lords, would that he could fondle her forever!

Alithia gave a gurgle of approval, arching her back and pressing her breasts against his hands, so generous in her enjoyment.

He shuddered at her eager response. She was soft where Taith was hard, open delight where his sword brother was quiet forbearance.

Phelan pressed against her, wanting to rub his body all over her yielding softness. Why had he hesitated? The sensations coursing through him at the contact were indescribable. His very bones thrilled to the feel of her on him . . . and Alithia had yet to touch his blade.

This was play?

How could Taith stand it?

She continued to nibble on his sword brother's length, her gurgles of delight and murmurs of praise sending chills of excitement over Phelan's arms and down his spine. He wanted her praise, too, wanted to be the source of her pleasure.

But the risk of embarrassing himself held him back, that and Taith's rare vehemence. His sword brother wanted this—Alithia playing with him—enough to insist on it when he seldom voiced his desires.

Alithia's back bowed, rubbing her rump along his belly. The brush of her thigh against his blade was nearly Phelan's undoing. His hand dipped between her thighs without his volition and found her wet sheath.

His breath seized. He'd dreamed of this for so long, had woken hard with need so often. The consummation of all those dreams was but a heartbeat away, her flesh a juicy temptation.

It would be so easy to take her.

By the Horned Lords! *Taith shook as wave after wave of dark* bliss flooded his veins, unable to suppress his groans. How could any man withstand such ravishment?

Alithia's face glowed, proof her brother had spoken truth. Southern women did delight in teasing a man. She played kissing games on his blade. The lilting murmurs she gave as she tongued and sucked him were unreserved in their approbation.

He could not endure her exquisite torture any longer. The carnal fire melted his rocks, blazed through his aching flesh in an unquenchable burst of pleasure. He lost himself to the eruption, a glorious outpouring of sensation—raw beyond belief—that left him shaken.

She winced, guilt darkening her blue eyes to green, horror replacing her earlier delight as she watched his release. "I—"

Taith never wanted to see that expression on her face ever again, not when she had given him more than he had ever expected—an exaltation fit for the Horned Lords. His heart pounding in his ears, he knelt before the bed and drew her into his arms, then pressed his mouth to her pink lips.

Alithia went still, tamely accepting his inexpert attentions. He had never kissed a woman before. Her lips were far softer than Phelan's, so soft he feared he might bloody her with harder contact. Just when he started to wonder if he was doing it properly, she responded, her tongue sliding along the seam of his lips in definite blandishment.

When Taith opened his mouth, she swept in, confidence in every supple stroke, branding him with her sweet heat and the salt of his release. She tangled her tongue with his, inviting him to duel, a purr of approval rewarding his acceptance. Her arms twined around his neck, pulling him close, pressing her soft breasts against him.

He groaned at the sensation, so different from her hands yet just as devastating. Nothing in his long-ago lessons or those countless sacrifices he had witnessed readied him for anything like this bewildering rush of delight.

"Now, me. My turn." Phelan pulled Alithia away, his hesitancy gone now that he had touched Alithia and felt her exquisite femininity, presenting his blade to her with laughable eagerness, except Taith did not feel like laughing.

He nearly protested the loss, torn between control and that seductive sweetness. But once his shield brother moved, precious little in the world could stop him.

She cupped Phelan's flesh with both hands, a mischievous smile on her lips. Her tongue darted out to lash his length, and his shield brother gasped, his hips jerking convulsively.

In no mood to watch—not again—Taith turned to more promising vistas. He wanted more of Alithia, wanted to see her writhing with pleasure from his efforts—no longer an onlooker.

Climbing onto the bed, he settled on the other side of her. Her belly was as smooth as silk beneath his hands and against his cheek, yielding yet hinting at strength. Soft and womanly.

Taith nibbled on her pale skin, tempted to mark her as theirs. So very tempted.

With his hair across his shoulders, his view of their audience was blocked. He could imagine they were alone—just the three of them. Remembering the pleasure she had derived from Rhi's mouth, he followed the slope of her belly to the damp red curls between her thighs and found the dark petals of her sheath. The scent of her pleasure filled his head with dreams of union, seductive beyond belief.

He licked her gently, savoring the warm cream forbidden to unbanded men—a salty sweetness that had him dipping back for more. In all his descriptions of this act, his blade father had never said just how luscious such delicate flesh could be. He snuggled down to feast, raiding his memories for those half-forgotten lectures on satisfying a wife.

Spreading her petals, he found the pearl hidden between them. If memory served, the swollen flesh should be tender. Would this bring her as much pleasure as her mouth on him had done? He tested the premise, circling the pearl with his tongue.

Alithia gave a cry of surprise as she shuddered, her hips rising to his kiss. Cream gushed from her sheath, coating his eager lips.

Taith's heart leaped in triumph, thundering such that he had to remind himself this was only the beginning. Once was not enough. He set his lips on her again, the scent of her desire even stronger now as her passion spilled across his tongue, hot and creamy. He dipped his fingers between her petals, gaining her sheath with tempting ease.

Her hand caught his, and he went still.

Had he done something wrong?

She pressed down, driving his fingers into her. A soft cry of pleasure reassured him. She taught him how to touch her the way she liked to be touched—and she wanted him deep.

Taith wanted the same.

His breath came quickly, each gulp bringing a taste of her desire. She was so tight around him. Despite the cream of her passion, her flesh balked at his exploration. That had to change if they were to win.

Determination cooled his excitement, returning to him the edge of control he needed. At least by letting Alithia bring him release, he could now focus on her pleasure.

He bent back to her delicate flesh and sucked her pearl between his lips, the better to tease her. This time he would not stop until her voice was hoarse from shouting her rapture.

Like Deighann and Kail, Taith and Phelan worked together to flood her senses with pleasure, distracting Alithia from her play. Phelan's rolling of her throbbing nipples sent another surge of delight through her veins, heightening the sensations.

His shaft pulsed in her hands, long and hot, his musk adding to the heady perfume in the air. She drew him to her lips, wanting to taste him the way she couldn't with Taith. The narrower girth of his shaft meant she could toy with him in comfort, unlike with his sword brother.

A moan greeted her motion.

Looking up, she met Phelan's eyes and smiled. Holding his gaze, she took him into her mouth and drew hard and deep.

He gasped, his body slumping as she sucked on him and played her lips along his length. "Sweet Lady of Heaven!"

She laughed around him, his reaction spurring her efforts. The feel of him in her mouth was a salty pleasure, his evident surprise unbidden spice to her play. She could feel his excitement pulsing against her tongue, a rapid flutter that belied his attempts at control.

But when he surrendered to her blandishments, the perfect bliss on Phelan's face as he took his release was a satisfaction all of its own. Triumph at her success buoyed her spirits. It might have been enough for her.

Then Taith growled something at his shield brother that she didn't understand. His hard fingers delving deep in her channel sparked a flare of pleasure and stole her breath. Now that he knew how she liked to be touched, he set to it with a will, rousing her hunger to startling effect.

Phelan stirred with a groan, taking her breasts in his hands and turning his lips to them—and proved talented.

Need and desire struck with the dazzling speed of lightning, searing her senses with Goddess heat. Alithia cried out, shocked by the violence of her response.

Taith and Phelan stormed her senses, applying mouths and tongues and teeth and hands, whipping the flames of her passion into a firestorm of revelation. Never had she imagined such heights of raw sensation. Her pleasure loves had never dared press more upon her.

Rapture swept her, a blistering surge of glorious abandon that ripped a scream from her lips. She writhed, lost in a whirlpool of carnal splendor.

Need built once more, its claws digging deep into her core. Alithia panted, dragging air into her lungs. At some point, Taith and Phelan switched places. She didn't know when, only that Taith's large hands now fondled her, thus it had to be his shield brother between her thighs. She didn't care who did what; they were both ruthless in their bed play, driving her from peak to peak on wings of ecstasy. She screamed again, needing to voice her delight. To celebrate the fact that she was alive!

Pleasure rolled through her, storm-tossed waves going on and on. The sea crashing into the shore. Heat swirled within her, surged and roared, the Goddess's touch unmistakable, swelling her senses with a hint of forever.

An endless moment later it was gone, little more than a dream. Then like a feather on a breeze, she floated back to herself.

Alithia slumped in Taith and Phelan's embrace, too raw from so much pleasure to speak, careless of their audience.

How, by the Maiden, could so much ecstasy be possible without union?

Nine

Her senses crept back with much meandering, lingering over memories of rapture, like waking from a dream of pleasure too potent to have been real. Alithia groaned, aching from a surfeit of ecstasy, wishing only to sleep the day away.

"Are you well, child?"

Well seemed too paltry a word to describe the feeling of utter well-being that suffused her—as though all the cares of the world had been lifted from her shoulders, as though nothing could possibly be wrong, as though she could defeat Gilsor's ferocious Hurranni monsters single-handed . . . if only she bestirred herself.

As it was, all Alithia wanted to do was snuggle deeper into the arms that held her. "Hmmm . . ."

"Is this trial complete?" From the grunt that answered Curghann, the question hadn't been directed at her. Then the hard pillows under her stirred, lowering her to the softer furs.

Fighting the heaviness of her lashes, she peeked out. Taith and Phelan were dressing themselves, concealing all that delicious virility from view. The sight sent another wave of bliss sweeping through her, slow and sweet, waking an answering ache in her folds.

"I take it there is no question as to the victors of the trials?" The gentle hint seemed to assume Taith and Phelan were her choice.

Alithia forced her eyes wider to consider the old trader's solicitous countenance and ignore Gilsor behind him looking grave. Curghann wanted a decision and deserved one—now, with the last trial done. He needed time to make whatever arrangements were left to be made if she was to depart for Sentinel Reach with all due haste.

Lassitude weighed down her limbs, dragged on her thoughts. She had never had so much of the Goddess's gift before and wanted nothing more than to have it again.

She tried to caution herself against impatience. This was no pleasure love, here and gone after a few days of dalliance. Her choice now would be her husbands—and not just till birthing.

Was it Taith and Phelan?

All the shield pairs had had their chance, but there was no doubt that Taith and Phelan had pleasured her the most, performing with a thoroughness and ruthlessness that boded well for other endeavors. They were the only ones to invite the humiliation of an early release, disregarding the expectations of the other shield pairs—that alone raised them in her estimation. Granted, they had had the advantage of being last, but none of the others had been willing to risk it after Mahon's experience. Even Slann had not dared that much.

Of certain, Taith and Phelan didn't have the unique appeal of Deighann and Kail or Lughann, but that was a minor detail and unworthy of notice.

Over the protestations of her body, Alithia forced herself erect, wanting a show of control when she gave her decision. Her pride would accept nothing less.

When she was steady on her seat, she looked over the waiting shield pairs, remembering Rhi's expertise, Mahon's stouthearted effort despite his embarrassment, the novelty of Deighann and Kail's matched set, Slann and Arghal's silks, Lughann's darkness and intensity, and his and Bronn's almost Lydian manners. But expertise could be learned, and silks could be acquired. She couldn't imagine Taith and Phelan acting Lydian, but they had shown it took more than an early release before their brethren to embarrass them. If they were willing to risk public humiliation, she imagined they would be willing to take other risks. Their determination and daring should stand her in good stead . . . and the thoughtfulness of their gift of flowers boded well for a life together.

Satisfied her decision was well reasoned, Alithia nodded at Taith and Phelan. "Them."

Strangely enough, her brother smiled.

"Them." That one word sent a jolt of desire through Taith. The trial was over. All the shield pairs bowed acceptance, the old father's presence silencing any protests to the contrary, though such was unlikely—training alone ensured that. Alithia had given her decision, and it was as binding as a priestess's decree.

Unlike the others, however, he and Phelan were now Alithia's husbands-to-be. Nothing but good manners precluded union and learning whether her sheath was as wonderful as her mouth—good manners and his shield brother's earlier restraint. Though sorely tempted to toss politeness to the flames, he withdrew with the others.

Once outside the chamber, Mahon clouted Taith on the shoulder, staggering him. "You lucky son!"

The other Swords were quick to add their voices, falling on him with mock blows and good-natured teasing. Phelan did not escape the Shields' congratulations. The rowdy well-wishes of the shield pairs came as no surprise to Taith. He knew them well, and though they envied him and Phelan and regretted their loss, their congratulations held no bitterness. They would have other opportunities and had lost nothing in the trial.

What took him aback was the response of the crews awaiting them outside. They received the news calmly, evincing no surprise, as though they had known Alithia's decision before the shield pairs' emergence. Devyn and their men were quietly triumphant, while the other crews resigned. The bets had already been counted and settled. There was none of the previous days' rowdiness, shock, or disappointment.

Once they were away from the others, Taith surveyed their crew, looking for an explanation for their strange calm and finding nothing.

"You're not surprised." As always, Phelan spoke before Taith could. "Why's that?"

Devyn smiled. "While you were inside, the Gray Lord rose to shield the Lady. Everyone saw. We knew then that you'd won."

Baillin slipped into the chamber, sidestepping the departing shield pairs, his face a picture of great excitement. Evidently, his presence was a violation of protocol as Curghann quickly stepped in front of Alithia, blocking her view of his servant. Rather than offering a bow of apology and awaiting the old trader's instructions, Baillin babbled something about the Lady and the Gray Lord, his breathless words tumbling one into another so that she could not make out their meaning.

She quickly slid off the bed and dressed, her fingers fumbling with the laces of her bodice.

"How is that again?"

Alithia exchanged stares with her brother as she twitched her skirt into place. Whatever was the matter had to be important, since Curghann failed to release the outrage that blazed in his eyes at his servant's appearance.

Behind her, Baillin gasped out a slower version of his report, painting an image of divine conflict. The sky had become twilight dark and the air bitter cold and all the animals fell silent. The Lady's fire flared from behind the Gray Lord's shield as He smote Her enemies from the sky. He kept His ward up until Alithia's cries were heard; only then did He stand down, returning to His rightful place—and the darkness and cold lifted. From his tale, the Hurranns had known her decision even before she made it.

She spun around to stare at Baillin, startled by the Hurranns' interpretation that her selection of Taith and Phelan had been intended. So the pale moon Egon had eclipsed the sun, and stars had fallen across the sudden twilit sky, bursting in great numbers—both unusual events, but not unheard of—that didn't mean the Lady of Heaven and Horned Lords had taken a hand in the trial.

"I don't know whether to be frightened or reassured," Gilsor whispered in Lydian, his sea green eyes probably as wide as hers.

May the Maiden protect her, she didn't know, either.

Ten

Standing in formal dress, its tiers of skirts trimmed with the purple braid due the first daughter of a clan, Alithia faced Curghann, wondering once again if she was about to do something wrong—violate some forgotten edict of the priestesses in Lydia by accepting the bonds of Taith and Phelan before the altar of the Lady of Heaven. This pledging ritual sounded so different from the simple signing of contracts that established a marriage in Lydia, yet another example of how Hurrann was unlike her homeland.

She stifled her doubts ruthlessly. Whether she was or not was beside the point. She had to take the shield pair as her husbands to journey to Sentinel Reach and complete her quest. Before leaving Lydia, she had made her decision to honor a Hurranni marriage. Nothing had changed.

Smiling so broadly that wrinkles nearly hid his eyes, the old trader straightened to his full height and, with his hands on his chest, gave her a formal bow in acknowledgment of honor done him. "You look beautiful, child. I am proud to attend you in this final duty."

Behind him, Gilsor shook his head in commiseration, knowing how she disliked the reference to immaturity. "It'll be fine. I think you made the right choice," he added, lapsing to the intimate mode of Lydian, the sound of their language a welcome reminder of clan.

"You do? Why?" she replied, in the same mode, as she made another—unnecessary—adjustment to the drape of her shawl.

Her brother grinned but merely shrugged, refusing to explain. Unfortunately, Curghann then gestured toward the door, indicating she should take the lead, and she didn't have time to extract clarification.

The temple was a building set apart from the others by gardens. Despite being dwarfed by Barda's high gates and the looming mountains, it had a majesty of its own, the tile work for which Hurrann was justly famous transforming its walls into works of art.

She stopped before the steps, pressing a hand over her heart to keep it in her chest, its pounding echoing in her ears like festival drums. From here on, she would be going where no Lydian woman had ever gone, risking defiance of the Goddess. For clan Redgrove.

"Child?"

Curghann's quiet voice stiffened her resolve. She had convinced the old trader to help her, faced the mothers, argued the necessity of this quest, and won. This was her duty, and only she could do it.

But despite her determination, she couldn't suppress a shiver as she entered the temple.

The serene features of the statue of the Lady of Heaven were like yet unlike the Goddess's in Lydia in Her guise of the Maiden. Like the Goddess, She extended the blessing of fire in one hand

and held the horn of bounty in the other—though Her statue was executed in bronze, not alabaster, and She did not bare Her breasts; instead, a necklace of some sort lay on the metal folds of her bodice. Still, Alithia drew a measure of comfort from the similarity. Perhaps the Hurranns' Lady wasn't so different from the Goddess.

Perhaps this ritual before the Lady's altar wasn't a denial of Her.

The Horned Lords, however, were entirely unique: warriors with thin crescents on Their brows—horned, indeed. The temple back home made no mention of Them. No statues were raised in Their honor. Here, They were menacing and severe, Their weapons fit to slay a gargant with a single blow—or so They seemed to her; Gilsor looked fascinated.

At the entrance to the sanctuary, a married woman in red floor-length robes wearing an elaborate necklace of beads across her breast greeted them, the first Hurranni woman Alithia had ever seen up close. Behind her stood two men in crimson and silver robes with the single bands of husbands. The priestess and her priests. If they felt any puzzlement at the arrival of a southern woman at their temple, it didn't show, their inspection surreptitious.

Alithia followed them inside, Curghann and Gilsor by her shoulders. Her skirts brushed her calves, unaccustomed finery she seldom had need to wear.

Though the Lady's hearth burned high, its milky crystal panels—so like those of clan Redgrove's altar—glowing bright, it wasn't what drew Alithia's eye. Neither was it what appeared to be bedding laid out on the floor in front of the altar. Her attention was reserved for the men who would be her husbands.

Taith and Phelan were already there, surrounded by a crowd of men, more than just the shield pairs who had taken part in the trial. Armed and armored men. In Lydia, they would have been the women of the husband's clan—and if they were armed and armored, it would not be as Hurranns understood it.

* * *

Phelan's lungs seized at the sight of their soon-to-be wife. He'd seen all of her before, kissed her beautiful skin for himself, tasted the dew of her pleasure. But seeing her now—like this—was different.

She wore a gold collar with only a thin shawl to veil her bare breasts above the laced bodice and a frothy skirt that reached the floor but was cut down the middle so her legs flashed with every step. She surpassed his wildest imaginings.

He had no eyes for anyone else. He'd dreamed of pledging for so long it was difficult to believe it was finally coming true.

Alithia's direct gaze met his across the chamber, the impact flooding his veins with excitement. Presence. Confidence. Certainty. The weight of her gaze made him shift his feet—whether to run away or run to her, he didn't know.

"Breathe or you'll swoon." Devyn's whispered advice was horribly suggestive, an embarrassment that didn't bear thinking upon.

Sucking in air, Phelan shot a glare at the older man, then risked a glance at Taith. His sword brother looked his calm self, as though a dragon couldn't shake him. He took comfort from that bit of normalcy.

Only then did it occur to him that the pledging meant change. They would no longer be two but three. No longer just Taith and him. There would be Alithia. From here on, her well-being would have to come first, their duty to her before and above everything else.

Their soon-to-be wife approached the altar, confidence in every stride, a woman who knew what she wanted.

The sight filled Phelan with renewed certainty.

Everything would be more than fine.

For all its ceremony, more ritual than a simple Lydian contract witnessing, the pledging passed in a blur of strange invocations for Alithia. At some point, Curghann and Gilsor stepped away, after accepting on behalf of the clan a casket containing a fortune in spices and gems, leaving her standing alone before the altar, the artfully arranged bedding behind her, while the priestess addressed her husbands-to-be.

"The *idkhet?*"

Taith and Phelan presented the items the priestess demanded. They were small open rings of shiny white *mythir*, barely more than bracelets and unadorned.

Alithia stifled a pang of disappointment at the contrast with Curghann's elaborately etched *idkhet* that spanned his forearms. It was her fault—in all likelihood acquiring more elaborate bracers would have taken time she didn't have to waste. The necessity of leaving for Sentinel Reach immediately also meant skipping many of the related ceremonies—offerings to the temple for the wife's health and the birth of daughters, feasts to celebrate the husbands' luck, music and merrymaking that lasted a sennight.

The priestess inspected the *idkhet*, handing them to her priest-husbands in turn. After they confirmed her inspection, she called down blessings upon the bracers, the Fire flaring high and dancing to her incantations. A rush of heat filled the room, a sudden breeze that stirred Alithia's loose tresses and set her skirts swirling.

An exalted expression on her face, the priestess returned the *idkhet* to Taith and Phelan, then stepped back from the Lady's hearth. The priests bore away the round crystal panels that spread the glow of the holy fire from their place on the sides of the hearth. Her husbands-to-be spoke as one, Taith's deep voice a stirring undertone to Phelan's fluid speech. "We vow to guard Alithia against all peril, to heed her wishes in matters of importance, to care for her through all our days, to attend to her as the Horned Lords attend to the Lady. To her, we offer our lives, our bodies, and our treasure with our bonds, forsaking all others."

Alithia's heart leaped to her throat as Taith and Phelan thrust their hands and *mythir* bands wrist-deep into the roaring flames to attest to the staunchness of their bonds. When they drew their hands back, strange patterns were etched on the white metal—nothing she could make out—and their arms were unscathed.

She exhaled slowly to steady herself. All of Curghann's lectures couldn't have prepared her for that sight.

"I take these bonds into my keeping, accepting Taith and Phelan as my husbands, to cherish as the Lady cherishes the Horned Lords." She recited the Hurranni vow by rote, the words the old trader had taught her just that morning sounding stilted to her ears. Would the Goddess take offense that she stood before another altar and spoke vows?

Alithia offered her bare forearms to her husbands. They locked the *idkhet* around them, the metal unexpectedly cool and far lighter than she thought it ought to be. The bracers were too large, sliding down when she lowered her arms and stopping only at her spread hands. If she wasn't careful, they could slip off.

But she didn't have time to worry about the fit just then. It was her turn to lock the *idkhet* around Taith's and Phelan's left forearms and complete the ritual. Theirs fit better—but still hung loose.

Was that an omen for the marriage? If it was, it didn't seem to be an auspicious one.

"It is witnessed. We leave you to complete your pledge with your bodies." With a gesture at the others to precede her, the priestess and her priest-husbands withdrew, closing the sanctuary's doors behind them.

Finally they were alone.

Alithia was no timid virgin faced with her first lover. She knew Taith and Phelan would pleasure her, but this would be the first time she would perform the Goddess's dance as a wife—and one with two husbands. In the temple of the Lady of Heaven. The prospect was daunting, no matter that she had had most of the summer to reconcile herself to the necessity.

But as her husbands undressed before her, the sight of all that male flesh—*hers!*—sent Goddess heat sweeping through Alithia, driving out all thought of duty. The holy fire gilded their warrior bodies in copper, the peaks and troughs of muscle gleaming softly, the shadows veiling their shafts from her gaze. Already she could smell their readiness—and hers.

She let her shawl fall from her shoulders, leaving her breasts bare, anticipation throbbing in the center of her being.

Moving as one, Taith and Phelan reached for the laces of her bodice and pulled them loose. She accepted their aid gratefully, fearing to lose her *idkhet*. With flattering haste, they disposed of her dress, leaving her as naked as they.

Taith knelt before her, his posture placing his head lower than hers. He should have looked docile that way—tractable—but nothing could disguise the warrior he was. The fierce light in his black eyes. The hard line of his jaw. The broad sweep of his shoulders. The scars that hinted at battle and peril overcome. The thick shaft rising between his thighs, daring her to take him yet promising fulfillment.

Phelan looked no less the warrior as he stood by Taith's side. The corded arms and brawny shoulders tapering to a narrow waist, the strong legs, his avid, unwavering gaze. The swollen shaft aimed in her direction. Despite the evidence of his desire, Phelan stepped back with a gesture toward his sword brother, surrendering precedence.

Either man would have roused the Goddess's heat in any Lydian woman. Both, together? She shivered, the center of her being already molten with hunger. After a season without union, she was more than eager for the final step in the great dance, to take a man's flesh into her body, feel him moving inside her.

But her necessities were about to deprive the shield pair of much of the celebration of their pledging. She couldn't deprive them of more by rushing this pleasure.

Burying her fingers in Taith's hair, Alithia bent her neck to kiss him. He met her with sweet pressure, asking for little. And again, the contrast of gentleness from such a large man.

She teased his firm lips apart, sweeping inside to claim his mouth.

He inhaled sharply, then after the slightest hesitation, his tongue met hers, warm and welcoming, offering a taste of sweet fennel as he answered her overture and countered with his own. Truly he had meant his pledge when he and Phelan offered her their bodies.

Alithia sank into the kiss, rejoicing in the promise of union and the freedom to touch without limits, pressing herself against the hard, smooth wall of his chest, so unlike the furry planes of her pleasure loves in Lydia.

His arms encircled her, pulling her tight to him. Heady strength, all warrior male. Hers, now.

Why had she always sought easy and tame?

Goddess heat sparked in her core, urging a faster pace. She rubbed her aching mound along his belly, rocking her hips in search of relief. She reached down, skimming resilient muscle, until she found the hard flesh she wanted.

Taith caught her wrist, his hold gentle but inflexible, denying her. "It must be union to complete the pledge," he murmured between kisses.

He thought she intended to play with him?

Before she could relieve him of his misconception, Phelan hugged her from behind, his body hot against her back, branding her with his heat, trapping her between him and his sword brother—except she didn't feel trapped.

His hands came around to embrace her and cup her breasts, his shaft nestled between her buttocks, turgid and insistent. He played with her, kneading firmly, his caresses surer than during the trial. His touch spilled delight through her veins.

The hunger inside her flared, desire a molten cream trickling down her thighs. Rubbing her backside against Phelan's shaft, she urged a deeper contact, her breasts heavy with need.

She tore her lips free of Taith's kiss to issue a demand. "Phelan, come to me."

He stiffened, his hands suddenly awkward.

Impatient now, she stepped away from Taith to arch her back, offering her tingling cleft, the entrance of her body. Taith didn't seem to mind, turning his attentions to her shoulders and breasts, but he couldn't distract her from his shield brother standing so still behind her.

With laborious care, Phelan set his shaft to her wet folds, all hot promise, his shuddering gulps for air suddenly loud.

Alithia shivered with anticipation. Finally, after an endless season without, she would join the Goddess in the celebration of life.

Phelan thrust into her convulsively, sheathing his flesh in her body in a single glorious motion.

"Oh!" Clinging to Taith, she rose to her toes, breathless sensation taking her by surprise. She had forgotten the fullness of union, the heady pleasure that having a man inside her could bring. He reached so deep inside her she could feel the tip of him against the center of her being. Her hips rolled unbidden, her body remembering the varied steps of the great dance, eliciting another wave of sheer delight.

"By the Horned Lords." Phelan's fervent whisper seemed to fill the chamber. Buried to the hilt, he froze inside her, his muscles quivering against the backs of her thighs. "Lady of Heaven!"

A snort erupted from Taith, an amused smile curving his lips. "Forget your lessons, Phelan?"

She stilled at the strangeness of his question. "You have never had union before?"

"Union is reserved for husbands and only with their wife." Taith glanced behind her, the light of challenge in his eyes. "This one forgets he is now a husband."

"Just you wait your turn. You won't be laughing then. Horned Lords, I couldn't have imagined—" With a soft groan, Phelan finally moved, tentatively at first—but this time it wasn't awkwardness but the slowness of appreciation. A man savoring a particular delight.

Alithia moaned softly, thrilling to the gentle prodding on her core.

Taith and Phelan froze—again. "Alithia?"

Panting to ease the tightness of her delicate flesh, she struggled for the correct words. "Do not stop. If you stop, I—I will scream."

A deep, rich chuckle full of joy answered her threat. "You have your orders, Shield. Move!"

Phelan *moved*.

He suddenly pulled out and drove back in, no rhythm to his thrusts, but his enthusiasm more than made up for his lack of control and artful ways.

Lightning blazed inside her, a bolt of sizzling heat that wrenched a gasp from her. Alithia closed her eyes to better savor the sensations. Surely her pleasure loves had been better, more experienced at bed play, but she couldn't remember any of them giving her such delight.

Large hands caught her hips, supporting her when her knees threatened to fold. Laughing softly, Taith lifted her off her feet then caught her lips, plunging his tongue into her mouth exultantly, mimicking the friction between her thighs. His tongue twined around hers possessively, a velvet caress that resonated deep inside.

Startled by Taith's sudden ardor, she clung to his shoulders, overcome by their forcefulness. Never before had a man so dictated the steps of the great dance with her. The added delight of Taith's kiss overwhelmed her senses. She could only hold on as they pleasured her.

Phelan continued his forceful shafting, reaching to her very core. His fingers pressed Taith's hands into her hips as he settled into a steady rhythm, his harsh groans melding with the wet slaps of flesh on flesh.

They rocked her between them, taking her mouth and cleft, surging in and out of her, as natural as the tides, stoking the hunger within her, building the fire in the center of her being into a conflagration.

Pierced both ways, her hungry body gloried in it all. She swung in the air, weightless, breathless, heedless, wanting nothing more than for the pleasure to go on and on. The rioting of her senses dominated her whole being.

Something coiled inside her—a feeling of imminence, rising as need rose. Ecstasy. It hung out of reach, tormenting her with the hope of the final step.

She wanted to scream at it to come, wanted the release it promised with everything within her.

Now, please, Goddess, now!

Phelan cried out, his hands digging into her thighs, his flesh pulsing inside her, warming her. His release flung her across the gap to her own.

Stars flashed before her eyes, rapture rising like a rogue wave to towering heights, inevitable and unstoppable, crashing into her and shattering her into so much spindrift. Floating on a turbulent sea of glorious ecstasy.

Alithia groaned, her senses reeling from the climax. Her heart thundered in her chest, her nipples throbbing to its beat. Her core quivered with the excess of pleasure so long denied, sending smaller waves of sweet bliss washing through her body.

The world swooped.

Startled, she opened her eyes to see Taith standing, carrying her by her spread legs, a look of fierce determination on his face. She clutched at him, her fingers slipping on sweaty muscle.

"Now, me." A thicker hardness nudged against her swollen folds, seeking entry. Shifting his grip to her buttocks, he worked his way into her in short, careful thrusts, driving slowly deeper. His shaft pressed into her sensitive channel, stretching her delicate flesh.

There was so much of him!

She gasped, panting to receive him. She had had similarly well-endowed pleasure loves and knew she should have no difficulty taking Taith. But while she was wet from Phelan's attentions, all that sensual friction now served to heighten her awareness. Taith's shaft felt larger, harder, his steady progress an ineffable force blooming inside her.

The hunger she had thought quenched flared to life once more.

Moaning, Alithia hooked her legs around his waist, trying to pull him deeper, faster. It was like straddling a log, so sturdy he didn't even shift his weight as she strained for more contact. Goddess heat burned in her veins, demanding she dance the great dance.

Then he was there inside her, stretching her sheath to breath-taking fullness. The pleasure that burst through her drove the air from her lungs. *By the Maiden!* He filled her so completely she could barely breathe.

Need uncoiled, a fierce catamount digging its claws into the center of her being. She writhed in Taith's arms, grinding herself against him to appease the craving for sensation. Fire sparked in her throbbing breasts, streaked to her mound to blaze in her core.

"Horned Lords—"

Behind her, Phelan gave a wheezing laugh. "Your turn, now. Move, Sword!"

If Taith heard him, he gave no sign, standing there hardly breathing, leaving her to arch against him and sate the demands of the Goddess. When he finally moved, it was to bend over her, his lips brushing her hair and temple and shoulder—all nice, but it precluded contact with that delicious chest of his. His shoulders were too wide to give her much purchase; she couldn't pull him back where she wanted him.

Alithia growled in protest. She needed him to be a partner, to help her build the passion between them to the ultimate step.

"You're too tall. Put her down here."

Taith stepped forward, his motions sending another jolt of delight coursing through Alithia. He laid her on the pallet and pressed a hard kiss on her lips. Then he started to move in earnest. Unlike Phelan, he didn't pull out; instead, he rolled his hips, rubbing and swirling his length inside her, igniting a storm of sweet sensation.

She couldn't help a gasp.

So much better.

Bracing her feet on the bedding, she arched up, driven to answer his actions with her own. She couldn't think, only move, only feel. The heft of him stretched her channel to satiety, the sensual friction sending ripples of sunshine delight through her blood, dazzling in power.

He strove with her, a warrior's grimace on his lips, grinding against her, his shaft churning the sweetness within her into breathless exhilaration. Rocking his hips, he quickly matched her rhythm, the primal beat of their hearts setting a relentless pace.

Soon. It would be soon. She could feel the end to the great dance approach, winding through the center of her being with the certainty of summer, building up to a frenzy.

Taith gave a choked groan, his hips jerking.

Between one heartbeat and another, the firestorm broke, a whirlwind of ecstasy blowing her cares into tatters and less than tatters, sweeping it all away. She lost sight of everything, caught up in the heart of the tempest, her world a furious flurry of sensation. Someone sucked her nipple, calloused fingers played with the other, teeth nibbled and scraped her shoulders, rough hands touched her all over, adding rapture upon rapture to her ecstasy.

Goddess heat consumed Alithia, inundating her senses. Pleasure rolled through her, sharp and sweet, a fulgent wave that went on and on. Another gathered behind it, all swirling delight and sensual madness, crashing down in turn. Then another. And still another.

Surely she couldn't take much more.

Something rose inside her. Something more than familiar need, more than imminent ecstasy . . . Pressure . . . Portent . . . Power.

The glorious firestorm within her kindled a presence beyond comprehension. A fullness. A vastness. As though she were standing on the edge of a cliff looking down into an eternity of stars, each one a spark of life. For a breathless moment, she hung there.

A heartbeat away from all the flames of the worlds.

Then she fell through the heavens.

The sense of aching fullness lingered, pinning Alithia in place with ridiculous ease while her whole being continued to quiver. Man to her woman as the Goddess intended. It had been so long since she had been filled so well that she was loath for it to end. Satisfaction weighted her limbs, a sweet fatigue beyond anything the trials had wrought.

"Horned Lords," someone groaned, pushing off her, taking with him a weight she hadn't been aware of off her chest.

She blinked at the wash of red that appeared before her, every muscle humming with the aftermath of rapture. It flickered and danced, the holy fire in the Goddess's—in the Lady's hearth.

The shaft in her channel slid free, the liquid sensation sparking a fresh wave of Goddess heat through her, reminding her of why she lay before a Hurranni altar in the arms of two men. The pledging.

Another tired groan drifted through the quiet sanctuary, its undertone of bliss filling her with intense gratification. She had worn out her new husbands.

"Union is even better than they said it would be." A happy rumble accompanied the fondling of her breast as Phelan nuzzled its curve. "Marriage is good."

Alithia froze in surprise. "You truly never shared pleasure with a woman before?" How could that be?

"We weren't eligible to pledge to a wife before now." The

amused explanation implied that the answer to her question was obvious. Perhaps it was—to a Hurrann!

Taith took her hand and raised it. "Wife." His statement was replete with satisfaction.

Phelan made a sound of agreement, stroking her uplifted forearm in a proprietary manner.

Just then Alithia noticed her *idkhet* were longer and narrower, snug from just above her wrists to almost her elbows. No danger of losing them now. The dark patterns etched on the *mythir* were finally recognizable—Phelan's *idkhet* bore flames while Taith's had trees and bells. And they were comfortable, as though sized especially for her.

Theirs had undergone a similar transformation.

Their pledge had been well and truly completed. Whatever happened, Taith and Phelan were now her husbands. She could only wonder what the mothers would make of them.

Blood Claim

Eleven

Phelan followed Alithia and his sword brother along the rocky path, his senses alert to danger . . . among other things, one of which was the eye-catching sway of their wife's rump. The dragon-scale tunic and trews she wore did little to conceal her womanly curves as she followed Taith behind the crag. Her sandaled feet were light, despite the long ride, kicking up loose pebbles that tumbled down and over the cliff edge mere strides away.

She carried a towel and a basket of what she called essentials. Never having witnessed a woman bathe, he could only guess at its contents. But he didn't begrudge her bath. She'd held up well under the pace of travel. Some of the men would have grumbled by now—save for her forbearance; since she said nothing, pride kept them silent. An unexpected advantage to traveling with her.

Having a wife was better than he'd imagined—and he'd done much of that even with his boyhood behind him. Her mere presence and her quiet smiles made the mornings brighter in a way he hadn't foreseen.

Taith scouted around before he called her forward and led them to the spring, a cheerful flow of water gushing from an outcrop to fall into a shallow pool that emptied over the cliff. Bright green moss blanketed the rocks around the water, the thick cover hinting at few visitors—at least of the animal kind.

Alithia gasped, the eager anticipation on her face ample reward for the hike. Setting her burden down, she dipped her fingers in the water. "Ooh, nice."

Phelan copied her and flinched at the keen chill. That was nice? Their wife had strange tastes, if so. He kept his opinion to himself, helping her out of her tunic while Taith climbed the rocks and took as his station the peak with its vantage of both approaches.

She immediately pulled off her shirt, sighing in relief as she stood there bare-breasted. Eyes closed, she held her pose for long moments, offering herself up to the touch of the Lady and the breeze. He got the impression of someone throwing off shackles, she seemed to revel so in her nudity.

He threw a glance over his shoulder to check the track. Luckily, there was no one else to see her but Taith and him.

An avid look of anticipation on her face, Alithia undid her sandals then stripped off her trews in impatient jerks. Finally, her hair came free of its tail, a red cloak flaring across her shoulders as she shook her head with another sigh.

Did she find it so constricting?

This wasn't the first time she'd gone bare-breasted.

They'd treated her with the gentlest of care as much as they could, still incredulous of their good fortune and wary of giving offense. But they were her husbands now and had to protect her from all dangers—including other men.

Alithia splashed into the pool with unnerving enthusiasm, apparently oblivious to its chill.

Phelan couldn't suppress a shiver as she stepped under the waterfall. How could she stand it? Yet she stretched and turned beneath its flow with every evidence of pleasure. He dug into his pouch in search of the beads with warming spells.

"There is no need to stand sentry." Their wife smiled at him through a veil of wet hair, her flowerlike nipples puckered into tight, dark pink buds, the way they did during bed play.

His blade swelled in immediate response. He had to clear his throat before he could speak. "Of course there is." The day-old scat Taith quietly pointed to beside the trail on the way to the spring had probably been left by a full-grown catamount. It could still be in the area and likely not alone.

Catamounts hunted in packs. Fortunately, they didn't consider wyverns prey, preferring the meat of gargant calves. But at times they also hunted men—those with the misfortune or temerity to cross their path. Thank the Horned Lords, it was nowhere in sight, but there were other predators that could be lurking nearby.

Making a face at them, she scrubbed her sweat-stained clothes, her breasts bouncing and jiggling distractingly. She was so natural in her actions, unmindful of her display. Every motion a graceful invitation to watch and stare and want.

Phelan forced himself to look away, to look around for danger. They weren't here for pleasure. The cliffside was too exposed for any kind of bed play, and he would be doing their wife no favors by dropping his guard. Despite the admonishment, his body hardened without his volition, the minor indiscipline a development that continued to take him aback.

Once satisfied with her laundry work, Alithia draped the garments on the rocks to dry, then fished in the basket for a purple bar—soap-root, he realized from the bubbles that formed when she rubbed it across her shoulders.

Stealing another glance at their wife, Phelan's mouth went dry. Until then, he'd never realized how alluring bathing could be. The bubbles veiled Alithia's vivid nipples, teasing him with hints of what he wanted to see. The sway of her gentle curves seduced with little effort—he remembered well how they felt under his hands, so soft and yielding.

She ducked under the waterfall, a delicious moan accompanying her quick shiver. Her red hair clung to her body, flowing down her back and around her breasts.

He swallowed, unable to drag his eyes away, sorely tempted to heed her invitation. He could already feel the weight of her breasts in his hands, feel her body writhing against him, hear her cries of pleasure as he drove into her. Bed play with Alithia still felt new and wondrous, each time like a gift from the Lady. He wanted to grab every opportunity.

"Phelan," Duty incarnate, that most stolid and implacable of warriors whom he'd chosen as his sword brother, growled under his breath. Most of the time, Taith followed his lead, but in certain matters, his sword brother had little patience.

With great reluctance, Phelan moved back, needing the added distance—however slight—from temptation. He was accustomed to seeking out what he wanted, on acting on his desires, to good effect: witness Taith, who might not have become his sword brother if Phelan had been more circumspect.

Stepping out from under the waterfall, Alithia frowned at him in bemusement. "Are you truly not joining me?" She pushed her wet hair out of her face, unmindful that her pose threw her breasts into heart-thrilling prominence. Her nipples peeked out between the strands, the flame red tresses only making her skin look paler.

Never had duty been more exacting.

He nearly strangled on his answer. "This is your bath."

She narrowed her eyes at him. "If you expect any bed play tonight, you had better bathe as well." Turning around, she tilted her head back to stare at Taith, her hands coming to rest on her hips. "That goes for you, too."

* * *

Taith sent up a silent prayer of gratitude to the Lady for the discomfort of the rock he sat on. Alithia's breasts were like flame sugar fruit, round and ripe for the plucking. The sight of the fiery curls between her thighs was almost more than he could bear. The knowledge of the pleasures awaiting him was a throbbing ache in his loins. If not for the Lady's boon, he might have succumbed to their wife's delectable invitation. And how would that serve her—beyond the obvious?

Diverting his aggravation at having to refuse so magnificent an opportunity, he glared at Phelan, who showed signs of weakness. If he had to suffer, he would not do so alone. He had no intention of sitting guard while his shield brother took pleasure with their wife and made certain Phelan knew his mind. "We will bathe in the safety of the camp."

"I could have bathed in the camp as well."

And place her in the center of their crew's fantasies? Out of the question!

He shifted his grip on the bow resting on his knee, having left the axe behind in camp in favor of the bow's greater reach. Though designed for use a-wyvernback, the bow was the better weapon for his present purpose, given the long sight lines in the mountains.

With his free hand, he rubbed the back of his neck where a throb gathered strength like a storm churning the sea. Alithia's penchant for undress made attending her difficult, but that was mere inconvenience. Not for all the gold in Sentinel Reach would he exchange her for a proper, temple-raised Hurranni woman.

"We thought you'd enjoy this more. There won't be many opportunities like this farther on," Phelan explained, casting a yearning look at their wife, then a guilty one at Taith. But his shield brother tugged his tunic and properly resumed his vigil.

To Taith's everlasting relief, Alithia ducked back under the waterfall beyond his line of sight, taking temptation with her.

Still, he forced his gaze back to the horizon, then to the slopes and nearby rocks. The sky was mostly clear with only high wisps to the west and a low bank of flashing clouds by the northern peaks. A lone gryphon wheeled above a lake some leagues distant, its bronze wings gleaming in the Lady's light—too far to be a danger.

Splashes of bright blue on the slopes swayed in the breeze, the spikes of delicate flowers a startling contrast to the granite. The cheerful turfs of rock lace did little to soothe his temper, though they were too small to conceal a man, much less a catamount.

Of the catamount that left the scat by the trail, there was no sign nor call nor scent. The only smell the wind brought him was a mix of soap-root and flowers, hardly cause for concern.

The remainder of Alithia's bath passed in restful tranquillity, hard-pressed though he was to ignore their wife's murmurs of delight. Phelan's fidgeting was spice to his self-denial; one might think his shield brother stood on an anthill, but this small deprivation would not hurt him.

Their wife finally emerged from the spring and into Phelan's solicitous care. He had a towel ready, warmed by a spell, though Alithia did not evince any particular distress—nor did she laugh at his assiduity, accepting his attentions in pensive silence.

Try though he might, Taith could not find anything in her expression to indicate a problem. Alithia and Phelan looked right together, the new *idkhet* gleaming white on their arms merely another tile in the mosaic, a part of them—as though his shield brother had always worn one.

He snorted to himself as he clambered down from his post. Likely he was reading too much into a quiet moment, a bad habit of Phelan's he had no intention of acquiring. So disposed, he started them down the path back to camp.

"Alithia!" Sand crunched as Phelan moved.

Taith spun around in surprise, nocking an arrow as he did.

Their wife was hunched over on her knees beside a boulder, his shield brother gripping her shoulder.

His heart stumbled even as he cast a ward and drew his bow, not knowing where to look for the cause of her distress. Nothing he saw could account for it, no danger in sight, so what had brought her down? He had to quash the need to check her for himself; that was a Shield's duty.

"Are you—what're you doing?" Phelan's voice rose in bafflement, not worry—their wife was unhurt.

Slotting the arrow back in his quiver, Taith turned to Alithia, breathing deep as his heart resumed its usual steady beat.

She dug at some plants behind the granite outcropping, ignoring the soil that clung to her freshly bathed skin and got under her nails. "Gathering." The exposed roots were a tangle of plump tubers embedded in the ground. She smoothed off clumps of mud, her touch almost . . . tender.

"Rock lace? Why?"

"We use it, both root and seed, in incense, but our supply comes from Caria, and they get it from elsewhere. We have not been able to discover where. If we could grow it ourselves, we would not have to beg for their leavings."

Ah, trade. That he understood well. An opportunity to improve the situation of her clan. He also detected a note of pride in her explanation, a good thing to have in a wife, especially theirs. Phelan would not deal well with a placid wife when he always looked to the next horizon for a challenge.

Kneeling on her other side, Taith stroked the feathery petals, too delicate to survive the journey, though the roots might. "Pretty. There are more over there." He gestured upslope. "Do you want them all?" More would improve the chances of something surviving to reach her homeland.

She stared for a long moment at the tuft he pointed to, clearly tempted. But in the end, she shook her head. "These should be enough."

Leaving Phelan to stand guard, Taith helped Alithia dig, sacrificing a knife to the enterprise. They soon freed the mass of rock lace, the blue flowers pungent with earthy spice and shivering as they took it out of the surprisingly large hole necessary.

Mud speckled their wife's hands and *idkhet*, a brown smear decorating her cheek. Sweat trailed down her neck despite the cool breeze. She had not spared her efforts despite his aid, now dirtier than when they had started out. She looked as if she had been in a fight, and perhaps she had—for her clan's future. Devyn had been correct when he said she had claws.

Taith braced himself, suspecting what would come next. "I assume you will want to bathe again?"

Stiffening in wordless protest, Phelan stared down at him, aghast at his suggestion. Taith could not blame him.

Another endless wait, taunted by her nudity, the sounds of her enjoyment, the thought of all that water flowing over soft, smooth skin. Knowing they had but to ignore duty in order to have her. Such torment was worthy of the Red Lord's hells.

Alithia gave him a puzzled look as she cradled her precious rock lace against her dragon-scale-covered breasts. "Of course."

He could only laugh.

Rank upon rank of tall peaks cloaked in green stretched as far as the eye could see, reaching for the sky and vanishing into the mists. Alithia stood in the opening of the tent watching the dawn paint the northern clouds pink then gold. Somewhere past those dizzying heights was Sentinel Reach. Seeing what lay ahead, it seemed impossible to traverse the distance in half a season, even at the rapid pace Taith set a-wyvernback.

It was becoming harder to judge the passage of the seasons as they traveled north. The deep valleys between the mountains were wet and held unfamiliar trees and exotic plants she had only seen before in apothecary records. These were swamps and marshes, but unlike the marshes around Lydia, these seemed to be always green and wet, refreshed by nightly rains.

Strange birdcalls punctuated the morning silence—chirps and whistles and chortles and clacks and warbles and fluting phrases. She could see none of the singers despite their seeming preponderance, but their songs were full of life, as though it were high summer.

Yet surely it would be autumn soon? Though she looked hard, she could see no hint of the coming season, and when she thought back through her lessons with Curghann, she could find no word in Hurranni for autumn. When she tried to describe what she sought, her husbands said the plants changed color only in the taller peaks near the southern border.

They had already spent days threading the pass, breaking off from the main track almost immediately. The track they now followed was barely a trail—and sometimes not even that. Gargants couldn't have taken it. Some portions were so steep their mounts clung to the cliffsides; others were split by deep fissures with edges that couldn't have supported a gargant's weight, though the wyverns leaped the chasms without balking.

That was nearly a sennight, as Hurranns measured time, the seven nights it took the red moon Adal to change from new to full. A fortnight was a full cycle by Adal from new to full and back to new—four and ten nights, and Curghann had estimated the journey from Barda to Sentinel Reach would take a few fortnights—the Lady permitting. If She veiled Her face and allowed storms to blow, it would take longer.

A tunic swung before her eyes, its pattern of yellows, browns, and black gleaming in the morning light. "The men will be up soon." Taith held up her dragon-scale armor with one hand, a shirt in the other hand. Her new husband towered above her, a giant of a man for all his quiet ways, the *idkhet* on his left forearm a discreet reminder of their alliance and his right to a voice in her life. There was no way she could miss the sheen of *mythir* against the golden darkness of his nudity.

In small ways, her husbands conveyed their preference for keeping her body hidden from other men's eyes. She didn't know if it was a Hurranni practice or something peculiar to Taith and Phelan, but while they didn't object to her meeting the dawn naked, they made certain she was dressed before their men were about. She suspected they suffered her dawn watch only because the tents set around theirs faced outward.

She donned the shirt first, then let him settle the sturdy tunic on her shoulders, still uncomfortable with their constant attendance. She had thought herself accustomed to having a man on hand from the journey to Barda, but Curghann hadn't been ever-present, and he hadn't required Gilsor to never leave her side. She hadn't minded Curghann's insistence on attendance so much because it satisfied propriety when they had been seeking husbands for her.

With Taith and Phelan, it was different, their attendance rooted in protection—as though she were a child to be told fire could burn, not just warm. They didn't prevent her from going anywhere nor insist she stay in one place, but they always seemed to be within arm's length. They stayed with her even at the spring when she bathed, not to watch or play but as if something would emerge from the rocks besides water.

She had never imagined having two husbands would be so frustrating, but at times their attendance wore on her despite their sincere concern. At least the guards of her retinue in Lydia gave her time to herself. Her sword and shield husbands—Taith and Phelan, respectively—went with her everywhere. And unlike with her guards, she couldn't bring herself to pretend her husbands weren't there.

Just another aspect of marriage she hadn't expected.

The first days of the second leg of her journey had been a disorienting flood of changes, new faces, and a different mode of travel amidst adapting to having husbands. Bidding farewell to Gilsor and Curghann had been unexpectedly heart-wrenching, her last connection to clan and home gone.

Devyn, the lone widowed man in Taith and Phelan's crew, had presented her with a tunic much like the ones her husbands wore. Dragon scale and made especially for her on the expectation of Taith and Phelan's victory, he had informed her with a proud glance at the shield pair, adding that the bulky attire was necessary for protection from the elements, the wildlife, and—most important—the covetous eyes of brigands.

Curghann had also surprised her with new clothes—mostly trews and shirts like a man's—explaining that her Lydian attire would not be suitable for travel in the stronger sun and warmer climes of Hurrann. She soon found herself grateful for his gift; the trews protected her thighs from chafing against Bulla's pebbly hide. Gilsor had told her about the wyverns, so the change in mounts hadn't come as a complete surprise, but he couldn't have known of the conflict inherent between a saddle barely large enough to cup the backside, Lydian skirts, and a wyvern's mobile neck.

Those days had also been a time of introduction. Until after the pledging, Alithia had spent hardly any time with Taith and Phelan, and she knew only what Curghann had told her. They couldn't have known much more about her.

Then there was their crew. Taith and Phelan led eight other shield pairs, and she had been introduced to every one. Save for Devyn, most of their men regarded her with a worrisome awe that she hoped had nothing to do with Baillin's babble about the eclipse. At least it seemed they were warming to her, setting aside some of that disconcerting reverence—to Alithia's relief; the respect due a first daughter was sufficient for her. Perhaps it had simply been the dearth of women in Barda?

Eoghann had even ventured a shy smile in her direction by the campfire last night. Of Taith and Phelan's crew, he reminded her most of Gilsor. Not that his looks resembled her brother's in any way, but he had a fondness for strange tales, which made him seem younger than the others, though he clearly was a warrior in his own right.

Taith seemed content to let her adjust in her own time, explaining the things she saw and confirming some of the stories Gilsor had repeated to her but otherwise biding his silence as his wyvern scampered down the mountainside.

Phelan, however, was full of questions, asking them at camp and rarely satisfied with a simple answer, particularly when it came to Lydian customs. She had never known a man to be so curious. Happily, that curiosity extended to bed play, where her shield husband displayed equal enthusiasm.

She laced up her trews, the coarse weave rough on her skin, her hands awkward with the leather cords. She still missed the softness and freedom of her skirts but had to surrender to necessity. Unfortunately, it made dressing slow; her husbands were dressed themselves by the time she was ready.

Taith straightened, and Phelan sprang to his feet when Alithia headed out of the tent. She slashed a hand and injected granite into her voice. "Stay. You do not need to show me the path. I remember how to get there." It was just a short trek to where she could see to her needs. She could find her way through the brush alone, and their time was better spent striking camp.

Time was of the essence. She could feel it trickling between her fingers, escaping in dribs and drabs, no matter how hard she tried to slow it. The seasons waited for no woman—or man.

Her husbands disregarded her words, Taith quickly taking the lead and Phelan trailing behind as she left the camp. Frustration stirred again at this reminder of their constant presence. A Lydian man wouldn't have flouted her.

"You need not bother."

"It's no bother," Phelan assured her, his absent tone saying his attention was elsewhere, barely paying her any mind.

She set out at a brisk pace, but Taith with his ground-eating strides didn't notice, and Phelan had no trouble keeping up with her. The path was worn and clearly blazed. There was no chance of her losing her way. Their persistence in treating her like some foolish child only made her resentment burn hotter.

Reaching her destination, she moved into the brush to tend to her needs, painfully aware of the two men waiting in the meager shadows with their hands on their weapons. They didn't allow her out of their sight, their posturing excessive. As if a brigand might lurk behind the low shrubs clinging to the rocks!

Alithia dug a hole in the hard soil and quickly relieved herself, filled the hole, and cleaned herself—all the while conscious of her audience. Done and burning from their disregard of her wishes, she moved onto the path to confront Taith and Phelan. At least they were far enough from camp that they wouldn't have an audience.

She had thought she knew what to expect with husbands constantly underfoot. She had lived all her life under guard, one way or another, but never like this. This was beyond her worst imaginings.

It couldn't be allowed to continue! If she didn't quash their overbearing protectiveness now, it would set a precedent—one she would have difficulty breaking the longer she delayed.

"Curghann did not insist on being on hand all the time. For most of the journey to Barda, only Gilsor attended me." Remarkably, she managed to keep her voice even despite the pounding in her chest.

"Only because there was no one else suitable." Phelan twitched a shoulder as though brushing off a fly, his hand on the hilt of his sword. "That isn't the case now."

The obdurate expressions on her husbands' faces didn't bode well for the future.

She inhaled sharply, air hissing between her teeth. Her hands found little purchase on the hard scales of her armor, her nails sliding over them as readily as her husbands ignored her instructions. Her thumbs caught on her belt, and she left them there, anchors for her temper. "Surely Curghann, a man with turns of experience in attendance, is a better judge of that?"

"He is not your husband; we are. Our judgment of the situation is what matters. Perhaps after we have gained the same turns of husbandhood we may agree with his thinking, but this close attendance is what we were taught. A Hurranni woman would understand."

Frustration at Taith's answer had Alithia struggling for calm. "I am not Hurrann. You cannot expect me to accept what a Hurranni woman would accept. I cannot live with this constant hovering, always thinking of how to behave with the two of you."

Phelan stared at her, confusion rounding his eyes, his jaw hanging slack, like Gilsor when he was caught out. "Don't worry about us. You're our wife, no matter what you do."

Despite their scars, they weren't that much older than she was, Alithia realized, and they were at as much of a loss on how to go on as she. With no experience to guide them, they relied on the training they had received—training for Hurranni wives, women who had been raised to know what to expect from such *attendance*.

She huffed, half tempted to throw up her hands at their incomprehension. Was it so hard to understand that there were times when a woman wanted to be alone? Their continual attendance made her feel more like a child than anything Curghann had done.

Alithia pointed to the sky where Egon waxed alone, its dark companion not having risen yet. "Even your Lady is not always attended by both Horned Lords all the time."

Taith nodded agreeably, clearly humoring her. "Truth, but you do not know the dangers of Hurrann. It is best this way."

There was no reasoning with them!

Fuming, she shook her head, at a loss for words at their unswerving certainty. She had never encountered such arrogance in a man before—not in Lydia. Even Curghann hadn't taken such an unappealing stance when he balked at helping her plan this journey.

Phelan caught her shoulder as she spun on her heel, his brows furrowed with undeniable concern. "We only want to make sure you're safe. We'll help you with whatever you're doing. We'll do everything in our power to get you to Sentinel Reach and anywhere else you need to travel. But you will have our attendance—even if it means you'll be uncomfortable. That's the way it has to be." The hard light in his dark eyes underscored his sincerity, unmistakable in the bright morning sun.

His sword brother added in a more conciliatory tone, "Alithia, grant that we know the dangers of Hurrann. Our vigilance is no mere whim. Even the temple of the Lady of Heaven accepts husbands' attendance as a necessity—and the priestesses would be the first to protest any arbitrary curtailment of their prerogatives."

She could muster no argument against that last. How could she, knowing next to nothing of the Lady's temple? If Hurranni priestesses were anything like the Goddess's priestesses in Lydia, his logic was unassailable.

They trailed her back to camp in silence, her frustration simmering between them like incense embers on a brazier.

"D'you think it's the imminence of her bleeding time?" Phelan whispered behind her.

Overhearing him didn't improve Alithia's temper. Who knew what sort of wild tales Hurranni men told about that?

Twelve

A break in the trees opened into a field where Taith and Phelan's crew was already unloading the wyverns. Alithia greeted the sight with relief, weary from bracing her legs against Bulla's sudden changes in direction, her backside numb and her stomach empty—the price of the long day of travel and her urgency. When Phelan had said they would do everything they could to aid her in her quest, he hadn't been placating her. Since their argument, her husbands had pushed hard for distance, maintaining a pace that stampeding gargants couldn't have matched.

She envied Taith his ease. He seemed always to know when Bulla was going to jump or veer, adjusting his balance without any awkwardness or overcorrection.

The leather riding straps that secured her to the saddle gave way with a little fumbling and Taith's help. He jumped down, a single smooth motion that belied any weariness on his part, then caught her as she swung her leg over his mount's neck. For a heartbeat out of time, he held her up, effortlessly, showing no strain as he drew her close and slid her down his large and very male body.

Just that quickly Goddess heat stirred in her, distracting her from her aches.

Then he set her on her feet, a smile flirting with the corners of his mouth. She had thought Taith the more sober-minded of her husbands, but that simple contact made her doubt. The rogue knew what he had done to her.

Laughing at his game, Alithia straightened her trews. After days of riding behind Taith, she was resigned to the necessity of them, much as she was becoming accustomed to the saddle straps. If only she could come to the same acceptance of her husbands' unnecessarily oppressive *attendance* . . .

She walked around to stretch her legs, working through the tingles as her backside regained sensation and waiting for the heat Taith had kindled to fade.

By this time, she was inured to the chaos of pitching camp. The view of golden peaks sinking into the twilight didn't hold her interest. Taith had said the morrow would see them leaving the shoulders of the mountains, speaking with some enthusiasm, but she wanted nothing to remind her of the long day that awaited her a-wyvernback. She turned her gaze to the nearby trees and the tangle of vines dangling from their branches.

Masses of white and red flowers on the vines caught her eye, the crescent buds something she had only seen in the clan's archives. *Moon blossoms!* Her heart leaped in excitement. If she could get seeds, perhaps they could grow them in Lydia. The oil from the flowers encouraged restful sleep and was sought by both perfumers and apothecaries. She nearly ran to the vines in her eagerness.

"Stop!"

"Alithia!"

"No!"

A sledgehammer slammed into her, flinging her off her feet.

Screaming, she threw her arms up as twigs and leaves flew at her. She landed hard, her breath forced out of her lungs. A heavy weight dropped on her back. Her heart in her throat, she pushed up, trying to throw it off.

"Don't move!"

The harsh command—Phelan's—shocked her into stillness. She tucked her head back down, her face pressed into her arms.

Feet pounded toward them, battle cries resounded, followed by thud after meaty thud in a battering that seemed to go on forever. A rich odor overwhelmed the smell of soil and sap, alien and unnerving.

"Safe." Taith's voice came from above them, quavery as though he had run a distance.

The tight arms around her waist released. Alithia turned over, wondering what had prompted all that, then stared. Above her and Phelan hung the mangled remains of a bloody serpent, its long, writhing body easily half as wide as her shoulders. She could see nothing holding it up. All the men around them had their hands on dripping weapons. That was when she noticed the beads in Phelan's braid glowing.

He stood up, then helped her out from under the gory sight and onto her feet, keeping a hand on her arm when she winced at the soreness the motion kindled. The glow faded, and the serpent dropped to the ground, its death throes flattening the grass.

"Well, at least we won't have to hunt for supper tonight."

Shaky chuckles answered Gair's breathless jest, rising until all the men roared with laughter.

"Too bad about the hide, though," Eoghann added, grunting as he picked up one end of the creature. He sheathed his sword to grasp the serpent with both hands. "Perhaps next time we should just put out bait."

Devyn's hand flashed out, clipping the back of Eoghann's head. "That's not funny."

"Alithia, what were you doing?" Taith thundered, his eyes

blazing, his nostrils flared, his face dark as a storm cloud. "You cannot just leave our side without warning."

Her heart pounded in her ears, loud and fast, the enthusiastic *boom-boom-boom* of a festival drum. Heat came and went from her face, leaving her chilled, her skin too tight across her cheeks. "I—the moon blossoms." The flowers gleamed in the dying light, so beautiful, as though the gore didn't exist. "I wanted to get seeds."

"Here, help me with this," Eoghann called to his sword brother, his arms full of serpent.

The size of it sank in, and Alithia's knees went weak, the pain in her side floating away as the edges of her vision darkened. She clung to Phelan, welcoming the sting from her palms as she fought to remain standing. An oath escaped him as he caught her by the elbows.

Taith gave a shout, then he was lifting her off her feet.

She transferred her grip to his tunic, the dragon scales hard yet slippery under her nails. She refused to faint like some silly kit. But she could see the serpent . . .

"Get the tent up," he ordered, his long strides rapidly distancing her from that nightmare.

"I am fine." Her voice emerged as a thin whisper. She tried again. "I am fine, Taith."

"No, you are not fine. You are as ash and quivering like a flutter-wing. You will be silent and rest. How can I yell at you if you look like a day-old corpse?"

Outrage forced back the darkness, but before she could say anything, he continued. "You cannot walk around in sublime confidence in your safety like your brother. You must be aware of danger—always—none of this rushing into the bushes without a word to your husbands."

The other men were quick to obey. Their tent was always the first one unloaded, and this time was no different; with so many eager hands, it was soon up.

"Tree serpents are known to hunt grown men. They coil around their prey until the victim dies for want of air. Its weight, the impact of its fall alone, could have killed you." Taith's embrace tightened in seeming mimicry, pressing her against his heaving chest. "Leaving our side—in the wild!—without giving us warning was pure folly, the height of recklessness." He set her on the pallet and made a mountain out of the jumble of pillows hastily unpacked. "This is why women need to be attended. We are your husbands. You must let us do what we were born to do."

Stunned into silence by the spate of words from one so miserly in speech, Alithia sank into the pillows gratefully, only now noticing the pallor of his cheeks, a sickly yellow tinge to the copper skin. She had frightened him, she realized, finally hearing the concern behind the fury.

"Now, will you rest?"

She nodded.

For some reason that made him frown all the more. He touched her cheek, then swore. "Horned Lords, you are cold." After piling blankets on top of her, he stalked out of the tent, shouting for Phelan, Devyn, and mead.

Now that it was over, her palms burned, abrasions from when she landed. Her side ached—probably bruised, but that was a bargain when measured against her life. She eased out of the dragon-scale armor and was surprised to find nothing worse than the cuts on her hands, due in large part to Devyn's gift and the now-sap-stained *idkhet*. The Goddess be praised!

Crawling out from under the blankets, Alithia reached into her saddlebag for her little-used sleep shift and checked where Taith was. He stood just outside the tent, casting about for Devyn and her shield husband. While his attention was diverted, she pulled off her shirt and found—as she had expected—mottled skin where Phelan's shoulder must have hit her when he tackled her. Not wanting Taith to see it, she hastily put on the shift, ignoring the pang in her side.

An oath told her Taith was back, but luckily he hadn't seen the bruise since he said no more—or perhaps he had simply run out of words.

Devyn came into the tent with him, bearing a flask and a cup and a guilt-inducing expression of concern.

"There is no need for that," she protested, having a fair idea of the cost, if the flask held the mead Taith had demanded. Her sword husband was overreacting to her stupid shivers.

Kneeling beside her, Taith took what the older man offered, and without any hesitation broke the wax seal over the flask's cork and poured a small measure into the cup. "Here, drink it all and quickly." He held it out to her, keeping possession of the cup when she tried to push it from her mouth.

"Alithia," he warned as he raised it to her lips.

The smell of honey and flowers reached her nose. Giving in to the inevitable, she drank. Sweet fire flowed down her throat and exploded in her belly.

As she gasped for breath, he refilled the cup. "One more."

By the time she got the second one down, warmth was spreading through her veins.

Taith peered at her, then nodded in satisfaction. "Better. Now for your hands."

He turned them over, exposing the scraped flesh. He must have felt the damage when she pushed the cup. To her horror, he splashed mead over her palms, using the expensive drink to cleanse them. The cuts stung, then quickly cooled to a gentle tingle. He inspected them thoroughly before finally corking the flask and handing it to Devyn.

Taith's silence left Alithia at the mercy of her thoughts. Her carelessness had brought on the serpent attack. She hadn't checked for danger. Despite her protestations of caution, she had proven her husbands correct in their judgment. *Bait, ha!* Clearly there was need for their *attendance*. The realization was a bitter potion to swallow.

Turning to Taith, Alithia forced out the necessary words. Delay would just make the unpleasant harder. If she waited for Phelan's return, she might not be able to say it. "I apologize."

"For what?"

She pressed her lips together, struggling for composure. If Taith wanted a thorough accounting, she owed them that much. "For the trouble I caused you."

"Not good enough," Taith ground out, the corner of his jaw twitching.

"What?!"

Devyn's troubled gaze bounced from her to him and back, then he shook his head. "It's not the trouble, lady. You nearly died. That's what matters."

"We are your husbands. Our purpose—our duty—is to attend to you. For you to just rush into danger without us is just . . ." Taith jerked his head, clearly struggling for words. "Mush head!"

He spun on his heel and glared at the older man. "Where is Phelan?"

"I'll look." Devyn made his escape.

Taith followed him outside, his obvious temper making the men approaching him swerve away.

Without anything to occupy them, her hands shook. Disgusted by the display of weakness, Alithia wrapped her arms around her bent legs and rested her forehead on her knees. She had been irresponsible, dismissing all the warnings about the dangers of Hurrann, so certain they were just stories. So eager to embrace a sense of normalcy—even if it was just harvesting—that she nearly got herself killed. Stupid of her. She had come this far and then risked her life for a handful of seeds.

Thoughtless, foolish mush head. Taith was correct to name her so. Blindly rushing forth, oblivious to the dangers. She had thought her husbands arrogant—what of herself? She believed she would get to Sentinel Reach; all that was in question was when. But it was clear her own temperament could lead her to failure.

Arrogance to think she would make no mistakes in Hurrann. How could she rail against her husbands' attendance when she needed their help to survive? Her pride wasn't the only thing at stake. What would happen to her clan if she didn't return with the tablet of mysteries?

Gentle fingers combed through her hair. Taith's from their size and blunt tips. Nothing was said as he stroked her neck, his anger nowhere in evidence in his touch, only tender concern.

But when she raised her head, that rich smell of earlier was there—and stronger. Her stomach rebelled, lurching queasily, though only mead filled it. Gulping, she slapped a hand over her nose and mouth.

He jerked back, hastily putting space between them. "I must wash. She smells the serpent blood on me." He swiped a line of wet from his cheek and grimaced.

Phelan stood just inside the tent, looking none the worse for his surprising absence. "Go on. I'll watch over her. You need to batter something before Bulla picks up your mood."

Taith scooped up her armor as he left.

Her stomach settled, now that the smell was gone. Alithia almost wished for the return of her nausea. With it gone, she had nothing to divert her mind from her folly.

She searched Phelan's face, trying to judge his mood. But the more easygoing of her husbands chose just then to school his features to impassivity. "Are you going to scold, too?"

"No, Taith's much better at it than I am." He paced restlessly, like a trapped wolf, then spun around, braid flying, to glare at her. "But don't you ever scare us like that again!"

"I am sorry. I should not have left your side." Alithia rubbed her watering eyes, ignoring the soreness of her palms. "I should not have doubted your warnings of dangers."

Phelan's face softened, his temper passing as quickly as a summer storm. "We only want to protect you. That's all."

"I— It is hard to accept." Because they were men? She didn't want to think so, but the guards in her retinue had always been women. On the journey to Barda, Gilsor and Curghann's attendance had felt more like companionship than protection. They hadn't tried to gainsay her will—could that be why it hadn't chafed on her? Had she expected unquestioning acceptance from Taith and Phelan because they were her husbands?

"Here, perhaps accepting this will be easier?" Phelan held out a leather bundle.

Frowning, she took the bundle and released the ties to find it full of hard black . . . pellets?

A red moon blossom covered her view, its rich perfume teasing her nose, and she realized in a rush of warmth what the pellets were: seeds. Precious moon blossom seeds! He had harvested some simply because she wanted them.

Blinking back inexplicable tears, she smiled up at her husband. "Thank you."

"Why'd you want them?"

Still stunned by the gift, Alithia stared at the flower, its crystalline petals glistening in the light of the amberlamp. "Moon blossoms used to grow in the garden—my clan's garden—ages ago. I wanted to bring them back."

"This?" He trailed a calloused finger along the edge of a petal. "They're a symbol of the Horned Lords, y'know."

"Are they? I did not know that. I want it for my clan. The oil of moon blossoms is expensive and hard to find." She forced herself to meet Phelan's eyes, needing him to understand that her impetuous act wasn't some careless whim. "It would be something else we could sell, another source of income, if—if this venture fails." She didn't want to consider the possibility, but reversals of fortune happened all the time, and one had to seize every opportunity to avert mischance.

Phelan grimaced and nudged the flower toward her. "Just get a sniff of that and rest. Taith'll have the grumps if he finds you still fretting yourself when he gets back."

Alithia bent over the dark red petals, her nose over the center cup. Cool breeze and fresh water. The sunlight scent of ripe berries on the vine. A rush of heady sweetness she could almost taste, rather like the mead Taith made her drink. Just a whiff of fragrance made her head float. *The old apothecary records don't say it's this potent fresh.* She didn't know when Phelan laid her on the pallet.

Phelan watched Alithia sleep, his heart still thundering in his chest despite a sip of moon blossom nectar while gathering the seeds, his ribs so tight he could barely breathe. He clenched his hands to hide the betraying tremors. If he shut his eyes, he could see the tree serpent's head again emerging from the branches, its thick body that mottled green and brown that was difficult to make out against the leaves, could hear the rustles and creaks of the vines as it swung down. Dropping . . .

"You are thinking too much again. Stop it."

Startled, Phelan spun around, knives drawn, ready to kick and slash—

To see Taith standing over him, hair damp from his wash, holding Alithia's dragon-scale tunic, both now free of serpent blood.

Phelan huffed in disgust, sheathed his knives, and settled back on his haunches. "You know I can't." His gut continued to churn from the fright their wife had given them.

"There is always a first time." His sword brother knelt beside him and slung a companionable arm across his shoulders. "Think on this. You were so deep in your thoughts that you did not know I was back. What if I had been a danger to our wife?"

Taith's words were like a dagger to the heart, his aim unerring. What if—

The arm across his shoulders tightened and shook him gently. "But not now. You did well. If you cannot stop your thoughts, I will stand guard."

Phelan buried his face in his hands and rubbed hard, trying to obliterate the memory of that tree serpent. "We almost lost her. Less than a fortnight married, and we almost lost her."

What did that say about their care for their wife? Unease slithered about his insides. Had he pushed them too quickly toward marriage? Were they not ready? Was there a good reason that most shield pairs were older when they pledged? Surely the Lady wouldn't have blessed their bond if they weren't ready?

He leaned against Taith, hoping some of that rock-steady confidence would seep into him and banish the tremors of his heart. Sometimes he wished his imagination weren't so quick to draw the possibilities, that he were more like his sword brother, focused on the here and now.

"But we did not. Because of you."

The tension in him eased at the unqualified approval in Taith's voice. He dropped his hands, needing to see Alithia safe. She looked so defenseless, lying on the pallet by herself, her arms clutching his second favorite pillow—the first kneeling beside him. "Do you think our fathers ever went through anything like this?"

A snort and a squeeze on his shoulders answered him first. "Of course."

"I can't imagine it." In boyhood memory, his parents were always together, happy and harmonious, with never a raised voice between them. His fathers never betrayed any frustration with his mother. She didn't have claws, as Devyn would say.

"I am sure your fathers would tell you so if you asked them . . . after they beat you for your insolence." A tug on his braid reproved him for his doubt.

"You think so?" The thought cheered him. If Taith could imagine it, then it was possible. His sword brother had this uncanny practicality that could cut through Phelan's fantastic speculation and state the obvious. "Really?"

"They just made their mistakes before you were born."

He frowned, not quite convinced. "Hmmm . . ."

"The Horned Lords attend the Lady for a purpose." An unusually fatalistic observation for his sword brother, who preferred to believe they could achieve anything they wanted if they had the wit and will to strive for it.

"This is harder than I thought it'd be."

Taith shook his head slowly in exasperated agreement, then threw a look of frustration at Alithia. "If she would just let us attend her as we ought . . . This resistance of hers courts unnecessary risk. Leaving our side without warning, wanting to walk alone, to be alone, she toys with danger all unknowing."

"We can't ask her to change. She's our wife—and a southerner. From what Baillin said, she's used to having her way, trained to lead her clan. Surely that's not unlike a priestess's training?" Phelan bit his lip as he walked the trail of that thought to its very end. "But if we don't, someday I'll be too late." He was the Shield, Alithia's last line of defense.

His sword brother grimaced, mouth thin and eyes narrow the way they did when he contemplated distasteful choices. "We cannot go on like this."

Thirteen

Taith kept a watchful eye on Alithia and Phelan by the campfire as he dug through his bags. Their wife wore a strained smile, putting on a brave face as she listened to Devyn holding forth, but clearly yesterday's scare still weighed on her spirits. Today she had informed them of her movements, raising no objection to their close attendance. As was proper.

He did not believe her change of heart would last. She would relax and forget—and he could not wish it were otherwise. For husbands, a fearful wife was a small step from utter failure—for it meant she did not trust them to protect her. Only a wife's death was more shameful.

Yet they could not continue down this path.

It was not that Alithia shunned their aid; she left the planning of the journey to Sentinel Reach in his and Phelan's hands, relying on their greater knowledge and asking for no concessions to her lesser stamina. As best as he could understand, she was too accustomed to the safety of the south—or so he supposed. The dangers that they took for granted and instinctively guarded against were fireside tales to her orderly perfumer's mind. She did not see the serpents amidst the leaves, the catamount in the bushes, the mire hole beneath the leaves, or the gryphons crouching on the cliffs, not until they were pointed out to her—or it was too late. Yet they could not expect her to learn everything they knew; only a lifetime in Hurrann could teach that.

With a temple-trained wife, they might have settled in a nearby town or at Black Python's clan house, avoiding much of the dangers from Hurranni wildlife, but with Alithia insistent on traveling to Sentinel Reach, that was not an option.

His fingertips brushed coolness, a rustle in the depths of soft leather. He closed his hand around the strand and pulled it out, reluctance a noisome weight in his belly. He would have given much not to have call for it, had hoped he would never pass it on. But he could not shirk his duty.

Leaning back against Phelan, Alithia wrapped her arms around her legs, a thoughtful frown creasing her brow. "But *mythir* is so expensive. What prevents a man—a shield pair—from offering their *idkhet* to another wife?"

Incredulous blinks met her question, the stunned silence broken only by the crackles from the campfire. Taith shook his head in wonderment. Such innocence. Were southerners truly so different from Hurranns?

"Once etched, they cannot be offered a second time. Only blank *idkhet* are honorable offerings, and they can be gotten only at the Lady's temples." Extending an arm to present the etching on his *idkhet*, Devyn stroked the *mythir* band, a habit of old, as he answered Alithia's questions. The easy smile he wore was that of a father humoring a favored child.

"And for most Hurranns," Phelan added, placing a hand on her shoulder, "the only way to win a wife is by facing trial at the temple."

Their third in command was safe, but Taith found himself

casting a sharp eye over their brethren and noticing how the unbanded shield pairs seemed to lean toward Alithia, like men warming themselves around a fire, hanging on to the sound of her husky voice as though bespelled. Even Gair had his head tilted in her direction as he blew a melancholy tune on his syrinx. Their response was understandable, as she was the only woman among so many men—and probably the first woman they had a chance to converse with in some time, perhaps not since they had last spoken with their mothers.

He should not mind that they were so concerned for her comfort, so aware of her presence—that could only help him and Phelan keep Alithia safe.

Yet he did.

It bothered him to be so suspicious of men he trusted to fight by his and Phelan's sides, brethren who risked life and limb at their say-so time and again. But they were unbanded.

Taith stroked his own *idkhet*, taking comfort from the warm metal band with its etching of the Lady's tree and its flowers. Though he had known from his fathers' stories something of what to expect during pledging, drawing the *idkhet* from the Fire to see them etched had still shocked him.

"But might they not offer to a southerner who would not know better?"

Startled glances were traded around the fire. The hands busy with cooking, honing blades, mending harnesses, or any of the endless other chores of a caravaner stilled.

"Perhaps so," Devyn conceded grudgingly. "But only men lost to honor would attempt that."

An uncomfortable silence descended.

Ducking his head, Eoghann shifted his weight, the cant of his shoulders warning Taith that the Shield was leading up to another of his outrageous questions; the youngest of their crew used humor as a ward against unease. "Do southern girls always share bed play with men before pledging?"

Gair poked him with his syrinx almost before the words were out of his mouth.

Instinctively, the Shield blocked the strike with his forearm, the exchange a familiar byplay between the two. "What? You're wondering the same thing!"

Alithia laughed, her color improving. "Bed play is the—the gift of the *Goddess* to all, not just those who are married."

Goddess? Taith puzzled over the unfamiliar word as he approached the campfire. It did not have the taste of Hurranni.

Despite Devyn's frown, Gair straightened from his slouch, his mouth gaping above the reeds of the syrinx, clearly intrigued. "So the temple approves of this? Women—girls!—sharing bed play with men not pledged to them?" He was not the only one to take notice, the other shield pairs also sitting taller.

"They say that, in the temples, the priestesses share their husbands among themselves," Eoghann offered with a quick glance at Alithia.

Taith swatted the Shield. "Where did you hear that rot?"

"In Barda, a Stone Bridge Shield." Eoghann rubbed the back of his head, eyes dancing, an unrepentant grin on his face. "You saying it's not true?"

"Someone was making a fool of you." Taith could not stifle a snort of irritation at the calumny. "Not that he had to work too hard, mind."

Eoghann laughed, doubtless not taking his comment to heart. For one who had passed his manhood rites, the Shield could be remarkably boyish. How he could willingly buy such wild tales, Taith could not understand.

"It doesn't matter. We don't aspire to a priestess's bond. But if southern women are all like Alithia, perhaps when our time comes, we'll look for a southern wife." Gair smiled in agreement with his shield brother's cheerful proposal—or perhaps merely mindful of Eoghann's lightning-swift fancies.

On that happy note, Taith invited Alithia back to their tent.

This gift ought not be presented before curious eyes. He refused to expose Alithia to embarrassment should she fail.

"So what other nonsense did that Shield tell you?"

"He said there were secret rituals that involve bed play."

Taith stifled a wince as knowing nods and titillated chuckles spread around the campfire as they left, the talk devolving to salacious speculation.

Phelan trailed them, silent, his gaze restless even in the midst of camp. With their wife's back to him, he did not bother masking his concern. However much he might dislike the implications of success, Taith had to do this, as much for his shield brother as for their wife.

And if she succeeded?

He would face that question only if he had to.

"Sleepy already?" Alithia gave him an arch smile, her determination not to allow her mood to darken their marriage bed pricking his conscience.

"Here, you will need to learn how to use this." Taith held out the necklace he had inexplicably included when he packed for the trip to Barda. A colorful fall of beads, the strands looked impossibly delicate in his large hand. The oranges and yellows of amber, dark red garnets, green malachite, turquoise, bright blue lapis, the purples of faience. Strung on silk thread, the stones were cool to the touch, despite the warm air, the etchings inlaid with silver and gold smooth, sliding between the fingers like a living thing—the creations of the finest artisans in Sentinel Reach strung into a masterwork of temple art. It had lain for so long among his things in Black Python's clan house at the Lady's Hills that he had almost forgotten about it.

"*Use* this?" She took the necklace cautiously, her eyes rounding as she got a better look at the beads. "For what?"

"Your protection."

Jerking back, Alithia stared up at him. "Protection?" Her surprise was understandable. Designed to cover the upper slopes of the wearer's breasts, the necklace was exquisite, its beads rendering a flame against a background of the sea, so fragile it could not stop a blunt eating knife.

He forced an explanation past clenched teeth. "Since you insist on leaving our side, you need a ward for defense."

Guilt and temper flashed in her eyes, quickly suppressed. "I admitted I was wrong."

Taith rubbed his brow in frustration. *Mush head.* He was doing this all wrong. "Forgive me, I should not have said that. What I meant to say . . . this may offer some protection, perhaps enough that we would not hover so much."

"This?" She raised the necklace to the light, the flame seeming to dance between her hands.

Phelan gaped. "But—"

Taith waved his shield brother to silence.

"How?" Her eyes sparkled with hope and speculation, the same way Phelan's did when his mind started swirling with all manner of possibilities.

By hushing Phelan's objection, was he raising her hopes unfairly? Giving her no warning that they may be dashed? Yet hinting at the difficulty of what he proposed might open the door to doubt, that bite of uncertainty making it real.

"You have to feel for the Lady's gift—the power set in the beads. I cannot tell you what it is like, because you are a woman. To us, it is almost like cold water on the skin. But we are told it is different for women."

He did not know whether he wanted her to succeed or fail. Whatever the implications of success, Alithia would still be a southern woman, not a temple-raised Hurrann. Success would not change that. But failure meant greater peace of mind—for him.

"It does not feel cold at all." Her fingers stroked the strands, lingering over the beads as though over silk or fur.

Phelan sent him a puzzled frown. "What does it feel like?"

"Warm." She flushed, her cheeks turning pink, the same as

when she was aroused by bed play. Her eyes fluttered down, her breath deepening as she held the necklace to her chest.

For long moments, nothing happened, and Taith dared a sigh of relief.

A bead started to glow, then another.

His mouth went dry, frail hope shriveling. Ash on the tongue. "Think of a ward, a shield all around you, covering you from head to toe." He shoved the words through the tightness of his throat.

Alithia bit her lip in thought, then the light spread, a sheen in the air, moonlight on still water. A bubble shimmered into being around her, a nimbus of blue sea fire barely seen.

"That's it."

At Phelan's murmur, Alithia raised her head. She made a strangled sound, her eyes as large as marbles.

The bubble burst.

But there was no denying she had potential.

"Again," Taith insisted. If she could raise the ward at will, on demand, perhaps they could ease the protectiveness she found so stifling.

She jerked to attention and shut her eyes, her brows furrowed in concentration. The bubble snapped back into being, stronger and brighter, power surrounding her like a cool breeze against the skin.

Then her hair stirred, streaming away from her body as though blown by the wind—save nothing else moved. No leaves rustled. No cloth flapped. No soughing could be heard.

Her features eased, a look of contentment settling across them. Euphoric, almost ecstatic. A soft sigh reinforced the impression of sensual pleasure.

The necklace glowed, not just two beads, but many. The stones that made up the flame shone bright, lit by an inner fire. The necklace glowed in the silence, reds and oranges and yellows shining between Alithia's fingers.

Phelan gasped.

Claws of dismay raked Taith's stomach, caught the throat of the faint hope that huddled there and tore it open. There was no question now as to their wife's success. He knew he should be proud of her accomplishment, but his heart sank. He had to remind himself she was a southerner; her use of power changed nothing. He prayed to the Lady it meant nothing. The priesthood with its flagrant rites was not for him. Ever.

"What is it?" Alithia murmured, her head tilted back, her lashes fanned shut, her lips parted, lost in a dream of power.

His shield brother pointed at the necklace, his eyes wide and shining with admiration. "Most women can use only a bead or two. Only priestesses can use that many."

Startled anew, she dropped the ward, catching a glimpse of the glowing beads in a quick, downward glance. "Truly?"

"In matters of power, I don't jest."

Blushing, Alithia slid a glance at Taith. "Perhaps if they were not told they could not, they would have tried harder."

Phelan followed her gaze. "Where'd you get it?"

Taith stared at the now-quiescent beads, unease sharp talons dancing across his shoulders. "It was my mother's. She gave it to me to give to our wife the day I told her we were a shield pair."

Among all her sons, she had chosen to bestow the necklace on him—another sign of her expectations for his future. How ironic that her gift found life in the hands of a southern woman. He drew some comfort from the fact that Alithia was not a priestess. Temple life was not what he wanted for himself.

"Is this all it does?"

All? She had cast an extensive ward!

"It has other spells—but that is the most important. You will probably learn the others with time and at need. It would take a lifetime to master all the spells."

She inspected the beads, rubbing them between wondering fingers. "How did they come to carry spells?"

"Temple artisans set the Lady's gift in the beads during their crafting." A single bead with a powerful healing spell took several fortnights to make. His mother's necklace represented a lifetime in artisanship worthy of a priestess, a burden of destiny that had terrified him.

Phelan watched Alithia practice calling power to cast a ward. She brought the full of her concentration to the matter the way she did everything else. He watched Taith watch her with equal intensity, his sword brother's reservations obvious only to one who knew him well.

He should have been relieved that their wife could now summon protection of her own, something that would allow her greater independence—something he hadn't considered possible and thus hadn't taken into account in his planning. But it bothered him that he hadn't known about the necklace. His sword brother had kept it a secret from him for nearly ten turns of brotherhood. Deliberately. Why hadn't Taith told him? He had to know Phelan would have found the necklace a puzzlement.

Perhaps that was his answer. Perhaps his sword brother had merely wanted to avoid Phelan's speculation. Truth, at times Phelan himself found all the thoughts dizzying. He wouldn't be surprised that Taith had kept the necklace a secret simply to save himself the aggravation.

Sometimes—as Taith would and had pointed out—the obvious explanation was the correct one.

With that question answered to his satisfaction, the wonder of it all filled him.

Taith's mother's beads. A priestess's beads!

To be given to their wife.

A gift entrusted to Taith in their early manhood.

And Alithia had brought them to life with very little effort.

A feather of excitement tickled Phelan's belly at the foreknowledge implied. While the grace of the Lady was welcome, all too often you didn't get that without the touch of the Horned Lords providing complications aplenty.

Life promised to be interesting with their southern wife.

Fourteen

A spear of rock, its underside pale and clear of lichen, jutted out of the mountain, pointing north. Taith welcomed the sight, its presence marking the end to the string of enclosed valleys they had been traversing. They had kept to the high slopes, skirting the marshes to avoid tiring their mounts on the ascents. Now travel would go faster.

Invisible power eddied up from over the cliff, cool and exhilarating. The Lady's gift.

Bulla rose on his hind legs, neck stretching forward as he ran, his flaps spreading to catch the rising flows of power; then, with muscles stretching against Taith's knees, the wyvern launched them off the ridge.

A squeak sounded behind Taith as they plunged toward the swamp. Alithia's arms tightened around his waist, pressing her soft breasts against his back, even as Bulla steadied and rose, gliding over still water. "You did that deliberately."

He grinned since she could not see his face, refusing to admit to anything. Having a wife who was not Hurrann was proving to be a delight in more ways than just bed play. Her open wonder made the world seem fresh once more.

Eoghann and Gair swept by on their wyverns, part of the defensive screen they would maintain around Alithia. The flight was arrayed above them, Swords gliding higher and Shields below. In the air, danger came more frequently from above. Save for them, the sky was empty. They were still far south of the dragons' range, but there was always a small risk of one going rogue.

This was his time with Alithia—which the glide signaled would soon come to an end. Once they reached the headwaters of the Nathair, he would have to surrender her to Phelan's care while he and Bulla flew ahead to guard against danger.

Resentment stirred at the thought, a twinge of possessive anger at the coming loss, unexpected and unreasonable. His shield brother had the skills to protect her better farther north, and Taith's role as Sword was to slay the dangers that sought his shield brother and their wife. Yet an insidious voice in his head suggested ways to prolong the time Alithia rode with him: a slower glide, a change in route, a claim of safety. The selfishness of his thoughts worried Taith. Why did he want to monopolize Alithia's company to Phelan's detriment? His cheeks heated with shame. His shield brother had seen him through peril and profit. This strange desire not to share their wife with him was unworthy of their turns of brotherhood.

The wyvern stooped suddenly, hooting as he lowered his head into the swamp waters. A large fish flapped between his narrow jaws a moment later, one he gulped down whole before rejoining the flight.

"Taith?" Alithia's embrace was tight, despite her calm question. She still struggled with trust, but her steady voice was assurance of her confidence in them; it banished the strange stew of emotion coming to a simmer in his belly.

Perhaps marriage was not so different from integrating a new shield pair into their crew. There was the unknown on both sides, the tentative decision to work together for a common purpose, the gradual extension of trust. He could only hope the rapport between him and Phelan and their wife would grow as strong as theirs with their brethren.

He stroked her arm in reassurance. "Easy. It is fine." The fish made a large lump in the wyvern's long neck as it made its slow way to the stomach.

After Bulla was level once more, her grip eased.

It was a good day for a glide, the wind cool and gentle, the clouds high and sheer, veiling the Lady's face just enough to ease the heat. They were all well rested and in good spirits.

Alithia leaned around him, her fingers digging into his waist as she stared at the trees streaming by below them, her cheeks the soft pink of dawn. The wind blew her hair across his face in a gentle caress. "This is so much faster." She turned to him, her bright eyes glinting blue and green like the sun on the waters of his boyhood home. "Does this mean we will arrive at Sentinel Reach sooner?"

That eager gleam faded when he shook his head. "We are making good time, but no more than that." When the rainy season started in earnest, they would not be able to travel as quickly.

Her quiet disappointment sent an unexpected pang through him.

"Why?" The question had plagued Taith for days, and now that Bulla's path did not require his complete attention, he could relieve his curiosity.

All the old father had told them was that they had to convey Alithia to Sentinel Reach and back to her home in the south before something called *budtime*, a period of leafing that apparently signaled the start of another turn of the Lady beyond the peaks. That had been one of the stipulations for vying for her bond. He had not explained why a southerner—and a woman at that—would wish to undertake the dangerous journey to the heart of Hurrann.

Taith shunted questions about budtime to the back of his mind. Phelan would have more than enough when reminded that in the south the start of the Lady's turn found all the trees and bushes standing naked for the whole world to see. Perhaps that was why Alithia's brother had not batted an eye when she proposed a trial of pleasure?

"The holy fire in our clan altar was extinguished—"

Surprise had him interrupting. "Extinguished? How is that possible?"

She sighed, resting her forehead on his back. "*Adal* and *Egon*—"

"What?"

Her fingers drummed on his waist as she gathered her thoughts. "Just before *budtime*, the *moons tide*—an unusually high tide called by the moons—coincided with the river's rise. The flood reached our clan house and entered the sanctuary. When the mud was cleared out, we found the Fire . . . gone."

The desolation in her voice made Taith regret his curiosity. He wished they were not aloft and he could take her into his arms to comfort her. All the saddle straps—and the danger involved in attempting such in midair—precluded that.

"Without it, my clan cannot supply the temples."

This journey, then, was more than simple trade.

She went on to explain something she called a tablet of mysteries that had been sent to the Lady's temple in Sentinel Reach. "If I get it back, perhaps we will be able to rekindle the holy fire. As it is, we may not return in time." Her hands fisted against his belly.

He rubbed her arm, the gesture insufficient to ease his guilt at causing Alithia distress. To think he had wished to delay their journey for selfish reasons.

Still, he did not wish to surrender her to Phelan's care. And no matter how much he struggled to suppress that niggardly whim, it continued to float at the edges of his thoughts.

* * *

*For the fourth time in as many days since they reached the Na*thair, rain fell. The drizzle started shortly after midday and continued sporadically. An irritation, nothing more. An unfortunate part of traveling Hurrann, however much Phelan might wish otherwise for their wife, and for long trips, a fact of life. While they could use beads to keep themselves dry, the effort involved was tiring and could leave them exhausted and in no condition to defend against an attack.

Anyway, this fickle rain was just an inconvenience. Soon enough it would be worse, as he knew well. The end of the hot season brought the torrents; then travel could become misery. At the moment, the clouds hovering low failed to veil the Lady, so they were wet but warm, and they could see for leagues in most directions. There was no cause for complaint.

He pointed to a stand of trees a short glide away, looming more than a gargant's height above the green canopy. "See those?" he asked over his shoulder.

Apparently resigned to the rain, Alithia merely pushed wet hair out of her face and peered where he indicated. "Yes, what of them?"

"Good nesting for tree serpents. Should have fresh meat tonight." Phelan forced himself to grin at her answering expression of disgust. Caution was good, but unreasoning fear could get her killed, especially with the return journey still to come, so they teased her. She'd grown accustomed to snake meat but hadn't quite overcome her squeamishness over its preparation.

She slid a doubtful look at him, her lips pursed in prim disapproval. "If you think that is incentive for bed play tonight, you are sadly mistaken."

Alithia's response surprised him into laughter so loud Dinglis eyed him warily, and Taith paused in his search for danger. Phelan shook his head, disclaiming any such notion, adding a gesture to reassure his sword brother.

The Lady was gilding the western peaks when the Sword at the lead sighted the campground and gave a shout.

A groan of relief came from behind him as Alithia laid her head on his shoulder. Their wife was clearly tired from the long day on wyvernback.

"You'll like this site. There's a pool for bathing," Phelan offered in encouragement.

"I should be stronger than this."

"Why? It isn't as if you travel for trade." After this, she would probably prefer to settle down among her kin in the south and do something that wouldn't require her to go far. Phelan didn't know how he felt about that. Travel and trade had occupied Taith's and his thoughts for most of the turns they'd been together. The possibility of all that coming to an end was something he'd never considered whenever he'd tranced over bonding a wife. He'd imagined a life together like what his parents had, but not the changes Taith and he would have to make, nor what having a southern wife might mean to them.

But that was past. Alithia was their wife, and her decision was what mattered, not their whims. It would take him time to adjust to that change, so used was he to doing what he wanted and knowing Taith would be agreeable. At least for now, they still had several more fortnights of travel to look forward to.

The site was wet but clear, the fire ring choked with leaf litter. From the encroachment of the trees, it hadn't seen much use in recent times—perhaps not since their flight on the trip to Spearspoint. Some of the branches would need to be cut while they set up camp, but it would do for tonight.

Most of the Shields landed their wyverns, spread out in a circle. Normally the first of the Shields to land, Phelan brought Dinglis in last, his mount alighting in the center of the circle. It still felt wrong not being the lead, but they had their wife to protect now. He had to keep her safety in mind and hang back, however much it chafed.

At Taith's wave, Gair and Eoghann wheeled off to hunt. If they were successful, Alithia would have fresh meat instead of the hardtack that took stewing to render edible. Roasting would also help them conserve charwood. They had sufficient supply, but one never knew what might happen; he preferred to have more on hand than risk raw food.

The Swords joined them on the ground. Dismounting, their brethren worked together with the ease of long practice to unload the wyverns and remove their harnesses. Taith joined Phelan to help him with Dinglis, then they switched to Bulla, both of them keeping an eye on their wife.

Gripping Dinglis's foreleg for support, Alithia stretched slowly, her other hand pressed to the small of her back, evidently stiff from travel. From the back, she looked like a slender youth in her trews and dragon-scale tunic, albeit one with a jaunty tail of strange red hair; she still refused to allow him to braid it for her.

Phelan smiled at the incongruity of appearances, the memory of what lay concealed beneath her clothes making his heart lift in anticipation and lending speed to his hands. The sooner they pitched camp, the sooner they might have her to themselves.

"Why your hurry?" Taith continued at his usual measured pace, checking Bulla's harness as he coiled it.

Rather than confess the direction of his thoughts, Phelan glanced at the sky. "Looks like more rain coming." Fortunately, the dark clouds bore him out. "I'd like to get Alithia out of those wet clothes and dry."

A snort coupled with a quirk of the mouth said his sword brother had seen through him. "*Out of her clothes* being of utmost importance."

He rolled his eyes at Taith as he gathered up the harnesses for safekeeping. "See to the trees. They're too close to the site to be safe."

His sword brother nodded agreeably and chose two shield pairs to help him, hefting his favorite weapon as he studied their targets. Cutting back the forest wasn't unusual duty. This wouldn't be the first time he used that great axe on wood instead of flesh or straw targets. If they left the trees to grow unchecked, the campground might be overgrown and unusable when they next passed this way. It was their responsibility to see that didn't happen. Any caravaner would do the same.

Bulla trailed after Taith, hooting in protest when the work party ignored him to chop at saplings at the edge of the clearing. The low cry set the leaves near him shivering.

The other shield pairs had already deposited their loads in the center of the clearing in tidy mounds of tents, trade goods, supplies, weapons, packs of clothes, and wyvern harnesses. As Phelan dumped his bundle beside Dinglis's smaller pile and rejoined Alithia, he shook his head at Bulla's antics, grateful once again for his own mount's more placid temperament.

Not one to overlook a tool, his sword brother pointed Bulla at the taller trees. The wyvern swiped at a branch, long claws slicing through wood with frightening ease. With a crack of protest, the shorn bough went tumbling into the bushes.

A startled shout went up where it crashed. A man stumbled out, holding a sword. From the outcry that followed, he wasn't alone.

"Brigands!"

Phelan shoved Alithia into Dinglis's side, planting himself before her and drawing his sword. "Shields!" Calling power for his spells, he bared his teeth, battle fury flooding his veins. With the wyvern behind them, their attackers would have to get through him first before they touched Alithia. Assured of her safety, he spared a thought for his sword brother.

Taith stood alone at the edge of the clearing with no one to guard his back. He swung his axe single-handed, an arrow shattering against it. Bulla took to the air, hooting angrily. At Taith's shouted orders, the two shield pairs with him retreated toward Dinglis—and Alithia.

The other pairs slotted into position before Phelan, Swords up front and Shields behind. Casting a ward around their wife, Phelan cursed. They were two men short: Gair and Eoghann had yet to return from their hunt.

Blades clashed at one end of the line. At least the attack was coming from only that side—thus far.

Alithia's eyes darted around in bewilderment, her face blank with incomprehension.

"The necklace. Use its power!"

She blinked at him, then understanding filled her face. "Oh!" Her hands rose to her throat, palms pressed to her chest.

Arrows shattered against his ward, the shards flying past her face. Alithia flinched, the power around her wavering.

"Focus!"

Squeezing her eyes shut, she took a deep breath. A ward shimmered into being around her, not as bright as he would have liked, but there all the same. One more line of protection. It would have to do.

Phelan turned back to the battle.

Arrows continued to fly from the trees, some brigands hanging back to take advantage of the overgrowth. The ones he could see were focusing their attack to his left, away from Alithia and Dinglis. They didn't seem to realize the flight had a woman with them, their target the readily portable flasks of blood mead. As he watched, two of the curs broke off to slash at the netting around the flasks while the rest kept the shield pairs at that end occupied.

The trader in him snarled outrage. The blood mead could mean the difference between profit and loss for their crew. He wasn't about to let these lazy curs have them without a fight.

Snatching up his bow from a nearby mound, he shot at the pillagers as he ordered a shield pair to join the ones already engaged. One of his targets fell, an arrow through the neck; his companion gave a shout. The brigands shifted their attack to get at Phelan.

He bared his teeth, daring them to come, ignoring the arrows shattering a handbreadth away as he took down the other pillager. Dropping his bow, he drew his sword and joined the fray, elation slowing the world until he could see every slow stroke, every twist and step, every bead of sweat on the brigands' faces. This was why he'd been born.

Side by side with his brethren, Phelan fought, Taith's absence a strange tingling at the back of his neck. He couldn't think about that now. Blades clashed amidst yells of aggression.

Fewer arrows flew at them now, archers in the trees holding their fire as the other brigands pressed closer. There were more of the curs, but Taith and Phelan's crew were better armed and trained—and had no intention of losing.

Then, too, the brigands used no beads. Perhaps they feared drawing the Lady's attention to their wickedness.

What wards their crew could maintain in the heat of combat evened the odds. The weaker spells could not prevent close-in combat, but they were sufficient to block the arrows.

Over the clamor, someone shouted: "Clear!"

Training had Swords and Shields disengaging and springing back. As the startled brigands froze at the unexpected maneuver, a serpent fell from the sky, pinning them to the ground. Those who weren't caught under it fled, screaming.

It took Gair's jeering howl for their crew to realize the serpent was dead. Laughter rose, and Phelan laughed with them.

Then he remembered.

Alithia! He'd left her side. In his outrage, he'd forgotten that his first priority should have been her protection. He whirled around—and found her still safe behind their wards.

Relief stole the strength from his limbs. He'd been careless, throwing himself into the middle of combat without thought to wife or sword brother.

Phelan sucked an unsteady breath and murmured a prayer of gratitude. Some of their men were bloodied, but no one was down. The wyverns were unharmed and their goods intact.

They'd been lucky. He'd been cursing Gair and Eoghann's absence, but that turned out to be a stroke of good fortune.

He waved at Devyn to deal with the brigands, wondering at Taith's silence when he should be giving orders. With Phelan as Shield to Alithia, most of the responsibility of command fell to his sword brother.

Just then, Taith staggered and dropped to one knee, his great axe slamming into the ground.

Phelan froze, caught by guilt between the need to rush to his sword brother's aid and the sure knowledge that his first duty was the protection of their wife. Alithia ran to Taith, relieving him of his dilemma. Thanking the Lady for giving them a wife with claws, he followed her.

Fifteen

Taith clutched his thigh, pressing together the edges of torn muscle along a gash leaking blood. A brigand must have caught him below his dragon-scale armor.

Alithia dropped to her knees beside her sword husband, the heart in her throat plummeting to her feet at the extent of his injury. She added her hands to his, queasily aware of the slickness that continued to flow between her fingers. "Do something, Phelan!" Her shield husband merely stood there, looking around, on guard, a spell glowing red above them—but nothing more. She wanted to scream in frustration. A ward wouldn't save Taith!

"He cannot. A healing spell is no use until the bleeding stops," Taith explained calmly, despite the tightness around his mouth and eyes. "He is doing what he must."

Scrambling out of her armor, Alithia doffed her shirt, folded it, and pressed the wad over his wound with trembling hands. "Have you dragonblood?" Besides its use in incenses, the powder stopped bleeding and prevented disease from wounds.

Devyn knelt on Taith's other side, his face contorting when he examined the wound. "There's none to be had. They sold it to make the journey to Barda."

"See to the others," Taith murmured between measured breaths.

"Be quiet. You're the worst off."

Alithia forced back the horror swamping her. "Get me bandages and the casket from my bags."

Devyn ran to Dinglis, shouting at the other men for bandages. He knew which she meant, having helped load her belongings on Bulla and Dinglis. He returned with the casket, its contents rattling as it landed beside her, and took over pressing her shirt to Taith's wound.

Her hands shook abominably, making her fumble with the lock. Stopping, she pressed a hand to her thudding chest, barely feeling the beads beneath her fingers, then raised those same cold fingers to her lips with a prayer to the Goddess for composure. Franticness aided no one.

She tried again. The clasp resisted her fingers but finally succumbed to her will.

Searching quickly, she passed over the alabaster perfume bottles and various ointment jars and found the vial of pearl root, wrinkling her nose at the pungent aroma that emerged when she uncorked it. Eyes tearing, she pulled the shirt away and poured the juice over the cut flesh with a liberal hand—dragonblood would have been better, but pearl root might be enough to prevent the wound from going bad.

Taith hissed, his leg jerking between his and Devyn's hands. "Red Lord! That is worse than the blade that got me."

"Hush, lad, at least we don't have to sear it."

Alithia's stomach flopped at the suggestion, her nose twitching at the imagined stench of burning flesh. To take a hot blade to one of her husbands! She raised the vial hastily, sniffing it to force away that nauseating thought, then replaced the cork when her stomach settled. This was no time for overly fine sensibilities.

Someone finally ran up with bandages. She sprinkled shell powder on the proffered fabric to make a plaster, silently giving thanks that the mothers had equipped her so lavishly for her journey. She had thought the expense of shell powder excessive—no longer.

"We will need to stitch it."

"There's no need for that! The healing spells should suffice." Holding one of the pouches from his belt, Phelan gaped at her, his eyes bulging as he took in her undress. "Horned Lords, put on your tunic, Alithia. There're archers out there!"

Taith's head snapped up. His abortive attempt at picking up her armor—to dress her in it?—convinced her to overlook her shield husband's commanding tone and comply with his request.

Once the wound was bound and the bleeding stopped, he handed Taith a softly glowing strip of beadwork. The lines of strain on Taith's face eased immediately—Alithia would have compared the effect to magic, except it apparently *was* magic.

She slumped in relief, her strength draining now that Taith looked to be out of immediate danger. She pressed a cold hand to her throbbing forehead. Her heart fluttered in her chest in a most distracting manner, one she didn't care to feel again.

"What of the brigands?" Devyn was back. He had left after helping her bandage Taith's wound to see to their crew. But now he crouched beside her, a frown creasing his brow.

At the question, both Taith and Phelan turned to her, clearly deferring to her as their wife—and the embodiment of the Lady of Heaven. To the Hurranns, the Gray Lord pursued wrongdoers and the Red Lord exacted punishment, but the Lady was the dispenser of judgment. Her husbands' expressions said they awaited her decision.

Weakness fled as a sudden fury rampaged in Alithia's heart. She wanted to demand their deaths for their cowardly attack, wanted to spit in their faces and curse them to the black waters of the Crone's abysm. She shuddered at the violence of her thoughts.

Goddess protect her, she had never realized she was capable of such vitriol.

"I care not what happens to them. Deal with them as you will." The words rasped her throat, but she managed to speak them without anger. At least if the brigands were executed, it would be due to Hurranni custom, not some ravening lust for vengeance on her part.

Once their third in command had her answer, Phelan stirred. "I wondered why the site was so overgrown. They must've been preying on the caravans that stopped here. The trees made for good concealment for their ambush. If it hadn't been for Bulla, they might have sprung their trap better."

"That sounds almost like a compliment."

If not for the lines of tension at the corners of Taith's eyes, Alithia wouldn't have known he was in pain.

"Merely the truth, no matter how unlikely. That sack of bad temper saved our hides." Phelan gave his sword brother a forced smile. "We need to make camp."

In the midst of taking his leave, Devyn paused, his frown shifting to her shield husband. "We can't stay here. Horned Lords only know how many more of them are left out there."

"Devyn is right. We must move on." Taith's knuckles whitened around the beads as he made to rise.

"You need to rest," Phelan argued, his eyes fierce. "The spell speeds recovery, but you still need to give yourself time to heal. If your wound opens, you could bleed out." He and Devyn held the larger Taith down with worrisome ease.

"There is no time."

Alithia shivered. Taith was right. She had only until the end of winter to return with the tablet of mysteries. Every delay could mean failure. And yet . . . she swore to cherish her husbands—as the Lady of Heaven cherished the Horned Lords.

She gripped her forearms, the etching on her *idkhet* just the slightest roughness to her fingertips and an indelible reminder of her pledge. "How long?"

Phelan stared at her, clearly debating how to answer. He averted his gaze, still silent.

"Devyn? How long must he rest?" The older man would tell her the truth, not what she wanted to hear.

"A sennight."

So long! Fear touched her arms with ice. Could she afford to lose seven days? She bowed her head, torn between husband and clan. As a first daughter, she had to put the good of clan Redgrove ahead of all other considerations. Husbands were for cementing alliances and begetting children; once their duty was done, they returned to their own clan. Yet that was in Lydia. Here in Hurrann, they were willing to lay down their lives simply because she was their wife.

Alithia tried to remember they were merely husbands—necessary only to travel Hurrann. But in the days since their pledging she had come to . . . care for them. And her heart quailed at the thought of her choice bringing them harm.

"Can we still camp here—at least for the night? Is it safe?" She stared at Devyn, willing him to speak truly.

He scratched his short, white-streaked beard in thought, then shrugged. "I suppose we could hold out, Lady."

Half of the men were guarding the surviving brigands. The rest kept watch against a resumption of the attack, weapons at the ready, wards cast around themselves and their wyverns. How much rest would Taith get here with the risk of another attack ever present? And what condition would their crew be in come the morning, if they had to stand guard through the night?

"There's another site, not as good as this one. It's a bit farther and near a swamp leopard's lair." Though it was his suggestion, Phelan's eyes blazed in angry protest.

"This one has brigands," she reminded him, her jaw aching from holding back curses. "Can we move Taith there safely?"

"I'll see to it."

Phelan's solution was a sling made from the spare harnesses, so Dinglis could carry Taith across her chest. No one wanted to let him ride Bulla, so the wyvern trailed after them, his low hoots full of confusion.

They left behind the bodies of the brigands, strewn across the clearing as a bloody warning to the rest of their ilk. Alithia couldn't find it in herself to regret their fate.

She spent the glide to the next campground staring at Taith's ashen features. He had given up his protests to suffer in silence. Her heart skipped each time his fingers jerked around the leather netting, taut knuckles straining a paler gold against his copper skin. Her bloodthirsty thoughts were of little comfort to her. Whatever punishments the Crone had in store for those honorless thieves couldn't be enough for the suffering they had wrought.

Thankfully, pitching camp at the new site passed without fresh excitement. She merely had to hold Taith down while their crew got on with work. Her sword husband had unrealistic expectations of himself, thinking he could resume his responsibilities despite his obvious weakness. It had been left to her to disabuse him of such notions.

The simplest means was to hint that she needed his *attendance*. To Alithia's consternation, her ruse wasn't so very far from the truth. Now that they were finally safe, her knees felt like water sloshing around in too large a jug, and her chest as if it were wrapped in cables. She sat down lest she fall, hugging herself against the tremors that fought to surface.

Strong arms enfolded her in warmth, pulled her into a tight embrace that belied any injury. "Alithia? What is wrong?"

She couldn't speak. It had shocked her to see Taith laid low, in pain because of her. For though she hadn't incited the brigands' attack, her presence tied Phelan to her protection. If she hadn't been there, he would have been fighting beside Taith—protecting him.

Taith had nearly paid for her quest with his life. She discounted the brigands—they would have preyed on other traders and killed or been killed—but Taith and Phelan had been separated in this instance because of her.

"Alithia, I am your husband. Tell me what I can do."

Even now his first thought was of her, not of the wound that had to pain him. He was the one hurt!

Despite the urge to pull away, to be strong as all first daughters were expected to be strong, she forced herself to lean against Taith and accept his comfort, allowing him to support her weight as she fought to regain her composure.

"Talk to me. Help me understand. If you could use spells to defend, why not to attack?" Talking would give her something else to think about besides the quavering of her heart—so fragile, as if the merest jolt would shatter it, leaving only shards of pain. How much easier the battle would have been if they had used magic against the brigands. Perhaps Taith wouldn't have been injured at all.

He stroked her back, the contact strangely soothing in the complete absence of carnal invitation. No man had ever touched her this way—offering reassurance. Even Gilsor had never taken it upon himself to comfort her in this manner. A first daughter was supposed to be above such weaknesses. "Power is the gift of the Lady. As the Horned Lords attend Her, so does She cherish Them. Thus power cannot be used to cause harm."

The simple explanation was uttered with utmost belief. Clearly Taith saw nothing strange in it. She clung to his voice, needing the even cadence of his words to banish this choking morass of vulnerability.

"You cannot use power to attack?"

"The spell is like to fail."

"What of the Horned Lords? Do They not . . ." She wasn't certain what she wanted to ask. She wasn't even sure she believed in the Hurranns' Horned Lords, let alone Their gifts, so why was she exploring this? The Goddess didn't have husbands, not in any of Her faces of Maiden, Mother, or Crone. Surely recognizing the existence of the Horned Lords contradicted the temple's teachings?

"Our weapons, the knowledge of their manufacture, and our brethren—all these are the gifts of the Horned Lords, given for men to protect women."

Alithia pulled away from Taith to study his face, taken aback once more at the Hurranni logic: a woman needing protection. Magan, the first of her guards, would certainly be surprised by such a concept. She couldn't agree with him, but at least their talk had eased the shuddering of her heart, and air no longer seemed to be in scant supply.

He raised his brows at her in silent question.

"That does not seem fair somehow."

"The Lady never promised fairness, only life. It is what we make of it." A curious undertone gave his words significance beyond what was said.

Before she could ask him what he meant, Phelan ducked into the tent, bearing a trencher of savory meats, his eyes darting from her to Taith and back in undisguised concern. Then the corner of his mouth tilted up as he took in their embrace. "I see you're feeling better. But don't you think that's too ambitious for now?"

Taith grimaced in mock disgust. "Mush head."

The meal passed in uneasy pretense, all three of them trying to act as if there was nothing wrong while Phelan watched her and his sword brother with troubled eyes.

She bit her lip, reminded that Phelan, too, had fought without a partner to protect him. In truth, she had been more worried about her shield husband during the attack, despite all the men who had been with him. Guilt pricked her that she had then forgotten about him in her concern for Taith.

The tender chunks of spiced meat now landed like a shower of hail in her stomach. She had never been in a situation like this in Lydia. While her guards had always been there, she had never faced the reality of their risking life and limb for her sake. Even more sobering was the knowledge that Taith and Phelan weren't doing it for profit but because they had given her their bonds. The responsibility not to squander their lives was a sudden weight on her heart.

Guilt was an uncomfortable pillow to rest one's head upon. The press of Alithia's breasts against his side didn't make it any easier for Phelan—a reward he didn't deserve. He was painfully conscious of Taith's choppy breaths on the other side of their wife and of his own helplessness. He couldn't take the pain from his sword brother, however much he might wish to. It didn't help that the air was brooding with rain, hot and prickly on the skin, the prelude to the torrents.

Alithia seemed to feel it, too, twisting against him restlessly, then wriggling backward out of his arms.

Taith stiffened with an indrawn hiss of pain.

She jerked awake, turning over—

"Red Lord's *bells*."

Phelan pulled their wife away before she jostled Taith again and made it worse. He lit the amberlamp with a call to the Lady and found his sword brother sitting up, his hands pressed to his thigh, gritting his teeth against the pain, the cords of his neck taut as strung bowstrings. If it were he, he'd be swearing a damn sight worse and probably at the top of his voice. Taith—as always—held it in.

"Taith?" Alithia reached out to him, her hand hovering in the space between them. "What happened?" Clearly she didn't realize she'd bumped him in her sleep.

Knowing his sword brother wouldn't welcome a fuss, Phelan drew her back. "I think we should give him more room to sleep."

"That might be best," Taith agreed in a hoarse voice.

Phelan split their pallet and set half the bedding across the tent, far enough away to preclude another accident. Alithia helped him arrange the smaller pile and settled back in his arms without protest. She'd probably deduced what happened.

The healing spell may have knit muscle back together, but the flesh needed time to recover from the outrage done to it. The wound could still open if they weren't careful—thus the sennight's rest Devyn prescribed and the delay in their journey.

His fault for not going to Taith's support. Instead, he'd urged their crew to attack the brigands—and left his sword brother to fight alone. Taith hadn't forgotten what was important, sending the shield pairs with him back to help protect Alithia. It was Phelan who'd gone his way and put both wife and sword brother at risk.

As if he hadn't learned from Devyn's regrets. The older man had told the story of the loss of his family more than once in the turns they'd known him.

A trembling pierced his gloom. Alithia shook, her hands clutching the bedding beneath them with desperate strength, her breath coming in quiet puffs. It seemed when it came to her own difficulties, their wife was another who preferred silence.

Phelan tucked the blanket around her, saying nothing as he pulled her into his arms, turning to his side to hide her from Taith's view, so as not to worry his sword brother. She'd been so strong all the while. It surprised him that she now succumbed to weakness.

But the greater surprise was the dread that clutched his heart. He hated seeing her pain and not being able to do anything about it; merely offering his body's heat felt so useless. Surely as her husband he could do more?

After a while, her shudders eased, and still Alithia said nothing. How like Taith in her forbearance.

"What was that about?"

She pressed closer to him, laying her cheek to his chest. "It is nothing. Go to sleep."

What could have provoked such a reaction? Only the attack of the brigands presented itself to Phelan—probably made worse by his abandonment of her. At least on this point, he could ease their wife's concerns. "There's no reason to be frightened. We'll take care of you." To himself, he vowed never to forget her safety had utmost importance.

Alithia pushed herself up to give him a penetrating look. "Who takes care of you?"

He stared at her, consternation tying his tongue in knots. Him? He was the one to blame for this debacle!

Apparently reaching some unspoken conclusion, she rolled her eyes. *"Mush head."*

Hearing those words from her lips shocked Phelan out of the doldrums of his thoughts. Rearing up, he snorted, then convulsed in cleansing laughter. "Don't tell me Taith's taught you to use that term?"

"If the sheath fits the blade . . ."

Amusement faded as he recalled his duties as a husband. His hand ventured down, sliding over her rump, under her sleep shift, and easing between her thighs to discover creamy interest. "And this one certainly does." His blade stirred in unmistakable anticipation.

"You are insatiable."

Phelan smiled at the approval in her murmur, bending down to press kisses along her throat. For the matter at hand, at least, he was not remiss in his attendance.

She arched her neck, giving him better access to continue his courtesies, her arms twining around his head to pull him closer.

He wandered down her shoulder, nibbling and licking. Dragging her shift above her marvelous breasts, he paid his respects to their soft slopes, reminded once again of their good fortune to have won her bond. He couldn't imagine that a Hurranni wife would welcome bed play quite as much as she did.

Alithia gave a choked cry when he tweaked her nipples. He laughed, delighted anew by her open enjoyment of his efforts.

A groan came from the other side of the tent. "If the two of you would let me sleep?"

"Shush, you'll have your turn when you're healed." Phelan didn't bother raising his head from Alithia's breasts, his lips busy worshipping her sweet nipples. "Besides, duty calls." He set about distracting her with a will, intent on building her pleasure to wild heights. If he tired her out, perhaps she'd get some sleep. At least one of them should.

Restricted to rest, Taith could only watch as his shield brother attended to their wife's needs. Averting his gaze did nothing to gain him ignorance. Even the amberlamp conspired against him, throwing Phelan's and Alithia's shadows against the tent.

A double punishment for his distraction in battle. He did not mind the pain so much—it was just another wound in the end. But to hear Phelan pleasure Alithia and be pleasured in turn, and to know he would have no part in that?

The Horned Lords were cruel in their amusements!

Draping an arm over his face, he tried to block out the sight and sounds of their bed play but failed miserably. Their tent was not large enough, and no amount of pillows could stifle the gasps and moans. Did Phelan have to put that much relish in his groans?

It was all his own fault. If he had been faster, had blocked that thrust sooner, he would not be suffering this solitude. He ground his teeth in futile envy, his body aching for remembered delights, his wound throbbing in painful concert. This was one consequence of slow reflexes his shield father had never mentioned.

Alithia woke to rain drumming on canvas with painful- sounding splats, a solid curtain of water veiling the entry of the spell-shielded tent, and thunder shaking the air. Phelan warmed her front, one leg between hers, his head sharing her pillow. It should have been a restful moment, but the sound of the rain and Taith's absence from her side made her restless.

Extricating herself from their bed proved less of a challenge than usual. Phelan only sighed as she pulled free of his embrace. Across the tent, Taith continued to sleep—on his back, not his side—his injured leg stretched out. His wound had to be bothering him. The bandage was unstained, pale linen against his dark skin—the bleeding hadn't resumed during the night. Thank the Goddess and the mothers' foresight for that.

Except that wasn't quite right—She wasn't the one Who healed Taith's wound. It seemed there was more to the gift of the Hurranns' Lady of Heaven than simple protection.

Alithia touched the beads at her throat, the sleek warmth beneath her fingers seductive. Could she have done that—healed Taith? Was it one of the spells of the necklace? Responsibility raised its insidious head, its nip a twinge of guilt for not attempting to master Taith's gift.

Coming to stand before the roaring, shimmering curtain, she wrapped her arms around herself against a mounting sense of unease. She had never seen anything like this endless cascade of darkness. If this were a blizzard or one of Lydia's summer southwesters, she would have some idea how dangerous it would be to be out in it—but this was Hurrann. Who knew what other dangers lurked out there besides the obvious risk of drowning?

So much water. She couldn't help a shiver. Even the spring rains that had fed the flood that extinguished the holy fire hadn't been this heavy. Relentless, yes, but nothing like this torrent that threatened to wash them from the land.

A light bobbed on the other side of the veil. Probably one of the men. She doubted a brigand would have dared this camp.

A scream tore through the steady roar. Feral and unhappy. The swamp leopard Phelan mentioned?

They were safe behind the wards, but the uncertain twilight gave no hint of the time of day. Was the sun still to set, or had they slept through the night? Was this still their first day in this camp or was it now the morning of the second? How long did these rains last?

Alithia pulled her sleep shift tight, though its thin fabric was little protection against a coolness she wouldn't have noticed in Lydia. It gnawed at her to be so ignorant. They were making haste for Sentinel Reach because of her urgency; given a choice, Taith and Phelan would probably travel at a more reasonable pace, perhaps stopping along the way to trade. She suspected they would have pushed on if that was her decision, despite Taith's injury. Would they let her push them into a potentially fatal misstep? Simply because she was their wife? She could only hope they had better sense than that.

Strong arms slid around her waist—Phelan's since Taith's would have circled her shoulders. "Looks like yesterday's attack wasn't all bad."

"What do you mean?" Anger flickered. He could find something good in an attack that nearly killed Taith?

"The pool in the other site would have overflowed by now. We'd've had to move camp, and in this weather, that wouldn't've been any fun."

"Is it safe?" She shivered again. After the previous days of heat, the air was cold—so she told herself.

Phelan made a noncommittal noise. "You can't see farther than your mount's snout. You can't travel straight. You have to stop frequently to make sure you're still headed toward where you want to go. The wyverns hate gliding in it, and no one can keep a rain shield up all day while riding, so everyone's wet and miserable and exhausted, and you end up making a fifth of the distance you'd make on a good day and miss the campsite you were making for. However, dragons and most other animals—including brigands—don't like to go out in it, either. That makes it difficult to find fresh meat, but mayhap safer. But really, you only go through it if you're desperate."

He pulled her into the heat of his body, tucking her head under his chin, and rocked her gently from side to side. "Devyn calls this wife-snuggling weather."

The whispered confidence made her smile, despite herself.

A snort came from deeper inside the tent where Taith watched them, a small smirk lifting a corner of his mouth.

Alithia suspected that meant there was more to the matter than Phelan's judicious explanation. "And how often have you traveled through rain like this?"

"Too often to count."

Phelan's shamefaced grin conceded the truth of his sword brother's statement, accepting responsibility for those incidents.

"Of course, if we had not taken the risk, others might have gotten to market first or bought what we wanted before we could. Our profit would have been less, and we would not be your husbands," Taith added in a tone of grudging concession.

She blinked, her heart skipping at that last unexpected detail. "Why not?" The thought of not having them as husbands alarmed, too soon after nearly losing Taith.

"We wouldn't've had enough funds." Phelan frowned as Taith rose painfully to his feet, one hand pressed to his bandaged thigh. "Where d'you think you're going?"

"Outside to piss. If you think I will do so in here, you are mistaken." Grimly determined, he staggered toward the tent flap off which water continued to cascade, promising chancy footing and unseen dangers.

Despite her concerns, even Alithia couldn't argue with his intent. "Do not get your bandage wet."

A grunt of displeasure paired with an outraged glower answered her. "My aim is not that bad."

Sixteen

With little to do but watch Taith fret over the passing days, Alithia soon found herself fidgeting and had to force herself to consider other, safer diversions. Joining her sword husband in his restlessness was not conducive to harmony or recovery. There was bed play, of course, and Phelan was eager to discharge his duties. But as much as she enjoyed the great dance, so much of it left her tender. Thus, when she caught Phelan hovering at the entry of their tent, a look of indecision beetling his brows, she was eager for diversion. "What now?"

"I need to see to Dinglis and Bulla. It'll take some time."

She frowned, not understanding. Their mounts needed little care that she noticed. On certain nights, her husbands had sent them off with the rest of the flight, apparently to feed, but other than cleaning and checking for sores, they didn't seem to do much.

"With the rainy season begun, we must apply an unguent to prevent smot," Taith explained beside her on the pallet. At her continued confusion, he added, "Smot is a fungus that thrives on wet scales. Infection can cause blood poisoning in wyverns."

And with Taith constrained to rest, lest he reopen his wound, Phelan would have to do both wyverns.

"Apply unguent? I can help." If she didn't have anything to do, she would feel obligated to remain by her sword husband's side despite the beautiful weather this morning. The memory of the swamp leopard's roar left her with no desire to venture out on her own—even if Phelan were to allow her to go unattended—but working outside should ease her restlessness.

"We can't ask you to do that! The first rub of the season is a whole day's work."

"You are not asking; I am offering. It will go faster with two of us." She stood up slowly so as not to jar Taith or betray her eagerness to be out—and aggravate the soreness of her nether muscles from the morning's great dance.

Phelan chewed on his lower lip, flicking a glance at his sword brother as so many concerns flashed across his face. She could guess what they were: Taith, her, and the wyverns, in one combination or another. "Not true, I'd have to worry about guarding you at the same time."

Sensing his resistance wavering, Alithia smiled. "If I help you, you won't waste time worrying about me with only Taith to attend me."

Still, he hesitated.

She pressed her hand to her chest where Taith's gift lay under her dragon-scale armor. "I do have the necklace, and I promise to stay within arm's reach."

"Ask Devyn to help guard," Taith suggested. Gone unsaid was the assumption that their third in command would be honored by the request.

At Taith's advice, her shield husband smiled, suddenly decided. "Good idea."

In a more cheerful frame of mind, Alithia accompanied Phelan to Devyn's tent, where he explained to the older man what they wanted. The air was pure, washed clear of the heavy humidity of yesterday. It felt good to be moving, to be doing something, if only tending to wyverns.

Their third in command stalked off, a man with a mission, shouting to Gair and Eoghann, who had watch over the resting flight, to lead Bulla over; Phelan hadn't wanted to leave her side to fetch Taith's mount. Heads emerged from tents, quickly followed by bodies as shield pairs investigated the noise.

Alithia was just glad she wouldn't have to work in close proximity to all the wyverns. While she had grown accustomed to riding the fierce-looking beasts, she had yet to view them with any complacency.

Devyn returned hefting a large crock on his shoulder. Glazed a pale jade green and decorated with white figures that reminded her of Curghann's writing, the crock yielded a spicy aroma once he pulled the cork free.

Her nose tingled as she tried to identify the scents: honey balm, smoky nightseed oil, cinnamon, some kind of pepper, hazel bark, something citrusy—lemongrass? oil of juniper?—with an undertone of myrrh and . . . bitter tatterleaf? The world blurred and swayed. She jerked back, shaking her head to clear it of the sudden drowsiness the mélange of odors induced. There were more, but another whiff might leave her in a stupor.

Phelan steadied her with a hand under her elbow. "Easy, it can be rather overpowering at first."

Alithia accepted his support gratefully. The unguent certainly smelled potent!

Once armed with old rags for the unguent, she allowed Phelan to present her to Bulla, not wanting to face all those teeth by herself. The wyvern grudgingly accepted her presence once he tasted Taith on her, his black tongue flicking at the juncture of her thighs with almost embarrassing insistence.

For some reason, her shield husband found that amusing, failing to muffle his snorts of laughter behind a fist.

She narrowed her eyes at Phelan as she suffered the beast's familiarity. "Do not just stand there. Do something!"

"Enough, Bulla. You'll make Taith jealous if he finds out." He shoved the wyvern's head away, the hitching of his shoulders betraying his continued snickers.

Shaking her head in mild annoyance, Alithia dipped her rag in pale yellow unguent.

Devyn led his mount over to the tents, choosing a position that allowed him to guard Phelan's back. But he wasn't alone. There was a mass exodus of wyverns from the field, and the campsite suddenly felt crowded with half the flight among the tents, attended by riders determined to apply unguent. The only ones not present were Gair and Eoghann . . . and Taith.

Their surge of industry banished her annoyance. How could she cling to irritation, however slight, when there was no compelling reason for the shield pairs to tend to their mounts at that very moment? They would be camped there for some days still, so would have other opportunities. Despite the pretext of work, it was clear that they were actually there to help Phelan protect her.

She and Phelan fell into a comfortable silence as they worked side by side on Bulla. She hadn't realized how much skin a wyvern had until now; the glide flaps connecting the fore and hind legs easily doubled the area they had to do.

The wyvern didn't appreciate their efforts, flinching away as they rubbed unguent into his gold and dark green scales, the skin under their hands breaking out in frequent shivers. Alithia found herself sympathizing with the beast. The unguent felt much like liniment and made her fingers tingle.

The work required little of her by way of thought. The sun shone down on their heads to soporific effect, a gentle breeze leavening the heat and fostering an air of contentment. She let her mind wander while her hands dipped and dabbed and rubbed.

All around them shield pairs exchanged banter while they tended to their mounts, two to a wyvern. She couldn't help but notice many of the Swords shared certain features with their Shields. None boasted the twice-born looks of Deighann and Kail, but the similarity was there: sometimes in a broad nose or bushy brows, the lines of jaws or the shapes of faces, or even the sound of their voices.

According to Curghann, the typical shield pair were cousins; it was rare for unaffiliated men to establish that bond. That meant Taith and Phelan were likely related.

She frowned, mentally comparing her husbands' features, as she wriggled her rag into the creases around Bulla's foreleg. She didn't see much similarity between them, yet they had been introduced as being of clan Black Python. When Curghann had briefly mentioned clans, she had been more concerned with trade potential, assuming they were like Lydian clans. Could this be another misapprehension on her part?

"How are you kin to Taith?" She rose to her toes to spread the unguent as high as she could.

Phelan clapped Bulla on the leg, cajoling the reluctant wyvern into crouching down so they could do the scales around his dorsal ridge, then swiped at a lock of hair that had come free of his braid, an easy smile on his face. "It's simple: Taith's shield father is the brother of my sword father. When we decided to form a shield pair, he entered Black Python."

Hurranns traced kinship through both fathers' lines—and changed clan affiliation when forming shield pairs? "Why?"

"Sword always joins Shield's clan."

"Always?" Alithia paused in her rubbing as she tried to imagine keeping track of who was kin to whom and in which clans—an impossible snarl of threads came to mind. Lydian kinship rules were so much simpler. Your clan was your mother's clan; that didn't change, and you were kin to everyone in the clan.

A grunt from her shield husband served as confirmation, Phelan's attention on uncorking a fresh crock of unguent.

"And the wife, does she join the Shield's clan, too?" Her shoulders tightened as she waited for an answer, the press of her rag drawing a disgruntled hoot and a shiver from Bulla, both of which she ignored.

Showing his usual consideration, her shield husband set the crock between them, downwind of her, so she wasn't subjected to another whiff of the unguent's vapors. "Oh, no," he assured her somewhat absently, his eyes wandering away after a quick glance in her direction to scan their surroundings for danger—as usual.

The tension within Alithia subsided. At least she hadn't been inducted into another clan all unknowing.

"She remains of the temple."

What?!

A furtive caress between her thighs made her yelp. Forgetting her question, she jumped away from the black tongue flicking back toward her.

"Bulla!"

*By the sixth night, Taith was impatient to continue on, claim*ing he was well enough to travel. Only Devyn's and Phelan's arguments convinced Alithia otherwise, so vehement was Taith's insistence. His sword brother wasn't a restful patient, his usual calm disposition nowhere in evidence. If it weren't unfair to Alithia, Phelan would have left his care to her gladly. At least with their wife, Taith strove to restrain his swearing.

"By the Red Lord's blade, I am not an invalid. There is no need to waste more time here, I tell you." Scowling, Taith stood with his fists on his hips, splendidly naked in the middle of their tent, while Alithia held the clothes she'd wrested from him behind her.

Since Alithia wore only a sleep shift—and that much only as courtesy to Taith's and Phelan's sensibilities—the confrontation between wife and sword husband held promise. Phelan would have cheered them on if Taith didn't have most of his weight on one leg, clearly favoring the other. But as thrilling as it was to hear Taith's vehemence, he didn't want it at the risk of his complete recovery. Bracing himself against his sword brother's rare display of temper, he set down the trencher with their supper and joined the fray. "Feeling neglected?"

He grinned at Taith's indecent gesture, then turned his grin to Alithia. "He sometimes gets these moods." Despite his teasing, he sympathized with his sword brother's frustration, knowing how he'd feel if it were he who was injured. He took pleasure in Alithia's pleasure, his heart lifting at her obvious delight in his strength. She made him proud to be strong—for her. For their wife.

What more Taith who was accustomed to being the pillar of strength and sound sense?

Alithia's answering smile was tinged with relief, the tightness of her shoulders easing. "What do you do when he is like this?"

"I distract him."

Taith glared down at Phelan as he approached.

Phelan didn't allow that to deter him. "If you fight me, you'll just injure yourself, and we'll have to stop longer," he murmured as he gripped Taith's arm.

"We do not have time to waste."

"This isn't waste. And it's our wife's place to judge what we can and can't risk. She's made her decision." While he agreed with it, Phelan could only hope she wouldn't regret it.

With a grimace, Taith allowed Phelan to help him back down on their pallet. The fact that his sword brother let him bear some of his weight meant Taith was hurting more than he let on.

Luckily, Alithia hadn't caught their exchange. "Distract him, is it?" Her smile bloomed into something more mischievous. "I think I have just the thing!"

Alithia rummaged through another pack. She had been wanting to try Slann and Arghal's gift for some time but thought to wait until they had proper lodgings. The current circumstances, however, called for strong measures if they were to keep Taith from further injury.

Her sword husband stretched out on the pallet, a delicious display of dark male flesh thankfully well on the way to recovery. "What are you looking for?"

She drew it out with a crow of triumph. "This!" The length of creamy silk unfurled in a dream of flight, hanging in the air as though made of mist before alighting on their packs.

Phelan blinked at her from beside Taith. "Wouldn't that be too strenuous?"

Anticipating their shock, Alithia wrapped the nubby fabric around her fingers, pulled it taut, and brandished it suggestively against her breasts. "Not if *I* use it on *Taith*." The fringed shawl was a gift of gratitude from Slann and Arghal, given shortly after the pledging.

At the blank surprise on Taith's face, Phelan doubled over in gleeful—triumphant—laughter. "You're right. That's definitely distracted him."

"Phelan!" A growl that did nothing to tame her shield husband's mirth.

Taith's stare grew pointed. "I do not need . . ."

"Yes, you do. I'll hold you down, too, if that's what it takes." Phelan leaned over Taith, a hand on Taith's chest, suddenly serious, the look in his eyes resolute.

A shiver of excitement washed through Alithia, Goddess heat stirring at the sight of her two husbands nose-to-nose. The promise of Phelan's help meant Taith wouldn't resist. Her sword husband was pragmatic that way. In his weakened state, he wouldn't win, and he knew it.

"It is the husbands' duty to pleasure their wife, not the wife's the husband," Taith argued through gritted teeth.

"I am sure doing this will bring me pleasure," Alithia assured him, a bubble of laughter dancing in her belly. "Do not worry on my behalf."

"Overruled." Her shield husband's smirk would have put a catamount to shame.

"When I am better . . ."

"Exactly. *When you're better.*" Phelan stroked him, his touch unerring as his fingers circled a flat nipple, going around and around the tightening peak. "But right now, you're not. Don't play the mush head, Taith. That's my role."

Taith's shaft hardened, his response unmistakable.

Alithia settled beside them on the pallet, feeling quite the intruder in this intimacy. "Perhaps there is no need for this, after all."

"Oh, no! You have to use it now!" Phelan protested, a roguish grin lightening his intensity. "I won't be able to sleep, otherwise."

Taith grabbed Phelan's braid. "Mush head."

That didn't deter him, his grin only growing wider. "Admit it. You want her to use it on you."

A stolen look of guilty speculation flashed toward the silk in her hands. Taith's throat worked, a tacit admission of interest, if Alithia knew men.

Her stomach fluttered with anticipation, relief infusing her with frothing, exhilarating lightness. He was as stubborn as a gargant, but she couldn't muster any irritation at his defiance, not when it was born of his concern for her—and her quest to save her clan.

She joined Phelan in stroking Taith, sliding the silk over his belly. He was firm beneath her hands, belying his earlier weakness. Surely he would recover completely, so long as they kept him from overextending himself.

"In collusion, are you?" Despite the admonishment in his tone, the muscles under the silk quivered, his shaft rising as though seeking more.

Remembering the sensation of silk over delicate skin, Alithia flirted the light fringe across his flushed tip. Taith sucked air, the sound making her heart speed and sending a thrill of excitement arrowing down to her folds. Goddess heat swirled in response, urging her to take what she wanted.

No, not yet—her pleasure could wait.

This time was for Taith.

He groaned when she repeated the motion, feathering that flimsy edge along his length. "That—" His hips rolled restlessly, a clear demand for more, as he gulped for breath.

Phelan's arm wrapped around his waist. "Just lie back, Taith. Don't strain yourself." Her shield husband groaned as well, his eyes widening as he watched Alithia's play. "Not that I blame you."

She bit her lip to hold in a laugh, bending down to nuzzle Taith's hip—and hide her smile. Having two husbands was so different from what she had imagined!

Then the musk of his desire, a heady perfume that conjured memories of pleasures shared, drove off all thought but the need to distract Taith.

Lying down alongside them, Alithia wrapped her hands in silk and trailed her fingers along Taith's inner thighs, then played the silk over his full pouch, netting its plump orbs and rolling them about. His black curls rasped on the fabric, the sound somehow absurdly titillating. She added her lips to the effort, nibbling on the tender skin of his groin.

The fresh scar on his thigh was a sobering reminder of how they had nearly lost him. She brushed a kiss over the outraged skin, strangely drawn to lick it. Its heat startled; she blew on it, wanting to cool it somehow, an action that drew another gratifying groan from her normally self-possessed sword husband.

But inevitably the thick flesh straining above her recaptured her attentions. She smiled in anticipation. That was where the silk would provide the biggest return.

Phelan's hand joined hers around Taith's shaft, fondling him with familiar knowledge. Alithia swallowed, remembering the contrast of calloused palm and silk, desire surging.

"Don't—" Taith's protest broke off on a gasp. "Phelan! The woman is supposed to be the focus of bed play—Alithia, not I."

"All these turns and you still haven't learned to accept pleasure graciously." Phelan pressed a kiss on Taith's chest, his tongue flicking out to tease a taut nipple. "You could try moaning, you know. Alithia does it to express her enjoyment."

Her cheeks burned at the jest and the ease between her husbands; clearly this wasn't the first time they had taken pleasure together. Then Taith sank his fingers into Phelan's hair, holding his shield brother in place, the fierce demand on his face at odds with his protest.

Tempted though she was to watch, she left Phelan to his teasing, focusing instead on her own efforts. She wrapped the shawl around his turgid shaft and behind his pouch, then slowly pulled it free, the silk sliding along his length as it unwound.

"Horned Lords," Taith choked out as a shiver swept him.

His audible approval warmed her with a thrill of accomplishment. She had given him that. It was little enough recompense for the pain he had suffered in her defense.

But they couldn't draw out their bed play lest they exhaust him. They had to finish this soon.

"No," Taith protested when she pressed her lips to his shaft. "After all this time, I want to be sheathed in you."

She froze. She wanted that, too; her body craved that union. But that would mean riding Taith—bracing herself on him as she moved. How could she do that without jolting his thigh and hurting him?

"Alithia?" His blazing eyes demanded an answer. His shaft rose full and proud, aimed at his flat belly. Pure temptation.

It was a struggle to remember her Hurranni. Her tongue felt too thick, clumsy, the words tumbling around in her mind. Needing distance to clear the fog of passion from her thoughts, she pushed herself to her knees. "I—I might hurt you."

"Here, let me." Phelan swung behind her, drawing her into his embrace, his arms under her breasts. When he straightened, she dangled in the air, his own shaft a hot brand against the crease of her buttocks.

She stilled at the sensation, uncertain what he intended. At his urging, they straddled Taith's hips, all without touching him; then with a flash of excitement she understood.

With his help, Alithia lowered herself, using her hands to guide Taith's shaft to her cleft and into her body, Phelan's arms keeping most of her weight off her injured sword husband.

She and Taith groaned as one as he slid into her, relief a palpable presence between them. Union with him was not the same as union with Phelan. Though longer, her shield husband's shaft wasn't as hefty. Taith's thicker shaft stretched her almost to discomfort—but not quite—and Alithia found she had missed that sensation of overwhelming fullness.

Phelan lifted her slowly, dreamily, rising along behind her, his hips rocking against her buttocks. So gentle in his motion. His stronger thighs bore their combined weight without any strain. He lowered them just as slowly, just as carefully, letting Taith fill her to satiety, then reversing directions.

Over and over and over.

Tireless.

Like the inexorable ebb and flow of the tides.

Alithia could only lean back in his arms and savor the glorious sensations coursing through her. Floating in a dream of bliss. Taith so thick inside her, Phelan's velvet hardness an artful stroking, his rough fingers plucking her nipples a spicy overlay to this sensual seduction. Pure pleasure, sweet beyond imagining. Demanding nothing of her. Lightning couldn't compare.

And still Phelan continued to rock them.

Goddess heat caught flame, billowed into sultry, torrid fire—warming, not consuming. Ecstasy gathered, the promise of perfect rapture sailing within reach. She rolled her hips, chasing that final step in the great dance.

Phelan groaned, his arms tightening around her.

"Yes, by the Lady, oh, yes!" Taith threw his head back, his hands clawing at the pallet, the cords of his throat working convulsively, his back arching, driving him deeper into her in a breathtaking burst of strength.

Voluptuous heat spilled into her as Taith found his release, bridging the gap to the Goddess's gift.

On that flash of triumph, rapture flooded her veins, irresistible in its power, a potent elixir that washed clear all fear, her concerns melting away. Surrendering to its urging, she collapsed into Phelan's arms, the warmth of his own pleasure trickling between her buttocks.

After long moments of panting, her shield husband dragged her off Taith and laid her between them on the pallet. He did so entirely without any help on her part—she was that surfeit.

"The two of you, together, are dangerous," Taith declared breathlessly, his chest still heaving from his release. His hand came up to play with her hair as he nuzzled her neck.

Phelan gave an easy chuckle, patting his sword brother's shoulder smugly. "Just thought you needed some exercise to work up an appetite." Rolling to his feet with enviable energy, he retrieved a trencher by the flap of the tent.

The contentment on Taith's face faded as he took in the food. "We are down to that?"

Setting the trencher before his sword brother, Phelan sighed, a strange glumness weighing down the corners of his mouth. "Unfortunately."

Looking from one somber face to the other, Alithia blinked, confused by the sudden lowering of their spirits, her euphoria dissipating. "What is wrong? What are you not telling me?"

Phelan pressed a warm tuber into her hands, refusing to answer until she took a bite.

She chewed with little appetite. It was dry with a hint of sweetness behind the ever-present ash. Of late, all the food had been roasted, the spicy stews and braised meats of before only fond memory. The rains likely made cooking those difficult.

"We're low on charwood, bread, and some other provisions."

Surprise held her silent. She had noted the fresh morel and roots she didn't recognize but hadn't realized what their presence in their meals signified.

Phelan cast a cautious look at his sword brother, hoarding his misgivings, but Taith just shook his head, not protesting his recovery. "We'll have to leave soon and stop somewhere to resupply. When we do so, you'll have to stay close—no walking around without us."

Alithia held in her objections. There seemed more to their reaction than mere concern for her inconvenience. "And?"

Taith took a swig of his cup, drink a necessity to wash down the food. "There is only one place we can reach that will not take us too far out of our way. Anywhere else will add more than a sennight to our journey."

"Table Rock." Phelan rubbed his hands together, distaste for the answer twisting his features. "It's a rough town, a gatherers' outpost and a market for wyvern fledglings. Mostly unbanded men. It's rare to see a woman there, even a matron. We'd hoped to avoid it altogether, be farther along before resupply." He glanced at Taith, apology and disquiet in one poignant exchange. "Now, we can't. We've been supplementing our provisions with forage, but we've exhausted what's available nearby. We can't search farther out without more men—not safely, not with that swamp leopard around—but that would weaken the camp's defenses."

"How dangerous is Table Rock?" If it was so dangerous, would it be safe for Taith? What little food she managed sat like a rock in her stomach. She had placed her quest at risk so as not to risk Taith's life. Was this another such decision?

Her sword husband spread his hands in a gesture of irresolution, bobbing them as though they were scales and he were weighing some intangible that was Table Rock. "Undesirable, certainly. Unlike the towns we prefer for resupply, there is no temple at Table Rock, so the denizens tend to be less . . . attentive of the Lady's teachings. Law is what you can enforce with sword, axe, or dagger. But for outright danger? Perhaps no more than what we might encounter by traveling the greater distance to a safer town."

Though he frowned at Taith's conclusion, Phelan didn't contradict him.

Alithia hid a sigh of relief behind another ashy bite of tuber. At least she wouldn't have to choose between husband and clan a second time.

She watched Taith behind lowered lashes, noting the stiffness in his seat and how gingerly he adjusted the position of his leg, and she balanced Phelan's continued concern against the sure passage of time. Despite his showing earlier, her sword husband remained in some pain. She could only hope that another day's rest would see him able to travel; she couldn't afford to wait until he was completely recovered. "The next morrow we leave for Table Rock."

Seventeen

The last wyverns made their pass over the narrow mountain lake and came up with jaws full of wriggling fish. It was unfortunate they couldn't provide for their riders, but the crew was short of other supplies besides food—charwood, for one. Few men ate raw meat willingly and only in desperation. Phelan didn't want to risk their wife's health when it could be avoided; he wasn't sure southerners could even stomach the poisons in raw fish and snake meat that cooking removed. Taith, he knew, would starve first before he let that happen.

There was no avoiding Table Rock.

Few stayed at the outpost throughout the Lady's turn, only the merchants and innkeeper who supplied the rest. Its inconstant population—spice gatherers in the dry and hot seasons and wyvern masters in the rainy season—made for a rowdy atmosphere, a society unfit for wives.

And they were bringing Alithia there, may the Horned Lords shield them and the Lady forgive them.

He raised his sunstone to the clouds, squinting at the resulting faint gleam to take their heading. They needed to go a bit more to the west.

The slight adjustment to their course soon bore fruit.

An enormous block interrupted the undulating flow of green, sheer cliffs rising out of the mist and trees, its flat top covered by tents and shacks in between wyvern runs. Countless waterfalls spilled down its sides, fed by the incessant rains and a pond on one side of the outpost.

Table Rock.

It grew rapidly, more details becoming clear with every heartbeat. Phelan could suddenly make out bright moss and stubby ferns on the dark rock as they glided up the cliff face. Then they were over the edge with the outpost before them.

The air was still, heavy with moisture. He would have welcomed another downpour to keep the dregs in their holes. Only necessity kept him from turning Dinglis from her course. Taith looked drawn, not yet fully recovered from his injury, despite his protests otherwise. His wound had to be nagging him.

There were more tents than Phelan had expected, but then it had been more than two turns since they'd last had reason to come to Table Rock—and that had been in the dry season to acquire a few parcels of cinnamon seed as a favor for the temple in the Lady's Hills. This was the time the wyvern masters sold off their fledglings, he now remembered, the auctions drawing buyers from all over Hurrann.

Rude huts, little more than dried fronds atop bundled sticks, clustered around five sturdier buildings. The long, broad leaves of sword reed were readily available from the lakes surrounding Table Rock. Its seasonal denizens didn't seem to feel the need for better roofing. Muddy tracks divided the outpost into nine sections, emerging from the center like the spokes of a wheel and leading to the wyvern runs.

One of the Swords gave a shout and a wave to the left toward a clearing large enough for their flight. Runoff from a tiny pond meant a ready supply of fresh water.

The empty run was near the cliffside, some distance from the shacks that served most of the residents of the outpost. At any other time, Phelan would have signaled the Swords to keep searching. But to his eyes, the nearby cliff only made the site more defensible.

With Alithia in their company, privacy was more important than convenience, even though they wouldn't have that much of it. The camps in the adjoining runs weren't that far away.

Their arrival drew little interest. Their neighbors probably thought they were there for the auctions. *Thank the Lady for that.*

Custom required Taith and him to handle the purchase of supplies. As Alithia's husbands, they were expected to represent her interests in any negotiations. However, neither Taith nor he wanted to expose her to the rabble that frequented Table Rock. When Alithia rushed to Taith's side, upon witnessing his cautious dismount, Phelan grabbed the excuse of his sword brother's weariness to suggest that their third in command handle the trade.

Taith grimaced but didn't object, retreating to their tent as soon as it was raised and taking Alithia with him. Devyn's immediate agreement said he, too, shared their concern. The rest of the men sorted themselves out, once the camp was in order, falling back on long-standing practice to decide who would stand guard and who had campfire duty.

It was Barda all over again—except noisier and louder despite the absence of gargants. So many wyverns in a relatively small space magnified the hooting, the cries resonating in Phelan's bones and shivering over his skin as though he were a temple drum. The sensation was distinctly unnerving. He could only hope they wouldn't be in Table Rock for long.

Surprise nailed Phelan in his tracks past the flap of their tent and a hazy ward. The pallet had been set out, the packs stacked on one side . . . and his sword brother lay naked, a bemused

Alithia in his arms, clearly intent on matters other than rest. "Taith, what're you doing?"

"I have been derelict in my attendance of our wife. I need to make up for my delinquency." His sword brother nuzzled her breasts, a look of bliss lightening the lines of weariness etched on his face as he pressed kisses on the pale mounds above him. "I could think of nothing else all day."

To distract himself from his weakness?

Phelan rubbed the bridge of his nose, gratified to have his sword brother insist on something he wanted yet frustrated at his choice of time. *Now* Taith voiced a desire? In the middle of Table Rock? "You mustn't tire yourself."

"I am lying down. How can this be tiring?"

He rolled his eyes at the stubborn obtuseness of the reply muffled against their wife's breasts. At least his sword brother was not so lost to his desire that he'd forgotten to raise a ward—not that Phelan expected otherwise.

As Taith returned to his nuzzling, Phelan suppressed a twinge of jealousy at his sword brother's evident preference for Alithia. After all, he, too, was guilty of the same, reveling in having all her attention to himself while Taith was too injured to take part in bed play.

Alithia laughed as Taith's busy hands disposed of her trews, roaming her body with a ravenous hunger that bordered on desperation. Such lust was most unlike him; Phelan was usually the one insistent on bed play.

Now, her sword husband sucked on her breast as though he had built up a bone-deep thirst, his lips and tongue kindling a bonfire in the center of her being, stoking the Goddess heat in her to sudden, fervid life. He sank his fingers into her wet channel, the urgency of his touch testifying to his continued recovery—not yet returned to full strength but no longer in danger of a relapse.

The sheer sweetness of his attentions forced a moan from her. Holding herself on hands and knees above him, she spread her legs in invitation, thanking the Goddess for his improved health. If ever there was an appropriate time to celebrate life, it was now. Then the swirl of sensation commanded her attention, and she gave herself up to the great dance.

Scorching pleasure leaped from breast to core, building the blaze within her higher. Her knees quivered, impaling her further on his skillful fingers. A bolt of keen delight followed, swift to find the center of her being. Then another and more—a quiverful coming in rapid succession and overwhelming her senses. She gasped in surprise, in delight. By the Maiden, he could bring her to the brink of rapture so quickly!

Taith urged her forward, his lips releasing their possession of her nipple, guiding her on until she knelt above his broad shoulders and astride his face. He grinned up at her with a very male look of carnal anticipation. "I dreamed of this."

She was so open to him, the aching folds of her cleft spread in welcome. The musk of her desire rose between them, a heady perfume that only fed her need, tinder for the flames.

With a groan, her sword husband brought her down to his mouth, his tongue finding the bud of her pleasure and rousing it with exquisite circles, fanning the flames of her hunger with a talent. Nibbling, licking, probing, teasing, he varied his play, not giving her time to grow accustomed. Just when she thought she knew what to expect, he changed tacks.

Passion blazed, a storm of exultation blowing through her body, flooding her with lush sensation.

"Oh, Goddess, yes!"

Arching above him, Alithia cried out, her words nothing Taith could understand, but the delight and approval in her voice needed no translation. Her hands dug into his hair, her fingers tangling in his braid and beads as she clasped him to her, giving herself over to his care.

Never had he felt so powerful!

He redoubled his efforts, stabbing his tongue into her sheath and along her slick petals in that rapid measure she enjoyed. The mere knowledge of her pleasure was a reward on its own, and he found he had a craving for it, but he had his own selfish reasons for his assiduous attention to husbandly duty.

Her thighs clenched against his shoulders, quivering as she convulsed in release and anointed his lips with her passion.

Taith caught her as she collapsed, confident she was now ready to take him. He lowered her onto his throbbing blade, sheathing himself in her wet velvet with a sigh of relief. She was still tight, but not so much that he feared hurting her.

He lay beneath her for an endless moment, immersing his senses in the rightness of her possession. He had craved this intimacy with an intensity that bordered on pain. The promise of this was all that had kept him upright on Bulla during this last long glide. Hoarding his strength for the journey to Table Rock, he had refrained from bed play after that night near the swamp leopard's lair.

She lapped on him, her small tongue almost tickling, her hands gratifying him with contented caresses up his sides. She pressed soft kisses on his chest, murmuring praise and encouragement as she grounded herself on him, her hard-tipped breasts bobbing against his belly.

Fire touched his blade with desperate desire, a tremor of need streaking up his spine. His rocks swelled to overfull, demanding relief. *Now.*

Grabbing her rump, Taith rocked her against him, wanting more of that grinding contact, craving the release that dangled just within reach.

Alithia gasped, her body clenching tight, squeezing him with all she was, fluttering along his length. That exquisite pressure was all it took.

Need shattered, splintering into countless shards of delight as he erupted in ecstasy. He shook with the strength of his release, his heart thundering in his ears, insensible to all but the rapture stampeding through him.

Devyn returned much later, wet from a passing shower, scowling, and scratching his beard in irritation, clearly in a mood. He headed straight for Phelan, not even slowing to speak with the shield pair guarding the break in the fence of the wyvern run that led to the muddy tracks that passed for streets in Table Rock.

Phelan paused in his weapons practice, having resorted to sword work to distract himself from the activities in the tent behind him. He could have joined the two in their bed play, but someone had to be responsible—and for once, that was him. He'd had more than his share of mush-headed scrapes where Taith had backed him to the hilt, so he couldn't begrudge his sword brother his rare lapse.

"Well, the charwood will be delivered on the morrow. But the proud worms refuse to talk trade. Leastwise, not with me." Devyn swiped back a gray lock straggling down his cheek, then tipped his chin toward the tent. "They know she's here and won't do business with anyone less."

"How'd they know?" Unbidden, Phelan's sword rose to a high guard position before him, his empty hand gliding along its spine to the tip: rainbow sword stance, good for both offense and defense. His legs shifted accordingly on the wet ground.

Their third in command gave him the forbearant smile of a father for a slow son. "A wife's cry of ecstasy cannot be mistaken for any other. They know."

*Unlike Barda, Table Rock had no stone structures to lend dig*nity to its composition. Beyond the wyvern runs, the prosperous tents of visiting flights were replaced by open-sided sheds—threadbare awnings or woven fronds lashed to rickety poles—barely large enough for a pallet.

Alithia was no stranger to hovels, having visited her share as first daughter of clan Redgrove—some of the gatherers who supplied the clan with herbs and spices for the perfumes and incenses they made preferred to live off the land during summer—so that aspect of Table Rock didn't surprise her, not after Phelan's description. But she hadn't envisioned anything quite like the contrast between the squalor of the outpost and the grandeur of the mist-shrouded mountains that rose around them.

As they got farther from their camp, the number of strangers around them grew: rough-looking men in hard-used leathers, bristling with weapons and feral vigilance. The shield pairs chosen to reinforce Taith and Phelan radiated a sense of greater wariness around those with unkempt beards and bare arms—in blatant disregard of the rules of Hurranni society. A beard was a symbol of fatherhood, an impossible claim for unbanded men. That these men didn't bother to shave marked them as little better than brigands.

The sheds eventually gave way to sturdier cabins huddled around the mud-mired track as though seeking warmth and a core of pole barns that served as market and taverns. Here, they found the crowds hinted at by all the occupied wyvern runs, eating, trading, gambling, raising their voices to be heard.

Alithia was painfully aware of the notice given her as she squelched through the mud behind Taith. How could she not when conversations lapsed into silence at her appearance and startled second glances were thrown their way in a visible wave of craned necks? The low susurrus that trailed their passage, barely louder than gentle rain, was also hard to ignore. This pointed regard wasn't the deference paid to a first daughter. It was more visceral, more insolent. Dangerous?

She frowned at Taith's back, now wishing they had brought

more men. Except more men were out of the question. The others had stayed behind to guard their cargo.

The only option was to buy the supplies they needed and quickly. Alithia hadn't missed the strain on Taith's face as he looked around, constantly vigilant. If she had her way, he would have remained behind to rest, but he dismissed the suggestion out of hand with Phelan in agreement. She recognized his stubbornness as one of those times when no amount of persuasion would move him. Rather than waste time, she had acceded—Curghann would have been surprised.

Her foot slipped from under her. Before she could grab Phelan's arm, he caught her by the elbow. The near mishap served to distract her from her nerves. Whispers and glances were nothing to embarrassment. She ought to pay more attention to where she was stepping, lest she end up facedown in the mud. The footing was treacherous; the constant rains and too many feet had churned the ground into a brown slurry.

The first and second pole barns were long, two-story structures with open sides on the ground level with pens full of small, restless wyverns, their whistles unexpectedly shrill. They passed those without slowing.

Taith led them into the third, which was a whirlpool of motion between stalls marked off by blankets draped over long lines tied to the rafters. Odors hung in the cool air, mainly leather and spices. Merchants haggled, arms waving in grand gestures, heads together in serious negotiation, toasting the completion of trade with small cups of sugarcane water.

Alithia almost smiled. Here was familiar territory, the smell of spices reminding her of younger days, of traveling with her mother to meet suppliers and learning the ingredients that went into the clan's perfumes.

Her sword husband revealed a different side of himself as he traded. He didn't resort to the theater of others, but his small gestures took on eloquence, conveying a range of emotions from grave misgivings, to polite interest, to cautious enthusiasm with a glance, a tilt of the head, a quirk of the brow or a stroke of his finger along his jaw.

She got the impression he was enjoying himself, the thought warming her heart. But the frequent glances of the merchants in her direction soon puzzled her. They didn't stare openly—Taith's and Phelan's stern miens discouraged such blatancy—but she could tell the temptation was there.

At first, she thought it was her appearance. From the tales the shield pairs told around the campfire, a southerner was a rare sight in Hurrann. Only gradually did she notice that they responded to her frowns as she translated the prices quoted in Hurranni silver crescents and copper shields to Lydian coinage. They seemed to gauge the acceptability of their offers from her expression and adjusted their bids accordingly. Did they think Taith negotiated on her behalf? Was that why they refused to trade with Devyn? Yet none of them addressed her directly. Was there some greater status attached to trading with a husband as opposed to a widowed man?

She exhaled sharply, frustrated by the convolutions of her speculation. Just when she thought she understood Hurranns she was faced with another example of how they were different.

It was a relief when Taith completed his negotiations. She knew he had yet to recover his full strength, and he had spent much of that at bed play.

The memory of his caresses sent a tingle up her arms, stealing all guilt at succumbing to his persuasion, and she spent a few moments reliving that interlude of delicious abandon as they returned to camp. Lost in her thoughts, she walked into Phelan's unyielding back—which shouldn't have been there.

Confusion erupted around Alithia in a clash of metal, battle cries, and Taith's roared orders. She froze. *Not again!* Shock, then fear, swept through her in icy waves, and at their heels came the welcome heat of anger. *How dare they attack us!*

But dare the motherless scum did, filling the muddy streets with flashing blades and the stench of their unwashed bodies.

The Lady's gift came at her furious call, flooding her with warmth and raising a bubble of protection around her. This time she wouldn't be behindhand, dragging on her husbands' sleeves when they had to concentrate on fighting. Not again.

Phelan turned to her—and grinned as another ward bloomed into being around both of them. "Good." He went back to fighting, his sword carving a gory chunk out of the tangle of men trying to attack him through the spell; there were so many brigands that they got in each other's way.

The ring of shield pairs defending her held, but they made no progress, trapped by sheer numbers.

She watched with horror as Eoghann slipped on the mud. She took a half step toward him and froze. If she ran to his side, it would sow confusion among her defenders, risking more lives. She wasn't even sure she could maintain her ward if she moved faster than a walk.

Gair fought to get to his shield brother, but for every brigand he cut down, two—three—more took their place. Too many.

Eoghann scrambled to rise, but the brigands pounced on his vulnerability, not allowing him to regain his feet. Knives and axes flashed, glanced off. His ward flickered. He rolled in the mud, kicking out and lurching aside to avoid another blow.

Alithia clawed at her dragon-scale tunic, at the warmth on her breast, fear for the young Shield a ball of ice in the belly. She had to do something!

"She be soothern. Temple willna claim her likes!" The shouted encouragement held the slur of eastern mines—Silver Ridge, Spearspoint, Longshore, and thereabouts. It confirmed Taith's suspicion that Alithia was their goal.

A stone blade shattered on his *idkhet* when his ward flickered, the blow numbing his forearm but thankfully nothing more. The press of men prevented someone else from taking advantage of his distraction.

Taith caught another blade between the horns of his axe, kicked its wielder, and swung down. Blood spurted, a hot, salty splash on the face. His return strike bit into flesh, a cry of shock cut short by the follow-through.

Before he could catch his breath, others lunged forward to give battle, working together now to get past his guard. Despite all his skill, only the Lady's protection kept him whole—and he was not the only one beset. They were outnumbered, pinned in the crossroads, their enemies attacking from all sides.

He risked a glance at Alithia and Phelan. They had to move, to somehow cut the numbers reaching them. Otherwise, sooner or later—unless they were lucky—the honorless curs would overwhelm them, once they were too tired to maintain their wards.

His leg twinged, the scarce-healed flesh overstrained. He gritted his teeth against the pain, bitter resentment welling up in his heart at his weakness. To fail Alithia this way!

Baring his teeth in defiance, he channeled the anger into his blows, determined to send as many as possible to the Red Lord's hells before they took him down. Each impact jarred his thigh, a hot spike searing muscle. He fought on, though his ward flickered and his thigh throbbed.

Then a surge of cool power blew over him.

His ward *flared*—smashing into the curs pressing him and throwing them back.

His was not the only ward that flared.

Several cutthroats went flying, flung off their feet by the impact and crashing into their fellows and through flimsy walls.

By the Lady that sheltered them all, what had happened?

Taith wheeled, checking the others. Wards glowed bright blue in the overcast gloom. Large spheres of light with their men nestled inside.

Alithia stood in the center of it all, hands clenched over her breast, a fierce scowl on her face, red hair streaming off her narrow shoulders like wildfire. The Lady in fury.

They had a chance.

"Fall back!"

Shield pairs straggled into a tighter ring around Alithia and Phelan, brilliant wards illuminating their positions. Gair pulled Eoghann to his feet, the Shield barely recognizable beneath a coat of muck.

"My left. Move." That road led to the cliff edge, which would reduce the number of men who could strike from that direction. With two other sides blocked by huts and wyvern runs, the brunt of the attack would come from only one direction. It would give their crew time to recover and for him to choose the best route back to their camp.

They moved while the motherless curs sorted themselves out, the moans and groans they left in their wake evoking only vengeful pleasure in him.

"Who's hurt?" Phelan took charge of ascertaining the condition of the others while Taith held the rear guard, keeping watch for another attack. Eoghann was the worst off, but nothing that could not wait—would have to wait.

They were not out of danger yet. As Taith understood it, Alithia was directing the power she called into their wards. She could not be expected to maintain it forever.

When they set out, another wave of cutthroats attacked, but the fight was short-lived. The very visible sign of the Lady's favor—of temple interest—took the hearts out of the curs.

Alithia collapsed as soon as they got back to camp, which came as no surprise. What had taken Taith aback was how long she had sustained the spell. The depth of her rage would have stunned better men than he. They had covered the distance at a slow walk to keep a close guard, and Alithia had stalked every step, cool power flowing from her in a steady breeze.

"What in the Red Lord's hells happened?" Devyn's glare took in Alithia cradled in Phelan's arms and the rest of them looking the worse for wear. Their arrival with wards so blatantly raised had brought their third in command running.

The four shield pairs who had stayed to guard the camp remained at their posts, but with weapons drawn, scanning the rain-swept night for trouble.

Impatient to check their wife, Taith forced himself to explain what had happened. Alithia would be fine with rest.

Once he had apprised Devyn of the situation, he limped off, confident the older man would do the needful. His leg could wait. He still had to check on the others. They had shield pairs who needed healing, Eoghann in particular.

But he could not forget the sight of Alithia glowing with fury. Even his mother had never summoned that much power. He could almost feel the stifling itch of formal robes, hear the gong summoning the priests to prayer, and the sanctuary doors closing behind him.

Eighteen

The mountains were lower and farther apart, younger cousins to the stern old uncles in the south, friendlier peaks lacking the giants that hosted the tree serpents, losing also the snowcaps and craggy ridges and secret valleys. The swamps and marshlands disappeared, replaced by thicker forest. The Nathair snaked between the trees on its way to Sentinel Reach and the sea, and the men rode with bows strung and quivers full of arrows.

Alithia leaned around Phelan, straining to find a tower on the horizon, but all she could see were trees. If they were less than a sennight from Sentinel Reach, surely she should be able to make out something of the temple from this high?

A cool breeze blew a tendril of hair across her face, a welcome change from the humidity below. Thankfully, Table Rock lay several days behind them.

Anger stirred at the thought. Futile anger. The motherless cowards who attacked them had disappeared into the forests. And she didn't have the luxury of time to have them hunted down.

Once again, she swallowed her outrage. Setting out for Sentinel Reach as soon as their supplies had been delivered was still the wisest course they could have taken. Unfortunately, her heart wasn't convinced, hungering for vengeance against those who had sought to kill her husbands and friends.

A deafening hoot of alarm scattered the flight. The saddle straps jerked tight on Alithia's waist and legs as Dinglis squealed and rolled to the left. For an endless heartbeat, Alithia felt herself leave the saddle, anchored only by thin leather and empty air beneath her. She grabbed on to Phelan, praying the straps would hold. A shadow skimmed the wyvern's twisting body, then something large plunged through the air where they had been just a moment earlier.

Arrows flew.

Bulla dropped after their attacker, howling in rage with claws outstretched, Taith on his back brandishing a spear. The impact startled a roar from the creature and slowed its flight.

Then she saw.

Enormous batlike wings. Four taloned paws. A large body covered in a pattern of browns and black and a pale belly. A long tail and equally long neck. A head like a wyvern's yet fiercer, striped round eyes with an unblinking stare. Gaping jaws full of fangs.

Dragon! Alithia stared in shock at this fanciful tale brought to life. Ice sliced through her veins as it roared again.

In what was surely a foolhardy attack, Taith stabbed at the beast, his spear scraping on its hide, then pulled his wyvern aside. The other Swords followed his example, while Bulla soared back to the flight. "Thunder Hole!" he shouted to Phelan just before Bulla dropped for another pass at the dragon.

Dinglis hooted in protest when Phelan urged her away from the battle. Despite the men's valiant efforts, only a few shallow gouges on the dragon seeped dark blue, mainly from wyvern claws.

The Swords maintained a string of attacks to keep the dragon at a distance while the flight fled for the place Taith had named—a splinter of mountain with a slit near its base. The slit was too narrow for the dragon's broad wings, barely wide enough for the wyverns to negotiate. As it was, harnesses and cargo scraped against basalt rock as Dinglis crawled inside.

Just ahead, Eoghann held up an amberlamp, using its light to explore their refuge. To Alithia's relief, a sizable cavern lay beyond, one that could accommodate the entire flight with space to spread out. A constant thunder rumbled, and the air was palpably cooler, but nothing sprang from the darkness to menace them, and the Shields ahead eventually waved approval.

There, they pitched camp for the night, laying charwood on older ashes, evidence they weren't the first people to take refuge in the cavern. Once the fire was lit, the men tended to their mounts and repaired harness straps strained and frayed by the wyverns' violent maneuvers.

They took special care checking their cargo: flagons of mead, wool, slabs of ashwood, furs, and the like. Small-volume, high-value items. Any profit they reaped from this trip depended on their care. The slightest tear or crack could ruin a load, costing several gold flames in losses.

Alithia paced between Taith and Phelan, feeling lost. Her heart continued to pound, her chest frozen around a shriek. Her hands shook, and if she didn't do something, she was afraid she would scream—or cry. A first daughter didn't cry, not where anyone could see. "I want to help. What can I do?"

She needed distraction, to fill her hands and thoughts with work—instead of what-ifs. She could still see Bulla's sudden swoop, so fast Taith's braid had flown like a banner in a wind of their making, could feel the lurch of her stomach as Dinglis twisted from under her.

Without a word, Devyn gave her a mass of leather and sat her down on a pile of packs.

Copying the older man, Alithia combed the long strips straight and free of tangles, then wove them into a single strap, focusing on her task with single-minded intensity until she couldn't hear her heart, couldn't hear her teeth, couldn't taste her fear.

Here at least she could be useful. Clinging to Phelan, knowing they wouldn't have been on this path if it weren't for her, had stirred guilt unlike anything before. Brigands, she could dismiss as a normal hazard of travel. But dragons—they might have taken a longer route that avoided its territory if not for her urgency.

A growl echoed through the cave, arrogant and hungry.

Leather bit into Alithia's fingers, treacherous strips that they were, jumping at the slightest noise. She forced them to ease and ignored the renewed flutter in her throat. "The dragon is still there."

"Don't worry about it." To her shock, Phelan's smile was a sliver of banked excitement.

"Are we trapped?"

"No," Taith hastened to assure her, looking up from the harness he was mending. "Come morning, there should be a patrol to roust it out. We are close enough to the garrison at Axe Peak for them to get out here."

"If the patrol does not come, what will we do?"

He pointed to the darkness on the far side of the cavern from where the soft thunder emanated—clearly the source of its name. "That is the Nathair. This stretch flows underground for some distance. It should get us out from under that dragon."

No one was in the mood for bed play by the time they retreated to their tent. Lying in the arms of her husbands, Alithia found herself staring into the darkness.

By the Goddess's grace, no one had been injured. But there was no telling how long that would last. Even their arrival at Sentinel Reach wouldn't see an end to the danger. There was still the return to Barda—and from there to Lydia.

Her heart lurched. In so little time, both her husbands had endeared themselves to her: Phelan with his thoughtful gifts, endless questions, and eagerness for bed play, and Taith with his quiet support, stealthy roguery, and deep-rooted refusal to worry about matters beyond his control. The prospect of losing either one to her quest shook her resolve, revealing cracks in the bedrock of her devotion to clan.

Her clan had never seemed so far away as today, her memories like wisps of fog slipping through her fingers. It was becoming harder to remember why she was doing this, risking the lives of so many men . . . for what? Pride? Tradition? Status? No one would die if they lost the temple trade.

Such thoughts shamed her. That she would put the good of husbands—men not of her clan—ahead of her mother, grandmother, sisters and brothers, cousins, aunts, uncles. Faces wavered before her mind's eye like reflections on water stirred by the wind. Courting the debasement of clan Redgrove was unworthy of a first daughter, a betrayal of everything she had been taught.

"*Hisst.* You are thinking too much." Taith's embrace tightened, his hand stroking her thigh.

"No, I'm not," Phelan grumbled sleepily.

"Not you, mush head."

"Alithia? What's wrong?"

"I was so scared." She twisted around to face Taith. "When you attacked the dragon, I thought it would kill you."

"It'd take more'n a dragon to kill him," Phelan grunted, nuzzling her breasts. "That's my job. That dragon has to get in line; that's a very long, long"—he yawned at this point—"long line."

Taith laughed softly and pressed a kiss to her shoulder. "You should listen to him. Every so often, he makes sense."

She smiled, strangely comforted by their logic. "I am glad you are my husbands. I cannot imagine making this journey with anyone else." Perhaps she was doing the other shield pairs a disservice, but she couldn't imagine any of them teasing her to distract her from her worries.

Still, the soft thunder of the river underground and the distressed hoots of the wyverns made for unsettled sleep.

A chill wind greeted them closer to the mouth of the hole, cold enough to draw unhappy hoots from the wyverns. They had waited long past first light for some sign of the patrol. In vain. They could not wait any longer, lest they emerge too close to the Lady's departure from the sky and nightfall to find a good campsite.

As the others made ready, Taith finished oiling Bulla's hide, checking for broken skin and taking particular care with the loose flaps stretching between his fore and hind legs. Alithia would ride with him because Bulla was the stronger glider and steadier on the wilder currents of power, not that his present deportment encouraged confidence in their judgment.

"Come, easy now," Taith coaxed, scratching the hard brow ridges above Bulla's eyes as his mount lowed at him, black tongue slapping his ribs in obvious displeasure. The other wyverns stood well away, avoiding the long, lashing tail. "Do not embarrass me this way."

Off on one side, Alithia smiled at him, her amusement clear even in the poor light straggling into the cavern. She did not seem to mind the wind that roughened his arms, standing near the hole and lifting the hair off her neck as if savoring its chill. Her pose displayed her *idkhet* for all to see, its *mythir* almost glowing against the darkness of their exit—a reminder of the good fortune bestowed by the Lady.

Finally, the contrary beast settled down, deigning to receive his harness and saddle and share of packs. Once Taith was mounted and Alithia seated in front of him, the rest of their crew followed suit, and they glided down, into the hole.

The Swords at the lead lit their amberlamps, pushing back the darkness for two wyvern lengths around. Something else to be grateful to the Lady for. Taith shoved the thought out of his mind—with Sentinel Reach within a sennight's travel, he did not want to draw Her focus to him.

Alithia patted his arm then pointed, her mouth moving, her voice lost in the river's noise.

Taith bent down so he could hear her.

"What are those?" She gestured at glittering specks beyond the circles of light.

He turned his head to speak into her ear. "Just rocks. The walls are overgrown with crystals." Some of his kin harvested the rocks to sell to temple bead makers; it was a surer way to amass a pledge gift, but such a life with its constant contact with the Lady's temples repelled him.

Between rock ceiling and water, there was barely space for a single wyvern to glide in safety. The river churned below, its wild rush kicking up so much spray the hair the wind pulled free of his braid now clung to his cheeks. The lights dimmed and flared at no set measure, in time to slight dips and lifts in Bulla's flight. Taith's mount was contrary enough to enjoy the challenge. Ahead of them, Gair's and Eoghann's mounts bobbed like fishing buoys in a rough sea, their bellies skimming the white waters from time to time. Like Dinglis, the younger wyverns had difficulty riding the surges in power.

Amidst the tumult of the river, other sounds died. Even the hoots of the wyverns were drowned out. Only the quivering of Bulla's neck muscles against his thighs told Taith that his mount continued to express his displeasure at the cold.

Alithia soon gave up her attempts at conversation. She leaned back against Taith's chest, a soft armful of sweet-smelling woman, content to marvel at the sights.

In the amberlamps' wavering circles of light, time stood still. If Taith were given to flights of fancy like his shield brother, he might have imagined the river went on forever in this roaring underworld. He knew better, of course. But the drapes of fantastic rock seemed endless, swimming out of the darkness then fading into oblivion like fever dreams, their colors vivid in that instant of clarity.

Uncounted heartbeats later, a thin line of brightness split the darkness, gilding the foam of the frothing river. It widened into a crack, then a beam of golden light reflecting off the water and revealing the wet rock above them.

They would soon be out.

Lady of Heaven, never had a day's travel felt so long. Yet perversely, never had he wished for a glide not to end.

Phelan brought Dinglis up from behind, waving to ask if they should stop and— His gesture broke off with a sudden grin. He shook his head and signaled Taith to disregard that last bit, though the plan was for Alithia to continue with his shield brother once they were back in open air.

Taith glanced down to see what had changed Phelan's mind.

Alithia had fallen asleep, her head tucked against his chest. She looked so peaceful, as though she did not harbor any worries despite the darkness surrounding them.

His heart turned over at the show of trust, a supremely uncomfortable sensation he did not want to explore. Regardless of what she had said last night about being scared for him, he had thought her words something she expected a wife to say. To his mind, action was more convincing. For her to surrender to sleep under these circumstances was . . .

Unthinkable.

He refused to speculate upon its meaning. Fortunately, they emerged into the golden afternoon, and he had to bend his attention to watching for danger.

Phelan took the lead, urging the flight for speed. The golden aspect of their surroundings meant the torrents were coming—the Lady's light streaming below the bank of black clouds advancing south and east was a warning to all to get to shelter.

The wind of their passage woke Alithia just as someone sighted a clearing high enough to be safe from the river. She took in their concern with a single glance, a hand on Taith's *idkhet.* "Why the haste?"

Taith gestured at the dark curtain sweeping over the land ahead of them. "The torrents." He did not have time to cast a rain shield, needing his attention for the turbulence that accompanied the gust front. It was all he could do to keep Dinglis in sight and guide his mount after Phelan's.

To his surprise, he heard Alithia laughing through Bulla's wild contortions as the wyvern struggled to stay airborne and level through the buffeting they received. When he shot her a bewildered glance, she only laughed harder.

It was a pity the joyous sound did not last long. The leading edge struck before they got beneath the trees, falling with punishing force, a pounding misery he would not wish on his worst enemy, much less their wife.

The crew raised Taith and Phelan's tent first, to get Alithia out of the rain. Taith left them drying inside while he saw to the rest.

When he stumbled back to the tent much later, favoring his weak thigh and cursing Bulla's bad temper, he found Alithia bundled in a blanket, pacing, with Phelan shadowing her steps. He frowned at his shield brother. The beddings were laid out. Why was their wife not in them?

She pounced on him before he could ask, ordering Phelan to help her strip Taith to dripping skin and towel him down, all the while asking after the rest of the crew and their mounts.

Bemused by her attentions, Taith put up no resistance, allowing her to undo his braid and comb out his beads.

When he was dried to Alithia's satisfaction, she left him to set out his weapons for drying and oiling, beside others already spread out on one side. "Phelan said we can expect more of these torrents—and every day." She resumed pacing while he worked, stopping frequently to stare out the tent's opening. His shield brother simply stayed by her shoulder; of course, he was one for pacing, too. Kindred spirits when it came to stewing over what could not be changed, the both of them.

"This is the rainy season," Taith pointed out, since Alithia seemed to expect a response.

"It will slow us down more." Her hands clenched when thunder rolled through the air, muting the roar of water.

"You have felt its strength. If Sentinel Reach were the end of our journey, then certainly we might push on. But we would be in a poor state when we arrived. The wyverns would need more than a sennight to recover." Not to mention the crew. Such a glide would push them to the limits of their endurance. "It would delay our departure—no one would dare the journey to Barda on an unknown mount." He laid down the last of his weapons, wearied by the long speech; he usually left such explanations to Phelan, who was unwontedly silent.

But when Alithia continued to pace and his shield brother did nothing to assuage her restlessness, he knew he had to act.

On her next pass, Taith caught her by the waist.

"What?"

"Tiring yourself this way is no help." He pulled her into his lap as he sat down on the pallet, ignoring the complaint of his thigh. "There is a better way."

Alithia stared up at him in surprise.

"I need some of your cherishment."

Bed play was a sure distraction. He suspected the knowledge of how close they were to Sentinel Reach was what fretted her, tormenting her with the thought of the end to her quest.

Phelan grinned at him in approval, suddenly coming to life.

Taith was not about to excuse his shield brother for letting Alithia worry herself unduly, the memory of her laughter still fresh in his mind. That joy was what she deserved. Before he got carried away, he made certain to tell Phelan, "Devyn will be by with supper. Keep an eye out for him."

His shield brother's face fell with comical inevitability, but

Taith counted the slight delay in joining their bed play small enough punishment for his dereliction of duty.

As Phelan stepped out of the tent, Taith pushed the blanket off their wife's fair shoulders, her damp hair cool against the backs of his hands. She was naked beneath it, all pale southern womanhood and the rich red curls at the juncture of her thighs. Though he sought to distract her, his need for her was no jest.

He seldom thought to ask anything for himself, the solicitation of special favors an unwelcome reminder of temple life and priestly duties. In this instance he could tell himself he was not demanding favors—he truly wished to ease their wife's disquiet. But with his hands full of their wife's soft flesh and her attention all to himself, it was difficult not to feel he was being selfish.

Turning to straddle his lap, Alithia wrapped her arms around his neck, a rueful smile on her lips. "*You* need cherishment? Did my pacing bother you so much?"

He kissed her smile, sucked on her lower lip, tasted the salty sweetness that was Alithia. "Only because you tire yourself to no purpose. You and Phelan with your worrying."

"I suppose I should apologize?" She rose to her knees, rubbing her mound along his engorged flesh, tracing a line of slick heat up his length.

The warm welcome he discovered between her petals made his heart race faster than fighting. "It is not the wife's place, not for something so trifling." But far be it for him to argue if she wished to.

Alithia bobbed down, the rasp of her curls against his blade sending a thrill through him as she took the tips of his fingers into her moist sheath. "Make amends, then?" The hard peaks of her breasts glided across his chest, painting him with lines of awareness with each quick gasp.

Excitement was a living, pounding presence between them, fed by the heat of their shared breath. Most nights he waited his turn, relying on Phelan to ease their wife into union lest his size hurt her. But this time it seemed she was in no mood to wait for his shield brother.

"If you wish."

"That I do." She reached between them and aimed him at the entrance of her body. He spread her petals, holding her open to him. Both of them groaned at that first hot kiss as she pressed down on the tip of him. She stopped before she went much farther, too tight to take the rest of him. She rode the sensitive tip, squeezing him intimately, sliding ever so slowly lower.

Taith swore softly. The heat of her called to him, impossible to resist. Despite his best intentions, his hands clamped on her hips, and he thrust up.

"Oh!" Her cry brought him up short. Then she softened around him and took more, her nipples blazing a path to his belly, a flush of bliss painting her cheeks. "You feel so much bigger."

Her praise had him swelling even more.

Clinging to his shoulders, she began to move her hips, slowly at first, then faster, until she rocked and swayed above him as though riding a galloping wyvern.

Pleasure arrowed up his spine, a thrill of delight that forced another groan from his throat. Horned Lords, he could not get enough of her!

Bending forward, he was too tall to reach her breasts, so he kissed her neck instead, licking the sweat that gathered at the hollow of her throat.

Alithia tilted her head in encouragement, moaning long and low, her hands sinking into his hair, clutching him closer. Her lashes fluttered down as she danced around him.

Just then Phelan settled beside them, already naked. He curved an arm around their wife as he bent to nuzzle her breast. His other hand, he wrapped around the base of Taith's blade, the rest of him that Alithia could not take, and quickly matched the rhythm of her hips.

Taith groaned at the added pressure; his shield brother knew just how to touch him. Still, he braced himself to yield his place. "I—"

"No, you finish." Phelan shot him a look of warning, then grinned. "Just count it as part of my punishment." He worked Taith's flesh, flooding his body with sweet sensation, making it impossible for him to refuse.

Alithia pulled on his hair, dragging his head down for her kiss even as she drew Phelan into her embrace. She writhed against them both, alternating her attentions now between him and Phelan.

Why he had wanted their wife to himself, Taith could not remember. Bed play was better with the three of them together. Alithia in their arms, her honeyed heat swirling around him, his shield brother stroking him . . . Pleasure was a wild river storming its banks, fighting to burst free.

He took Phelan's own blade in hand, needing to share the delight. And as he should have expected, Phelan sped his hand, that competitive spirit of his roused.

Helpless to deny Phelan's urging, Taith's hips rose off the pallet. Alithia cried out, her release spilling over him. Her muscles quivered around him, countless waves of pure sensation rippling along his length and easing him the rest of the way in. His control snapped.

Falling back on the pillows, he thrust again and again. Driving himself into the flames. Chasing the ecstasy hovering within reach. Glorying in Alithia's gasps of delight.

A part of Phelan relished Taith's hard fingers on his blade, moving in concert with his thrusts, the sweet ache of his burgeoning hunger. Part of him reveled in breathing the heady perfume of desire—both hers and Taith's—in helping bring their wife to release. But the rest of him plotted how to do the same to Taith. His sword brother could be frustratingly selfless at times.

He rubbed the pearl between Alithia's petals, his heart jolting as his fingers grazed Taith's flesh driving in, then pulling out, hot and slick with the cream of their union. The two people in the world who meant the most to him.

"That's it. Let go." Whether he addressed their wife or his sword brother, even he didn't know. He'd watched them while waiting for Devyn to arrive, his hunger rousing as they moved together, sweeping him up in their desire.

Alithia moaned, the sound even more voluptuous than the last. A cry of exultation and triumph, of power. As she flung her head back, he almost felt a cool breeze flowing across his hot skin.

Then Taith gave a harsh grunt, recalling Phelan to himself. Yes, there was still his sword brother's pleasure to see to. This time, Taith would take his release first—Phelan intended to make certain of it.

Phelan turned to Taith lying on his back, all that hard muscle bunching and gleaming in the amberlamp's soft light as he strove for completion. His energetic motions sent thrill after breathless thrill through Phelan. Bending over him, Phelan used his mouth and hands, nibbling and caressing, focusing his attentions on his sword brother's pleasure points.

"Red Lord's hells." Taith's grip slid away, his arm coming around to drag Phelan up into a hard kiss. They rocked together, Phelan rubbing himself against Taith's hip as his sword brother's motions grew wilder. Taith stiffened suddenly, his back arching off the pallet as he gave a hoarse shout.

Yes! Grinning at his success, Phelan gave in to the hunger coiling within, eager now to share the same ecstasy. As he pressed closer, his flesh was caught in a delicate grip.

Alithia lay on Taith, a blissful smile on her lips. Her fingers toyed with Phelan gently, yet that knowing tweak of the tip of his blade was shattering.

Raw sensation lashed him, the thundering in his ears louder

than the rain outside. The scalding release emptied him in a flood of breathtaking delight.

When Phelan recovered his wits, he found their wife had succumbed to sleep. "Your plan worked." He stifled a yawn, then lay down himself, stretching an arm across Alithia's back and Taith's waist. The contact soothed something inside him.

"The day was long, and worrying did not help." Taith stroked their wife's hair, his expression soft with wonderment and—dared he hope?—growing affection.

The scene reminded Phelan of his boyhood, of the devotion between his fathers and mother. That was what he wanted for the three of them, not simply duty, though he'd hoped their pledging would provide some advantage to Black Python.

Could they have what Phelan aspired to?

From what he'd seen of Taith's parents, their relationship was more formal, Taith's mother preoccupied with her temple duties. Would it be the same with Alithia? He himself had compared her responsibilities to a priestess's. Would the burden of leading her clan preclude the love he craved?

Nineteen

The mountains were visibly lower, weathered old fathers worn down by the elements and vegetation, all gnarled and knobby. If they had the time to allow Alithia to explore the tree-covered slopes for her beloved herbs and roots, she probably would've been ecstatic. It wasn't possible, not now nor on their return.

The Nathair at that point was a churning, roaring beast, its white waters crashing over rock and deadfall, as it wound its way to the sea. They followed the river north, gliding deep in its narrow ravine and venturing out only to make camp at twilight. No one wanted a repeat of that dragon attack.

Late in the afternoon of the fifth day, a cry of "Stone bridge!" went up from somewhere ahead.

Alithia stirred in Phelan's arms where she'd been drowsing, all soft and sweet. "What is it?"

It was safe for her to ride in front of him this near their destination. Should they be attacked today, they'd only have to hold

As Dinglis climbed the bridge, Alithia could see downslope what looked like a pack of gargants—if gargants had black or brown coats and larger ears.

Phelan followed her gaze. "That's the holding of clan Stone Bridge." He had to mean the crenellated structure on the far side of the meadow. When she pointed to the beasts, he merely added: "Gargants aren't allowed into Sentinel Reach."

Naturally something as familiar as gargants were also different in the north. Again, she was reminded that Hurrann was not Lydia. It would be wise not to forget that.

At least Sentinel Reach was better than Table Rock.

The guards at the gate didn't give her more than a second glance. Once they spotted her *idkhet*, they immediately looked away, and no furtive whispers followed. Inside, the buildings were made of stone, substantial and prosperous-looking, with sculptured walls and planters bursting with flowers. Down a side street, she noticed some women behind what seemed to be market stalls, attended by men, but there. Their easy smiles were reassurance enough. There would be no repeat of Table Rock here.

Devyn led the way down the main street, the only one sufficiently wide for wyverns. Their progress slowed to a plod, blocked by the sheer number of people. Merchants and mendicants, travelers and entertainers, all had come to Sentinel Reach.

The street curved, following the outer wall, choked with carts and oxen and other flights of wyverns. At the intersections stood slender obelisks inscribed with flowing Hurranni figures and topped by amberlamps.

It was surreal how Sentinel Reach could be so different yet so similar to Lydia. A yearning for home pricked her. The trees would be turning color soon, the reds, oranges, and yellows of autumn. She would miss that. In Hurrann, everything was green.

But then would come winter.

Alithia craned her head around, straining for a glimpse of towers above the rooftops. "The temple?"

"That way." Phelan tipped a hand to the west—or perhaps a street they had just passed. "But it's too late to go there now. The Lady has left the sky." When she continued to stare at him, he added, "The priestesses have retired for the night. We have to wait for the morrow when the Lady is high."

Resigning herself to further delay, she turned her attention to the stalls lining the street. Countless odors assaulted her nose: leather, incense, spices, roasting meat, and many more she couldn't name. An alley beckoned, its mouth spilling with lilies and the perfumes of hundreds more. A pang of longing surprised her at the reminder of home.

The next obelisk they passed had a banner hanging from it. When she pointed it out to Phelan, he called it a signpost and said the banner announced the arrival of a new shipment of Beartooth incense, a blend popular with eastern miners.

She straightened at the explanation, excitement driving back fatigue. Sentinel Reach was a temple city and would have need for the suppliers that catered to the needs of the temple. "Are there merchants here that sell sanctified oils?"

Phelan's smile was apologetic. "Not during the rainy season. Any supply not bought by the temples would've been sold to the aftermarket by now."

Disappointment redoubled her weariness. "Aftermarket?"

The street widened into the caravaners' quarter, which gave to the outer crescent where pack beasts were stabled.

"Towns with shrines or the clans that need sanctified oils for products sold to the temples—or prefer them over ordinary oils."

"Such use is a point of pride for some people," Taith added with a wry smile, from beside them, having slowed Bulla so that his mount now paced Dinglis.

"On our last trip—the one before we went to Barda—sanctified oils made up the most part of our goods. The freshest, soonest, earns the most profit."

Of course. She had known of such, but clan Redgrove dealt mainly with the temples, so that detail had slipped from memory. If she failed, her clan would become part of that aftermarket, begging for the scraps from towns with shrines. Her nails bit into her palms at the reminder of what was at stake.

Torches were lit as twilight deepened, the flickering flames throwing strange shadows. After stabling for the wyverns was arranged, they walked a short distance to the tavern of a Black Python clansman, the crew ranged protectively around them.

Their arrival was cause for an outpouring of news and remonstrances over Taith and Phelan's prolonged absence. Alithia smiled, distracted from her thoughts by the tavern keeper's voluble discourse. It seemed the long arm of clan was the same everywhere.

"But what's this? You're bound? Since when?" The tavern keeper raised Phelan's arm to inspect the *idkhet* there, his gaze then darting to Taith's similarly banded forearm. Of a height with her shield husband, though somewhat heavier in the chest, he was clearly a cousin, his bearded face bearing a marked resemblance to Phelan's.

"Last season." Phelan's grin could not have been prouder.

"Last—" The other man frowned. "But the trials were before then, and you weren't here." He rattled out names in a two-beat rhythm that implied shield pairs. "They were the only ones to come for the trial."

Phelan shook his head. "This was in Barda."

Taith drew her forward then, into the torchlight. "Alithia, this is our kinsman, Colle, clan Black Python. Colle, our wife Alithia."

"Clan Redgrove," she added with a smile.

The tavern keeper blinked down at her, his mouth working in silence, his bemusement making him look younger than the sprinkling of silver in his hair suggested. "You're . . ."

"Lydian," Alithia offered, when it seemed her husbands' cousin had lost his tongue.

"In Barda," he repeated absently. "You took the fast route, then."

Colle's eyes widened and his head snapped up, his glare entirely for Phelan. "You risked her life in the valleys?! Of all the mad, irresponsible—"

"The need for haste is mine," Alithia interrupted. "I insisted."

"But, lady, the danger involved!"

How dare he criticize Taith and Phelan for doing their best to help her succeed in her quest! Frowning, she took a breath to rake him—and was gratified when his gallant but misplaced outrage wilted beneath the weight of her glare.

"Forgive my impudence, lady. I've traveled the valleys myself, and there is no fit place for a woman to rest."

"So long as you know it is no fault of my husbands."

"Of course, I meant no insult." He waved some boys over, introduced as his sons, and directed them to take Taith's and Phelan's packs. "Please, be welcome in our house. Eryn will want to celebrate your pledging."

Colle's prediction was quickly proven right when they entered the dining hall. A woman and her husband appeared in a doorway that apparently led to the kitchen, raising glad cries of welcome when they saw Taith and Phelan. By the patterns on their *idkhet*, they were Colle's wife and . . . the other half of his shield pair. From what Alithia overheard, Phelan was a favorite of the woman, Eryn, who did insist on hosting a banquet that very night.

And celebrate they did, though the banquet was unlike clan Redgrove's celebrations or any Lydian feast that Alithia could remember.

First was the preponderance of men. While Alithia had two younger brothers and quite a number of uncles and male cousins, she had never been in a room with so many talking, laughing, cheering men. There had been more in Barda's great hall, but that vaulted space hadn't felt this packed. Their voices thundered to the rafters, filling the air with their presence. Phelan claimed they were all kin of one sort or another, greeting everyone who approached by name and reminiscing about mutual acquaintances and boyhood escapades.

A long table along one wall was set aside for the few women in attendance and their husbands, Colle, his wife Eryn, and his sword brother among them. The rest were claimed by unbanded men and the widowed, with the younger of Taith and Phelan's sword pairs surrounded by avid listeners. Alithia could only imagine the stories being told; the animated gestures hinted at wild tales.

Tray after tray of food was paraded then served, such dishes that Alithia had never seen before with special plates reserved for the three of them. Phelan took an unseemly delight in identifying for her those ingredients intended to rouse a wife's passion. That the tavern keepers could prepare such a feast in so little time was a source for marvel.

Flasks of blood mead were broached, and filled cups were raised in salute. Low voices mingled and rose in songs of jubilation with Alithia a wide-eyed witness to the revelry. Perhaps Lydian warriors acted in much the same manner, but she had never heard the like.

All this to celebrate a pledging? It was more like midsummer festival, the height of the Mother's season.

Proving he noticed her amazement at their hosts' largesse, Taith leaned over to murmur, "Such generosity attracts the favor of the Lady—and spreads their name among caravaners and other travelers." A minor benefit that more than compensated for the expense, his smile seemed to imply.

Unbanded men came up to offer toasts for fertility and the gift of daughters, invoking the Lady for her or the Horned Lords for Taith and Phelan, then to touch the *idkhet* of her husbands—in the hopes of sharing in their good fortune and perhaps a little envy.

A beat started up, a complicated rhythm that had Alithia's foot tapping. Pipes and horns joined in, weaving in and through the drums. Someone pulled out a seven-stringed kithar, lending its clear, ringing tones to the harmony.

Before long, the unbanded men were dancing in the cleared space in the middle of the room—a swaying line of tall, dark warriors, bristling with weapons, stomping and high-kicking and clapping and cheering, all as one to the tinkling clash of cymbals. They almost seemed to be fighting, and she said so.

Taith shook his head. "It is tradition. They dance for the Horned Lords' favor, for strength of arms on the day of their own trial."

Unwilling to drag Taith and Phelan from the celebration—her necessities had already deprived them once of the traditional pledging rituals—Alithia stayed longer than wise, until her fingers were tingling from clapping and too much mead. The long day weighed on her limbs, but she took as much pleasure from her husbands' enjoyment as from the well-wishes of their clan. Though Taith wasn't as exuberant as Phelan, she did catch him humming along with some of the songs. His chest vibrated under her cheek when he did—a delightful discovery as her eyes felt too heavy to keep open. She almost didn't notice him gather her into his arms.

With a soft laugh, Taith carried her to their room, over her yawning protests. Phelan trailed behind, offering their excuses. But once there, the urge to sleep abandoned her, ebbing like the tide as they undressed her.

The merrymaking continued in the courtyard, the drumming now distinguished more by enthusiasm than skill, the snatches of song bawdy. Toasts drifted up, the cheers giddy though goodhearted, celebrating the good fortune of kin. The airy resonance of Gair's syrinx floated up, a reminder of fireside tales on the nights when Devyn had unbent to share and talk.

Alithia was suddenly struck by an absurd longing for clan—for her discussions with Astred and Arilde about their plans for the clan, for Magan's quiet reports, for Dagna sighing over a handsome musician wandering the Perfumers District, for Gilsor's wild tales, even for her younger sisters with their endless questions, so eager to leave childhood behind, impatient for their Maiden rites and their first pleasure loves. Fighting back useless tears, she pulled away from her husbands, ignoring Phelan's laughing exclamation, to lean out the window in search of something of home.

Torchlight flickered, the dancing flames of little challenge to the night sky. The stars above Sentinel Reach were passing strange. She couldn't find the Galley or the Fisher or the Gargant or the Unicorn that roamed the autumn skies over Lydia. Here, they had the Wyvern, the Dragon, the Porpoise, the Catamount, and the Serpent—none of which helped her judge the season among the forever green of the northern forests.

Could it be winter already?

She couldn't remember how many days they had taken to travel to Sentinel Reach, the count blurring in stark memories of shock and fear: the brigands, the fight in Table Rock, the dragon attack. In her secret heart, she feared she would be too late to save her clan.

And her quest would be for nothing.

Yet how could she have sped their journey? Should she have disregarded her husbands' sound advice? Sacrificed Taith's life for the chance of arriving a day earlier—and risked not arriving at all for want of his assistance in her defense and his command of their crew? Forced them on through torrential rains, only to arrive exhausted, unable to undertake the return to Barda as soon as she had the tablet of mysteries?

The stars shimmered through her tears. She let them, too tired to blink her eyes clear. It felt like forever since she had conceived this quest and argued for the mothers' support. Time vanishing into the air like summer ice from glaciers, save that the coming winter wouldn't restore the lost days to her.

"Come to bed." Taith stepped in front of her, the breadth of his chest blocking out the strange night sky—interposing his body to protect her from attack.

Fatigue might have dulled her senses and frayed her self-control, but she still noticed that.

As Taith gathered her into his warmth, Phelan pulled down the window screen, a faint glow the only hint of power summoned. Even in Sentinel Reach, amidst kin and celebration, her husbands remained vigilant against danger.

She had learned not to argue the point.

Twenty

Resonant bells announced the dawn, accompanied by mellow horns, a solemn yet exultant melody rejoicing in the return of the sun—the rising of the Lady of Heaven. Alithia's heart leaped at the sound of home. So, too, did the temple of the Goddess in Lydia greet the day. She didn't recognize the melody, but the voices were the same. It had been seasons since she had heard its like. Yesterday they had been too far to hear the bells, and if Barda observed the dawn ritual, the animals drowned out the sounds.

Today, they would finally go to the temple. In light of the urgency of her quest, Devyn would handle the sale of the goods they had carried from Barda while her husbands accompanied her.

She slid out from between her husbands, sweaty from their heat. With a grunt of displeasure, Phelan slumped over to rest his head on Taith's chest, still mostly asleep. They looked so right together, despite Phelan's broad, unmistakably masculine shoulders. Her delicious men.

Her sword husband, however, immediately opened his eyes, watching in silence as she made do with a quick wash, a small complimentary smile curving his lips. He raised his hand for her attention as she dressed. "You should wear the necklace outside your tunic today."

Alithia touched his gift doubtfully. She had taken to wearing it under the dragon-scale armor because the sight of it seemed to bother Taith as much as protection for something so delicate. "Outside? Are you sure?"

Sliding onto his back, Phelan pushed his hair out of his face, then nodded in yawning agreement. "You'll be safer if people see the necklace. Truth be told, if those brigands at Table Rock had seen it, they mightn't've tried to steal you." He shared a dark look with Taith.

"Someone thought the temple would turn a blind eye to your abduction," Taith added, his mouth thin. "Because you are not Hurrann."

Disquiet crept down her back with feet of ice. She shivered. While there was danger in Lydia, especially for a clan's first daughter, no one had ever tried to abduct her simply because she was a woman.

The dragon-scale armor went on under the necklace.

As she did up the laces, Taith got up, swatting Phelan on the buttocks to roust him out of bed, then made short work of his own preparations, though he took time to rub scented oil on his body. Despite a lazy start, her shield husband, too, was ready soon after.

Her hair took longer, tangled from sleep and riotous from long days of humidity. At any other time, she would have just scraped it back into a messy tail, snarls and all. But for the temple, she had her position as first daughter of clan Redgrove to consider; one didn't present anything less than her best face to priestesses—especially when seeking their cooperation.

She muttered under her breath as the long tresses resisted her efforts. Never had she missed the maids in her retinue more.

"I'll do that." Phelan took the comb from her, displaying more patience as he teased the snarls loose. "It'd be simpler if you'd just let me braid it."

Not wanting to jostle his busy fingers, Alithia twitched her head the slightest bit side to side in the negative. "It is too hot to leave it down, but I am not yet a mother. I cannot wear my hair the way you do."

Taith handed Phelan a leather strip to tie off her hair, a smile teasing the corners of his mouth.

"Something amuses you?"

Her sword husband laughed, a belly-deep rumble that danced across her arms, straight to her nipples, then wrapped around her heart. "At least he has you to fuss over now—that is a benefit to having a wife I had not expected."

*Despite all the people milling in the streets, they soon ap-*proached the outer precincts of the temple. Alithia suspected the shield pairs who ringed them had something to do with the celerity of their passage. After the attack in Table Rock, their escort seemed only prudent.

In the light of day, the temple of the Lady of Heaven in Sentinel Reach was nothing like the Goddess's temple in Lydia in anything save size. Red granite walls were surmounted by the twin crescents of the Horned Lords and covered with sculpture, a dazzling array of the bounty of the Lady and glossy plaques inscribed with a flame framed by two crescents. Every twenty paces was an outpost bristling with armed and armored guards.

What need had a temple for such formidable defenses?

The strange sight quickly dispelled the comfort Alithia had taken from the dawn ritual, a reminder that Sentinel Reach was a Hurranni city, not Lydian. "What is it like, inside?"

Phelan shrugged, an apologetic smile twisting his lips. "I've never been to the sanctuary, just the temple grounds." He shot an expectant look at Taith, who shook his head.

Broad, curved steps led to a wooden bridge over a bubbling creek. On the other side, more steps became a staircase that wound up a rocky cliff. The landing on top afforded them a commanding view of Sentinel Reach with benches for those who wished to linger. Here, they left the shield pairs.

"We will be a while," Taith warned.

The senior Sword of the shield pairs nodded. "No dealings with the temple ever go quickly."

Alithia forced herself not to fidget like a child while Taith and Phelan took their leave. A first daughter was controlled—so she reminded herself. A display of impatience would impress no one. That didn't prevent her from studying the gate into the temple she had traveled so far to reach.

Metal bosses studded an enormous door that rose four times Taith's height, the grain of its thick timbers a bold pattern of red and silvery white. It was large enough to admit a gargant. Had there been a time when the beasts were allowed into the city?

Visitors were admitted through a wicket in a steady stream. The three of them joined the flow, a gap opening for them as soon as they stepped forward—without their escort. Uncommon courtesy. Alithia was accustomed to the self-important insisting on precedence. But perhaps that was just in the south?

A troop of warriors stood just inside, helmets gleaming, shields strapped across their backs, leather cuirasses studded with bronze—widowed men one and all, scarred and wary. Their presence struck Alithia as unusual; in Taith and Phelan's crew only Devyn wore two *idkhet*, the rest were unbanded shield pairs. The warriors relaxed at the sight of her and—she later realized—the *idkhet* marking Taith and Phelan as her husbands.

Their reaction pricked her curiosity. "Why the troop?" she asked as they took a stone path into lush gardens. The temple in Barda hadn't had any guards in evidence, though that might have been because it was in the middle of a garrison. But even the Goddess's temple in Lydia wasn't so blatantly defended.

"Some brigands are more presumptuous than most."

Taith's answer provided little enlightenment. She glanced over her shoulder at the warriors at the gate. They actually expected an attack on the temple in the middle of the city?

She forgot the vagaries of Hurranni thought as soon as she faced forward.

Massive red trunks thicker than two gargants were wide curved away to either side, their branches impossibly high.

Shading her eyes with one hand, Alithia stared up, gripping Phelan's arm for balance with the other. She was wrong—not all the trees in Hurrann were green. Far, far above, golden leaves danced, shimmering in the wind. The trees looked nearly a league tall. This close to the giants, she couldn't see their tops or the temple that had to lie behind them. "What are they?"

"Sentinel trees," Phelan murmured, his words ringing with pride, "the temple's first line of defense against dragons."

She understood now why the city had been named Sentinel Reach. The trees' size was a statement of the generations the temple had seen. Testament to the power of the Lady of Heaven.

Taith left them staring at the trees to enlist a guide. Of the three of them, he had the best chance of obtaining an audience with a priestess for Alithia—so he had insisted and Phelan agreed.

Alithia didn't mind his departure, welcoming the chance to regain her equanimity. She expected grandeur from the preeminent temple in Hurrann, but she had imagined imposing architecture, pomp, and self-important officials—this was beyond comprehension. Nothing of the Goddess's temple in Lydia could compare to this.

Childish voices penetrated her abstraction, drawing her gaze to a garden on one side of the stone path.

Girls! She gaped in astonishment. The clearing held more girls than she had ever seen in one place, even in her clan house. Despite all the women they passed in the traders' quarter, she now realized she hadn't seen any girls.

The girls played a skipping game familiar from her own childhood; she and her youngest aunts and the older of her cousins had passed many a summer day chanting what sounded like the same singsong words as they took turns hopping between and around the crescent and full moons scratched into the ground. Nonsense words, she had thought at the time. But in hindsight, they could have been *"Gray Lord, Red Lord, Sword and Shield. Lady Heaven, power wield."* In badly mangled Hurranni.

Of course not. Alithia shook her head in amusement at herself. She must have misheard. It had to be one of those coincidences. They couldn't have been chanting Hurranni. Curghann hadn't taught them that game; ages of clan Redgrove had played it before the old trader entered their lives.

"They're raised here in the safety of the temple."

Phelan's voice recalled Alithia to herself. Her shield husband stood at her shoulder, a wistful expression on his face.

Of the temple.

Curghann had said the temple had domain over girl children, and her husbands implied that they were . . . clanless or perhaps not bound by clan?

She sat on the low wall alongside the path. "What of those not born to priestesses?"

"All daughters are brought to the temple when they have seen two turns of the Lady." He watched the laughing children with a pensive smile, a critical eye on the warriors standing guard at the edges of the clearing, his usual protectiveness given over to someone other than herself.

She suddenly wondered what Hurranni fathers were like. In Lydia the man who stood as sire returned to his clan once the marriage contract was fulfilled. She herself didn't know who had sired her, though a copy of the contract lay in the archives. Yet

Hurranns—at least the males—grew up with two fathers. She glanced at the girls. They apparently had none—or many more.

"I had a sister once. She was so small when I last saw her." A self-deprecating laugh. "She's probably a mother by now and taller than you."

Her heart clenched at the wistfulness in his eyes, the pang stealing her air. "You never saw her again?"

"It's for the best." Despite his answer, a slight crease appeared between Phelan's brows. Regret?

"How can you say that?"

"The temples are the safest places in Hurrann. The turn my sister was brought to the temples, a swarm of dragons came to the Lady's Hills. They made off with several of my kin—boys caught out—but they didn't get anywhere near the temple."

Alithia studied him. His statement was so matter-of-fact, so accepting of horrific loss, that she didn't know what to say.

Thankfully, Taith returned just then with an older warrior in his wake, one with a weathered face, a deep groove puckering his brow into a sardonic crook and extending in a line of white into his hair, and *idkhet* on both arms marking him as widowed. Despite the austerity of his features, he couldn't hide the surprise that widened his eyes when Phelan stepped aside, revealing Alithia.

"He will take us to the sanctuary."

She hid her surprise with the excuse of straightening her tunic as she got to her feet. *As simple as that?* No officials demanding to know her business? No insistence that she wait her turn? Her sword husband had wrought a miracle!

Crossing his arms before him and clasping his *idkhet*, the warrior gave her a deep bow, so low she could see the whole length of the sword strapped to his back. "It is my honor to serve you, lady," he assured her with apparent sincerity.

What had Taith told him? She would have suspected bribery, save that he had never done so that she had witnessed. But what could he have done to effect an immediate audience?

The warrior led them up a broad sweep of stairs, the blocks of red granite polished by time and thousands upon thousands of footsteps to a fine sheen, so wide they took two full strides to cross to the next. The ghosts of choral chants floated through the air, drifting down from the galleries they passed and echoing against the stones. She lost count of the steps and was hard-pressed to hide her winded state by the time they emerged into sunlight and onto a terrace surrounded by shimmering golden leaves and busy with clusters of warriors and traders and functionaries and servants, all caught up in animated conversations. They were mostly men, though she saw a handful of much older women among them.

Perhaps now came the wait?

Alithia expected some difficulty in navigating the crowd, but they quickly gave way after their eyes dropped to her necklace. A few of the sumptuously dressed strangers made to approach her, their attempts deflected by a frown from their guide, and were soon left behind bowing regret.

The sight of those bent heads disturbed her. What offense were they making excuses for?

As they mounted another flight of stairs, this one coiling around the outside of a tower, the wind tugged at her hair, forcing her to gather the heavy mass before it was hopelessly snarled. The men with their tight braids suffered no such danger, she noticed with some envy.

Her thighs and knees were protesting the exertion by the time they completed several full circuits, climbed above the uppermost branches of the sentinel trees, and achieved a wide balcony facing east where the stairs finally ended.

Grateful for the rest, Alithia gulped air greedily, her cheeks feeling overly hot. Taith and Phelan, on the other hand, looked as though they had gone on a stroll, breathing as easily as their guide. *Hurranns!*

This high up, she could see sunlight sparkling on the waters of the Nathair in the bottom of the canyon, could trace its winding path from the mountains, through the trees, and north to the sea. To the south, beyond the shimmering treetops, she found the traders' quarter of Sentinel Reach, and to the west she discovered that the city continued on, sprawling farther than she imagined. As amazing as the sights were, they weren't why she had come, and she gave her back to the vista.

A door pierced the wall before her, large enough that three men with Taith's shoulders could walk abreast without touching the sculptured edges, rising twice its width and curving to a spear's point. The stones around it were decorated with sigils and swooping lines in lacy designs that teased the memory—as if she had seen them before.

Bronze tubes on either side of the portal gave a resonant, tuneless hum that hung in the air, the protracted sound eerie in its steadiness. Unlike the wind, a piper would have had to stop for breath long before.

It was here that their guide turned aside, an air of expectation settling across his shoulders like a cloak. He spoke no words, made no sound, holding himself in readiness.

And nothing happened.

The door remained shut while the wind swirled around them, murmuring blandishments in her ears, making the pipes hum, and setting the beaded fringe of her necklace to clicking.

Alithia stared at the door, its weathered timber carved with the ubiquitous flame and crescents. She could see no hinges, no handle, no break in the wood. It was as though the panel was made from a single slab, unwarped and unblemished.

Their guide waited, attentive. Taith and Phelan stood at her shoulders, equally silent, vigilant even in the heart of their Lady's temple.

Something was expected of her. She couldn't bring herself to ask what. This was no language lesson where she could afford to show weakness. Needing to think, she pressed her hand over the necklace to quiet the distracting clicking.

Stone lace lured the eye, the chiseled grace of their loops strangely fascinating, their patterns almost like writing. If she stared long enough, perhaps they would relinquish their meaning. The need thrummed within her. To look. To see. To understand . . .

It took a gathering of will to wrench her gaze away. She wasn't here to understand, merely reclaim the tablet of mysteries one of her foremothers had sent to this temple.

But first she had to gain entry into the sanctuary.

Alithia forced herself to ignore the stonework—it was a distraction. The door was what barred her way.

Some unknown wood, gray from the elements, its raised grain scattering the light. Centered above her, just where the door started to narrow: the Flame with its attendant crescents.

So similar to the design on her necklace.

Symbol of the Goddess's—the Lady's gift.

The Flame filled her vision, suddenly more than carved wood. The holy fire.

Despite the cool wind, heat licked her cheeks.

Beneath her palm, beads warmed, pulsed. A quiet throb of power.

Like a dream, like morning fog burned away by the sun, the wood faded to nothing. It didn't part. It didn't rise. It vanished, the Flame and crescents flaring bright then disappearing to reveal the inner chamber.

Twenty-one

Alithia's heart skipped at the door's disappearance. The doors of the Goddess's temple in Lydia hadn't done anything like that on her visits there.

The wind died down to the barest puff, no longer tugging at her necklace. Now that there was no more need for the reminder?

If its subsidence was happenstance, the timing was uncanny.

Inhaling deeply to calm her nerves, she let go of her hair and entered the sanctuary, schooling her face to show only confidence. She was a first daughter of clan Redgrove. It wouldn't do to display uncertainty. Taith and Phelan's silent support made retaining her composure easier than she expected.

After the full sunlight, the interior was dim by contrast, drawing her eyes to the only light in the chamber: Her hearth. Red fire burned in it, the darker red of fresh blood and rubies, fulgent sparks leaping high, frisking in the air before fading. She could feel its heat from where she stood. Soothing. Balmy. Strangely . . . welcoming.

Once Alithia's eyes adjusted to the shade, the three statues beyond the hearth were hard to miss. Rising more than four times Taith's height, they filled the round chamber with awful splendor.

The Lady's statue was made of some age-darkened wood, Her robes gold-laced ivory, the blessing of fire She offered enameled in bright reds, the necklace She wore similarly enameled with a ball of fire instead of a flame. Her features were much the same as those of Her statue in Barda, but with the darkness of the wood Her features seemed unlike those of the Goddess of Lydia.

And yet . . .

Her robes left Her dark breasts bare beneath the necklace, what looked like laces seemed to pull Her bodice tight. Her skirts fell in graceful tiers that parted in the middle to reveal the shape of Her forward leg.

Am I dreaming?

The Horned Lords flanked Her on either side, facing outward as though watching for intruders, Their weapons bright with the gleam of honed edges. Their armor had the iridescence of pearls while alabaster and red onyx crescents rode Their brows.

Phelan inhaled sharply, the hiss of surprise cutting the waiting silence.

A faint hint of musk and spices teased Alithia's nose, a complex blend that said *Taith and Phelan* to her at a level below thought. Her husbands' scents reassured she stood in the sanctuary of the temple in Sentinel Reach, not wandering in some strange walking dream.

Enervating relief swept through her, sapping the strength from her limbs. She was here. At last. After so much effort and peril, she would soon hold the tablet of mysteries in her hands.

A woman stepped from behind the Lady's statue, tall and stern, her black hair gathered at the top of her head in a cascade of ringlets, an elaborate necklace much like Alithia's draped atop her linen vestments. She was trailed by two men swathed in heavy robes of silver and crimson. By their attire and their presence in the sanctuary, they could only be the priestess and her priest-husbands.

She spread her hands, the gesture revealing red scars in the centers of her palms. "Sister, be welcome in the temple of the Lady of Heaven." Unlike their guide, she evinced no surprise at Alithia's appearance.

The strangeness of the salutation gave Alithia pause. *Sister?* Surely that was simply because she was a woman, therefore, by Hurranni lights, of the temple? *No matter.* "I am Alithia, first daughter of clan Redgrove of Lydia. I have come to retrieve a tablet sent to this temple for safekeeping."

The priestess heard her in silence, her unreadable gaze lingering on Alithia's necklace. "Perhaps you are capable. You must perform a Blood Claim." She turned to one of her priest-husbands, who drew something from inside his robes.

When the priestess faced them again, a naked blade rested on her palms, etched *mythir* as long as her hand. Phelan and Taith stiffened visibly when she offered it to Alithia.

The blade was narrow, made for stabbing, not slashing. A dagger. It felt too light in Alithia's cold hands, an alien device unlike her eating knife.

The priestess offered no explanation, provided no advice. She merely gestured toward the altar with its bronze tripod holding the hearth, a circular slab of obsidian, above waist level—and the Fire that burned unfueled.

Yet another test.

As she approached the hearth, Alithia stroked the etching on the blade, hoping for some clue on how to proceed. Cool metal flowed beneath her seeking fingers. There was no answering warmth, no sense of the Goddess's—the Lady's!—touch within it. If this was indeed another test, it wasn't one of power.

She faced the holy fire, the dagger's handle biting into her palm. Standing so close drew sweat to her cheeks yet stole her breath, the heat so much fiercer than she remembered from when she had faced the altar in the Goddess's temple in Lydia.

"A Blood Claim must be made by a Daughter of the House." That had been the message given.

Alithia scoured her memory for everything she knew or heard of Hurranni ritual: Devyn's stories of the tests of manhood, Taith and Phelan thrusting their arms into the holy fire during their pledging, Curghann's suggestion of a traditional trial of arms for winning a wife. The priestess's scarred palms flashed before her mind's eye.

Mere barbaric traditions or true ritual?

Hurranns seemed to set great store upon courage. Was the Blood Claim a test of her courage, of her certainty in the veracity of her suit?

She licked dry lips, daunted by the answer that unfolded.

Did she have the right of it? The future of her clan depended on her success. But if she did as instinct suggested, she would be bowing to the Hurranns' Lady of Heaven, not the Goddess of Lydia. Turning her back on ages of clan Redgrove's obedient worship.

The sea roared in Alithia's ears as she teetered on the precipice, a step away from irrevocable decision.

No other possibility presented itself. To save her clan, she needed the tablet of mysteries.

She plunged the dagger into her palm, ice bursting in her veins. She gasped. For a moment, there was nothing but silence; even the Fire made no sound. Then she pulled the dagger out, blade grating against bone, and the world swayed around her.

Phelan's touch steadied her.

Before she lost her courage, Alithia thrust her wounded hand into the bright red flames, blood dripping from her fingers. The holy fire erupted with the vivid orange and rich yellow of poppy and mustard flowers around her hand.

She gasped.

Power surged up her arm, stronger than the bold crash of towering waves, louder than the keening howls of the fiercest winter storm, flooding her veins with the Goddess's—the Lady's ineffable presence. Her essence filled Alithia's mortal body to overflowing.

Daughter.

The Voice was life and everything that could be. All voices, all music, melding into a resounding note of perfect balance singing through all the ages of the world. For a single moment of eternity, Alithia understood everything.

Then silence surrounded her, the peace of a starlit night, in the embrace of her husbands, and she returned to herself. Back to the confines of her merely mortal mind.

Something appeared within the leaping red flames of the Lady's hearth. She grasped it—and her hand didn't hurt. When she pulled it out, she found the stab wound healed and scars on her palm and the back of her hand, shiny and pink.

But more important was the black stone tablet she held.

I did it.

Strong arms caught Alithia as her knees folded from under her. The world floated away.

Power flared as Taith lowered Alithia to the floor, his shield brother not taking any chances with the safety of their wife, their presence in the Lady's temple be damned. With his other hand, he balanced the hard-won tablet. His heart had stopped when he realized how she intended to use the dagger, his fear having nothing to do with a husband's duty. It had taken every bit of his control not to stop her.

"Taith?"

He checked Alithia's hand and pulse, his hand trembling like a flutter-wing in a stiff breeze. "She fainted." He sighed in relief, taking his first easy breath since she accepted the dagger. "Just fainted."

"Thank the Horned Lords." Phelan knelt beside him and helped him take Alithia into his arms, then took up the tablet and reached for the dagger their wife had dropped.

"Leave it. She is more important."

Reminded of the priestess's presence, his shield brother flushed and banished the spell he had cast, embarrassed by his temerity at raising power in the Lady's own temple.

Taith turned to the red-robed priest. "The Shaft?"

The priestess stared at him. "You're temple bred."

"The Shaft," he insisted, beyond rudeness. Alithia needed rest, and she would rest better in their bed.

The red priest nodded and led them to an arch behind the altar. The floor of the chamber beyond was pierced by a single hole a few paces wide and leagues deep, its edge described by a mosaic of red and white tiles: the Shaft, which connected the sanctuary to the rest of the temple, its stone walls falling away to a bottom dizzyingly far below. If one truly listened, one might hear the waters of the Nathair as they flowed past.

Fear for Alithia had Taith summoning the Lady's gift, waking the spell in the walls without hesitation. A glow filled the empty air. Carrying their wife, he stepped off the edge, his shield brother a mere heartbeat behind.

They fell—

As a feather fell.

Softly. Slowly. Raising no wind with their passage.

The priestess and priests joined them, their eyes full of questions. As were Phelan's.

He ignored them to watch the stones float by and the arches that opened to other levels. His neck prickled from the spell he had hoped never to use ever again—one he had not cast since his boyhood. The mosaics on the wall changed as they dropped, the dominant color of the designs shifting from the red of the sanctuary to the orange of the teaching levels, the yellow of the living quarters, then the green of the gardens. Just as green was about to become blue, they stopped. This low, one did not have to strain to hear the Nathair nor to feel the cool breeze from its waters.

The arch before them was flanked by glyphs of sentinel trees, informing anyone ignorant that they had arrived at the public grounds. Taith stepped out of the Shaft and released the Lady's gift with a silent prayer of gratitude.

Phelan overtook him and walked ahead, acting as Sword to his Shield—a reversal of roles that felt unnatural, especially with their high-ranking companions.

As they approached the gate, the priestess laid her hand on Taith's elbow. Training stopped his feet without his volition. "When it is done, tell our sister we stand ready to receive the tablet. It is our honor to keep it."

Our sister. The words shook Taith. Would that they lied.

"We'll tell her," Phelan promised hurriedly, throwing worried glances at Taith's burden as they left the garden.

At the sight of Alithia in his arms, their crew drew blades, closing ranks around them and maintaining a protective cordon all the way back to their lodgings.

Phelan paced the narrow confines of their room, all sorts of horrors suggesting themselves to him. Alithia was so pale, so still, lying in the middle of their bed. Her hand was healed, but she continued to sleep, her bright hair the only color on her. "Are you certain she's fine?"

He swiveled around to retrace his track, needing to move. With nothing to fight, he couldn't stand still. His heart continued to shudder, not with the fear of failure and dishonor, but at the pain she must have suffered. Stabbing himself would've been easier.

Taith looked up from where he sat on the floor watching their wife. "She is breathing. Let her rest."

They'd made better time returning to his kinsman's tavern than on the morning's walk to the temple. The priestess had augmented their crew with a squad of temple guards and their scarred guide in command. The evidence of temple favor sped their passage through Sentinel Reach's busy afternoon streets. Taith must have said the right words to have gotten someone so senior to guide them—but he hadn't expected anything less.

Phelan shoved the memory of their rapid descent from the sanctuary to the back of his mind for later consideration. His sword brother had only done the expeditious thing, no matter how startling. What was more important now was Alithia.

Just then she stirred, her lashes fluttering.

His sword brother glared at him, apparently blaming him for rousing their wife, but Phelan paid him no heed as he knelt on the bed beside her, too relieved by her recovery to mind.

She opened her eyes, the look in them vague as her gaze wandered the room, though some color had crept back to her cheeks. "Where . . . ?"

"You're in our room, back at the tavern." He caught the hand she pressed to her head, the strong beat of her pulse added reassurance. "How're you feeling? Does your hand hurt? Can I get you anything?"

Taith rolled his eyes at him, a not so subtle hint to rein in his questions that Phelan chose ignore.

"The tablet, it was not a dream, was it?"

Of course that would be her first concern. She hadn't watched herself lie dead to the world for most of the afternoon after standing by and doing nothing while she impaled herself. Groaning, Phelan rubbed his forehead. That thought didn't make sense even to himself.

"Do not trouble yourself. It was no dream."

Alithia pushed herself up, reluctantly accepting Taith's support as he sat behind her, her focus on the stone tablet on their saddlebags. "Is that it?"

The square of black glass, obsidian born from the Red Lord's hells, looked like a game board, straight lines scored on its face in some strange pattern with *mythir* pegs sticking out where the lines crossed.

"It's a tablet, there's no denying that." Fetching the hard-won slab, Phelan traced a finger above its lines, feeling for power. Alithia called it a tablet of mysteries and said her clan needed it to rekindle the holy fire in their altar; surely such an object would reverberate with power?

There was nothing—less power than in the beads they used to speed healing, not even enough to light an amberlamp. He sat beside them on the bed, forcing back his unease.

Taith twitched his brows at him, silently prompting for his verdict, not wanting to worry their wife. His sword brother had probably sensed the absence of power when he held the tablet at the temple but left the drawing of conclusions to him.

Except Alithia had eyes like a dragon. She frowned at Taith then at him. "What are you not saying?"

Phelan touched a peg. It shifted by a hair, the slightest quiver of power responding to his fingertip. He pulled it out and found he held the handle of a tiny dagger.

Alithia tapped his arm in a heartening display of impatience. "Stop delaying, and tell me what is wrong."

Sighing, he met her gaze. "It doesn't feel powerful. If this is to kindle a holy fire, I can't imagine how."

She stared at him, nonplussed. "But it came from the hearth. It is the tablet of mysteries."

He shrugged, glancing at Taith for help. "If you say so."

"Since this is what the Lady gave, this is what is needed." The look of unease on his sword brother's face belied the certainty in his words, but Alithia seemed to take heart.

"What do you suppose this is?" Phelan raised the tiny dagger to the light, noting the fine design etched on both sides of the blade. The dainty thing was smaller than the tip of his smallest finger, a toy that would prick, perhaps drawing a drop of blood, but no more.

Leaning closer, they frowned at it, accepting the diversion. The etching seemed to change depending on how one held the dagger. Viewed along one edge, he saw waves; from the other, breasts; from the hilt, a line of peaks; from the tip, hooks. He could almost see it as writing, but not temple script. Was the design simply decorative, or did it have meaning?

Of course, it was a Lydian artifact, despite the Lady's temple holding it in safekeeping. What would he know of such devices?

"It is a mystery," Taith stated with finality, his expression entirely serious.

Alithia gave a shout of laughter, her hand coming down on Phelan's thigh as she leaned into Taith. "Surely that is too simple an answer," she protested with unwonted giggles, the flush of her cheeks a marked improvement from her earlier paleness.

They couldn't help grinning at her amusement.

Phelan slid the tiny dagger back into the sheath incised in the stone. "What now?"

To his regret, the question silenced her laughter. "If this is the tablet of mysteries, what we need is the second mystery." Alithia touched the *mythir* hilts one by one as she thought. "But how can we tell which one it is?"

Watching her finger's wandering, Phelan realized the visible handles formed a spiral pattern. "If this is the first"—he pointed at the one closest to the edge of the tablet—"this should be the second."

They stared at him, Taith expectant, Alithia surprised.

He explained his reasoning, showing how the daggers circled inward.

"But why would that be the first? Why not this one?" Alithia indicated the center of the pattern.

Phelan blinked at her, taken aback by her question when the answer was obvious. "Because it's all a mystery, not just the daggers but the tablet itself. Like a snail's shell or a gargant's tusk, the outermost is the least mysterious."

Taith snorted, his mouth twitching. When their wife transferred her frown to him, he explained: "The tip of the tusk is a known danger, but what makes the tusk is the true mystery."

Alithia's eyes darted between Taith and him, then she shook her head, clearly dismissing the matter as irrelevant. "That must be a Hurranni saying."

He exchanged relieved smiles with his sword brother, their wife's manner reassuring them better than words of her recovery.

"So, this is the second mystery?" Alithia examined the dagger Phelan said was the one she needed. It did seem puny for what it was expected to accomplish. Had she been mistaken?

The blade bit into skin, on the verge of drawing blood. She returned it to the tablet, drawing her threadbare certainty about her, hoping desperately Taith had seen clearly, that the Goddess—or the Lady of Heaven—had given her what she needed. She had only to discover how to wield it.

Trust that it will all come right. She hadn't worried when the world enfolded her in darkness, secure in the care of her husbands, a surprising development in itself. Though it went against the grain to leave her fate—and the fate of her clan—in the hands of the Goddess, she had to believe she would unravel the second mystery.

Her heart trembled in her chest. She had come this far; she couldn't doubt the wisdom of her plan now—nor Her blessing upon it. The memory of the power that had filled her was too fresh for that.

Or perhaps it was the Hurranni Lady's?

Alithia had never felt anything like that before—and it had been at the altar of the Lady of Heaven. Here in Sentinel Reach, not in Lydia. Could that presence truly have been the Lady of Heaven?

She shook her head. That was all useless speculation. She had what she had come for. All that remained was to return the tablet of mysteries to her clan.

But would she be in time?

Sacrifice

Twenty-two

Phelan floated on a dream of pleasure, moist heat, soft sighs. Delight rippling through him. The low, intimate chuckle of his sword brother, rarely heard and thus more precious. The heady sweet scent of their beloved wife. Such a glorious dream. He didn't want it to end.

But when he clung to the dream, it frayed.

And he began to wake.

To a harsh breath. His lungs heaving. The muscles of his groin quivering in strain.

Need coiled inside him, a tight harness set to snap.

He woke on his back.

To the unexpected sight of their wife straddling him . . . and to pleasure that was no dream.

Smiling, Alithia squeezed his swollen blade with her sheath, rolling her hips with voluptuous relish. She leaned forward, resting her hands on his chest as she slowly impaled herself on his throbbing flesh. Again and again and again.

Stretched out on his side, Taith traced lazy circles on Phelan's belly, using the ends of Phelan's own hair to tease him. He, too, smiled as his hand wandered lower to more sensitive regions.

A thrill shot through Phelan at their play. Their focus was entirely on him. While their wife rode him, his sword brother reached down to tickle the tender skin of Phelan's inner thighs.

He gulped, his hips lunging upward in determined pursuit.

"Such haste. Always so impatient," his sword brother chided him, amusement glittering in his eyes as he brushed Phelan's quivering, burgeoning flesh.

The two paid no heed to his groans, persisting in their efforts. They lingered over him, Alithia with her languid seduction, Taith with his deliberate challenge. Building his need in slow measures. Stretching out their assault on his senses for long moments. Until he could barely breathe in anticipation of their next foray.

Desire spun a glittering web around his rocks and pulled taut.

Tight heat and feathery lightness—Phelan squirmed beneath the doubled lash of sensation. The contrast narrowed to the keen edge of an obsidian blade. Need shattered, release a sudden outpouring of sweet delight.

Lady of Heaven! Absolute bliss flooded him, filling him with a surfeit of well-being. If it weren't for their wife on top of him, he might have floated away.

"Good morning." Alithia gave him a quick kiss, looking much too alert for his liking, though Phelan couldn't fault her for her cheer. They'd taken him entirely by surprise.

"Without doubt."

His sword brother chuckled, a rare, intimate sound, then pushed hair off Phelan's face. "Warm now? The Lady should be on the horizon."

Phelan groaned at the unwelcome reminder. Leaving their warm nest and the soft curves of their wife bordered on banishment from the Lady's halls to the Red Lord's hells—though in this instance, it would be more properly "to the Gray Lord's hells," if He had hells.

The amberlamp hanging in the far corner of the palanquin swung to the gargant's stride, gifting them with a gentle light but no heat. The outer leather walls shuddered before the wind. He couldn't imagine anything less inviting than that flogging sound.

But someone had to go out and look around, keep watch for danger, ready to defend their wife. It was his turn.

"It will be cold again today, so we thought we would start you hot." Alithia gave him a mischievous smile as Taith drew her into his arms, her back to his chest, and under the blankets.

We? He rolled his eyes. It seemed someone had overheard his grousing of the night before—and it wasn't his sword brother.

A sweet laugh confirmed his guess.

Without leaving his blankets, Phelan cleaned himself, waking more at the touch of the cold towel, then wriggled into his clothes, adding spare shirts and leg wrappings over his usual attire. Only after he'd donned those did he drag his reluctant body from the warmth of the blankets and pull on his dragon-scale tunic. All the same, he had to suppress a shiver. His breath smoked when he exhaled.

Furs on top of his leg wrappings. More around his sandaled feet. Then the gloves. Then his hair.

He tied beads with warming spells around his wrists; lately, he needed them to keep his fingers supple. Once satisfied they were secure, he tugged his fur cap around his ears, snugged the veil that protected his nose and mouth from the cutting wind, and made certain his cloak wouldn't hamper his sword. He couldn't help an envious look behind.

The soft murmurs of approval that reached Phelan's ears left no doubt in his mind of the pleasure he would be missing.

For a moment, he doubted the wisdom of abandoning their nest of relative warmth. Who in his right mind had thought that someone standing guard outside—in the Lady-forsaken cold—was a good idea? Oh, yes! He had.

Shaking his head at his mush-headedness, Phelan quickly

stepped out of the palanquin, made certain the flap was secured behind him, then through the outer tents that shrouded it to trap the heat of the gargant. Into a world that was fit for neither man nor beast.

Well, most beasts. They'd had to leave Bulla and Dinglis behind in Barda, since wyverns couldn't survive snow.

This bull gargant, however, appeared to be thriving. The beast had stopped to use its long tusks to sweep clear the snow by the edge of the road, plucking the withered, brown grasses it uncovered with efficient greed. How so large a creature could subsist on so little was a marvel to him.

They'd been lucky Curghann had left his steward in Barda to handle preparations for Alithia's journey back. When they arrived from Sentinel Reach—more than a fortnight late because of the wyverns' sluggishness in the cooler high mountain air—Baillin had been waiting with a caravan to bear them south.

Balancing on the gargant's broad back, Phelan surveyed his surroundings, struck once again by the contrast with Hurrann.

What a dismal, Lady-forsaken land.

White hummocks stretched out in all directions, broken only by the black pillars that marked the road and the peaks of Hurrann sinking in the far north. Snow swirled as though the very elements sought to erase all signs of their passage.

The wind clutched at the lungs, searing in its chill, bereft of the Lady's kindness. Clouds veiled Her gaze, more often than not, yet even when She shone down upon them, Her touch was distant. If the Gray Lord had His own hells, this was how Phelan imagined they would be.

Some days the wind blew strong, and snow flew sidewise from bank to bank, forcing the caravan to struggle to make any distance—and Taith and him to argue long and hard with Alithia about remaining in the palanquin. On those days when they could barely see the gargant ahead of theirs, he had difficulty imagining there could be an end to this white wasteland.

But when they were blessed with cloudless skies, they traveled into the night, pitching camp in the middle of the road long after the Lady had left the sky and setting out before She had risen. It wasn't as dangerous as it might have been in Hurrann. The myriad stars of the Lady's Shawl above the peaks cast so much light that they could see for some distance.

Phelan stared at the larger hummocks but couldn't spot the catamounts that had shadowed them from the foothills, their clouded fur blending with the snow-covered bushes. They'd seemed almost desperate enough to risk hunting a full-grown gargant. Save for the caravan, nothing moved in the white wilderness.

With the aid of a rope, he descended the side of their gargant, more than thrice his height, and jogged to the head of the caravan, where he was certain to find the old trader's steward. He kept to the road, not wanting to test the true depths of the shoulder-high snow. According to Alithia, the road was built up above a floodplain. Walk too far on either side, and it was likely his body wouldn't be found until the snow melted—*drowned in ice* had been Taith's helpful comment.

The memory of heat—the scorching sands on the beach of Crescent Bay in the dry season, the sere, treeless peaks that were the heart of the Gryphonclaws and root of the Silver Ridge mines, the pungent, smoking rocks at Dragon's Foot—was like some idle fancy. Even the Red Lord's hells promised ease from the chill. It seemed impossible there could ever be floods in this white wasteland—for surely that required heat?

Climbing up the lead gargant was easier since the bull's pace was slowed by the need to clear snow from the road. Crouched behind the gargant's handler, Baillin greeted his arrival with a grunt.

"No catamounts today."

The wiry older man gave a shout of laughter, snow clinging to his grizzled brows adding turns to his age. "Told you there's little to fear from the creatures."

Truth, most hunters wouldn't dare a herd of gargants, but Phelan had difficulty believing the south was that safe. They traveled through a blighted land—what little green could be seen had faded quickly to nonrecognition. The bones of trees in the foothills of Barda had been bare and gray or shrouded with dry brown leaves hanging limp. Surely the beasts that roamed would be equally desperate?

Phelan huffed in disappointment. An attack would've relieved the gray monotony of their days and gotten the blood in his veins flowing—not to mention the lucrative market for catamount furs, fangs, and claws.

He stared at the tops of the pillars that stood like a line of black swords stabbing the snow. They rose perhaps thrice a man's height above the whiteness, taller than the gargant they rode. "Is it always like this?"

"The tales say those were raised after a caravan with goods for one of the southern temples was lost in a great storm. The snow was that high"—Baillin pointed to the base of the flame on top of the nearest pillar—"and they couldn't find the road, so at times it's worse. Most traders don't travel so far this late in the season, but it couldn't be helped."

Perhaps the older man meant that as reassurance, but the thought of a storm covering the road with snow deep enough to bury a gargant didn't sit well with Phelan.

Talking with Baillin helped time pass. The older man's tales of service with Curghann made for interesting and enlightening conversation, but the cold and the Lady's descent to the horizon eventually drove Phelan back to their gargant.

Partway up the rope, he hung from the gargant's side to look back to where they'd come. The peaks of Hurrann had disappeared from sight in the time he'd spent with Baillin. He returned to the palanquin without further delay, his heart heavy with unexpected grief at the loss. It was unlike him to view the unknown with dread, but this alien landscape leeched the spirit. Here, the Lady's gift was harder to call—as though locked in the ice around them. The warming spells on his least-used beads took much more effort to maintain.

The white expanse seemed endless, a sea of snow broken only by drowning stands of skeletal trunks and branches. He'd never imagined there could be a land without mountains and the horizon an unbroken line from east to west. How could they tell distance with so few landmarks? If you left the road and didn't have a sunstone for when clouds hid the Lady's face, you could travel in circles and not realize it—which was probably what had happened to that hapless caravan in Baillin's story.

This must be what the ocean was like, if you took a boat out far enough. Many of Taith's milk clan were seafarers, and his sword brother had tried to describe it to him once, but Phelan hadn't understood.

Now he thought he did.

Yet the sea held life. This cold wasteland seemed the opposite. How could so much bleakness have given birth to someone as vibrant and full of life as Alithia?

Black obsidian greeted him at his return, the tablet of mysteries gleaming in the amberlamp's faint light, unchanged from the countless other times Alithia had unwrapped it from its bed of lint. Of late, their wife had taken to brooding over the strangely marked slab and the tiny daggers it bore. Having mastered the art—if one believed Taith—Phelan knew the signs.

A rush of affection banished the heaviness of his spirits. She took her responsibilities so seriously.

From behind Alithia, Taith pointed his chin at a flask wrapped with glowing beads; the look of resignation that accompanied his gesture said their wife had been worrying over the tablet of mysteries cradled on her lap for some time.

Phelan exhaled loudly, adding a rather exaggerated—though

sincere—shiver as he threw off his cloak. "Gray Lord's hells, I don't believe anything lives here. There wasn't an animal out there that wasn't a gargant."

Alithia's hand jerked away from the *mythir* daggers, her head following suit; clearly she hadn't noticed his arrival. Then she laughed up at him. "This is—*winter.*" She used what had to be a Lydian word, rolling her eyes as her tongue failed her. "Snow season. Many animals sleep through it."

"*Snow season?*" Used together, the Hurranni words didn't make sense. Phelan glanced at Taith, wondering if they made sense to his sword brother. Snow was the white stuff that settled on the taller peaks where it was cold, the field around them notwithstanding. There were traders crazy enough to mine snow and ship it down, packed in straw, to sell in temple cities during the hot season. The southerners had a season for it? How bizarre.

Then understanding struck, a blade of ice cutting deep into his belly. "You mean we'll have *fortnights* of this? We're not just passing through a valley of snow?"

Unlike Gilsor, Alithia's husbands were not content to ride in the palanquin. Each took turns walking alongside or riding up front by the handler, while the other attended her. But as the days grew colder, and the snow persisted in blanketing the fields, they turned to snuggling her against their hard, welcome heat, and Taith insisted she teach them Lydian. The lessons proved challenging—particularly the interruptions.

"What's Lydia like?" Phelan propped his head on the fist of his cocked arm as he lay on his side. His loose hair spilled over his shoulder and across his broad chest in unintended distraction.

How to describe her home to a Hurrann?

Alithia's thoughts ranged back to last spring when she first delved into the differences between Lydian and Hurranni societies. Little had she suspected just how vast those were.

When she asked Curghann about Hurranni marriage customs, he had said that widowed men wore two *idkhet*, their own and their wife's, one on each arm, which served as a sign of mourning and their widowed state since a husband wore only one. *"What if they marry again? If they are young enough to stand as sire . . ."*

The old trader's forthright dismissal of the possibility had taken her aback. *"Marry again? A man who has failed one wife cannot be trusted with the safety of another one."*

Perhaps explaining that most basic difference would serve as a start. "In Lydia, men do not form shield pairs, because women do not need attendance."

Her husbands met that statement with open disbelief, so many thoughts flashing across Phelan's face as he gaped at her. Throwing a bewildered glance at Taith, he sat up, tangling in the blankets in his haste.

Alithia continued before they gave voice to questions. "Marriage is between a woman and only one man—and only until a child is born or the contract is ended without issue. Men might marry several times, if that is what the mothers decide."

"They break their pledges?" Taith looked up from his inspection of the knife he was honing, a frown of disapproval darkening his face.

"N-no!" Dumbfounded by his interpretation, she stammered in answer. "No pledges. Lydian marriages are contracts only."

Despite the many questions, the lessons eased the monotony of travel and provided a distraction from her useless worrying, especially with the towns few and far between.

Snow squealed under their gargant's feet, winter's grip still strong, though the Fire Heart, the red star on the crest of the Diadem, was above the horizon. Its appearance heralded springtide and the warm northern winds that would melt the ice.

How had her clan fared in the seasons she had been gone?

Inventory had to be running low, but soon demand for incense and sanctified oils for the budtime rituals would soar—and empty the clan's storehouse.

They were making better time now with the road mostly clear of snow, the dirty remains evidence of other travelers. The ridge Baillin's gargant approached looked familiar—but then, everything they had passed these last handful of days looked familiar. They had seen the Lone Rock standing in icy, solitary splendor, shortly after leaving Susa in the foothills by Barda and entering the Flats, the vast floodplains on either side of the Orinde. They had reached that mighty river and since left its banks to cut overland at the first of its many loops. What came next was a blur. Alithia traveled the route home so often in her dreams of late that she had difficulty remembering what was yesterday and what was still ahead.

They were so close, but would they be in time? She hadn't seen Egon and Adal in the last few days or nights, couldn't remember what the faces of the two moons were supposed to be by now. How much longer did she have before the budtime festival?

Alithia shivered, chilled by a sense of foreboding. She resented the bite of ignorance. If she had taken time at Rinna to contact Arilde through the Fire, she wouldn't feel so helpless now; but there were no more towns between here and Lydia, therefore no temples. She could no longer ask a priestess to send a message to her clan, even if she dared risk it.

Phelan draped his cloak over Alithia's shoulders, noting the distant expression on her face. Their wife's brooding had deepened ever since the first star of what she called the *Diadem*—as he understood it, some sort of hair ornament of the Goddess of Lydia—had made its appearance in the east just before the Lady's rising.

She accepted his care with a quiet smile, no longer arguing against their right to attend her.

The bitter coldness of nights past had eased once the road had joined the river and followed its course. Truth, it felt warmer now, allowing them to dispense with the added fur wraps, but he still worried it was too much for Alithia, despite her claims that she'd faced much colder weather.

Far ahead, Taith swung down the side of the lead gargant, barely needing the pause in its pace that ensured he was clear of its massive legs. He moved well, with not a hitch in his stride from the bandit attack. Keeping to the road, he headed back to them at an easy lope, a well-dressed bear in his thick snow season garb, uncaring of the wind that made his cloak flare behind him when he stepped beyond the gargant's sheltering bulk. A man in his element. His sword brother had adjusted to the cold with little difficulty.

As he made for their gargant's side, the beast stretched out his flexible snout to wind it around Taith and pass him between his tusks and over his head. The gargant's handler merely laughed, lending the Sword a steadying hand while he got his feet back under him. The first time their gargant had done that, it surprised a shout from Taith. But now he took it in stride, and the handler hadn't bothered lowering a rope for him. Clearly the beast recognized his sword brother as the man who cast the healing spells that kept the gargant hale.

At camp, Alithia practiced her healing spells on the gargant, too, but luckily, the creature hadn't tried the same with her but once. A faster learner than a wyvern.

"Just saw the river," Taith informed them as he reached their side, his bulk sheltering them from the wind. "Baillin thinks we will be in Lydia before the Lady is high."

Alithia clutched at his cloak. "Truly?"

His sword brother shot him a questioning look as he gathered their wife against him, his cloak settling around her like great wings. "Truth."

Phelan made a wry face. She'd hoarded her thoughts. He hadn't been able to get her to share her concerns—not that talking would've changed anything. They'd made the best speed they could and had to trust to the Lady they'd arrive in time.

They topped the ridge, and Phelan's heart stumbled in shock at the sight below.

The gargants' field was a patch of churned brown full of the pack beasts and piles of straw, devoid of snow. It stretched to the river—the same one they'd left behind several leagues back, from what Baillin had said at camp last night, but was now a far wider ribbon of black choked with ice and cargo-laden flatboats riding low in the water.

Beyond them rose a city. Rank upon rank of strangely wrought buildings lined the opposite riverbank, naked towers piercing the blanket of white, spreading for leagues in both directions. More buildings than he'd seen anywhere in Hurrann.

"It's larger than Sentinel Reach." In his shock, Phelan forgot his lessons in Lydian and spoke Hurranni.

Alithia tilted her head to one side as she considered the sprawling city and his statement. "Perhaps not," she replied, likewise in his milk tongue. "I think they are of a size, but Sentinel Reach is hidden by the trees and its height. With Lydia, you see everything."

He continued to stare at the snow-covered city, feeling like an unbanded boy instead of a man full-grown and pledged. The few towns they'd stopped at along the road from Barda hadn't prepared him for *this*.

Mist veiled the scene, like smoke rising from the river or the clouds that were the Gray Lord's domain. Eerie. He'd thought the expanse of icy wilderness they'd traveled through the Gray Lord's hells, but surely this was the true portal.

Twenty-three

Leaving Baillin to see to their baggage, Alithia hired a flatboat to bring them into the city from the gargants' field, carrying only the tablet of mysteries, still wrapped in lint and gauze, a heavy weight on her back. Even with winter holding sway, the Orinde continued to flow to the sea. Going by water would be faster than taking a coach over one of the far bridges.

Fog hovered over the black waters, so like wisps of steam it belied the ice that nudged the flatboat. Taith and Phelan regarded their transport with extreme suspicion—or perhaps it was the proximity of the river. They seemed to expect some creature to jump out of its icy depths with jaws bared. But they reached the opposite bank without mishap, and the boatman let them off with a cheerful smile for the extra coin she gave him.

As they left the riverside and headed upslope, past the new storehouses that replaced the ones destroyed by the flood, Alithia found herself walking slowly, as though in a dream, the cold and the people around her of little consequence.

Lydia looked different, as if she were seeing it for the first time. The soaring towers of the temple compound no longer seemed so tall, not to one who had slept on the shoulders of the snow-capped peaks of Hurrann. The colors looked pale, the silvery wood bland compared to the tilework and sculptured walls of Sentinel Reach.

Of course, when she had left in spring, the ones nearer the river had still been knee-deep in mud. Now, the streets were clear and walls clean. But still, the contrast disoriented her.

She hadn't expected anything to change. Now, she was home—yet she felt like a stranger. Her guard was wrong. Her hair with the tiny braids she had allowed Phelan to weave to hold back the rest of the loose tresses was wrong. Even her garb was wrong: the cut of her cloak, Hurranni; her dragon-scale armor, nothing that had ever been seen in Lydia.

For the first time since their pledging, the *idkhet* hung heavy on her bare arms.

Suddenly, Alithia dreaded seeing the clan's estate. Would it have changed as well?

Taith and Phelan did nothing to speed her steps, content to follow as her feet dragged, watchful shadows eyeing the people on the street with such wariness that a bubble of space opened around them as though spellcast. Would her husbands' manner have been different if it were summer, instead of almost spring, and the women dressed as she had been when she had first come to Barda?

An intersection revealed the spires of the Goddess's temple in the distance, barely visible against the cloudy sky. She dutifully pointed them out to her husbands, feeling most un-Lydian in her discontent. The land was so flat not much more could be seen—so different from her first awestruck sight of the Lady's temple at Sentinel Reach.

Her feet slowed further, fear for what she might find at the end of her journey clinging to them like mud.

Even in the cold, Alithia knew when they entered the Perfumers District by the cleaner, sweeter smell in the air. Not of flowers but of the freshness of herbs growing in hothouses. Phelan and even Taith murmured appreciation, their guarded expressions easing into smiles.

Sparse green rising above the steep rooftops announced the proximity of clan Redgrove's estate. Her heart swelled with pride, a response she had half feared wouldn't come after the dismay at her first good view of Lydia. The grove of flame trees had no equal in the south. The next closest stand was said to be in the foothills of the northern mountains far to the west of Barda. Other clans had attempted to cultivate their own groves, but none had flourished.

The sight of those young leaves sent a thrill of happiness through her. Suddenly, she couldn't wait to be home.

Alithia broke into a cautious run on the snow-packed street, grateful now for the space her husbands' glares afforded her. When the familiar red granite walls of the Redgrove clan house came into sight, she made for the shop instead of the family entrance, recalled to duty and intent on seeing for herself how dire the situation was.

Taith entered first, careful not to brush the wood tongue of the traditional bell of welcome, a metal tube that hung in the middle of the entries of most businesses. He paid the two guards just inside the door no mind, seeming to dismiss them as little threat.

The smell of incense tickled the nose with hints of dragonblood, clove, sandalwood, and sweetgrass—a traditional blend she had learned at her mother's knee.

At first glance, the shelves were well stocked. Dark blue and green vials filled the tiers with no space left bare. A closer look, however, revealed the show of plenty for the sham it was. Many bore the same labels, and only a few were the more expensive blends—even the shelf for samples of sanctified oils bore lesser scents. The way light gleamed through some vials led her to suspect those were next to empty.

Behind the counter, Dagna bent over a ledger, blond corn-silk hair held away from her serious face by a plain green fillet, taller and lacking the plumpness around her cheeks of the previous spring.

Under Phelan's curious hand, the bell rang, its voice a single low resonance almost like a wyvern's hoot of greeting. She had heard bells higher and sweeter, but the clan's had always sounded thus. Her husbands smiled at the tone as her cousin looked up, a distracted look on her face. She took in the three of them, her eyes darting to their *idkhet* and widening. "How may we serve you, lady?" she asked in tolerably fluent Hurranni, stumbling only over the honorific.

Alithia smiled, amused by her formality. They must seem so prosperous, wearing the proof of Taith and Phelan's lifelong hard work on their forearms. How simple it had seemed when she made her plans last spring. The reality was much more complicated. "You may welcome me home, Dagna."

Her cousin blinked, silent for so long she was intensely conscious of the braids that Phelan had woven to keep her hair out of her face and of her dragon-scale tunic. "Alithia?"

"None other." She gave thanks the rest of her hair hung loose, not laying claim to unearned status.

"You're late!" Hurrying out from behind the counter, Dagna threw her arms around Alithia, catching her in a desperately tight embrace of white tea scent. "Thank the Goddess you're safe. Maybe now the mothers will tell us what will happen."

The spate of fluid Lydian brought tears to Alithia's eyes as she hugged her cousin in return. She hadn't realized how much she had missed the sounds of home. "Happen?"

Dagna cast a surreptitious glance at the shelves. "You must've noticed; our stocks are low—very low. But the mothers won't say anything."

"The Fire?"

Dagna's stricken look confirmed Alithia's suspicions: the clan altar remained cold. Her cousin attempted a weak smile. "I'm sure the mothers are doing something—even though they won't tell us what. They've been busy."

So even now the mothers had kept the purpose of Alithia's journey secret—in the hopes of it not being necessary.

Her cousin caught her up with recent gossip, her voice singing with the lilt of clan. The unexpected comfort she drew from the flow of words diverted Alithia from her purpose, and it was a while before she remembered she wasn't alone.

With a guilty start, she released Dagna. "These are my husbands, Taith and Phelan." She completed introductions in Hurranni with a wave to the younger woman. "My kinswoman, Dagna."

Her cousin craned her head back, eyes going wide as they flitted between the two men. *"Husbands?"*

"Didn't Gilsor explain?"

Dagna shook her head slowly, goggling as though she had never seen a husband before—though to be fair, the clan had never hosted a Hurrann as a husband, and the many weapons they carried marked them as warriors. They were worth a stare. "He didn't have much of a chance to talk to anyone. His return was delayed because of something or another. The mothers married him off almost before his feet touched the courtyard."

Alithia winced inside. She and Gilsor were the first of their cousins to reach marriageable age, available to strengthen alliances or forge new ones, but she had hoped he would be here to greet her when she arrived. "I had best present myself to Arilde." If her mother learned of her return from someone else, life would become difficult.

"I'm glad you're first daughter." Dagna finally pulled her gaze from Taith and Phelan to give Alithia a smile of commiseration. "I wouldn't have dared gone north."

As she made to leave, her cousin tugged on her arm. "Bera's been all storm and gloom. You might want to step softly."

Alithia grimaced at the news. Born a day after her mother, Bera had never overcome her disappointment at not being the first daughter of her age and had set herself up as Arilde's rival. When her first breeding resulted in a son—the day before Alithia's birth—her bitterness had hardened to stone. Their aunt had made her displeasure known in subtle ways during Alithia's childhood. If she was stirring the waters, Arilde's temper would be uncertain.

The weight on her back reminded her of her duty. Some days she was tempted to wish Bera's firstborn had been a daughter—and had survived to adulthood. But if being the first daughter of her age meant having Taith and Phelan as husbands, she was glad Bera's ambitions had been thwarted.

Lydia was an astonishment to Phelan. He'd never conceived of a land where women walked about unattended, so many he'd lost count even before they'd left the river. Alithia had said it was so in her homeland, but it'd seemed like some fireside tale older boys told the young ones during treks into the jungle—complete with a Lady Who claimed no Horned Lords as husbands.

But here he was, and alone the women were.

They followed Alithia through the wareroom, leaving her kinswoman to mind the shop—with unbanded men for guards who, from the lack of greeting or introduction, weren't kin! She led them to the back, where a door gave on to a plain corridor lit with torches and fragrant with herbs and flowers, though none was in sight. They passed several barred doors, their wood dark with age—probably storerooms—then took corner after corner in bewildering succession.

Their wife wended the labyrinth without hesitation, nodding at the people they passed, ignoring the starts and acknowledging the greetings with equal confidence. A woman on a mission. A wife with claws.

Phelan hid the smile the thought provoked.

Another door opened into a tiled hall—the fine Hurranni work on its walls as unexpected as it was welcome. Here was where kin lived and the wealthy entertained, the extensive artwork announced with understandable pride. The mark of a successful clan.

Alithia's steady progress up one of the curving arms of the grand staircase didn't give him much time to study the lagoon mosaic, but he could tell it was old—he'd only seen its like in the temple at the Lady's Hills. The bright blue green tiles used in the sparkling waters weren't made any longer, ever since the ore at Weeping Rocks played out when his old fathers were boys. The other source of chrysocolla resulted in a greener shade. Had that long-ago artisan taken inspiration from his home waters, or did the mosaic depict some southern lagoon?

He stole a last glance at the mosaic over his shoulder as they left the hall. It didn't seem possible that the snow-swept south could have so colorful a sight, yet it was the land of their wife's birth. Perhaps his imagination was too limited?

As they ventured deeper into the building, the stones underfoot grew warm, though he could see no source of heat. A breeze drew his attention forward, its warmth redolent with the Lady's favor. *Here in Lydia?* Startled, he glanced at Taith to see if he, too, had sensed the flow of power.

His sword brother nodded as he met Phelan's gaze, using his chin to indicate an open door. Perhaps after their wife presented herself to her mother, they could explore this wonder.

Alithia's rapid gait slowed to a more measured pace as they approached the junction with another corridor. Their wife seemed to brace herself for battle, drawing a deep breath before turning the corner.

A fine-looking woman dressed in sumptuous furs led a group of women in their direction, striding boldly like a priestess in her own temple, lacking only *idkhet* and priest-husbands to complete the image. Her thoughts seemed far away, her gaze flicking neither left nor right nor reacting to their presence. Her cinnamon hair was woven into a cloak of braids around her shoulders—in Lydia, the badge of a mother. Its color reminded Phelan of Alithia's brother; touched with gray, it was perhaps a shade lighter than Gilsor's. Her brow shared the same graceful line of their wife's, as did her jaw, though her nose was a trifle long in comparison and her mouth drawn tight.

It came as no surprise, then, when Alithia stopped before her. "Arilde."

That their wife's and her mother's names both started with the first letter in the Lydian alphabet meant they were the first daughters born in their corresponding ages, he'd learned during the long snow season traveling south. They were expected to lead the clan when their time came. Without doubt, it was a position of influence and responsibility.

The duty apparently weighed heavily on the older woman.

*"Alithia." Happiness and welcome brightened Arilde's face be-*fore she brought her features under control, mastering them to stern lines. Judging by her furs, she had been out, and in this season that likely meant a consultation at the temple.

"I have it." Alithia laid her hand on the strap that carried the tablet's weight.

Her mother's glance took in Alithia's silent shadows, a brow rising in equally silent inquiry.

She performed introductions, her husbands responding with formal bows.

Arilde nodded, her eyes cautious, then led the way into her rooms. She dropped her furs into the waiting hands of her maid Ildi. The heavy winter coat she wore beneath them followed, leaving her standing in a formal, short-sleeved jacket that bared her breasts and belly to the navel and a many-tiered skirt that reached the floor, the wool leggings around her calves and feet her only concession to the season. Proper attire for a Lydian woman.

Unlike her.

Alithia suppressed a twinge of discomfort at the comparison, reminding herself that she was dressed as was practical for her travels, despite the present warmth. Presenting herself as soon as she arrived was more important than changing into more appropriate clothing.

"Leave us. I wish to speak with my daughter in private."

Arilde's guard bowed obedience and withdrew to the outer chamber, Ildi with them. Taith and Phelan, however, turned identical frowns to Alithia in obvious disapproval.

Resigned amusement had Alithia shaking her head at their reaction. After all this time, they still occasionally insisted on strict attendance.

"She is my mother. Surely you can leave me alone with her?" While Alithia could understand her husbands' concern—Hurranns in the strange south—she couldn't insult Arilde by allowing them to remain, not when Dagna had warned of Arilde's uncertain temper. What her mother might forgive at other times might not be excused now. Here in Lydia, there were dangers other than rampaging beasts and brigands; antagonizing her mother and strongest supporter was one of them.

Phelan turned troubled eyes to Taith, who gave her a hard stare before jerking his chin toward the balcony. "We shall wait over there, if that is acceptable?"

Alithia nodded assent, relieved they weren't going to argue the point.

Still, her husbands dragged their feet with many a look over their shoulders and a suspicious stare at the door through which Arilde's guard had disappeared, in no hurry to obey.

"My, they're certainly excellent specimens."

After Dagna's warning, Arilde's congratulatory comment wasn't what Alithia expected to hear, but from the twitch of Phelan's shoulders, it hadn't been intended for her ears. By the quickening of her husbands' pace, it had had the desired effect—though the appreciative gleam in her mother's eyes said the sentiment was sincere.

"I didn't expect them to be so young."

Confused, Alithia frowned. "Why not?"

"The *pledge gift*"—her mother stumbled over the Hurranni words—"was worth a goodly sum." The casket of spices and gems Curghann and Gilsor accepted from Taith and Phelan on behalf of the clan—the payment she had teased Gilsor about so long ago.

"Nothing like those," Arilde continued with a wave that encompassed the *idkhet* Alithia wore. "But still something I expected of older men. Most younger men wouldn't give anything of such value—nor afforded it."

Alithia smiled, unable to refrain from glancing toward the balcony where her husbands waited, Phelan glowering with some impatience. "You're thinking of pleasure loves, not Hurranns."

"Are they so different?" Maternal concern darkened Arilde's grass green eyes to malachite—concern for a daughter, not just for a first daughter. She couldn't protect Alithia from the consequences of her own decision, but that wouldn't stop her from worrying.

"Like no southern man I can think of—Lydian, Carian, or any other." The memory of her former expectations of Hurranns made Alithia smile. How ignorant she had been then.

"You intend to keep them as husbands."

She stiffened, taken aback by the implicit suggestion to the contrary. Taith and Phelan were hers! She couldn't imagine a life without them. She reined in her outrage in favor of a more temperate response. "Of course. Hurranns marry for life. We knew that from the start." To end the marriage would be to break faith, not merely with her husbands but with the Hurranni Lady Who had blessed their pledging.

Her mother's forced smile hinted at reservations. "How was your journey?"

"Except for the lingering snows, nothing unexpected." There was no point in speaking of the brigand attacks or of dragons and tree serpents. Those dangers were past. Arilde could do nothing about them, and anyway, Alithia had survived. What was important was claiming the tablet of mysteries.

Arilde's eyes narrowed. "Three messages through the Fire and one from your brother were hardly sufficient to keep me apprised of your progress," she observed in a neutral tone.

"I didn't believe you would appreciate being summoned to the temple merely to hear we were making the best possible speed on our journey," Alithia countered. "You had better things to do, and frequent messages might have piqued the curiosity of the priestesses."

"Impertinent."

"But true, nonetheless."

Arilde's answering smile was tacit acknowledgment—and approval—of Alithia's retort.

"How much time do we have?" The budtime festival was held when waxing Egon and waning Adal were perfect crescents, and the Diadem was entirely visible above the horizon just before dawn. Alithia knew that, but with all the cloudy days, she had lost track of the moons' aspects. The clan would be expected to deliver the sanctified oils to the temples twelve days before to give time for preparation.

"Eight days."

Alithia stared toward the balcony, at the flame trees in bud, her heart constricting. Eight days wouldn't be nearly enough time to make all the sanctified oil necessary—they couldn't start until the flame trees bloomed. Even if they were lucky, there would be nothing left over after supplying the temples . . . save the clan's reputation.

But only if the second mystery rekindled the holy fire.

"What is this tablet of mysteries you went to fetch?"

Recalled to the discussion, Alithia drew the strap over her head, pulling the parcel that was the tablet off her back. Unwinding the gauze, she carefully freed the tablet from its bed of lint. The *mythir* hilts seemed to catch the light, glowing against the shiny black stone. The lines etched on its face looked as mysterious as ever. It was hard to believe the fate of the clan rested on the slab of obsidian and a single stud of white metal.

"We think this is the second mystery the histories mention." Alithia pulled free the tiny dagger.

Arilde hissed in surprise. "*Mythir?* All of them?" By itself, the dagger was not significant, but the tablet held several—a minor fortune. "How would this rekindle the Fire?"

Alithia bowed her head. "I don't know."

"What!"

She described the Blood Claim ritual at Sentinel Reach and the result. "This is what the holy fire returned. I have to trust that the Goddess will show the way to use it."

Except it hadn't been the Goddess Who had answered her plea. Alithia hardened her heart to that whisper of doubt. This had to work.

"It's a dagger. The blade must mean something." Arilde took the second mystery from her, turning it to catch the light.

"The only way we can find out would be to attempt it at the altar. We don't have the luxury of time to study it further." Neither she nor Taith nor Phelan could fathom what the mysteries were supposed to do, and they had tried during the long journey to Lydia. She didn't think the mothers could solve it with only eight days between the clan and disaster.

Arilde tapped her lips in thought. "It must be done before the mothers. All must bear witness, or you'll have problems later on." Caution about Bera and her coterie? Her mother was more concerned than she let on.

"And Astred?"

"You know your grandmother will support you."

"Because I'm first daughter."

"Not to the detriment of the clan," Arilde corrected her sharply. Closing her eyes, she sighed, suddenly looking careworn as she rubbed the lines between her brows, her face slack, her shoulders slumped. "They offer only opposition, not solutions, not alternatives."

Alithia frowned, the seeds of dismay taking root in her belly at the signs of weariness in her indomitable mother. "None?"

"Not a one. And still they refuse to approach the temple."

"You don't want that any more than they do."

Arilde's narrowed eyes smoldered with frustration, glints of yellow lightening the grass green slits. "We've tried every fire ritual Eldora could find and some we inveigled from priestesses—those were just as futile—and all they say is, 'That's not the way it's done.' As though they can do any better. With each failure, Bera sits there and gloats, building her support."

Alithia ground her teeth at the news, biting back curses. This was worse than she feared: the clan tearing itself apart with disunity.

"If this succeeds, we'll be able to replenish most of our sanctified oils faster than the Carian clans can deliver—anything save flame tree oil, and only if they have a ready supply, which I doubt. Your plan offers hope. Of course, Astred will support you." Arilde's posture straightened, her chin coming up, as though drawing strength from the thought.

"Has it been that bad?"

"That flock of old hens are scared. Tradition is what they know. They dig like crabs in the sand and hope the tide won't take them." A sly smile curved her mother's mouth, belying her weariness. "There is a reason the Goddess made us first daughters."

Taking heart at Arilde's recovery, Alithia smiled back. "What now?"

"You will want to bathe. Best you change out of that as well."

Arilde nodded at her, her eyes dipping to indicate Alithia's armor—what she thought of it, she kept to herself. "Take your husbands to your rooms. The mothers must be summoned, and that will take time."

When she stood to obey, Arilde rose as well and hugged her tight. "Welcome home, Daughter."

Alithia's nose prickled as she returned the embrace. The hint of burnt incense clinging to her mother's braids was only the beginning of temple interference, should her attempt fail.

Twenty-four

Taith stood by the railing, far enough away that their wife's and her mother's voices were merely murmurs, frustration tight in his belly—and pointless. They had known before the pledging—even before accepting the old father's invitation to try for her bond—that Alithia was a southerner. Lydian. Despite half a turn of marriage, there would still be adjustments. Where her safety was not in doubt, they had to give due consideration to her wishes. Leaving her alone with her mother was one of those times, no matter how much he and Phelan might dislike the separation.

He forced himself to ignore the roiling in his belly and look around. Alithia had said her clan house was built as an open square; he had to take her word for it. He could not see any of the other sections; the trees were too thick and the sides too far away. Balconies faced the inner court, and that was where he stood, staring at the trees that filled the garden, breathing in the fragrance that in Hurrann signaled the start of a new turn of the Lady, while they waited for their wife to finish her conversation with her mother. The garden was a pleasant surprise, reminding him of Crystal Bell's clan house.

Despite the snow and ice they had walked through and the cold that had nipped at his face, here the grounds were clear, the air warm, though the sky beyond the branches was gray. Power rode the air, likely the same spell they had sensed earlier and the means of their snug environs—a tangible demonstration of the Lady's favor, however much Alithia might doubt with the clan altar standing vacant.

The compound had surprised him in another way: it was made of stone. Most of the buildings they had passed along the way were of wood, their roofs steep cliffs, their walls blank, their portals and posts so wonderfully carved they appeared to be covered in lace. Quite unlike Hurranni buildings.

Phelan joined him, perching on the railing with his back to the grove, his attention on their wife.

Taith shook his head in amazement. "A forest in the middle of a clan house." Crystal Bell's garden had been more modest in scale, used to grow herbs—quite unlike the garden of the temple at Crescent Bay that he had reveled in the difference. It was strange what details he could find in memory. He fancied if he closed his eyes, he would smell the sharp tang of bloodwort, made familiar by boyhood scraps, but the silence beside him was distracting. "You are brooding again. What about?"

"What if Alithia wishes to remain here?"

He raised a brow at the question. "You mean in Lydia?"

His shield brother merely grunted.

"We make plans after the holy fire is lit."

"But what if she does?" Phelan persisted, his fingers tapping a restless cadence on his thighs.

"Alithia is our wife. We knew she was a southerner when we chose to vie for her bond. Our place is at her side." A gentle breeze blew warm, hinting at growth and renewal. *Budtime,* Alithia had named it, the *spring* season they had raced across the desolate southern lands to overtake.

"But she doesn't need us here. It's so quiet. We haven't been in a decent fight since that little town in the cliffs, and that was barely a skirmish."

Taith suppressed a smile, though he agreed with Phelan's assessment. He had not even worked up a sweat when Alithia's appearance put an end to that tussle; calling it a skirmish when no blood had been spilled gave the drunkards who accosted the caravaners more dignity than they deserved. "We saw guards on the streets. There must be a need for them."

"When they have matrons and girls serving as guards?" Phelan huffed, casting a dubious glance toward the chamber and the door through which those matrons and girls had withdrawn.

"Do you want to leave?"

His shield brother straightened of a sudden, slipping off the rail to stand with a wary readiness that meant their wife had concluded her business with her mother. Perhaps that was an answer in itself, yet it worried Taith that Phelan was so silent. Did his shield brother truly entertain doubts as to the wisdom of Alithia holding their bonds?

Alithia watched Taith stalk through her rooms, wary, like a catamount scenting danger. He had shed his cloak of stoat fur and the wool shirts under his dragon-scale armor, his darkness looking very much out of place against the pale gold of the granite walls and ashwood furniture. The aura of ready violence clinging to her husbands seemed more pronounced of a sudden, now that her meeting with Arilde no longer occupied her thoughts.

Having followed Taith's lead in divesting himself of extra clothes, Phelan now stood by her side, balanced on his toes, his eyes darting around as he studied the outer chamber with avid interest—as though he hoped a serpent would tumble down from somewhere. "What now?"

Remembering her mother's advice, Alithia smiled. "We bathe."

Her husbands traded such resigned looks she had to laugh.

She opened her clothes chest, the light sweetness of lilies that wafted up still fresh despite the seasons of storage. For a heartbeat, the folded dresses awaiting her looked exceedingly outlandish with their abbreviated bodices, like nothing she might have worn—say, rather, nothing a Hurranni woman would have worn. They were perfectly proper Lydian attire, the very same she had worn since her Maiden rites.

Why then did they feel like someone else's clothes? A stranger's?

Alithia took a deep breath to banish that odd sense of alienation. She was home, in her rooms. These were her clothes—ones fit for a first daughter.

Still, it took a force of will to take one out.

The fragrant folds of its short skirt swung before her, nothing that hadn't happened in the past more times than she could count. But her memories of those days were like a dream half remembered.

She sighed. Clearly she couldn't take up the threads of her life as though she had never left. Her journey to Hurrann had changed her in more ways than just the constant attendance of two husbands.

With some reluctance, Alithia pulled off the dragon-scale armor, then the fur-lined smock. The shirt she wore beneath them was hopelessly travel-worn and embarrassingly threadbare. She caught sight of herself in the metal mirror. Stripped of Devyn's gift, she looked more like the woman she remembered—Lydian. First daughter. Only the necklace with its warm beads and the *idkhet* covering her forearms hinted at any change.

Arilde was correct. A bath was in order. She couldn't appear before the mothers looking like some waif. It wasn't wise to start a campaign from a position of weakness.

As she reached behind her neck to release the necklace's clasp, large, calloused fingers caught her hands in a gentle grip. "Keep it on. Please."

"Even here?" They were in the heart of her clan. What need had she for the necklace's protection here?

"Even so." Her sword husband nodded gravely, his black eyes tight with unspoken reservations.

Alithia stared at Taith, then glanced at Phelan, who also nodded. Wearing the *idkhet* while bathing would look strange to her clan but could be explained away as a Hurranni marriage custom. The necklace was something else altogether—an indication of the interest of the Lady of Heaven, even though they wouldn't know. Wearing the necklace to the baths would be eccentricity in the eyes of her clan.

Yet if she who had grown up Lydian found what should be home strange, what more her husbands who didn't have that advantage? She lowered her hands. Let her clan look askance at her. Some caviling was a small price to pay if Taith and Phelan felt more secure amidst the strangeness of the south. "Very well."

She picked up the dress she had chosen and left her rooms, suddenly eager to wash the stains of travel from her skin. Perhaps once she was clean and back in Lydian clothing, she would feel more like her former self again.

"Lady." Magan, the first of Alithia's guard, came to attention in the hallway, pressing her fist to her cuirass, the leather armor rubbed dark above her breast from countless other salutes. "Rumor said you had returned. I'm glad to see it spoke true." Reproach couched in gruff welcome.

Alithia chose to let it pass. "My husbands are always with me. There was no danger."

Gray eyes widened in Magan's weathered face as she tilted her head back to stare at Taith. "Your husbands? They?"

Smiling inwardly, she performed another round of introductions. She didn't know who was more bemused by the situation:

Taith and Phelan who blinked at the sight of armed and armored women, or her guards who seemed to have taken her husbands for hired warriors.

"Any problems I should know about?" Alithia asked as she took the stairs down to the baths, falling back on long habit. Many was the time the first of her guard had given her reports as they walked these halls.

"Agents of Snowroot have been sniffing around," Magan reported, naming one of the clan's Carian competitors. "They suspect; but if the temple shares those suspicions, they're not saying anything."

They had time then. Snowroot was the most aggressive of the Carians. If they were merely sniffing around, Snowroot would be in no position to take advantage of Redgrove's short supply of sanctified oils—so long as Alithia was successful in wielding the second mystery. "What else?"

"Speculation about your journey—mostly good. People saw it as confidence." A small smile penetrated Magan's austerity. "Your cousins believe you wouldn't have gone if the problem with the altar were grave."

That much the mothers' secrecy had achieved.

Damp heat rolled up the steps to greet them, enfolding them in an embrace of mist redolent with herbs and flowers. Taith filled his lungs with moist air, suddenly reminded of the grotto in the gardens of the temple at Crescent Bay with its fern-edged spring. His arms prickled with presentiment. It was not simply the heat that conjured up those memories. It was—

"D'you feel that?" As ever, his shield brother was first to give voice to their suspicions.

"Feel what?" Alithia stopped halfway down the stairs to look back at them, dreamlike in the mist.

Stealing a glance over his shoulder at the matron who led their wife's guards, Phelan waved his hands before him as though touching something that could not be seen. "That."

Alithia closed her blue eyes, a small furrow forming between her brows as she sought what he and Phelan could not help but sense. Her eyes flew open, bright green with surprise. "*Power?* You mean the Lady's . . . ?" She bit her lip, her gaze sliding past them.

She felt it, too, and did not want to discuss it before others. Taith did not know whether to be reassured by her confirmation of what they had sensed since arriving at her clan house or concerned by the strength of the Lady's presence so far from Hurrann.

With a small shrug, she resumed her descent and, perforce, they had to follow.

The foot of the steps fanned out into a spacious chamber, and Taith finally understood Alithia's fondness for bathing.

At first glance, the baths were very similar to the grotto. Near the entry, water cascaded off a ledge into a large pool in a constant deluge. Pink petals floated on top, surfing the eddies. Inviting to all the senses.

Shrieks of laughter rose above the splashes, echoed against the pale stone walls. He tensed, nearly raised his axe in surprise, and stopped himself only because Alithia's guard evinced no alarm.

The sounds were his first indication the baths were unlike those in Hurrann. The next was when Alithia's guard did not object to his and Phelan's presence, despite the evidence of their ears that there were girls in the chamber.

But surely he and Phelan had no place here?

As though hearing nothing out of the ordinary, their wife walked to an alcove along the wall, her bearing one of ease as she started to undress.

Taith stared at her, thrown into confusion by her disregard.

"You cannot expect to bathe with your weapons," Alithia exclaimed in Hurranni, amusement lilting her words. Laying her dress on one of the shelves that lined the alcove, she took off her shirt and trews as though they were alone. Many of the shelves already held piles of clothes.

It was clear she expected them to join her. Not to do so here, before her kin, would display discord, something that might undermine her position.

"If you promise to keep the necklace on." While their wife might trust her safety to her guards, Taith preferred the certainty of the Lady's protection.

She touched the beads, a warm gleam appearing in her eyes. "Very well. You have my word." Her agreement came too readily.

Schooling his features to blankness, Taith laid his axe on an empty shelf, then his knives, and untied the laces of his dragon-scale tunic. "Will they be safe here?" He could feel the gaze of Alithia's guard on him as he bared his scarred body.

Phelan frowned at him doubtfully but did not protest, displaying unusual restraint. He merely set his sword beside the axe and stripped down to naked skin. The body he bared was no less scarred than Taith's after a lifetime in Hurrann, perhaps even more so from running wild as a boy; his shield brother had always been one to seek excitement and adventure.

The back of Taith's neck itched when he turned to follow Alithia, presenting his spine to her guards. Phelan's white-eyed glance told him his shield brother was entertaining similar misgivings. To distract both of them, he tugged on Phelan's braid in passing. One thing they had learned was never to display weakness before predators—guards surely counted.

Alithia created a furor when she passed through the curtain of water and entered the pool. Girls just budding into maidenhood and others ripe enough to pledge cried her name in tones of amazement, relief, and welcome. In less time than it took to draw a sword, their wife was engulfed by a sea of pale arms and smiling faces.

Wiping deliciously warm water from his face, Taith had to

force himself to keep his eyes off those bodies for fear of embarrassing himself.

Light from square windows set high in the walls sparkled on water, the swordlike leaves of strange plants at the sides, and the mosaics on the walls. The pool they stood in was shallow near the deluge, the water's edge only hip-high to him, though almost waist-high for Phelan.

The rough tiles underfoot gave good purchase. Should they have to fight, slipping would not be a worry.

Whether that was a valid concern was still uncertain. Though Alithia was surrounded by a bevy of well-wishers, there were men lounging in another pool deeper in the chamber—with a direct view of their wife! If it came to a fight, Alithia's guards, who had remained at the entry, would be of little help.

He returned the men's stares with hostile interest, quick to dislike all strange men who saw Alithia naked, an action that had several of them sitting up. The Lydians had more body fur—much like southern gargants had more fur than their northern kind. They were paler, the lines of their muscles less defined. Softer somehow. He had thought their wife's brother merely young, but even these older men lacked the scars of experience.

Remembering Gilsor, he now saw similarities in face between him and these men. Though some had darker hair, almost to black, and others lighter, even the color of chaff, the lines of their brows and nose and jaws were alike enough that he would venture a guess of kinship.

It was the men's attitude of idle relaxation that drove home to Taith the understanding that he and Phelan were truly beyond the peaks. The snow season could be dismissed as weather—at times uncomfortable and dangerous in its own way, but still just weather. The journey south had been in the company of Baillin's caravaners, all fellow Hurranns.

But here, the only men about were all in the pools, at their ease. Save for Alithia's guard waiting by the entry, he could see no protection for the girls. To his mind, the Lydian men did not count—they were unarmed and unwary. At least he and Phelan had their beads.

Such confidence in their safety! This sort of inadvertency would be unthinkable in Hurrann. Though they stood within a clan house, it was no temple. He could only marvel that so trusting a people had survived a flood that could extinguish the holy fire.

The Lady of Heaven truly held them in Her favor.

A squeal of surprise jerked Taith's attention back to their wife. One of the older girls held up Alithia's arm, displaying her *idkhet* to the rest. "This is *mythir*! Goddess, you're wearing a fortune—even for a priestess." Envy gleamed in the girl's pale eyes, calculation giving them a cold light.

Indeed, *mythir* was precious, but its value came from its use by the temple. The Lady's rituals demanded *mythir* because the white metal was the most responsive of all materials to the Lady's touch. In Hurrann, a man was lucky to inherit *idkhet* from one of his old fathers since the temple could use its *mythir* to make a new *idkhet*. It seemed, however, that southerners held *mythir* as precious all for itself.

Even as Taith noticed the girl's envy, Phelan moved, closing the distance to their wife. Taith followed, a step behind. Their motion drew the attention of Alithia's well-wishers, sparking a flurry of giggles and glances from him and Phelan to the men in the pools.

To Taith's surprise, several girls came up to them, flaunting bare breasts, high and billowing with the Lady's bounty. They fluttered their lashes at him and Phelan, unmindful of the *idkhet* on his and Phelan's forearms. They circled around them, much like sharks or a pack of direwolves scenting prey.

The image roused a twinge of disbelief. Him, prey? Taith had never thought of himself in those terms before, but the sharp gleams in their eyes could only be described as predatory. The experience was disconcerting.

"Now, now. There'll be none of that," Alithia chided her kinswomen, a tolerant smile drawing her reprimand of any fangs. "They're my husbands, not pleasure loves."

"Husbands?" a bolder girl echoed, her voice lilting high and dripping with sweet disbelief. "These?" Her wet honey brown hair clung to her curves, emphasizing the buoyant slopes of her ripe bosom bobbing on the pool's gentle waves. Unlike Alithia's, hers would be more than a handful—even for him.

Taith shoved that inappropriate thought from his mind, lest his blade betray him. That response belonged to their wife.

A questioning chorus of doubt rose from all around them, impudent eyes sweeping them like breeders judging an urux bull for stud.

These were their wife's kin?

Phelan backed against him, trying to avoid curious hands. Hidden by the light sparkling on water, inquisitive touches along Taith's thighs and rump told him he did not have room to maneuver. Schooling his expression to blandness took most of his control; some of the contact bordered on intimate. Only training—bone-deep reflex to protect daughters—stayed his hands.

"Enough. You will treat my husbands with all due respect." The crack of command had the girls instinctively stepping away, even as they turned wide-eyed stares at Alithia.

Despite her nudity, their wife exuded authority, the beads of her necklace glinting with power. Taith had no doubt she would be obeyed.

The last one drew back with great reluctance, her eyes clinging to Phelan. "You need only one for breeding."

"Nonetheless, they're both mine."

Phelan took advantage of the sudden space around them to wade to Alithia's side. Only someone who knew him well would notice the stiffness in the set of his shoulders. His shield brother had to be fighting outrage.

Taith followed, his back feeling absurdly vulnerable amidst all these girls. The water rose to his waist as the pool sloped deeper, providing welcome cover, however slight.

Despite their pointed scrutiny, the Lydian men kept their distance, apparently deterred by Alithia's presence. From the mutters carried over the waters, there was no doubt their wife's kinsmen recognized her.

If her kinswomen felt a similar reticence, it was not obvious from their behavior.

"There was no contract signing announced. From which clan are they?" The green eyes of Alithia's honey-haired questioner widened when she caught sight of his and Phelan's *idkhet*, then narrowed in speculation.

"*Black Python.*" Even to Taith, the Hurranni sounds of their clan name fell strange to the ear in the midst of the conversation in Lydian. At her audience's looks of confusion, their wife added, "I married them in Barda, a Hurranni pledging."

Shock met her announcement, quickly followed by a spate of questions.

"You did *what*?"

"When?"

"Is that where you've been all this time?"

"Without the mothers to witness?"

"Yes." She said no more, evidently judging her answer sufficient, displaying that same serene confidence she had shown a chamber full of shocked Hurranns.

Disbelief and admiration in varying measure showed on the girls' faces. A reassessment of her position and—perhaps by extension—of his and Phelan's worth? Wondering looks were cast at their *idkhet*, the calculation behind them as inevitable as Bulla's unruliness; though from their wife's explanations, that calculation had its roots in expectations of great wealth, not the Lady's favor.

As if there could be any trade worth the loss of Alithia and Phelan—and his own honor. *Foolishness.*

Not one to disillusion her kin, Taith said nothing.

Following the flow of water, Alithia led them to one of the many downpours under the windows, choosing a spot under a square of sunlight—one unfortunately that was far shallower than the rest of the pool, the water's edge reaching only to her waist and not even that high for him and Phelan. Putting them on display for all her kin to see?

A nearby ledge bore those purple bars she used for bathing, a rendering that included an extract of soap-root. From the examples of those under other downpours, this side of the pool was where the actual bathing was done.

The girls trailed after them, watching with expectant eyes as he turned to stand opposite Phelan.

"Formal introductions will have to wait until later."

Despite the obvious hint, their audience remained where they were, the crowd growing as more girls waded over.

"Are they as vigorous as they look?" Pushing her honey hair out of her face, Alithia's questioner of earlier appraised Taith's and Phelan's bodies with avid eyes. Her gaze lingered on their blades, the tip of her tongue darting along the seam of her lips.

"That is none of your concern, Blas."

"If they make good sires, the mothers may contract for them again." She looked down at Alithia, the gesture calling attention to the difference in their heights. "Perhaps their intention is to have taller children in the next age."

Sending up a silent prayer of gratitude that he and Phelan were well and truly pledged to Alithia, Taith reached for a bar of soap-root, preferring to ignore the unnerving discussion of Lydian contract marriages. Even in the temples, the priestesses had never spoken so bluntly of begetting. The selection of wives for shield pairs was left to the trials and the Lady of Heaven—none dared interfere with such decisions.

He bided his patience, sensing undercurrents he did not understand, treacherous to the unwary. Like entering a new market for the first time, it was better to watch and learn.

Alithia made a noncommittal sound as Taith lathered her soft breasts, leaning back against him as though he bathed her all the time. "If so, they will have to look elsewhere." She arched into his strokes with a murmur of approval, her taut nipples hard against his palms, her overt response a surprise. While she had not seemed to mind the presence of Devyn and the rest of their crew, she had not been so open with their intimacy.

The pretense reminded him of temple intrigue, a game of manipulation. But despite his suspicions, he had to smile at her open delight—and her display of trust. She did not doubt they would play along.

Phelan joined him in washing their wife, working with uncommon silence. Though he glanced at Taith from time to time, his shield brother looked remarkably complacent.

"Why do you say that? The contract would be fulfilled and their clan free to negotiate a fresh one."

"You didn't hear me earlier? I accepted their bonds in a Hurranni pledging. There is no end to that contract." Alithia smiled up at him, her body completely at ease.

Certain she had good reason for her actions, Taith pressed a kiss to her upturned lips, content to be claimed before her kin. Her hand hooked the back of his neck as she rose on her toes, her ardent response nearly making him forget their audience. As he raised his head, he caught a start from Phelan.

His shield brother gaped at them like some unbanded boy receiving for the first time the collected wisdom of how to pleasure a woman. The mush head's blade even had the temerity to stir and swell for all to see!

Still bent over their wife, Taith glared at him, wordlessly promising all manner of dire fates if Phelan did not bring his unruly flesh under control.

Alithia giggled, her amusement spilling over in breast-jiggling distraction that had Taith—and her kin—staring. She reached over and tapped Phelan's mouth. "Later."

Despite her implicit promise of bed play, their wife lingered at her bath, seeming to delight in running her hands over him and Phelan as they washed her, then themselves. Taith did not dare ask her what she was about. The voices echoing through the chamber meant any question could be heard by all.

Most of their audience wandered away when Alithia continued to insist on postponing introductions. The handful that remained spoke of trade and unfamiliar names, of changes and concerns they had not felt comfortable bringing to a mother's ear, though they seemed not to mind a husband hearing.

He tried to remember those names that drew a response from their wife, so he might ask her about them at a later time, but the whispers of farther away were more intriguing. He discarded the titillated conjecture on their bed play bruited about behind cupped hands, in preference of what sounded like comparisons of him and Phelan and Alithia's former pleasure loves. Since their wife was scrupulous about not voicing any comparisons of her own, the whispers were too great a temptation to ignore.

To his frustration, his Lydian proved inadequate for the task. The splashing water garbled the sounds that reached him such that he could not be certain he heard correctly.

Phelan was of no help. His shield brother seemed to have focused on bathing their wife to the exclusion of all else—even the ripe bodies of her kinswomen. A sound strategy on his part, after that earlier lapse.

Finally, Alithia signaled her readiness to depart, evidently satisfied that she had accomplished whatever she had set out to do. They emerged from the pool to discover thick towels awaiting them and clean trews and shirts folded on top of their dragon-scale tunics. That the servants had found clothes that fit him in the time they bathed was a marvel to Taith—one that fled his mind as soon as Alithia donned the clothes she had brought from her rooms.

His lungs seized when she turned to them.

Their wife was the very image of the Lady in Sentinel Reach! He had forgotten his shock at Her statue in the horror of the Blood Claim ritual and Alithia's subsequent collapse. Now, the necklace on her breasts recalled his first sight of the Lady's statue in the sanctuary at Sentinel Reach—so were Her breasts bared beneath Her necklace. The memory of their pledging rose to taunt him with the sway of Alithia's skirt as she entered the sanctuary at Barda, baring her legs in the same way the Lady's skirt had bared Her leg in Sentinel Reach.

Foreboding stabbed at the reminder, a sharp knife sliding deep into his gut, ice-edged and jagged. Coincidence could not explain the likeness. The temple at Sentinel Reach was the oldest in Hurrann; he remembered that much from his lessons. The statues in its sanctuary were equally ancient; all others were inspired by them. Why then would the Lady be garbed in southern attire?

Twenty-five

His sword brother was withdrawn on the return to Alithia's rooms; no expression crossed his face at their escape from the baths nor the incongruity of a matron protecting their backs. This wasn't Taith's usual silence but something else altogether—a rare brood.

Phelan cudgeled his memory for the cause. Surely not the outrageous behavior of their wife's kin? He might have given the matter more thought, but he had his own worries.

Everything he had seen of the south—from that minor scuffle with the drunkards put to naught by Alithia's arrival in the little town in the cliffs, to the matrons and girls serving as guards, and the general lack of concern on the part of her male kin—all pointed to the absurdity of their attendance. Beyond the peaks, what need did Alithia have for two husbands? He felt as useful as dry, flaking scales on a wyvern, fit only to be cast off and trampled underfoot.

When the door shut behind them with her guards left outside,

Alithia surprised Phelan by turning around, laughing up at him as she cupped his cheek. "Was it so terrible?"

The question jarred him out of his introspection. The sight of all that fair, nubile flesh at the baths flashed before his mind's eye, making his blade stir without his volition. His boyhood self would have thought he'd died and woken up in the Lady's halls. He shook his head in rueful embarrassment. "Words can't describe just how much."

Watching Alithia and Taith kiss had only fanned the flames of his arousal. Thank the Lady for Taith's dagger stare—which was all that had saved Phelan from making a fool of himself before Alithia's kin.

"I did say *later*. And you were so good to put up with that lot." She caught his arm, holding it against the side of her breast as she led him to the inner room and its waiting bed. "Come."

The contact focused his thoughts with admirable efficiency.

"Taith?" Alithia stopped at the threshold to look over her shoulder. His sword brother stood by the door to the balcony, staring at them in silence, his brow furrowed, his thoughts unreadable. He made no move to join them.

"Trouble?" Phelan could see nothing to warrant concern.

Taith shook his head and averted his gaze. "Go on."

"Truly?" From Alithia's tone, she expected an answer.

"Truth, I have to think."

Frustration at his sword brother's taciturnity was an old friend. Long experience had taught him the uselessness of trying to talk to Taith before his sword brother was ready; asking only earned him tetchy grunts and no answers.

Phelan gave Alithia a resigned half smile. "Best leave him alone. I tell myself it's good for him to brood, if rarely. Otherwise he'd be perfect, and who could live with perfection?"

A snort came from the balcony.

"Only if he wakes still in a brood is there a problem."

She cast a last look over her shoulder, then nodded. But inside, she sat Phelan down on the bed with a stern eye. "You have that moody look, too. What is it? You, I can make talk."

Of course, she'd noticed their change in spirits and chosen to tackle them individually.

"This is not about that silliness at the baths. You of all men would laugh that off."

He cupped her breasts, left bare below her necklace by her Lydian bodice, ran his thumbs over her flowerlike nipples, and watched with fascination as they furled into tight buds. He buried his face in the valley between, conscious of the pettiness of his complaint. Hadn't they sworn their lives and bodies to her attendance? "Here, you've guards to protect you."

Alithia drew away, tilting his face up for her scrutiny. Warm concern softened her gaze to azure. "That is a problem?"

"I need to be more than—what did you called it?—a *pleasure love.*"

Surprise flickered in her eyes, turning them a greener hue. "You are more than that. You see me as myself, not some first daughter to be pleasured for advancement. That is a gift beyond measure. I do not want guards. I want my husbands." She undid the laces of his shirt and pushed the garment off and down his arms. "I need your care, your teasing, your laughter, even your scolding." She punctuated her words with soft kisses on his lips, neck, shoulders, and throat as she urged him onto his back.

Phelan's heart leaped, joy spreading in a flush of warmth. He pushed her hair back, wanting to see her face after that astonishing revelation.

Her smile assured him, love sparkling in her blue eyes. "I need your questions, your thoughtfulness, your fierceness." Crawling over him, she licked her way down his body with wet little lashes that sent shivers across his skin. The heat of her mouth and the resulting coolness roused him to aching desire.

Her hands slid under his trews, freeing him. "My guards can't give me that," she whispered over the weeping tip of his turgid blade. Then she took him into her mouth.

Horned Lords!

The sight of her lips around him, sucking him in that most unthinkable of kisses, touching him as no temple-raised Hurranni woman would have done, excited him beyond belief. The thrill of her touch, her encouragement, her words, shattered his control.

He couldn't—

Raw pleasure erupted in a scalding release, wrenching a shout of delight from his throat. Torrid sensation poured through him in a flood of ecstasy—and still she sucked on him, drawing on him, taking him deep. Until his strength was spent.

Only then did she smile and unhand him.

Floating on a wave of bliss, Phelan panted for breath, Alithia snuggled against him. Never had he felt anything like what had happened.

She laid a hand on his pounding heart, her touch possessive yet . . . protective. "This is not all of my life. As first daughter of clan Redgrove, I have to travel. You will have your fill of attendance, then."

Truth, his fears had been shortsighted. A single season's loss could still become a profit at the end of the Lady's turn.

Phelan lay there, content. Only one cloud darkened his joy: Taith hadn't joined them.

Servants arrived bearing platters of food and the customary tea for the noon meal. Alithia directed them to a small room with lounging cushions on thick carpets, reminiscent of the tents of their travels and far more welcoming than the formality of the outer chamber. A window offered views of the balcony and garden and allowed the entry of a warm breeze.

Despite the aroma of strange spices drifting up from the covered pots, Phelan's stomach growled audibly—though Taith failed to hear. Their wife, on the other hand, laughed at his grimace of embarrassment as she poured tea for all of them.

"What was that about?" Phelan gestured toward the baths as he set his sword on a pillow beside him. Having regained his equanimity, his curiosity stirred anew.

"You will have to be more specific."

"The challenge from the exceedingly ripe one."

"Exceedingly ripe one?" She paused with her cup halfway to her lips, her head tilted in query.

He scooped his hands in front of his chest in explanation, giving his wrists a voluptuous twist.

Alithia spluttered into her free hand, her eyes dancing with mirth. She drew a few shuddering breaths before recovering enough to answer him. "You mean Blas." She shook her head at him in smiling reproof. "It seems she spent my absence cultivating my younger kinswomen. I expected her to do something of the sort. If she had not, one of the other girls would have."

"She . . . tried to usurp your authority?" The idea was surprisingly difficult for Phelan. No Hurranni wife would attempt to claim the prerogatives of another woman. Within a clan, that meant the bonds of her husbands; all other rights were a matter for the temple. Did that mean this Blas wanted to take Taith and him from Alithia? The thought certainly shone a different light on her calculating looks and bold touches. His heart clenched, his hands itching for his sword. "Why?"

"People seek the comfort of the familiar. In my absence, some turn to an older kinswoman to provide the guidance—no, the reassurance—they need from a first daughter. As the second eldest of our age, Blas is the obvious choice. Certainly her own mother would expect her to act."

"Politics." That he could understand, though in Hurrann such rivalries were between clans, not within clans; if the temples had the same, he'd never heard of it, possibly because his sword brother was so closemouthed. No matter that they were beyond the peaks, it seemed some things remained the same.

Reassured, Phelan turned to the pots on the table. His appetite returning, he tore a chunk from a loaf and dipped it into an innocuous-smelling sauce that Taith found unexceptionable to judge from his steady chewing.

"Now I have a question for you. At the baths earlier . . ." Alithia's voice trailed off, her face troubled. She sipped her tea before continuing. "You sensed power."

Phelan smiled at the memory, around a mouthful of flowery, creamy blandness. "The Lady of Heaven. We'd sensed Her favor earlier, and Her presence is even stronger here."

"Here?"

"Why do you think this garden can be so warm though it is open to the sky and snow lies outside your clan house?" Taith set down his bread, a frown darkening his brow. "The spell is a powerful one."

Alithia rubbed the necklace on her bare breasts, now visible for all to see. The memory of the beads shimmering with power in the baths was still fresh in Phelan's mind. He hadn't felt the cool touch of the Lady, but he knew the light of Her gift, and the necklace had had that added spark then. It only confirmed his supposition that the Lady had plans for them.

He forgot to chew as he considered the odds against pledging to a Lydian woman whose clan—among all the southern clans—happened to find favor with the Lady. Surely that had to be destiny? The Lady had to have a purpose for guiding Alithia to Hurrann and into accepting Taith's and his bonds. Why here in all the south? Why this clan?

The prolonged silence suddenly impinged on Phelan's awareness. He'd been lost in his thoughts again. He glanced at Alithia then Taith, wondering what he'd missed. Curiously, the two looked grave, not at all what he'd expected from talk of the

Lady's favor. The undercurrents he sensed between them were like to drown a wyvern!

Taith stared back in unhelpful silence. There were times when it was tempting to shake his sword brother. Unfortunately, the attempt wouldn't do any good—save to amuse their wife.

"I never thought I'd be so glad to see trees." Phelan embellished his statement with a deliberately melodramatic shudder, hoping to lift her mood. "All those fortnights seeing that white expanse of snow plain was unnatural. Is the south truly so devoid of green?"

Alithia gave a forced laugh, her hands worrying at her food, bread crumbs piling up in front of her. "Most of the trees along the shores of the Orinde were downed by the floods last spring, not that there were that many left."

"What happened to the others?"

"The histories say they were cut down long ago to build the city. All gone now." She stared out the window at the sparse leaves as though drinking in the little color.

Phelan put an arm around her and pulled her close, hoping the contact would ease the shadows in her eyes. Taith drew them under his arm, his hand on Phelan's shoulder, holding Alithia between them.

"Is that why there isn't much meat to this?" Phelan sopped a bit of bread in the sauce, pretending not to find anything more substantial. "No tree serpents?"

She smiled at him, a reluctant, lackluster curve of the lips, but at least she stopped picking at her food enough to eat more than just a few bites. Once Taith started asking about ingredients and where they were bought, she took more interest in what lay before them, and the meal passed in talk of trade within the south and between southern cities and Hurrann.

They were occupied thus when word came that the mothers were assembling in the sanctuary to witness Alithia's attempt to rekindle the holy fire.

* * *

The setting sun painted the clouds in colors of spring flowers, the blaze of orange, pink, lavender, yellow, and touches of red and purple surprisingly heartening. Though Alithia didn't subscribe to the Hurranni belief equating the sun with the Lady of Heaven, the festive display as she and her husbands crossed the garden to answer the mothers' summons felt auspicious.

She touched Phelan's arm, then pointed to the sky as they walked. "See? Lydia is not all bleak snow."

He grinned, somewhat abashed, the expression surprisingly boyish. Away from the men of her clan, her husbands didn't seem out of place, just themselves.

Yellow torchlight spilled out of the sanctuary—the one chamber in the clan house that had never needed it—staining the granite floor a sickly orange instead of its rightful red. She had forgotten about the torches, their use inconceivable to memory. A faint whiff of soot tainted the air, a violation of the pristine sanctuary and a mockery of the clan's history. The profane offering seemed almost a portent of what was to come. A shiver of dread sought to quench the tiny ember of hope the sunset had stoked.

Those two absonant notes underscored the truth that the Goddess's hearth remained cold—despite the seasons she had been gone and all the mothers' efforts at a remedy. The tablet of mysteries Phelan bore was their only hope for rekindling the holy fire—and they had no guarantee of success.

Had she frittered away any chance of contracting future alliances to strengthen the clan . . . to no avail? Certainly, Bera's coterie would argue so, if she failed.

Twenty-six

The sanctuary doors closed behind Alithia and her husbands with a quiet thud of finality. A sea of faces turned at the sound.

Astred stood before the altar, the torches along the walls throwing strange shadows across her features. Her grandmother's gaze was unreadable as befitted one who led the clan. The other mothers were equally inscrutable, betraying no reaction to Taith's and Phelan's presence.

"The clan is gathered. You may begin." The dispassionate words offered no encouragement. Astred stepped aside, clearing the way for Alithia to approach the cold hearth.

In all the time since the tablet had appeared in the Lady's hearth in Sentinel Reach, they hadn't discovered how the second mystery with its glimmer of power was supposed to rekindle the holy fire. Now that the moment was before her, Alithia still didn't know what to do. Taith believed the Lady had given her everything necessary to fulfill her task—she could only hope he had the right of it. Feeling the weight of her clan's attention, she kept her pace steady, drawing on her husbands' silent support for strength.

The altar didn't match the one of childhood memory—but not because her perception had changed. Without the Fire to claim her attention, she saw more: the obsidian hearth borne by the bronze tripod wasn't a pure black but was shot through with streaks of *mythir*; the crystal panels that looked so drab without the holy fire to light them were held in place by curved bronze prongs shiny and untouched by time; even the tripod didn't show any hint of ages past, gleaming as if new.

Alithia nearly flinched from the wrongness of it all. Without the blessing of fire—the holy fire—it was just so much metal and stone.

With great solemnity, Phelan turned to her to present the tablet of mysteries, holding it with both hands. He had volunteered to be its bearer, eager to play a part in the rite.

She chose the tiny dagger that they agreed was the second mystery, hoping she wasn't making a mistake. It seemed unchanged from the last time she examined it, a sliver of *mythir* with an ambiguous pattern etched on its blade; whether it had hooks or waves or flames or vines, she couldn't tell. In form, it was a miniature of the *mythir* dagger she used for the Blood Claim.

Was she supposed to wield it in the same way?

Doubt assailed her. Sentinel Reach was a temple to the Hueranns' Lady. Why should the same ritual apply to a Lydian altar? And yet the statue of the Lady of Heaven in Barda looked much the same as those of the Goddess in Her face of the Maiden.

Even more telling, the mysteries were made of *mythir*, a rarity in Lydia . . . and were daggers.

But perhaps the Goddess would recognize the intent?

Alithia held the second mystery over the scar on her palm. The dagger looked insignificant in comparison, too small for the task required of it. At least it shouldn't hurt as much as the first time.

The blade pricked the pink scar.

Power slammed into Alithia, whipping her hair around her in a whirlwind of sensual heat, filling her with that ineffable Presence she had felt only once before.

The Voice that spoke should have shaken the chamber, yet none of the others seemed to hear it.

Cleanse Our altar and rededicate it to Our service.

As quickly as the Presence had come, it was gone, leaving her shaken. Clutching the dagger against her itching palm, she staggered into Taith's arms. *Cleanse the altar?* But the hearth was clean. *Rededicate it?* Wasn't that the purview of the temple?

"Are you well?" Taith's rumble was more felt than heard. She nearly laughed. As ever, her husbands' first concern was her well-being, not her purpose.

Alithia repeated the message she had heard.

"But it has been cleansed," Astred protested, her face flushed in affront. As the eldest surviving first daughter, the care of the altar was her responsibility.

"Was sanctified oil used?"

Silence met Phelan's question, no one expecting to hear a man's voice in a matter for women. The strangeness of it smothered the sparks of argument.

Unaware of his violation of custom, he continued in careful Lydian, "You need sanctified oil. The priests always use sanctified oils to polish the hearth and shields."

"Shields?" Arilde repeated, her arms crossed under her breasts. Her mother looked as uneasy as Alithia felt—would have felt if not for Taith's support.

"Those." Phelan pointed to the crystal panels—which the altars in the Goddess's temples didn't have, but the Lady's temples in Barda and Sentinel Reach had.

Two shields. One on each side of the hearth. Curving slivers when seen from the front.

Like the plaques on the walls in Sentinel Reach with the crescents framing the Flame?

Round shields when viewed from the side.

Like the moons when they were full?

Attending the holy fire?

The way the Horned Lords attended the Lady?

Alithia's thoughts whirled in confusion.

Taith studied the crowded chamber, still bemused at being in the midst of so many women with only him and his shield brother in attendance. Much though he preferred to carry Alithia from here, he could not interfere unless her safety was in question. It should have been Phelan holding her, but his shield brother had charge of the tablet of mysteries.

"It was cleansed. But was sanctified oil used . . . ?" One of the older women glanced at the others, soliciting their recollection and receiving only murmurs of uncertainty.

A gray-haired woman standing apart shook her head. "I doubt it was. We dared not ask the temple, and the supply is limited. Nothing in the records or the histories that can be read addressed such an eventuality. All mentions of when the altar was raised or what rituals were done claim the First Record as their source." From her words, she had to be Eldora, the keeper of the archives, who had helped their wife find the references to the tablet of mysteries.

More murmurs rose, much like the gush of a river or the roar of a waterfall, too many words in too many voices for him to make out. None of their wife's quiet lessons in Lydian prepared him for this babble.

"The holy fire has always burned in living memory, a sign of the Goddess's favor." Heads turned, everyone else falling silent as the oldest matron he had ever seen spoke. Closing her eyes for a moment, she pressed a hand to flaccid breasts, then to wrinkled lips. "If the hearth needs cleansing to regain Her favor, then it must be cleansed." That venerable mien changed little when she transferred her stare to his shield brother. "Do they use a particular oil?"

"They use the oil made from the blossoms of—" Dismay swept Phelan's face as he struggled for the correct words in Lydian. "The Lady's tree," he finally blurted in Hurranni.

Blank incomprehension met his answer.

How could they not know?

But even Alithia did not understand. "The Lady's tree?"

Phelan looked to him for aid.

"The trees outside." Forcing an arm to release their wife, Taith pointed toward the garden.

"Flame tree oil? Out of the question!" A flaxen-haired matron of an age with Alithia's mother made a sweeping gesture of dismissal. "There is only one jar left. If we open it, there will be nothing for the budtime rituals."

"Bera speaks truly," someone in the crowd said in a ringing voice. "Our stock of sanctified oils is low. Dare we spend it on supposition?"

At the acclamation, the flaxen-haired matron's chin rose, a hard light in her eyes, an almost visible cloak of triumph settling around her shoulders. A swamp leopard in Lydian dress. Vicious if crossed.

Taith's arms drew Alithia deeper into his embrace of their own accord. Here was no friend to their wife; this matron would rejoice in Alithia's failure, regardless of who else may suffer.

The venerable elder clasped wrinkled hands around a walking stick, her face troubled. "Yet if we do not make the attempt, our stores will eventually run short."

Phelan looked to Taith, his eyes tense, urging him to argue. For once, his shield brother's tongue failed him.

Taith forced back a scowl, hating the feeling that he was failing Alithia. He had tried to avoid learning such things—had gone so far as to become a trader and pledge himself to a southern wife. But there was no help for it.

He straightened his shoulders, resisting the instinctive urge to silence. "In his boyhood, Phelan went to the temple . . . often. If he says the priests use the sanctified oil of *Lady's tree* blossoms to cleanse the altar, that is how they do it."

As a boy, Taith had avoided those chores, wanting nothing to do with the sheltered, stifling existence that was temple life nor its more daunting responsibilities. But a sinking sensation in his belly told him his efforts had been in vain.

The Horned Lords had to be laughing at his folly.

*To Alithia's relief, her mother and grandmother argued in sup-*port of the attempt, despite their initial resistance. With Arilde and Astred on her side, only the most intransigent of the mothers opposed the proposal for long—and even Bera could not disregard the concurrence of Henia, the clan's oldest living great-grandmother. Someone was sent to fetch the precious oil.

She urged her husbands to one side, while everyone else waited for the jar's arrival. "What then? How should the cleansing be done?" she asked in Hurranni.

Phelan's gaze flicked to Taith. "The priests did all the polishing—with the traditional invocations. I think it'd have to be the two of us." By his tone, it was clear he didn't like the thought of leaving her unprotected. Her sword husband's answering frown said he agreed with the sentiment.

Though their concern made her heart flutter, Alithia rolled her eyes, shifting out of her sword husband's arms to stand on her own feet. "I will be right here, watching you—surrounded by clan and kin. Surely that is safe enough?"

Taith shifted his frown to the cold hearth and the separate clusters around Arilde and Astred, the dissenting mothers, and Henia. "This is necessary." He didn't look happy about it.

His shield brother evidently took the statement as acceptance, his mouth twisting in resignation. "We'll both need two squares of soft cloth, one for oiling and the other for polishing. The hearth is cleansed first, then the shields."

Of course. The Lady, then the Horned Lords. "And the re-dedication?"

Phelan gave a tiny shake of his head—hiding his doubts from the mothers. Protecting her. "I don't know. None of the priests ever spoke of kindling a holy fire or dedicating an altar, at least not within my hearing."

Alithia schooled her expression to calm. Any display of uncertainty on her part was bound to raise fresh dissent. She could only hope she could unravel the second half of the Goddess's directive before any of the mothers remembered it.

Taith tipped her head back with a gentle finger under her chin, distracting her from the fears struggling for the upper hand. "The answer will come. The Lady has guided you this far." The sweet smile he gave her quieted the roiling of her stomach.

Then his words sank in: the Lady, not the Goddess.

"Yes, trust in the Lady. She gave you to us, didn't She?" Phelan's grin was unrestrained, belying his earlier doubts.

With a laugh, she pulled his head down for a kiss, reassured by their confidence. In the interest of fairness, she had to kiss Taith as well.

She ignored the indignant mutters behind her.

Soft cloth was easily obtained, ready before Dagna's white-faced arrival bearing, with the help of a younger cousin, a jar nearly half their height.

Taith and Phelan set to work under the critical eyes of Alithia's clan. Cradling the tablet of mysteries her shield husband had passed to her keeping, Alithia gave thanks to the Goddess that most of the mothers agreed with Phelan's reasoning. If priests had the responsibility for cleansing the altar, then her husbands, as the only men present who knew the invocations, were the best suited to perform the task.

The men's voices rising in prayer before the clan altar made many of the mothers uncomfortable; Bera's visible fuming was only one of the more notable displays. Even Henia, seated on the stool accorded to her by her great age, who must have seen much in her many springs of life, bit her lip at the invocation of the Horned Lords, her mottled hands restless on her staff.

As Taith and Phelan took down the crystal panels, Alithia was reminded of their pledging and the priests who had done the same in the Lady's temple in Barda. Here was another instance of similarity with Hurranni rituals—in her clan altar.

Was it simply coincidence? Yet all the records agreed that the altar was dedicated during the establishment of the Redgrove clan house. Why was it different from the altar in the Goddess's temple? Had the Goddess given her Hurranns as husbands for a reason?

Or was it the Lady's hand stirring the waters?

The image of a hand stirring brought to mind another hand and a similar motion. Writing. Unfamiliar figures.

Curghann and his notes, char stick moving over vellum. The strange figures seemed to glow black with portent. Burning themselves into her mind's eye.

She had seen their like before. Somewhere.

Swirling lines. Like the sculpture around the door to the sanctuary in Sentinel Reach. But that wasn't it.

Wasn't what she thought she remembered.

It was more . . .

Alithia closed her eyes, trying to think. The colors inverted, now glowing bright against the red of the inside of her lids—like pale writing on red lacquer.

That was where she had seen it!

Suspicion teasing her with hope, she drew Eldora aside. "Can you bring me the First Record?"

"What for? No one can read it."

"I think—" The idea was so wild Alithia hesitated to say it aloud, questioning the wisdom of blurting out such improbable speculation.

"Yes?"

Her grip on the tablet of mysteries tightened, the weight of the obsidian slab with its precious *mythir* daggers fortifying her resolve. "I think it might be written in Hurranni."

Eldora stared, her mouth opening and closing in silence before she found her voice. "Hurranni?"

"I've seen their letters. If memory serves, they're similar to those on the Record. My husbands might be able to read it."

Made of neither parchment nor vellum, the First Record was a book of sticks—literally. More than a thousand flat-sided sticks lacquered red and tied together into a scroll. Some long-ago keeper of the archives had etched numbers on the ends of each stick to preserve their order should the threads break. Those numbers were the only part anyone could read of it. But tradition held that the ancient scroll told the origins of their clan and was thus the most important book in the archives, held closely and shown only to a select few at any time.

As a child, and last spring when she sought an answer to the question of rekindling the holy fire, Alithia had been allowed to see it, as was her right as a first daughter, though she had yet to become a mother. She suspected those viewings had been a mark of Eldora's favor. Now, she hoped that regard was high enough that the keeper of the archives would defy tradition and permit her husbands to examine the First Record.

The older woman rubbed her chin, her eyes unreadable. "Do you truly believe it's written in Hurranni?"

"I think there's a good chance."

"And if it is . . . have you considered the implications?"

It would overturn the history of clan Redgrove as they knew it. If the First Record was in Hurranni, that meant their foremothers' first language was Hurranni—that perhaps they had been Hurranns. They exchanged troubled looks.

"Surely saving the clan is more important?"

Eldora pressed her hand to her breast, then raised its first three fingers to her lips in silent invocation of the Goddess, her gaze dropping to Alithia's scarred palm. After some thought, she sighed. "I'll fetch it."

No one minded Eldora's departure, their attention bent on the men cleansing the altar. Probably waiting for a drop of sanctified oil to hit the floor, ready to cry waste.

Alithia drifted closer, drawing comfort from the deep-voiced chant of her husbands. They were polishing the crystal panels now, their motions respectful, concentrating on the importance of their task. Soon they would be done.

Her grandmother waved her over. As Alithia joined the cluster around her, Astred asked the question she had hoped to avoid: "What do you propose we do next?"

"We wait."

Frowns met her answer. Once again she wished she weren't standing before them with her loose hair declaring her maiden status. Married, yet not one of them—a mother. Surely the braids Astred and the other grandmothers looped around their heads served as reassurance? Announcing for all to see the Goddess's blessing of a strong and fruitful lineage.

"For what?" Arilde prompted in a murmur, stealing a glance sidewise toward Bera and her coterie. Did her mother look forward to the day that she, too, wore her braids in a circlet, when she finally would be above the challenge of her cousin?

For the first time, the twinge of doubt Alithia suffered was for the regularity of her bleeding time. Despite frequent bed play, she had yet to breed.

"You spoke of a rededication, not just cleansing," someone mused from behind Astred. "What ritual is this?"

Alithia shook her head, delaying the inevitable response. Even her mother's support would go only so far.

"Daughter, you shouldn't spring a surprise on us when we might have to argue in support. We need time to prepare."

Recognizing the merit of Arilde's statement, she nodded acquiescence but gestured for the mothers to move closer, to hide their faces from Bera.

They frowned but followed her lead. Keeping her voice low, Alithia repeated her speculation. As she expected, they rejected the possibility out of hand.

The First Record written in Hurranni? Preposterous!

At that moment, Taith and Phelan resettled the crystal panels on the hearth, backing away with stiff but obviously respectful bows to the cold altar. They then went straight to Alithia's side, the lack of any hesitation showing they had tracked her progress even through the cleansing.

With a quick smile, Phelan reclaimed the tablet of mysteries. Despite his reluctance to leave her unattended, it seemed he enjoyed acting as priest.

Eldora returned just then, escorted by two of Alithia's cousins bearing a folding table between them, wide-eyed girls overwhelmed at being in the presence of so many of the clan's mothers. The red mass Eldora bore could not be mistaken for anything other than the First Record.

Alithia swallowed a sigh of relief. She had feared the keeper of the archives would change her mind.

"No!" Bera stalked forward, the tiers of her skirt flapping, outrage painting livid spots high on her cheeks. "It's bad enough that we must suffer men not of our clan in this chamber. You cannot—"

A loud thump interrupted her tirade. Leaning on her staff, Henia got to her feet, her age-spotted fingers white-knuckled. "You forget yourself, Bera. The holy fire may be extinguished, but this is still the sanctuary."

"But, Henia—"

Thump. "You will speak with the respect due the Goddess." The austere expression above her wizened frame evoked the gravity of the Crone. Only the most imprudent would dare defy that face.

Bera took a deep breath, then continued in a more moderate tone. "I demand to know why the First Record has been brought here."

All eyes turned to Alithia.

By force of habit, she pressed her hand to her breast, then kissed her fingers, the gesture doing little to calm her pounding heart. "I believe it is written in Hurranni."

"Outrageous!"

Knowing she would never convince Bera, Alithia turned to address Henia and the others. "Why then would our foremothers send the tablet of mysteries to Sentinel Reach for safekeeping—into the hands of the Lady of Heaven—when the Goddess's temple is within the city?"

Taith and Phelan exchanged confused looks. Of course they wouldn't understand the significance; she never told her husbands about the First Record.

Ignoring the discussion, Eldora gestured to the girls to set up the table, then dismissed them once she laid her burden on it. She summoned Alithia with a glance as she untied the ribbon that held the scroll together.

Marching to the small table, Bera slashed out her hand in command. "Eldora—"

The older woman stopped her with a hard look. "*I* am keeper of the archives. This is my decision." To Alithia, she exposed a hand's length of the scroll, revealing scratch marks pale against the red lacquer that ran the length of the sticks. "Is this what you remember?"

Unlike the straight lines of Lydian letters, the marks beguiled the eye, flowing from one elaborate pattern to another. It made it hard to say where one ended and the next began.

"It looks very similar." They didn't quite match the figures Curghann had used, but perhaps that was because they were scored on the wood, not written with a char stick.

She stared at Eldora, silently urging her for permission to

summon her husbands. While she was the first daughter of her age, she could flout clan traditions only so far.

Doubts swam in the pale green eyes of the older woman, wallowed in her indecision, then drowned in a flood of resolution. The keeper of the archives nodded.

Alithia called Taith and Phelan over. "Does that not look like Hurranni letters? I saw Curghann use the like."

Bending forward, Phelan reached for the scroll, his motion stillborn at a warning hiss from Eldora. He tilted his head from side to side, peering at the marks, then froze in an awkward pose as though about to tip over. "This—it's temple script!"

Looking to his sword brother, he pointed at a pattern. "Here, look here. Doesn't it look familiar?"

Taith nodded thoughtfully. "It is, indeed, similar but not quite the script I know."

Alithia couldn't see what Phelan found so exciting about it, but Taith gave a grunt of discovery as he copied Phelan's pose, draping an arm around her shoulders as he bent lower. "*Dainthe*," he murmured thoughtfully. A Hurranni word that meant *fireplace*—or *hearth*.

Her heart leaped. She grabbed Taith's belt, reining in her excitement. That didn't necessarily mean a temple hearth.

"Can you read it?" Eldora's expression warmed, the keeper of the archives lured by the possibility of unlocking the First Record's secrets after ages of mothers had lost the skill.

"You are holding it upside down," Phelan informed her with a boyish smile.

She blinked, then quickly shifted the scroll until Taith and Phelan could hold their heads straight. It left the sticks standing on one end with the bundle unfurling to the left.

The two men leaned closer. Phelan's mouth moved in silence, a finger slowly tracing a line in the air above the scroll. At one point, he stopped and threw a perplexed glance at his sword brother. "Is that what I think it is? *Priests?*" he murmured in Hurranni.

Taith grunted, his brows beetling.

"Well? Can you read it, boy?" Henia perched on the edge of her stool, hope and impatience struggling for control of her features. "What does it say?"

"This portion here tells of commissioning the crafting of a hearth, lady, specifying dimensions and material and payment. The dimensions match those of this hearth." Taith waved toward the cold altar they had just cleansed. From the unsettled expression on his face, her sword husband wasn't entirely forthcoming in his answer. What had stirred his reservations?

"Of course he would say that. It's what you want to hear." Bera's open scorn was scathing, the sneer she swept the chamber with condemning them for gullible fools. "Men only seek to please."

Wearied of the bitter woman's invective, Alithia gave her back to Bera to address the mothers, confident that Taith and Phelan were on guard. "If you have doubts of his reading, why not consult Curghann? He may be better versed in this writing."

Surely the old trader's many springs on retainer to the clan would give his words weight with the mothers that her husbands didn't have?

Twenty-seven

Alithia studied Taith as Dagna walked ahead, leading the way to the hall where the mothers waited to receive Curghann. "Is there something about the First Record you did not want the mothers to know?" she asked in Hurranni, that language feeling more natural for conversation with her husbands.

His head jerked to her at the question. "No, why would you think that?"

"You seemed to have reservations."

Her sword husband looked aside, though there was nothing to see down that corridor. "It is an old scroll, is all." His face was set in resolute lines, definitely unwilling to speak further on the matter.

She glanced at Phelan to see what he made of Taith's manner, but he only frowned back at her, in similar puzzlement, not disapproval nor concern. Whatever lay behind Taith's strange reticence, she could only hope it had nothing to do with rekindling the holy fire.

When they entered the hall through a side door, the old trader was already paying his respects to Astred, Arilde, Henia, and the representatives of the various factions among the mothers, which unfortunately included Bera.

Dagna stopped short of entry, having no place inside unless summoned for an errand. Alithia almost envied her cousin the opportunity to avoid what promised to be a contentious meeting. The sentiment was fleeting; she was too well trained as first daughter to cavil at something this important to the clan's future.

Knowing what she did now of Hurranns, Alithia watched Curghann's intercourse with the mothers with fresh eyes. Despite their worship of the Lady, she had thought Hurranns dominated by men, since she hadn't met any Hurranni women in all the springs she had known the old trader. Now, she noticed the—not deference, but . . . regard. Yes, that was it—the regard he gave the mothers, even Bera, though she interrupted him.

Her husbands' attendance was slowly changing to something similar as they three grew accustomed to marriage. It had started after Taith had given her the necklace, Alithia now realized. Perhaps if they had to return to Hurrann after this, life wouldn't be unsupportable.

She couldn't imagine Taith and Phelan being content to remain in Lydia. From their travels together, she knew they enjoyed the trade too much to set it aside. She couldn't, in good conscience, ask them to do so. Whether the holy fire was rekindled or not, they would have completed their side of the bargain struck at Barda when they pledged themselves to her. To require more of them would be doing them a disservice.

Though she was first daughter, they were her husbands, so pledged before the Lady of Heaven. She had tried to treat them as any Lydian woman would treat her husband but had failed. Their happiness was important to her; she accepted that now.

Curghann looked unchanged from the last time Alithia had seen him, his robes a festive green, the white hair that hung halfway down his back, restrained by two thin braids from his temples, the beads woven into them the sort for warming spells. His face brightened at their arrival, though he said nothing, no doubt mindful of the critical eyes among the mothers. But then his eyes widened with a flash of astonishment to stare at Taith.

As Alithia puzzled over that betrayal of emotion, Bera scowled, pale and ugly with outrage, her nose wrinkled as though she smelled a rotting corpse. "They shouldn't be here, none of them." From her gimlet glare, there was no question whom she held responsible for the ruffling of her sensibilities.

"I am first daughter. It's my right to be present." Alithia raised her chin, defying the older woman to argue otherwise. While Arilde and Astred might support her, she refused to hide behind their skirts. "My husbands stay with me, as is their duty."

Bera's coterie joined her, their tacit support emboldening Arilde's challenger. "Your *husbands*? This *permanent* marriage of yours is an insult to the Goddess. And to suggest the First Record—and by extension our clan—is not Lydian!" She held her head high, her shoulders back, in a pose of self-righteous dignity that struck Alithia as a shade melodramatic.

"Is it?" She tilted her chin skeptically, her heart strangely calm before the bane of her childhood. Perhaps suffering dragons, brigands, tree serpents, and the sometimes overzealous attendance of her husbands had their advantages. "Then our foremothers were heretics who supplied sanctified oils to the Goddess's temple."

The mothers before her inhaled sharply.

Not waiting for them to muster a reply, Alithia walked around Bera's coterie, staying out of arm's reach as she did, to join her mother and grandmother. She didn't look back.

Bera said nothing—Alithia didn't expect her to. The protest had been a matter of form. Her aunt focused her energies on opposing Arilde. As yet, she considered Alithia to be a nuisance at best. Alithia almost looked forward to the day that changed.

Nearly a head taller than Alithia, Astred stood with quiet dignity, alone in the midst of grandmothers. The large ruby of the eldest first daughter nestled on the thin white braids wound around her head gave the impression she wore a priestess's diadem. She greeted Alithia's arrival with a grave nod that withheld judgment, her attention reserved for her husbands. Her grandmother had always had an eye for men, and as Arilde noted, Taith and Phelan were fine specimens of their sex.

"Well played, Granddaughter, and an excellent brace for your efforts." The speculative looks Astred flicked at Alithia's husbands said she complimented her for them, not her *idkhet*. "A canny throw."

"I was fortunate." How fortunate remained to be seen. Taith's confidence in the Lady's generosity had proven correct, thus far. Alithia could only hope the solution to rekindling the holy fire truly lay within the First Record.

And that the mothers would accept Curghann's translation.

Behind her, Bera took her argument to Henia. "There is no need for this. The priestesses of the Goddess can interpret the First Record if it is so important."

"Finally, you want to approach the temple? And what—surrender the clan to their behest? To grow what they tell us to grow? Harvest when they tell us to harvest—when the priestesses' lackeys think we should harvest? To withhold our oils from those they deem unworthy?" Alithia's mother crossed her arms, framing and lifting her still-prime breasts to greater prominence. She turned her gaze to the mothers around Bera. "Do you truly wish that upon our clan, upon your daughters?"

Confidence faltered in some eyes.

Bera threw her chest forward in answer, aggression in every line of her body. "Better that than this heresy."

"Heresy?" Arilde stalked toward her challenger. "Heresy when it comes from the First Record? The words of our own foremothers? You toy with truth, Bera."

The two were of a height, equals in most ways that mattered, their hair woven in the braids of motherhood. Few held the death of her firstborn against Bera, ascribing his fatal illness to misfortune. A number of older aunts of Arilde's age supported Bera—those born the same spring as she and Alithia's mother. The ones with the most to gain if Arilde lost influence, that was Bera's coterie, the whisperers of poisonous reason.

Alithia watched the confrontation in silence, painfully conscious of her loose tresses. Though she was a first daughter and thus permitted to observe, this was a matter for mothers.

"You waste our time with your caviling, Bera. This issue must be resolved immediately for the good of the clan." Astred gathered the mothers in the hall with her gaze, the adamant will that had steered the clan for most of Alithia's age demanding and receiving their acquiescence.

The unusual—and successful—display of authority inspired awe. Somehow Alithia doubted she would ever be capable of such when her time came.

Despite the open dissension, Curghann betrayed no curiosity, his control of his body absolute. Like the canny merchant he was, he waited for the mothers to open negotiations and reveal their hand.

Astred now turned to him, her manner softening. "We have in our possession a record in writing unknown to us. It has come to our attention that you may be able to read it." She waved Eldora forward. "Of your kindness, would you make the attempt?"

The first crack in the old trader's even mien was a sudden quirk of his bushy, white brows when the keeper of the archives revealed the First Record. His eyes blazed with sudden emotion. "Why, that is a temple scroll! Where did you get it? How did it come into your hands?"

At his words, disconcertment flashed across the faces of the mothers present. "Temple scroll?" Henia repeated from behind three fingers. "Are you certain of this?"

Curghann stared at her, his jaw slack at the question. "The red lacquering is unmistakable."

"We have never seen such in the temple." Astred smoothed back a tendril that dared fall free of her circlet of braids.

"Forgive my ambiguity. Such scrolls are used in the temples of the Lady of Heaven. One of my sons is bound to a priestess. I know temple scrolls well. You wish me to read this?" The old trader's gaze darted toward Alithia, his black eyes puzzled.

"If you are able."

Eldora surrendered the First Record reluctantly, hovering as if tempted to snatch it back.

He handled the scroll with reverence, laying it on the table at the same aspect that Phelan had said was correct, then carefully unrolling a hand's length. Resting his hands on either side, he bent over the lacquered sticks, squinting at the scratched figures.

Alithia smiled at the corroboration of her speculation and consigned herself to patience. A display of anything else would gain her only discredit in the mothers' eyes.

Taith drew her back to rest against him, whether for comfort or concealment, she couldn't tell. Her husbands were doing their best to blend into the hall's mosaicked walls.

At last, the old trader sighed, his shoulders easing. He raised his head to Eldora and laid the tips of his hands on sticks he had exposed. "These laths are the end of the record."

The keeper of the records reared back as if he had slapped her. The portion he indicated was the start as the sticks were numbered. The accepted wisdom was that that much understanding as least had been retained of the First Record.

He pointed to some figures. "From here, it tells of the decision to establish an altar in the house that would be raised in this new land."

New land? The words flew through the hall on the wings of murmur.

"New land, yes. There is a reference to the granting of property to the clan. The priestess of the time commissioned a certain clan Clawfield to build—"

Astred clapped her hands, cutting through his discourse. "While your success delights, we do not need to know how much the altar cost or how it was built. Suffice that it was. What we need to know is how the holy fire was kindled."

Though disappointment marred the old trader's face at the scorning of his scholarly zeal, he nodded understanding. Provided with parchment, he copied some figures, the fluid motion of his char stick confirming his claim of familiarity with what he called temple script—as had Phelan. The thoughtful frown as he tapped his chin with the char stick then absently rubbed off the consequent mark with the back of his fist was a comfort to Alithia, a reminder of childhood afternoons spent nibbling sweetmeats and listening to the old trader's lectures on Hurranni, and in turn, declining nouns and conjugating verbs.

When Curghann finally set down the char stick, it was with a sigh. "Lady, there are few specifics. It may be that certain rituals were presumed to be known to all and thus not recorded, or it is here but beyond my meager capacity to understand."

"Speak of what you read, then."

He combed his fingers through his wispy beard and consulted the parchment. "The clan gathered in the new sanctuary to stand as witness. Before the new altar, the priestess and her priests offered a sacrifice, and their celebration of life ignited the holy fire."

Taith stiffened behind her, his arms suddenly tight.

Consternation showed on the mothers' faces, their expressions reflecting Alithia's own emotions. A sacrifice and the ritual concluded with a celebration of life?

How would—

Of course!

Alithia's heart raced as her thoughts leaped, chasing the scent of inspiration that was almost divination. During the pledging in Barda, she had sensed a Presence within her—the Goddess, or so she had thought. But the power they summoned had sealed their pledge—their *idkhet* had changed form then, lengthening and narrowing to fit their forearms. She had felt that same Presence in Sentinel Reach—the Voice of the Blood Claim. Had heard that same Voice when she used the second mystery.

Had that Presence truly been the Lady of Heaven?

Was that power how the holy fire had been kindled, back in the days of their foremothers?

If they raised a similar power, would it rekindle the Fire?

Confusion erupted throughout the hall as the mothers argued over meaning, but Alithia paid them no mind. Deep inside, she knew what had to be done.

Opposition came from an unexpected quarter.

Twenty-eight

Stunned by the announcement, Taith stared at their wife, amazed that she could propose such an enterprise. "Out of the question!"

All those women . . .

Air came in shuddering heaves, his chest tight—as though a gargant had its snout around him. "Even for our pledging, only the Lady and the Horned Lords witnessed the completion."

"For the rededication of the clan altar, there is no way I can convince my mother and grandmother—let alone Bera and the rest of the mothers—to leave the sanctuary." Alithia had waited until they were back in her rooms before revealing her understanding of what the ritual required: union with the three of them in the roles of priestess and priests. Hearing the explanation in Hurranni did not make it any more palatable.

He traded white-eyed stares with Phelan. Even his shield brother's adventurous spirit quailed at the prospect of bed play before all the women of Alithia's clan.

Their wife sat on the couch, acting for all the world as though her proposal were nothing out of the ordinary. "It is just like the trial. You stripped naked and took your release before the other shield pairs."

Taith swiped cold hands over an equally cold face. "No, that was different."

"How?"

"That was before brethren." There was a level of trust between brethren because of their mutual goal. Too, those shield pairs were kin, which made for stronger confidence. Here, they were among strangers—not that Alithia considered her kin as such.

She rubbed her forehead, deep furrows appearing between her brows. "It is different before the mothers?"

"Of course it is! How could it not be? The trial did not include union!"

Phelan's gaze darted between them, his loyalty torn.

"And—" Taith tugged on his braid. How could Alithia not understand? The thought of displaying himself—of performing such intimacies—before the sort of people he had been raised and trained to protect was . . .

The nightmare of his boyhood.

He could not find the words to explain.

"They are women!"

"So?"

"Men are supposed to protect women, not parade ourselves before them."

Alithia brushed his objection aside with an impatient wave of her hand. "That is of no import. This is the only chance we have to rekindle the holy fire. In a greater sense, this ritual is for my clan's protection."

He stared at Phelan, willing him to talk. Surely his shield brother could think of some argument that would convince their wife not to ask this of them.

But Phelan stayed silent.

"We are not priests." Taith turned to grip the window's edge, blind to the colors of the waking garden. "Cleansing the altar is one thing. This—" He could not help a shudder as he took a deep breath, his nails aching against the granite. "This is entirely something else altogether. We have not the training."

An incredulous laugh answered him. "None of us are trained for this. All we know is it culminates with a celebration of life—and for *that* neither of you have need for training."

A surge of pride silenced Taith at her easy dismissal of any problems he and Phelan might encounter in the ritual. But the feeling was soon overcome by the thought of standing naked before all those women. Their scrutiny would be worse than what they had faced in the baths. Then to have to pleasure Alithia while they watched, with success dependent on performing to the Lady's satisfaction?

"I never aspired to the priesthood. I saw the dissatisfaction of my shield father and want no sip of that cup." That was the closest he could come to confessing his cowardice.

Phelan blinked at the declaration. They'd known each other for more than half their lives—with nearly ten turns of that as a shield pair. He'd have said he knew Taith well, that nothing his sword brother did could have surprised him, but he'd never suspected he harbored such reservations. "Dissatisfaction?"

"He wanted the road, the trade. It was what he enjoyed most." Taith ran his fingers along the windowsill. "But Mother was already being trained as a priestess."

That was why Taith's shield father had spent so much time with them discussing routes and what sold well and where? Had trained them in sword, axe, and knife? Why Taith had slipped away from the temple every chance he got?

He understood better now why his sword brother had welcomed the chance of pledging to a southern wife.

"But I am not." Alithia stared at Taith's back, her arms wrapped around herself. "This is just to rededicate the altar."

Phelan wanted to go to her, to assure her of their support. His heart yearned to embrace her. But selfishness held him back, that and sympathy for Taith's position.

"It is the first step." Taith turned to them with a bleak smile. "Why else would my mother have given me that necklace? I had five brothers older than me and three younger; she could have chosen one of them—or one of the children in the temple."

Frustration drew Alithia's mouth tight, the corners staked down. "You are willing to die to protect me—but not do this?"

"If we die in battle," Phelan gritted, "we won't have to face your disappointment after."

Her face cleared, a thoughtful look in her eyes. "You do not have anything to worry about. And once they see you, they will stop wondering why we are still married. Since you are my husbands, they cannot insist you share their beds."

A cold wind blew through him at her words, colder than any blast from that frozen wasteland they'd crossed.

Wondering why we are still *married?*

Could the mothers of her clan unmarry them? She'd spoken of contracts—*marriages*—ending without issue. It wasn't the thought of clan Black Python's shock and disappointment at such an unprecedented loss of wife that chilled him, but the prospect of not waking with Alithia in their arms, not seeing her curled up in thought, not having her scowl at them in outrage at their overprotectiveness, not see her face light up with happiness.

He gripped his *idkhet*, the warm metal beneath his fingers of little reassurance. Surely the Lady wouldn't allow such, not when She had blessed their bond?

And yet—

At the baths, Alithia's kinswomen had dismissed them as mere pleasure loves, unworthy of being Alithia's husbands. He shivered at the memory of those covetous hands, touching him as though they had every right when only Alithia and Taith did.

Anger flared. To have come so far, only to lose Alithia?

Taith's eyes bored into his, warning him to leash his temper. His sword brother had the right of it. Their wife had done nothing to earn his anger. But reining it in was difficult, like swallowing gravel. Phelan paced, a hand tight around his sword, the leather strips wrapped around the hilt a familiar roughness that helped steady him.

"Still married?" Taith repeated, to Phelan's relief, as he couldn't seem to get his throat to work.

"That would be how they would see it." Alithia looked away. "Even Arilde."

Had her mother objected? Fresh worry stoked his anger.

"Do you want to . . . *end the contract*?"

Phelan couldn't believe his ears—Taith had said the last in Lydian. There was no mistaking his meaning; the words didn't have the same nuance in their own tongue. The idea of ending a marriage didn't exist in Hurranni, not even after death. The survivors continued to wear their *idkhet* to honor the memory of the one they'd lost. Ending the contract in the Lydian sense would mean . . . that they had never pledged at all?

"No!" Alithia spun back, her expression one of open horror.

Thank the Lady!

"But the—the mothers of your clan don't believe we should be your husbands?"

A careless wave dismissed the objections of her elders, but her averted gaze roused unease. "They can express concern all they want, but they cannot censure me. I entered into the contract for the good of the clan, with the full support of my mother and grandmother. Only a small faction would cause trouble, and rekindling the holy fire will silence them."

Phelan could imagine what would happen if Alithia failed in

her quest: the objections raised, the concerns . . . the doubts. That matron who was so hostile would gain influence. Then would come more opposition, questioning Alithia's judgment, undermining her authority. What kind of future was that to offer their wife? How happy would any of them be, knowing that Taith's and his refusals had brought it upon them?

His anger died, leaving only regret and guilt in its ashes. All this time, he'd tried to draw his sword brother out, to get him to express his desires. Yet now that Taith had taken a stand, Phelan couldn't support him.

"And if the ritual fails to rekindle the Fire?"

A brave but tremulous smile crooked her mouth, the sight of it tugging at his heart. "Then we can go into imports. The clan will need another source of income to replace the temple trade, so Curghann will just have to suffer more competition."

But she would fight tooth and claw before she let it come to pass. That was her entire purpose for traveling to Hurrann.

Could they do any less?

He looked to his sword brother. By the unhappy resignation on his face, Taith had already come to the same decision. They had to help Alithia. However much performing such intimacies before women might embarrass them, however much his sword brother might dislike acting as priest, they had to do it.

Taith turned to their wife, his shoulders braced, accepting unpleasant duty the only way he knew—completely. "You should know that what is expected of this celebration of life is not simply bed play. The priestess—you—offers up the pleasure gathered in the rite, as much pleasure as can be gathered. The gathering of pleasure—that is the sacrifice."

Stunned by the revelation, Phelan stared at Taith. "You mean all that gossip about secret rituals wasn't just idle chatter?" Priestesses and priests truly did perform bed play as sacrifice behind the closed doors of the sanctuary?

"We do not speak of it." His sword brother gave him a forbidding look that discouraged further questions, picking up his great axe to run a finger along one blade. He'd probably reach for his whetstone any moment now.

A weight like a gargant's foot settled on Phelan's belly. Now he understood why Taith had never wanted to become a priest despite growing up in Crescent Bay's temple. If he'd known this could happen, would he have been so eager to win Alithia's bond?

Twenty-nine

Taith struggled to ignore their audience, to forget everything but Alithia. It was hard and more than hard. Their training taught them to always be aware of their surroundings to protect their wife. Danger could come from anywhere. Even here in the bosom of her clan, Alithia had her enemies. He had seen the abiding hatred in the eyes of the matron she named Bera.

It did not help that formal robes had been found for them—heavy silk, thankfully in the bright blue of lapis, not some shade of red or gray, but similar enough to priests' robes that wearing them made the back of his neck itch. Taith's actually fit his shoulders—a miracle in itself, according to Phelan. He disliked what they represented.

He reined back a sigh. A night's sleep had done little to reconcile him to the necessity of this rite. But Alithia needed them to perform this sacrifice—to celebrate life before the mothers of her clan. He, too, needed to do this, to prove himself worthy of their wife's trust . . . and to face his boyhood aversion of priesthood.

He had spent half his life trying to avoid temple service; it was time he stopped running.

Alithia stood so straight and brave before the cold altar, in the dress she had worn for their pledging, her gaze upraised to where the flames would reach if the holy fire burned above the hearth, the beads at her breast glowing like low embers, as they would for any priestess. The tablet of mysteries at her feet seemed to glow as well, the obsidian slab a square of pulsing blackness.

They had not dared leave it in her rooms. Even discounting the tablet's purpose in ritual, the *mythir* daggers were a temptation for thieves, and the matron who led Alithia's guards had refused to detail anyone to watch it, pointing out that the guards' duty was to ensure Alithia's safety. But perhaps the tablet was supposed to be here as well and not simply the second mystery.

He could not help a spike of pride amidst the strangling panic that wound tight around his chest. Though he had never wished to serve as a priest, there was rightness in standing by Alithia's side that he could not deny.

"O Lady Most High, we are come here before You and Your husbands to dedicate this altar to Your worship."

A start of surprise went through Alithia's kin, young and old, consternation twisting the features of those in Taith's sight. A small frown crossed her grandmother's brow, though she kept her silence.

Their wife paid them no heed—as she should not, for this rite was dedicated to the Lady of Heaven, Who Alithia speculated may also be the Goddess of Lydia. Confidence woke in his heart at her unswerving gaze, the unwavering certainty she displayed before her entire clan, so dedicated was she to their welfare.

He straightened his spine, drawing strength from Alithia's promise that whatever happened, she intended to hold them to their bonds. Keeping him and Phelan as her husbands was her choice, and her strength of purpose would see them through, no matter what her elders wanted.

Despite all the people within, the sanctuary held a touch of coolness he associated with the Lady's gift. How could they not feel it?

Alithia chanted the prayers calling the attention of the Lady of Heaven and the Horned Lords to this place. They had worked long into the night refreshing their memories of the prayers, then teaching their wife the proper cadences and intonations used by the priestesses—a task made more frustrating by their lower voices.

Priests had their own chants, blending with but not repeating the priestess's invocation. Even concentrating on the privileged words, he could not ignore the pallet before the altar—there for their use when he had hoped pledging would be the only time he would have need for one in a sanctuary. Only a priest lay before an altar more than once in his life.

As one, he and Phelan knelt and, still kneeling, raised the tablet of mysteries to their wife's hand. Phelan had insisted on the formality, arguing its necessity in a ritual unknown to Alithia's clan and conjured from beyond the mists of memory.

She plucked the second mystery without hesitation and set the tiny dagger to her scar. Holding her hand above the hearth, she pressed down.

Taith held his breath. This time, no rush of power answered to reassure them of the rightness of their actions.

A single drop of blood emerged from the wound, a red bead that trembled on the tip of the *mythir* blade for a heartbeat, then fell.

The instant it stuck the hearth, power swirled around them, the cool breeze of the Lady's gift stirring their robes and lifting tresses left unbound.

He shivered at Her touch and the strange sensation of his hair rising off his back and baring his neck, his heart stuttering as it never had in battle. There could be no doubt they had the attention of the Lady of Heaven. From the awestruck expressions of Alithia's kin, they, too, felt Her presence.

Together, he and Phelan set down the tablet and stood, sharing a white-eyed look of unease. Even his shield brother was not so mush-headed as to welcome the next step.

Forcing his features to a calm he did not feel, Taith shed his robes, the last barrier between himself and the mothers of Alithia's clan. The heavy silk slid off his shoulders with only a whisper to mark its departure.

Murmurs rose when he and Phelan bared themselves, whispers too soft to make out, a rustling like pine needles sliding underfoot, treacherous to walk upon. Yet he had to ignore that inkling of danger, the roiling of his gut, to focus on the ritual. Their wife was relying on them to do their part, and he would not disappoint her.

Mustering desire before all the eyes around them was even more difficult. His blade was as limp as a dead eel, unresponsive from the avid press of attention and expectation. This was worse than the most wretched of his boyhood nightmares of priestly service.

Alithia laid her hands on their wrists, her grip commanding their attention.

Welcoming the contact, Taith stared at her face and the pale slopes left bare below her necklace, willing his blade to respond. It remained flaccid, his rocks shriveled in protest. Doubt assailed him. Nothing good could come of that.

With a smile of understanding, Alithia curved her arms around his neck and drew him down into her perfumed embrace, her hair sweet with the oil of some flower he could not name. Taith sank to his knees, sank into the determination in their wife's sea blue gaze. Confidence glowed in her eyes, absolute trust in him and Phelan, her belief pure and unshaken.

Submitting to her urging, he pressed his mouth to hers and drank deep of her certainty. He immersed himself in her taste, a warm sweetness that was uniquely Alithia. She filled his senses, commanding his attention with her kiss. Her tongue seduced him, compelled he answer with his own, engaging him in a delicious duel. A lick, a stroke, a lash—pure temptation and entirely irresistible. She pressed herself against him, the soft comfort of her breasts awakening memories of long nights of rapture and breathless release and the sublime clasp of her possession.

Delight shivered through him, and he forgot himself and all else that was not Alithia. Their wife. His love.

The sight of Taith kissing their wife awakened hope in Phelan as his sword brother's honest ardor grew. If Taith could ignore their audience, perhaps he could, too—though how his sword brother was doing it, Phelan couldn't imagine. He was acutely aware of the eyes bent on them, critical and covetous. Waiting to challenge Alithia's claim on their bonds.

"You are thinking too much again, Mush head, tying yourself in knots." Perhaps that was the secret of it. Don't think, don't give the doubts room to take root. Trust in the Lady to see them through in safety. She had led them this far.

His blade stirred as he watched his sword brother's large hands glide over their wife's familiar curves, swelling with every beat of his heart. His hands itched to follow those same trails, to cherish this woman and no other. She was another gift of the Lady, a wife they could be proud to be bound to, and he didn't intend to fail her. Whatever happened, this ritual was a confirmation of their pledge.

One step was all it took. He was committed, and suddenly it was that easy.

Pushing aside Alithia's floating tresses, Phelan wrapped his arms around wife and sword brother. The musk of their desire enveloped him, both lure and reward—sensual invitation and heady intoxication all in itself. But he couldn't give in, someone had to remember their purpose . . .

The sacrifice. To rededicate the altar of Alithia's clan to the Lady with a celebration of life and rekindle the holy fire.

Yes, that was it.

Phelan reached between Alithia and Taith to untie her laces, his task made more difficult by the hot flesh against his hands, tempted by memory to raise his hands and fondle the soft mounds above them—or turn them and stroke the hard chest pressed to their wife's breasts. Unfortunately, either motion risked distracting Taith when his sword brother needed to focus on their wife.

But once the laces were released, he discovered another hindrance. Brushing his lips down the side of Alithia's neck, he whispered, "I need your arms down."

Thankfully, their wife wasn't so lost in the kiss that she didn't hear him. She lowered her arms in turn, not releasing Taith, but allowing Phelan to slide her sleeves off and her dress with them.

Taith took immediate advantage. His hands roamed her back, stroking bare skin, his so dark against her fairness.

Following his example, Phelan dropped to one knee to nibble on her shoulder and couldn't suppress a shiver as her hair billowed across his body with almost knowing insistence.

He leaned into her, seeking pleasure. The double caress of wife and sword brother sent a spike of delight to his rocks, a familiar sensation from all their nights of bed play.

Then he remembered Taith's description of sacrifice.

Delight rippled through Alithia at the touch of her husbands, their knowing hands and the press of their bodies fanning the flames of her passion. Pride swelled inside her at their valiantness. She had forced this on them, pushed hard for their agreement, yet they displayed none of their reluctance, doing their utmost to support her.

This sacrifice was one she would never forget.

Her channel moistened, aching with readiness, her folds already swollen and spread, anticipation a potent philter. Goddess heat suffused her, coursing through her veins and blending with the heat of her husbands' bodies. Sinking her fingers into Taith's hair, she poured her need into their kiss.

Phelan's hands trailed down her sides and slid to her inner thighs, so fleeting they might have been the breeze. But as they rose higher, their touch firmed, parting her wet folds with sure confidence and testing her welcome.

She thrust her hips into his caress, eager for the next step in the great dance—one unlike any they had danced before. A nudge from him, and she widened her stance, anticipating what would come. They had no time for slow, lingering play.

The blunt tip of his shaft grazed her cleft, featherlight, teasing contact, then the true rush of breath-stealing entry, reaching so deep inside her that he nudged the center of her being. He pumped his hips, setting a rapid pace that jolted her body and ground her against Taith.

Passion spiked, a surge of need that flooded the center of her being. Pleasure erupted with unexpected suddenness. Alithia cried out, startled by the torrent of molten sensation. Her legs trembled as Phelan slipped free.

Dropping to his haunches, Taith caught her as she fell. She landed straddling his lap, his turgid shaft between them. But he did nothing more than resume kissing her, leaving it to her when to take him and as much of him as she would.

As she guided her sword husband into her, Phelan scooped up a robe from the side of the pallet. "Remember this?" he whispered just before he set silk along her back, the contact sparking inordinate delight. The internal stroking of Taith's shaft combined with Phelan's silken caresses fanned her desire to blistering.

Taith and Phelan took turns filling her, neither one leaving her to the other, changing places only to regain their control. Intent on driving her to madness. They combined their caresses, their kisses passionate, not seeking release for themselves—that, too, was part of the sacrifice.

Goddess heat overwhelmed her, ecstasy flooding her veins, a scalding wave of raw pleasure tumbling over her in a fury of rapture. Another climax, then another, as her husbands continued to lick and suck and thrust. Each one following on the heels of what came before. It was like their trial all over again, all that glory sweeping through her in an endless parade of release.

How could any woman survive such ecstasy?

Alithia gave herself up to their attendance. Each thrust stoked the hunger inside her, fanning the flames of sultry power. Then she felt it begin. Rising from the center of her being, that ineffable Presence that had filled her before.

That fullness. That vastness.

She hadn't understood before.

Goddess heat blazed within her—yet not the Goddess. The Lady of Heaven.

Another surge of exquisite pleasure, and her senses flared.

Once again, she stood on the edge of a cliff looking down into an eternity of stars.

The essence of power. A conflagration of the senses poised to consume her.

She pressed her hands to her chest, over her heart drumming so hard she feared it would leap out. The beads shone between her fingers—

No, her hands, arms—her whole body glowed as though lit from within. An alabaster lamp wrought in flesh.

Taith and Phelan seemed to share that inner glow, though darkly, their skin burnished to a brighter bronze than torchlight could explain.

Her glow reflected in Taith's eyes as he gave her a fierce smile. "Yes." Clearly he expected this to happen. Another of his non-warnings to shield her from fear of failure. He brushed kisses up her arm and along her shoulder with complete disregard for the light emanating from her, withholding nothing from the sacrifice.

On a rush of emotion, Alithia caught her sword husband by the hair and tugged him up to kiss him. In each their own way, he and Phelan took such good care of her—perhaps better than she deserved.

But the power pouring into her soon swept her up in a torrid wave of glory that went on and on, filling her with more. She gasped at the pool of stars that continued to widen at her feet, waiting for her to fall. Her heart leaped. This had to be it. There had to be enough of the Lady's gift here to kindle the holy fire.

All that was left was for her to release it.

Gladly. She didn't think she could hold any more.

Hold, daughter.

The reproach in the Voice reined back her burgeoning ecstasy. Alithia shuddered. Surely she couldn't. She was swollen with power. Too much. Surely her skin would split open.

With every kiss and thrust, every lick and caress, Taith and Phelan built her pleasure higher. Brighter. Hotter. Honing its edge to greater keenness.

The Presence within her *burned*.

She screamed, unable to contain the power pounding inside her. No woman could hope to embody the Lady of Heaven. And still her husbands stroked her. She shook with the immensity of Her presence, incapable of denial. Bound to the ritual, she could not stop them even in her extremity.

Why?

Do not your husbands deserve a reward for their sacrifice?

The sacrifice was sum of their efforts—all three of them. For the ritual to succeed, culmination meant release for all, not hers alone.

This time when Phelan came to her, she rode him on the pallet, frantic in her necessity. Flames seemed to lick at her skin, burning through mere flesh.

"Alithia?"

"Now." She writhed around him, using her channel to urge him to release. As he gasped, she found that spot behind the base of his shaft and rubbed.

Gaping at her in surprise, Phelan gave himself up into her keeping, his body tensing under her. Exaltation transformed his face as he took his release with a shout of joy, all his cares erased. With a final jerk of his hips, heat bathing the center of her being, he fell back to the pallet, completely spent. In his surrender, he looked springs younger.

His ecstasy served to magnify the power within Alithia. She panted, struggling against her mortal weakness to hold it in. She could not take the final step in the great dance—not yet.

Taith wrapped his arms around her waist and drew her back and off Phelan, reaching between her thighs to set his shaft at her cleft.

"Hard and fast," she urged him with what little voice she could force past her throat. Power beat on her senses, drowning her in Goddess heat. Too much. She needed release.

Obedient to her instructions, he drove into her, fingers biting into her hips as he held her in place for his shafting, in and out with forceful insistence. The pressure within bloomed to breathless intensity. She pushed back against him, meeting his thrusts in carnal dance, a wild fling up the dizzying heights of pleasure.

With a groan, Taith ground himself against her, burying himself to the hilt, his thumb finding her bud and adding that final spark to the conflagration of her senses.

Yes.

Power rushed out of her in a torrent of primal pleasure. She screamed in relief and triumph, ineffable rapture flinging her through the stars.

A hollow roar answered her, sensual warmth banishing the ghost of winter chill in the sanctuary.

Alithia collapsed on top of Phelan, Taith landing on top of

her, his shaft sliding free of her quivering channel. Her heart thundered, her body its drum, her bones shuddering to its roar.

Her flesh was hers once more, not sheath to indescribable power, the beads of her necklace no longer ablaze with color. Relief was a tremor that started at her fingertips and quickly spread throughout her body.

"By the Horned Lords." Phelan stared, sparks reflecting from his wide eyes.

Mustering her last drops of strength, she turned her head.

Fire burned in the altar—the holy fire!—red flames leaping high and putting the torches to shame, the sanctuary restored to its proper light.

They had succeeded.

The knowledge stole the dregs of Alithia's energy. She closed her eyes and laid her head on Phelan's heaving chest, using him for a pillow while Taith served as blanket. They were enough. Her husbands were all she needed.

Silence surrounded them, an awestruck quiet so profound she could hear the dancing of the holy fire. Her euphoria kindled the hope that it would last.

She should have known better.

"Sacrilege!"

In her daze, Alithia barely made sense of the shout. The depth of emotion imbued in the word should have frightened her, but she could scarcely twitch her fingers. Blessedly, Phelan understood that feeble motion, pushing himself up and lifting her with him. Only his support got her upright. Taith held himself above her, his attention on the scene behind them.

Bera stormed out of a cluster of similarly perturbed mothers, her white shawl spreading wide like an erne's outstretched wings. "How can you countenance the desecration of the Goddess's hearth?"

Astred drew herself up to her full height, pulling her dignity around her like a cloak of age, the ruby on her braids sparkling like the Fire Heart of the Diadem. "I believe the Goddess has given ample demonstration of Her approval." She extended a thin hand to indicate the Fire.

Red splotches dotted Bera's cheeks, her nostrils flaring as her breasts heaved and her knuckles whitened across her fists. "The Goddess?! They invoked the Lady of Heaven and the Horned Lords! Hurranni deities have nothing to do with the Goddess."

A flinch rippled through her audience, piercing Alithia's languor with foreboding.

"See! Now, they understand—"

"If the Goddess disapproved, surely She would have struck down Alithia during the ritual." Arilde crossed her arms under her breasts, uncaring that she had interrupted Bera. "The holy fire has been rekindled—through no action of yours. Have the grace to accept the truth."

Bera's face paled, her gray eyes erupting with venomous fury. "No, I refuse to be party to this!" Darting to the altar, she snatched up the tablet of mysteries at its foot and brandished it above her head. "This is the root of your heresy. I will not permit it to continue."

With a gasp, Alithia tried to move, to lunge to her feet, to stop what was about to happen—but her limbs were weighed down with lassitude, spent from the sacrifice, her body tender from her husbands' attentions. Taith and Phelan caught her up in their arms, their first instinct to shield her.

Bera swung down, a sneer of triumph twisting her features.

The flames leaped up, spilling from the hearth, engulfing the slab and the older woman, the last thing Alithia saw before Phelan landed on top of her and Taith. Heat billowed out, sweltering, suffocating, pressing on them like a heavy hand.

Fear seared her. *Taith! Phelan!* At that moment of terror-fraught darkness, her only thought was for her husbands—not clan, mother, or grandmother.

Only them.

"Red Lord!" Phelan's voice, shocked, but not hurt.

In the next breath, the punishing heat was gone.

Simple warmth replaced it, a balm to the senses.

For a while longer, Alithia clung to her husbands, her heart as unsettled as the sea after a waterspout's passage. Thank the Goddess they were unharmed.

Then she remembered.

The tablet of mysteries! The focus of seasons of travel and effort, of the risks Taith and Phelan had taken—that had almost cost Taith's life.

She didn't want to look at the hearth and see the destruction Bera had wrought. Only the sure knowledge of Taith's and Phelan's safety gave her the strength to urge them off her, and even then she nearly averted her eyes.

The Fire had subsided, its red flames dancing between the crystal shields as though nothing unusual had happened. The hearth was intact in the arms of the tripod.

But the tablet was nowhere to be seen. Claimed by the Lady. For though Alithia stared, she saw no shards around the altar nor any *mythir* daggers, which surely there would have been if Bera had succeeded in shattering the tablet of mysteries.

Someone screamed.

Bera's coterie was staring with open horror at . . . the hearth? Something beyond the hearth?

Alithia rolled over to see what transfixed their attention and recoiled at the sight, clutching at Taith's arm around her waist for strength.

It was Bera. And yet not.

Her hair was gone. The long, blond braids that proclaimed her motherhood, her haughty brows were no more, without even stubble to show where they had been. Instead, a black flame smirched the middle of her forehead—death's hand, the mark of the Crone.

The Goddess—or the Lady—had passed judgment on Bera.

By the black flame, she was now the Crone's—stricken from the clan's rolls, cast out, and divested of all possessions—to await the end of her days, however long that might be. The temple had the charge of those so claimed. No one would raise a hand against them, but to one and all, they were as already dead.

Epilogue

Taith fancied the air was warmer, the Lady smiling down at them. Even the voices coming from the garden sounded more cheerful. Truth be told, his own heart felt lighter, now that the sacrifice was over and done and the matron who had held such enmity for Alithia sent to the temple of the Goddess of Lydia, the fangs of those who had supported her drawn.

"Priests? Us? Who'd've ever imagined?" Sitting on the balcony rail, Phelan shook his head in bemusement.

"You, I am not surprised, not with the attraction the temple held for you. But I . . . I was never so inclined."

But looking back, it was as though every step, every decision he had made—from his boyhood rebellion and his choice of Phelan as his shield brother, his acceptance of his mother's necklace, and on—had led him to this point. To Alithia and clan Redgrove. Guided by the Lady. Was that why his priestess mother had given him her necklace?

"Does this make a difference? The holy fire has been rekindled. I have accomplished what I set out to do. But we have never really spoken of what we would do . . . after." Alithia was trying to appear dispassionate, but the fingers stroking her necklace gave away her worry.

Normally outspoken, Phelan was unwontedly silent.

A surge of deep, abiding love welled up inside Taith, its strength stealing his voice. He found a smile on his lips, albeit a crooked one. He was no Horned Lord to defy Her, and he wanted believe he was too pragmatic to spite himself. "It seems Lydia is where the Lady wishes us to be. We will just have to find something to do."

"Stay here? Are you sure?" Alithia blinked rapidly, her eyes suspiciously misty. "We could return to Hurrann, resume your trading. We do not have to remain here if you do not wish."

Taith's heart melted at the offer. Never had he expected a woman to consider her husbands' preferences. Despite her responsibility to her clan, she was willing to leave them and turn trader for his and Phelan's sakes, to face dragons and brigands and tree serpents anew. She would choose them over her own kin! That she even considered making such a sacrifice only proved the rightness of his decision.

"Lydia is where you belong, and our place is beside you." It surprised him to realize he meant exactly that. Nothing in Hurrann drew him as much as their wife, and he had no wish to risk losing her to the wilds of their homeland.

"You're sure this is what you want?" Phelan frowned at him. "You wouldn't be dissatisfied?" Clearly he was thinking of Taith's shield father.

"The Lady's trees are about to flower. That is a good omen, I think. You thought we would miss it."

His shield brother scowled. "Be serious, Taith."

"I am. I tried running from the temple most of my life—and look where it got me."

Phelan smiled at Taith's adamant statement.

"What of you?"

"Me?"

"You would be happy to remain amidst all this quiet and bleakness?"

His shield brother gaped at him, his eyes darting in embarrassment toward Alithia. "I was hasty. *Budtime* should be different. As you said, the Lady's trees will bloom."

Alithia stared at them, concern still furrowing her brows. "If you have a change of heart, we can always go back."

Taith scooped her up into his arms and hugged her tight, the joy of his spirit spilling over into delighted laughter. "What a wife! Surely there could be none better for us."

Unlike his shield father, he knew he had his wife's and shield brother's support whatever happened.

Alithia clung to him as he spun around, unable to restrain his elation. "Taith!"

Grinning, Phelan came to her rescue, throwing his arms around them both, his weight dragging Taith to a standstill. "Now you're acting the mush head."

Taith denied the accusation with a quick shake of his head. "Merely showing proper gratitude. We have been blessed with an exceptional wife." He kissed Alithia, trying to convey in that paltry salute all the love and joy rampaging inside him. When he raised his head, her cheeks were gratifyingly flushed as her eyes fluttered open.

"So you are happy with this?"

"At least it is just a shrine, not a temple." Taith shrugged in belated abashment at his lack of restraint. It might have been proper gratitude, but he was not accustomed to handling their wife so indiscriminately outside of bed play.

Alithia did not seem to hold his loss of control against him, leaning into him as she turned to his shield brother. "Phelan?"

He, too, kissed her, drawing her into his embrace for a slow cherishment. No one could doubt his shield brother's sincerity when he released her. "It's a feasible solution, I think. You needn't worry on our behalf."

Still holding Alithia within the circle of his arms, Phelan looked to Taith, the pleasure in his eyes dimming. "We'll have to inform Devyn we're not coming back."

Taith suffered a twinge of regret at the reminder. They had been through so much with their crew. "There was always a chance we would decide to remain. They will not be surprised." Still, he would miss Devyn and their brethren.

A faint hint of perfume from the Lady's trees tickled Phelan's nostrils with promise. Anticipation raised its head, emboldened by their wife's and his sword brother's happiness. A new city to discover and sights to see. He was more than ready to bid farewell to the snow season. Anything else had to be better than the Gray Lord's hells, but snow was a minor inconvenience, if they were happy.

Alithia pulled free of his embrace, eager to be about her business. She glanced down the garden toward the sanctuary, where even now her clan elders were making haste to prepare for whatever they did to produce their oils, then turned to her rooms—their rooms, now. By the light in her eyes, it was clear to Phelan she'd thought of something.

"What now?"

She dug through the bags remaining to be unpacked, then with a cry of triumph brandished a leather bundle—the moon blossom seeds Phelan had collected for her. "The next thing I have to do is plant these. Where would they grow best?"

He smiled in delight at his gift's reappearance. She'd remembered; after all the fortnights of travel, he'd forgotten about them. "They'd do well among the Lady's trees, I think." The crescents belonged by the flame, after all. Just as Taith and he belonged with her.

Another reminder of home and the promise of color—an end to the bleakness. His heart felt ready to take flight as they followed their wife down to the garden.

Until faced with the possibility of never seeing Hurrann again, he hadn't realized how much he depended on returning home to the Lady's Hills and the Black Python clan house in between their travels. He whom Taith called intrepid—and at times reckless to a fault—longing for the sights of home! The irony wasn't lost to him. At least he would have this.

And he gained so much more—the love he'd dreamed of between wife and husbands.

Alithia led them to the heart of the grove, to where the pale great roots of the Lady's trees rose like buttresses, living walls more than a man's height and nearly as broad. The ground underfoot was soft from leaf litter, the familiar sensation comforting. If he didn't see the distant walls of the clan house, he might imagine they were in Black Python holdings. They could sling an awning across the roots—as he'd done as a boy—and sleep in comfort within the grove; perhaps he'd suggest it when the Lady's trees bloomed. The prospect made an already beautiful day brighter.

Taith stood guard while Phelan helped Alithia plant the black seeds in the damp soil around the trees. His sword brother had changed since their pledging. There was an ease to his stance, an openness, that hadn't been there before. That fire that Phelan had known was there now made occasional appearances. He doubted Taith would ever put his desires ahead of theirs, but at least now he expressed them.

Who could've imagined they'd find what they had with a southern wife?

"You should pray over them," Taith advised from where he sat on an exposed root, his axe resting across his thighs.

"Pray?" Alithia repeated.

"Consign them to the Lady's attention."

"I suppose it would do no harm." Despite the concession,

their wife gave his sword brother a doubtful look, clearly still uncomfortable seeking the aid of the Lady of Heaven instead of the Lydian Goddess.

What are you about? Phelan mouthed the question at Taith as their wife knelt, cupping her hands over a tiny mound of soil, visibly bracing herself to call power.

His sword brother merely smiled and shook his head, hoarding his secrets.

A cool breeze swirled around Alithia—not the bitter, bone-numbing chill he now associated with ice and the snow season, but the welcome kiss of power. The ends of her hair stirred then rose, blown into the air by the Lady's gift. The malachite beads on her necklace glowed the bright green of sunlight through thick leaves.

Alithia's lips moved as power continued to surround her, her eyes shutting out the rest of the world. After a while, the power subsided, leaving the air smelling somehow cleaner and more vibrant.

When she lifted her hands, green shoots were poking out of the soil. She startled at the sight, nearly falling over before Phelan steadied her. "How . . . ?"

Taith smiled that indulgent smile of his, once again the stolid sword brother. "The spell is akin to healing. The temples always have the best gardens."

Oh, yes. Phelan nodded, finally understanding, and cursed himself for a mush head. He'd forgotten about that.

But Taith wasn't done dispensing advice. "If you pray over the Lady's trees, they will bloom sooner."

Comprehension came in a flash of surprise. "They'll be able to harvest earlier, could—"

Alithia's arms around him cut Phelan's speculation short as she threw her head back and laughed. He didn't mind, though her jubilation leaked a few tears. The latter made his heart trip with trepidation. With embarrassing haste, he got her to stand, gazing at his sword brother to plead for succor.

It was Taith who was the author of her joy, after all, not Phelan. By rights, his sword brother should be the one wiping their wife's tears.

Smiling, Taith slid off his perch to embrace them, the circle of his arms more than wide enough to encompass Alithia and him.

Phelan savored the happy moment, secure in knowledge of Taith's and Alithia's contentment. Her clan would be safe. That was what she'd set out to do, and she'd succeeded—with their help. Taith and he would make a place for themselves in Lydia, and whatever happened, they'd be at the side of their wife.

Even now, it seemed the fragrance from the trees was stronger, the buds above them a bit fuller. The clouds parted, revealing the face of the Lady, Her touch warming the garden.

He could believe all would be well.

Curghann approached them in the garden as Alithia bent over the last of the moon blossom seeds, Baillin restored to his side. By the old trader's expression, he had something of import to discuss, but he kept his distance, as was proper, until she acknowledged his presence.

She released the power she had called, the sensual warmth flowing away until her hair cloaked her shoulders once more. Elation rushed through her at the green sprouts that appeared under her hands. She had followed Taith's advice, but the response of the seeds was more immediate, visible reassurance that the flame trees would bloom sooner than expected—enough to allow the clan to build up some inventory, now that the holy fire blazed in the clan altar once more.

Brushing the soil from her knees, Alithia waited for Taith and Phelan to join her, their presence now a comfort after seasons of travel. Only then did she nod welcome to Curghann, noting the formality of the robes he wore. While the old trader had never been casual in his dress, the gold brocade was more suited to a presentation at the temple. Even his long white hair was drawn back in a complex weave of beads and braids, and his beard was carefully groomed.

"Lady." He gave her a full bow, complete with spread arms, palms bared to display his peaceful intentions with their emptiness, the look in his deep-set eyes cautious—approaching her as priestess. "I am told the ritual was consummated to great success. What are your plans now?"

Alithia had thought she would welcome the change when the old trader finally ceased addressing her as a child, yet she suffered a pang of loss at his newfound wariness. Suddenly self-conscious, she rubbed at the dirt staining her hands.

As though he sensed her discomfort, Taith bowed to Curghann with Phelan following his lead a heartbeat later, her husbands drawing her visitor's attention from her. "Old father."

Old father? She stared at her sword husband, her thoughts thrown into turmoil as she struggled to translate the Hurranni term. *Father's father?* "What does that mean?" she whispered to Phelan as Curghann and Taith shared a warrior's grip, hand on forearm. Seeing the two men standing face-to-face woke a strange sense of . . . recognition.

"He's the blade father of Taith's blade father. Thus, he's Taith's old father."

"But not yours?"

"Taith and I are kin through his shield father," Phelan reminded her.

Alithia studied the old trader now clapping Taith's shoulder in affectionate greeting, noting now the semblance in the lines of their brows, the formidable height and broad shoulders now masked by age, and something in the set of jaw veiled by a wispy beard. "Hurranni kinship is so complicated."

She gathered her composure to approach the two. "Such formality for one you called child. Surely I do not merit all that." She smiled, glancing down to indicate Curghann's robes.

His face brightened at her overture, the stiffness of his shoulders easing until the kindly trader who had spent long afternoons teaching her Hurranni slouched before her once more. "There is no loss in displaying proper respect."

At Alithia's lead, they retired to her balcony.

"Daughter." Curghann took her hands in his and pressed a solemn kiss on the back of each one, his gaze lingering on her scar. That look confirmed her suspicions. In his eyes, she was now a priestess of the Lady of Heaven. "I rejoice in your triumph."

"You have my gratitude for your aid." Greased with sincerity, the rote formality came easily to her lips. If not for him, she wouldn't have accepted Taith and Phelan's bonds and might have failed in her quest. She had truly needed husbands, not merely to travel Hurrann but to rekindle the holy fire.

It struck her then that the flood was responsible for her husbands' presence in Lydia, the reason they were on hand to represent the Horned Lords among a once-Hurranni clan. Had that been the purpose of the Lady? Was it the absence of the Horned Lords that She sought to correct? A welling confidence suggested there was merit in the thought, that she was on the proper path.

Alithia took heart. Perhaps the demands of Her service wouldn't be onerous; after all, She had allowed ages to pass without a priestess in Lydia.

"But speak of your plans. What do you intend to do now?" Curghann's glance encompassed her husbands.

"We'll stay here, of course," Phelan answered from his perch on the balcony rail. "There is much to be done. The keeper of the archives wishes the First Record translated to Lydian."

The success of the rite convinced Eldora that clan Redgrove descended from Hurranni traders who had migrated to Lydia. She suspected much knowledge had been lost when the clan embraced the worship of the Goddess and wanted to recover what she could of the clan's history. The mothers had agreed to the undertaking after Alithia informed them that the Lady's gift was responsible for warming the clan house in winter.

A small, cunning smile creased Curghann's aged features. "It pleases me to hear that."

"Why?"

"Perhaps you would consider something more."

Taith and Phelan exchanged puzzled looks then turned to Alithia, leaving the discussion to her. "You have a proposal?"

"I am in need of heirs to train, men who can learn the southern trade and take up the reins of my affairs." Once again, that crafty smile made an appearance. "I believe your husbands would be suitable."

Taith straightened on his bench, the glance he sent Alithia urging her to seek details.

"Us?" Gaping, Phelan slid off his perch. Rather than resume his seat, he joined Alithia on hers.

"How did you come to such a conclusion?"

Curghann smoothed the drape of his robes, a habit he indulged when he wanted to draw out the suspense for a young girl; it made her want to laugh despite her impatience. "It was simple, truly. I decided that whichever shield pair wins your bond would be my heirs."

"But why?"

"I need heirs. I will not be able to oversee trade with the south forever. This seemed the best way to choose men who could deal well with southerners."

"Based on my choice? It could have been anyone, perhaps complete strangers. It might not have been Taith and Phelan."

Smiling in bemusement, her shield husband shook his head. "Mahon, Bronn, Slann, Deighann, Kail, and Taith were all born to Crystal Bell from his sons."

"I was born to Crystal Bell, but my shield brother was clan Fire Lake, so I joined Fire Lake. But many of our sons were fostered to Crystal Bell and eventually joined it." Curghann waved at Taith, his gesture encompassing the other Swords not present. "Their sons went on to join other clans."

"So all the shield pairs you invited were kin?" Alithia couldn't remember the proper Hurranni word, so she settled for the less specific term.

"I did say I would find you suitable husbands." The old trader smiled, a glint of satisfaction in his black eyes.

"All the shield pairs who came were willing to pledge themselves to a wife who was not Hurrann. This boded well for my purposes, but it did not resolve my problem. They are all my youngermost sons. I could not be impartial," he continued, using the Hurranni term for *son's son*. "You were wise to stipulate a trial of pleasure as you did. It was a perfect demonstration of the differences in northern and southern sensibilities. A trial of arms would not have been as effective."

Silence descended as Alithia and her husbands absorbed his reasoning.

"Wouldn't Bronn and Lughann be a better choice?" Phelan finally asked. She wondered the same, remembering the shield pair's almost Lydian approach during their trial.

Again that sly smile. "They were too cautious. She would have ridden them ragged within a turn. A good marriage is a subtle balance between wife and husbands."

Alithia stared at Curghann in admiration. He had gone to incredible lengths to arrange an alliance between their clans—without the mothers knowing. "Still, why? You trade with other clans. Why single out clan Redgrove?"

"You sought my aid and were willing to pledge Hurranns as husbands. The opportunity was a gift from the Lady." Curghann looked at each of them in turn, his eyes searching. "What think you of this proposal?"

From the fire in Phelan's eyes, he was already imagining the travel involved. Taith kept his opinion to himself, but from the easy way he sat, he had no strong objections. It would give her husbands something to focus their energies on besides her and get them out from under the eyes of her cousins.

She smiled. "I believe it holds promise. But I wish to discuss it with my husbands first."

Taking her hint, the old trader took his leave with many graceful courtesies.

After Magan ushered Curghann and Baillin from her rooms, Alithia turned to Taith and Phelan. "This changes things."

"Of course, it does. Now, we'll have something to do besides hone our swords and frighten your kinswomen."

Alithia had to laugh at the picture Phelan's words painted. "That is not what I meant."

"Truth." Taith nodded, his eyes smiling. "Your kinswomen are like to tease than take fright."

She shook her head at their lighthearted banter, though the reminder of her cousins' behavior stirred irritation.

"What, then?"

"If you accept Curghann's proposal, there is no need to give up your crew. If Devyn and the rest are willing, they could join you in learning the southern trade." The company of the other shield pairs—friends all—would surely ease her husbands' hearts.

Phelan's face brightened, a mischievous grin slowly unfolding as he considered the possibilities. "Perhaps Gair and Eoghann will have their southern wife, after all."

The merits of such an alliance appealed to her. If the Lady of Heaven wished to establish the Horned Lords' presence in the south, bringing over more Hurranns could only be to the good.

Taith, though, wasn't diverted. "So you approve of this?"

"I think it would benefit us all. You do enjoy trade."

"You are not just saying that to protect us from your kinswomen?"

Her eyes narrowed at the memory of her cousins flirting with her husbands, flaunting their nubile bodies before them and taking advantage of their courtesy. "More like moving them beyond the compass of my wrath."

"Then it seems we will be traders in the south." Her sword husband smiled and kissed her, a gentle brush of his lips that still managed to stoke the Goddess heat in her. "Such a change. To think this all happened because some old mother of yours, ages past, sent the tablet of mysteries to Sentinel Reach."

Phelan drifted over to put an arm around her and Taith. "What if you need it again?"

"The tablet of mysteries?"

He nodded.

"Should we ever have a need, I am sure it will appear from the holy fire."

"Unless the holy fire has been extinguished."

"If there are no priestesses and priests here to rekindle the holy fire, then a daughter of the blood will have to repeat the journey to the temple in Sentinel Reach." Alithia smiled at her husbands, raising a silent prayer of gratitude to the Lady of Heaven for their bonds. "For now, there is no need to summon the tablet of mysteries. It has served its purpose here."

Perhaps in answer, light glistened on the first blooms on the flame trees filling the air with heady perfume.